BAD FAITH

A HARPER ROSS LEGAL THRILLER

RACHEL SINCLAIR

SUNRISE BOOKS

ALSO BY RACHEL SINCLAIR

For information about upcoming titles in the *Harper Ross Legal Thriller* series, sign up for my mailing list! You'll be the first to know about new releases and you'll be the first to know about any promotions!!!! https://mailchi.mp/2e2dda532e99/rachel-sinclair-legal-thrillers

Johnson County Legal Thrillers (Kansas City, Missouri)

Bad Faith https://amzn.to/3jko0tz

Justice Denied https://amzn.to/3j8s2b2

Hidden Defendant https://amzn.to/3yypUjH

Injustice for All https://amzn.to/3lmZpJY

LA Defense https://amzn.to/3A313EW

The Associate https://amzn.to/3jeXqVF

The Alibi https://amzn.to/3ykjnZL

Reasonable Doubt https://amzn.to/3C9HBYH

The Accused https://amzn.to/3jiTL94

Secrets and Lies https://amzn.to/3fowW2V

Until Proven Guilty https://amzn.to/3CbQukz

Emerson Justice Legal Thrillers (Los Angeles)

Dark Justice https://amzn.to/2Vhg72L

Blind Justice https://amzn.to/3A44DyE

Southern California Legal Thrillers (San Diego)

Presumption of Guilt https://amzn.to/3A6duQ2

Justice Delayed https://amzn.to/3lpWOiG

By Reason of Insanity https://amzn.to/3ymyz8H

Wrongful Conviction https://amzn.to/3looT6J

The Trial https://amzn.to/3jeKG1c

ONE

HARPER

"The body of Gina Caldwell was found and your client has been arrested. Do you have any comment?"

Flash bulbs popped in my eyes, blinding me. I felt bile travel from my stomach to my throat and swallowed hard. I had a headache that would have blinded me if those damned flashbulbs didn't first.

I didn't want to deal with this, even though I knew I would have to, eventually. Ever since my former client, John Robinson, had been arrested for killing his current girlfriend and dumping her body in a ravine, I knew this day was coming. My day of reckoning.

"Yes," I said, putting my hand over my eyes to try to shield them from any more insult from the popping flashbulbs. "My client, John Robinson, has a Sixth-Amendment right to counsel, same as anybody else in this country. I was simply fulfilling my constitutional duty in defending him."

My statement wasn't something I'd practiced in front of a mirror before leaving my house this morning. I didn't dream there would be reporters camped outside my door. After all, I lived in a quiet neighborhood in Kansas City called Brookside – I had restored one of those rambling turn-of-the-century homes the Brookside area was so famous for when I won my first big case and the offers and new cases came pouring in. It was always my dream to own a large older home and I achieved this. This home became my enclave, my space where I could decompress.

Now, it seemed, it was my prison. The place where the media camped out to get some kind of word from me about how I felt to, essentially, be an accessory to murder. At least, that was how the press framed it – I was the lower-than-scum who managed to free my client on a technicality even though I surely knew the guy was guilty. Blood was on my hands.

I didn't have time to think about what had happened to that poor girl, Gina, before the media besieged me. I was suddenly surrounded by all these people who wanted to talk to me about how I could get this guy off.

John Robinson was a Kansas City Chief's fullback who'd been charged with brutally murdering his business partner with a baseball bat. He owned a bar downtown and his partner was found in the back room, bludgeoned to death. I knew the dude was guilty – he told me as much. But he expressed remorse, breaking down in my office as he told me about how he came to fear for his life around this guy, and how the victim, a known drug user, charged at him late one night with a large kitchen knife.

The whole thing became "he said he said," of course, because the victim was the only person who could tell me what happened and he wasn't talking to me or anyone else. Still, it seemed like a pretty cut and dried self-defense case and I only needed to make the jury buy his story.

I also had to constantly quell my own misgivings about my client's story, which didn't really add up. My client John was

6'6" and 250 lbs, while the victim, a slight Jewish man named Anthony Gold, was a foot shorter and one hundred pounds lighter. John insisted to me that Anthony had a drug problem, but I could find no evidence of this. When I did my investigation, I spoke with Anthony's closest relatives and friends, all of whom described a quiet, slightly nebbish man who loved animals and never lost his temper.

Not that any of this meant Anthony didn't charge John with a kitchen knife. But it certainly seemed like Anthony wasn't the type to do such a thing and my gut was telling me something was off.

I ignored my gut and went into the case full speed ahead, the media following the case every step of the way. It turned out John flunked a lie detector test, which pretty much sealed it for me – I was representing a guilty man. And I would give him the same treatment I gave everyone else – I would go balls to the wall and give him all I got.

What I actually ended up getting was a mistrial. The prosecutor introduced the polygraph evidence without warning, I immediately objected because the judge had previously ruled the polygraph evidence couldn't come in, and that was that. The jury was sent home, and the prosecutors, tired of the media glare, decided not to try him again. The judge ruled the jury was tainted by the surprise admission of the polygraph test and the fact that John flunked it, so there was no way they could make an unprejudiced decision.

And that was that.

Or so I thought.

I tried walking to my car, but the throng of reporters were surrounding me, essentially blockading me from my black Beemer SUV. They were all asking me for a comment, but, of course, I wouldn't give them anything juicy.

"No comment," I finally said. "Now please back up and let me into my car before I call the police."

I shoved a few reporters to the side, pushing one so hard she fell to the ground. I just rolled my eyes, not bothering to help her up. She was the enemy, or was part of the enemy squadron, and I couldn't care less about whether or not she tore her panty hose and skinned her knee on the pavement.

I finally put my car into drive and got the hell out of there.

WHEN I ARRIVED at my office, I could finally process the news that my client was in jail again for a brutal murder. Well, he was no longer my client, because my contract with him only lasted for the length of his murder trial, with the option that I could write the appeal if it came to that, which it didn't. But he was my client, and, because of me, he was free to do what he did to that poor Gina Caldwell.

I felt sick so I opened my purse and brought out some Tums. I drank a glass of orange juice and sat back in my chair.

This isn't your fault. It's not your fault. It's not your fault. If you didn't take this case, somebody else would've and he still would've been free.

I shook my head. It didn't really work that way. Alternative universes with alternative endings didn't really go in a linear line – if I didn't take the case, it was possible John would've never walked free, because perhaps, with his alternate attorney, the whole accidental polygraph courtroom admission wouldn't have occurred. Maybe a different attorney would've pled him out to 25 to life and Gina never would've met the guy. Who knew what would've happened if I didn't get involved?

As I sat looking out the window of my office at the expanse of the Country Club Plaza below, my mind kept going there - to my guilt in getting off this John, which enabled him to do it again. Deep down, I knew this day of reckoning would come. I always knew it, from the moment I was a baby lawyer and working at the Public Defender's Office. I always knew I'd do my job so well that I'd one day unleash a monster back on the streets and would end up with blood on my hands.

I'd been practicing for 10 years, and, thus far, it hadn't happened. Now it did, and I felt...haunted. Sickened. Like I couldn't get the picture of Gina - so young and beautiful and full of life – out of my head. Gina had two girls who were only 11 and would be without their mother for the rest of their lives. They would grow up knowing their mother died in the worst, cruelest way possible, outside of being burned alive. Gina worked at the animal shelter as a volunteer and had rescue animals at her home. She had grieving parents, devastated friends and a life ahead of her. A life cut short because I chose to give John the best defense I could give, even though I knew, deep in my heart, he was guilty as hell.

"Hey," Tammy, my law partner, said as she peeked her head through my door. "I saw you on the news this morning. And I saw what happened with John. Tough break, huh?"

I smiled, feeling that the words "tough break" were the most hollow, meaningless and understated words I'd ever heard. "Yeah, tough break."

I didn't invite her in, and, ordinarily, that wouldn't have been a big deal. She and I always practiced an open door policy so it went without saying that we could always come into one another's office and bounce ideas off each other or just give encouragement when one of us was down. We often celebrated together when we won a big case. Ironically, the last really big case we celebrated was my getting John off his murder charge. After hours, we blasted '80s new wave classics out of our stereos and she drank champagne while I stuck to my sparkling cider – I'd just gotten my one-year chip from my local AA and was determined not to blow it – and we ended up going downtown to a seedy bar and dancing the night away.

Now I felt like the only appropriate song for the situation was a dirge. A funeral dirge. That was how I felt – like somebody close to me died. And, in a way, something *did* die – my soul. My ethics. My sense of right and wrong. What the hell was I doing with my life?

While I didn't invite her in, she sat down anyhow. She was sitting in the swivel chair I reserved for my clients and rocked back and forth while she carefully watched me without saying a word.

"What?" I finally asked her. "You're looking at me like I've grown another head."

She grimaced and plopped both of her elbows on my mahogany desk. "You're not okay," she said, stating the brutally obvious. "Listen, you were-"

"Just doing my job," I finished for her. "Blah, blah, blah." I felt the rancor building up inside of me. The rage over what had happened and about my career path and life in general. "No, Tammy, I wasn't doing my job. Not at all. If I did my job, I would've pled that bastard when he flunked the polygraph. I would've listened to my gut that was screaming at me to make sure that guy didn't walk out the courtroom door a free man. Or I would've-"

Out of nowhere, I started sobbing uncontrollably. Tammy came behind me and put her arms around me and I clung to her like I was a small child clinging to her mother.

"Shhh," she said. "If it wasn't you who walked him, somebody else clearly would have. He had all the money to get the best hired gun in the world. He would've gotten somebody who would've walked him just like you did. Don't blame yourself."

I shook my head rapidly. I suddenly felt I couldn't breathe.

I felt like I was under water and my lungs were filling up with fluid.

"No," I finally said between sobs. "That's not true. You know that's not true. He was guilty as sin and maybe he would've hired a lawyer who would've done the right thing and pled him out. Or maybe that whole polygraph debacle wouldn't have happened with another lawyer and the case would've went to a jury, who might've fried him."

Tammy sighed as she let go of me and sat back down on the chair across from my desk. "What's this? I've never known you to have a dark night of the soul. Ever."

I looked at her. What she just said to me was *not* a compliment. Like I had no conscience. I knew there were attorneys who apparently didn't have a conscience, and, for them, winning was the only thing. They would take the news that John did it again in stride, figuring they weren't to blame. Only John was. That kind of thinking drove me crazy – as if, in a situation like this, there was only one person to blame. That wasn't true. It was never true. Yes, John was to blame, because he apparently had a problem with his temper, to say the very least. But I, too, was to blame for what happened. I was. There was just no getting around it.

"Dark night of the soul." I looked out the window and realized it was starting to get dark. I'd decided to come to work late after I found out the news and it was December, so the darkness started to fall at 4 PM. In about an hour the entire Country Club Plaza would be lit up which ordinarily would've cheered me up. Ordinarily. Tonight, though, nothing could cheer me up.

I sighed. "I guess I should go to the funeral," I said.

Tammy raised an eyebrow. "Are you sure that's a good idea?"

"No. But I need to do it anyhow." I dreaded doing that, of

course. I would be faced with the consequences of what I did. Of what I set loose. John was back in jail, and, no doubt, would be calling me to represent him again. If he did, I'd hang up on his ass so fast...I'd represented repeat offenders before but they were low-level things. One guy getting a million DWIs, for instance. As long as these guys didn't kill people while drinking and driving, I pretty much took their case again and again and again. But in this case...no. Just no. I wouldn't touch that guy with a twenty-foot pole ever again.

Tammy put her hand on mine. "I'll be there for you," she said. "If you need me to go with you to the funeral."

I shook my head. "No. It's something I need to do myself. But thank you, though." I swallowed hard. "I wonder if the vultures are lying in wait to ambush me as I leave my office tonight. Maybe I should just stay here." I had a couch in my office as well as a chest of drawers in my closet that held pajamas, a change of underwear and a toothbrush. I also had two fresh suits hanging up. I spent the night in my office on occasion, whenever I was working a big case, so those things were necessary.

"Just stay here," Tammy said. "I'd stay here with you, but I have Buttercup at home," she said, referring to her 100 lb pit bull.

"No, that's okay. I need to be alone tonight, anyhow." I didn't really want to be alone, though. I wanted to be with Jack. Jack Daniels. I'd just received my one-year chip last week from AA and all I could think about was drowning myself. I was responsible for two little girls being orphaned and I simply couldn't handle it.

Tammy finally got out of her chair. "Well, I really should be getting out of here. Got an early depo in Harrisonville tomorrow," she said, referring to the bedroom community about

40 miles outside of Kansas City. "And gotta prepare for it." She put her hand on mine again. "You going to be okay?"

"Yeah," I lied. "I'll be fine."

Tammy left and I pulled out my couch and lay down. I fell asleep in my suit while I listened to the late-December rain pelt on my window.

TWO

A few days later, Gina's funeral was held. I'd spent the last few days fending off the news vultures while trying to maintain a normal life. I'd canceled all my new client intakes and pawned off my laundry list of depositions and hearings to another lawyer in my building who was always good for a cover. Once I had everything covered, I retreated into my home and turned off my phone. I wouldn't talk to anyone, not even Tammy, who apparently tried calling me again and again – I didn't know for sure, because I refused to turn on my phone – so she ended up on my doorstep with some kind of baked goods in her hands.

I didn't come to the door, though, so even though she stood on the porch ringing my doorbell again and again, she ended up leaving. The baked goods were placed, with a bow, in front of my swing.

As I looked outside on the day of Gina's funeral, I saw the snow piled up on my front porch and the steps that led down to my car, which was parked in my driveway. I shook my head, cursing that I had to do the dusting-off-the-car ritual and doubly cursing I would have to spend my day at services for a dead girl that should've never been dead and probably would still be alive if not for me. The only good thing was the news channels decided to finally leave me alone as they seemed to get the message that I wouldn't talk to them. I wasn't talking to my closest friend, Tammy, I wasn't talking to my brothers and sisters or my mother and father, so I sure as hell wouldn't talk to them.

Wrapped in a heavy winter coat, under which I wore a black pantsuit with a black fedora hat, I made my way to my buried car and took my big broom and wooshed away the piled snow. I was running late, so I didn't have time to scrape the windshield with my hard plastic scraper. I had a small bucket of hot water ready to pour over the ice. I was always told not to do this, because it might result in a cracked windshield, but desperate times sometimes called for desperate measures, so I would chance it. It was an emergency way of getting that damned ice melted. Having to attend a funeral at 1, while just getting to your car at 12:30, would be just that kind of emergency in my book.

Five minutes later, I was crawling along the side streets of my neighborhood. The snow plow had not yet gotten to my enclave, so I drove gingerly and carefully through the neighborhood streets, until I hit the main drag, Wornall Road, which was thankfully plowed early that morning. I had to make it all the way over to Leawood, where the services would be held at The Church of the Nativity on 119th Street. As much as I didn't know what to expect, I knew one thing – I would have to face them. The daughters. The Mom and Dad. The cousins, aunts, uncles and best friends from college and beyond, all of whom would be staring accusing daggers into the back of my skull and probably right to my guilty face. I would have to face it and I would have to do it bravely.

I cleared my throat and looked at my unopened bottle of

Jack Daniels I kept on the seat next to me. I did that because I wanted to show myself I was stronger than the drink. That I could be around it and not succumb. So far, I'd resisted the siren song, even though I was increasingly having weaker and weaker moments. I kept the Jack on the seat unless I had a passenger in my car, in which case I would relegate the bottle to my glove compartment. I was weird but I didn't want the whole world to know just how weird I really was.

****

After the service, I found the children. I'd watched them from my vantage point in the back of the room and saw how devastated they were. They were identical twin girls, Abby and Rina, age 11. They looked devastated.

I bent down to look them in the eye. "Hello," I said to one of the dark-eyed twins. They were both wearing tiny black dresses with even tinier black shoes and their hair was curly and notched up in pony-tails. "How are you?"

Neither twin said anything but looked at the woman holding each of their hands. "My name is Hannah," she said. "I'm the social worker assigned to their case."

"Hi," I said, extending my hand. She let go of one of the children's hands so she could shake mine. "My name is Harper Ross. I need to know what will happen with these children."

She cocked her head slightly. "I'm afraid I cannot divulge that to you," she said. "It's confidential."

I cleared my throat and got out my wallet, so I could flash her my bar card. "I'm an attorney," I said in a low voice. "And I..."

She crinkled up her brows. "An attorney? Why are you here? Are you a loved one or a friend of the deceased?"

Here we go. Of course everyone was suspicious of me. Nobody knew me from Eve, this was a private service and Gina had been splashed all over the news just about every night. The sharks were coming out and many more were kept at bay. This woman probably assumed I was there for the wrong reasons.

"No," I said. "I just want to make sure these girls have a guardian or somebody who will care for them."

"And if they don't?"

My heart sunk. That would be my worst nightmare, really, that Gina's girls would end up orphaned and in the system. They might be split apart as one family takes one and another family takes the other. They might remain in the system where they'd end up abused or neglected or shuffled around from one place to the next. They might grow up haunted - without a mother, without any family, and without each other. I did too many Family Court cases to ever think these girls would have a happy ending if they didn't have somebody solid to care for them.

All because of me.

"If they don't, I can take them," I blurted out. "I make a decent living and have my own rambling home in the middle of Brookside. Five bedrooms. I can even afford child care to watch them. I can-"

The woman nodded. "Here's my card," she said. "If you're an attorney, then you probably have access to their court files, even though they're sealed. If you're really interested, then start the process. In the meantime, we need to get over to Gina's house. We're meeting there for refreshments. You're welcome to come."

I wasn't listening to her at this point. All I could hear, if I read between the lines, was these two little girls had no place to go. They had court files and this woman was encouraging me to "start the process," which I assumed meant fostering the children in hopes of eventually adopting them. If there was a guardian in place, or, at the very least, a close relative who could take them, this woman wouldn't be saying these things to me.

That was one more thing on my plate – I was about to possibly be responsible for these two little girls growing up in a foster care system that didn't care a damn for them. Maybe they'd get lucky and be placed with some wonderful people.

Or maybe not.

They would roll the dice.

That was on me, too.

THREE
SIX MONTHS LATER

My bucket was officially empty, and there was no way I could imagine going back to the office. I was staying home and had been there for the past three weeks, ever since I broke down after being denied the right to adopt Gina's two little girls.

I got certified as a foster mother and took them in and they'd been staying with me for the past six months. Then, out of the blue, they were taken away and given to another family to foster. It came time for me to apply to adopt them, and I was refused, just like that. Apparently, my "lifestyle" - being a recovering alcoholic single woman with a full-time job - wasn't stable enough for them.

And that was the final straw. I wanted to make sure Rina and Abby were safe. After all, I was why they were orphaned. And having them under my roof made me want to re-evaluate my choices and life.

And I decided to get out of criminal law. Yet, I couldn't think of an alternative path.

I didn't have a real interest in other areas of law. Estate planning involved too much tax law and I hated tax law. Family law was...no. Just no. I couldn't imagine putting myself into the middle of a child custody or divorce mess if my life depended on it. Personal injury was an okay line of work but extremely saturated and cases were getting harder and harder to come by and even harder to win. Besides, anybody who had a really decent PI case would go with one of the larger firms that handled that sort of thing. That meant tiny two-woman operations, like Ross and Warner, which was the name of mine and Tammy's firm, would get the scraps in that particular line of law.

I was a criminal defense attorney through and through. I had to admit to that. It was what I was born to do, in a way. It was what I did straight out of law school when I took my first cases with the Public Defender's Office. It was all I knew and I was good at it.

Too good at it, as it turned out.

Having those girls in my house made me happy and gave me a sense of purpose. After they left, I found my newfound sense of purpose was gone. I felt burned out by my law practice and fantasized about giving it up completely and doing anything else. Anything else at all. Selling my body, working in a slaughterhouse, digging ditches along the side of the road... anything seemed preferable to going back to my office and facing one more criminal case.

The problem was, I was running out of money. I spent my life savings on my home. Turned out buying a 100-year-old home came with some 100-year-old problems – the plumbing, the electrical wiring and the floors all had to be replaced. That cost me a mint and the house did as well. The Brookside area was one of the most desirable in Kansas City and houses didn't necessarily come cheap. Even the fixer-uppers, like what I bought. The median price for a home in the area was $350,000. While some areas of the country would laugh at that price – like in San Francisco, where $350,000 would only buy you a shack in the worst part of town, if anything at all, in Kansas City, $350,000 bought you a very nice home. My home was less than that but I'd put so much into it that I was tapped out.

I'd hoped a products liability drug case might bear some fruit for the lawyer I referred it to in return for a 10% finder's fee. But that one fell through even though the case was won, because it was overturned on appeal.

I had to eventually return to the salt mines or face losing my home. And since I still wanted custody of those little girls, I couldn't do that. I had to figure something out.

Just then, I looked out the window and saw Tammy walking up the drive. I groaned, not wanting to face her. She would try to drag me back to the office and I didn't want to face it.

I opened the door anyhow, feeling embarrassed that I was still in my pajamas. "Hey," I said to her. "Come on in. Have a seat."

She sat down, a pissed-off look on her face.

"Harper," she said. "I won't beat around the bush. You have to come back to the office and back into life."

I shook my head. "Can't do it. Can't risk springing another jackass who'll be free to do it again. I'm tapped out, Tammy. Tapped out."

"You want some cheese with that whine?" Tammy looked at me skeptically. "Listen, you have to stop dwelling on what happened, Harper, and come back. All the pity parties in the world won't bring Gina back. Nor will they bring those two little girls back into your home. In the meantime, you've become an absolute waste who's no good to anybody." She stood up and put her hands on her hips.

"I'll dwell if I want to." I would be stubborn about this,

because I didn't want to face up to facts. I wanted to push the world away and keep it there. Safe in a cocoon of my own making.

"Harper," Tammy said. "You need to come back to the office. Our books haven't been healthy since that products liability drug case fell through on appeal. We both were hoping for a decent settlement there and now it looks like no checks will be cut for a long time, if at all. We need money coming in and that means both of us need to get out there and make it. In other words, if you don't get your ass back into the office and into life, I'll have to dissolve the partnership and find somebody who'll be active in the business."

I turned on the television so I didn't have to face up to what she was saying. I knew I had to make things right.

"Okay," I finally said. "I'll come back to the office and try a little harder. It was nice having this vacation for awhile, and thanks for letting it go on as long as it did. But I'm not doing any more criminal defense, so don't even ask me to."

She sighed. "About that..."

I groaned. "About what?"

"I signed up a new client today. While you were here at home, I signed her up. Her friend came in and paid a $25,000 retainer."

I shrugged. "That's good. If she's a criminal defendant, then you try the case. I'm fine with that. You can give me all the..." I shook my head. All the what? What cases did I want? After the whole Gina thing, I knew I was gun-shy and didn't want any case where there was a chance I could totally screw up somebody's life if I lost or, God forbid, I won and the bastard went on to do it again.

That pretty much left very little for me to do because attorneys always had their client's life and livelihood in their hands at all times. If an attorney lost a custody case, the client was devastated. Losing a criminal case was even worse, as the client could literally lose his or her life, or be behind bars for the duration of his or her natural-born years. The stakes with a personal injury or medical malpractice case was that a loss meant your client might be living in chronic pain with no compensation for the rest of his or her life.

To top it off, all of those outcomes could also mean a big, fat malpractice suit against me and the firm. Being a lawyer meant constantly playing with people's lives and livelihoods and, if you rolled the dice and lost, it also meant possibly answering to the State Bar and possibly getting sued and losing the practice.

I had no desire anymore to deal with any of that.

"Harper, you know I don't do criminal cases."

That was true enough. Tammy pretty much stayed on the "safe" side of the law while bringing in the big bucks. She settled estates, set up corporations, constructed trusts and did the occasional will contest. That was as far into litigation as she dared wade into. A criminal defense attorney she wasn't.

"Yes, I know that, but you apparently will be doing at least one criminal defense case since you saw fit to sign one up without my knowledge." I glared at her. I knew her game – she would force my hand. She saw me as a prize fighter who took one punch too many and decided to get out of the ring. The best way to get that prize fighter back on his feet would be to sign him up for a fight and make him face his fears.

I wasn't about to fall for that, though.

"If I took this case, there would not only be a malpractice claim coming down the pike, but also an appeal for ineffective assistance of counsel. My ass would be dragged through the mud by a strong mule," Tammy said.

"True that, but Tammy, you should've thought of that before you signed this girl up. Now, here's what will happen. You'll give that girl her retainer back and give some referrals to people who actually would like to take her on. And you're going to lay off me and let me come back on my own time schedule."

She finally sighed. "I didn't want to do this. I really didn't. But I need you to know that I've already seen an attorney about dissolving our partnership. She said I'd have grounds to do just that, seeing as you've checked out of our business altogether this past month or so. She's drawn up papers. All I have to do is sign."

I couldn't believe what I was hearing. She was going to blackmail me into doing something I didn't want to do.

I had to give her credit. I didn't think she had it in her. I never pegged Tammy as being a shrewd businessperson, but when the chips were down, she was showing her true colors. I had to grudgingly respect that.

"I'll think about it."

"Well, don't think too long about it. Her initial appearance is at 1:30 today and she's likely to be assigned to the rocket docket. Especially since this case is pretty high profile."

The "rocket docket" referred to the cases assigned to Judge Reiner in Division 33. He was known as a judge who didn't mess around with continuances and had no patience with dragging things out. He generally wanted his criminal cases tried and gone within a year, maximum, and, most of the time, he demanded cases be done within three months. The ones allowed to go for one year were truly exceptional. Like high-profile capital cases. I hoped and prayed this case wasn't one of those.

"How high profile?"

"Very. The name of the defendant is Heath Morrison, and-
"

"Heath Morrison. You mean Heather Morrison, don't you?" I'd heard about this case in the paper. I didn't read too much about it, except that Heather Morrison was a transgendered youth accused of stabbing her mother to death. It was one of those things the media decided to blow up, for whatever reason, and the whole thing had been front-page since it happened.

"Heath Morrison was his birth name, so that's the name on the docket. But, yes, you're correct. Heath Morrison has been known as Heather Morrison for the past three years."

I shook my head. "No. Not doing it. No way will I allow myself to get in front of that spotlight again. It's bad enough you sneaked me into a criminal defense case, when you know damned well how I feel about that. But to get me into something where the media will be crawling up my ass again…no. I mentally can't handle this right now. Or ever for that matter. You tricked me into this and you'll get me out of it. You'll visit Heather in jail and explain the bad news. In the meantime, you'll contact Tom Peabody or Rex Arnold. Those two love the limelight."

Tom Peabody was nicknamed Tom Peacock by most of the Missouri Bar and it wasn't meant as a compliment. The guy preened worse than any multi-colored bird with fabulous plumage. Rex Arnold was just as bad. Those two would always fight over who would get the big cases that would make them famous. If there was something the media was blowing up, they were both on the case like flies on shit. One or both had probably already visited Heather and tried to steal her away with promises of a book deal when everything was said and done.

So be it. Either of those men could deal with this because I certainly wouldn't.

"You *are* doing it, because if you don't, I'll sign that paper dissolving the partnership. I have grounds to do that. You know I do." She crossed her arms in front of her. "1:30 is quickly approaching. Tick tock."

Tick tock? Tick tock? She had her nerve.

"Go to the initial appearance. You know nothing happens on that docket," I said.

That was true – initial appearances were pretty much a reading of the charges and entering a plea of not guilty. After that, the case would be turned over to the grand jury, and, after that, assignment to the permanent docket, arraignment and setting a trial date. There was very little in the initial appearance that necessitated my being there.

"Nothing doing. Heather wants to meet you. I've already told her you'd be her attorney, and that means you'll be with her every step of the way. That means every step, even this first little baby one. Besides, she'll have a bond set today. She needs you to argue forcefully the bond shouldn't be astronomical, and she should only have to come up with 10%. Only you can do that, Harper. I wouldn't do her justice."

"What's her bond now?"

"$250,000 cash," she said. "Obviously that means she'll have to stay in jail unless you do something about it."

I rolled my eyes. $250,000 cash? For most defendants, that bond was completely out of reach. Might as well be $250 million.

On the other hand, if I could convince the judge to make it $250,000/10%, Heather would only have to post $25,000 to get out of jail. If she jumped, she'd be on the hook for the whole $250,000, however. That was how that worked.

$25,000 might be doable, or at least it was for many defendants. They'd get their aunts, uncles, cousins and friends to come up with a thousand here and a thousand there. A house or two would be mortgaged and that would be that. At least that was my experience – most criminals had multiple people who care enough about him or her to get that person out of jail.

I knew I'd be sucked into this Heather Morrison case

against my will. I didn't want to lose Tammy as a partner and if I had to take this case in order to keep her, I'd do it.

I ran one hand through my hair.

"I hate you."

Tammy smiled. "I know."

"Well, I better put on the old monkey suit. Sounds like this Heather needs me."

And, just like that, I had a purpose again.

FOUR

By the time I arrived at the jail to see Heather, I had a tension headache screaming towards a 75 on a scale of 1 to 10. I'd just arrived at the common area, where I'd meet my client, when I saw her. She was slight, about 5'2", with features that looked like she'd been born a girl. She had long chestnut hair pulled in a high pony, big green eyes with long dark eyelashes, a tiny nose and full pouty lips. She probably didn't weigh 110 lbs soaking wet.

Not bad. If this is her pre-op, then she doesn't have far to go to look completely like a woman. I'd had experience with men who fancied themselves as women, even though their features were completely masculine. Caitlyn Jenner came to mind. Although Caitlyn was a beautiful woman, she had to work for the look with a lot of makeup to try to tone down her naturally butch face. But with Heather...she didn't have to do much. She already looked just like a female.

"Hello," she said. "Harper Ross, I presume." She sat down at the table with me and peeked at the guard standing in the room.

I raised my eyebrow at the guard as I needed for him to leave. I literally couldn't talk to my client if another person was around, because, if I did, anything Heather told me wouldn't be confidential. That was the rule – the attorney-client privilege only was good if there wasn't a third-party around to hear everything said.

"You presume correctly." I continued to stare at the guard, who didn't seem to be taking the hint. I didn't need this. I was running late as it was. "Excuse me, uh, Mr. Spaulding," I said, reading the guard's name tag. "I need to speak with my client confidentially. That means you need to leave."

The guard gave me a look but glanced over at the other guard behind the glass. That other guard was motioning him to leave us alone, so he just nodded and walked through the door without another word to either Heather or me.

"Oooh, you made that boy disappear just like magic," Heather said, snapping her fingers, which seemed to be difficult for her to do, considering she had on cuffs. "Wish I could have those same super-powers."

"They're not super-powers, they're called rules. I can't speak to you confidentially if other people are around. That guard probably should've known that." I shook my head. I had no idea what kind of training these guards had, but it was clearly inadequate. "Anyhow, there's not much time before your hearing. I just wanted to meet you and let you know what will happen, from start to finish."

"Good. Is this the part where I tell you about why I iced that old bag?"

I cringed. The "old bag" in question was Heather's own mother. Not that that mattered to Heather or to people like her, but it certainly mattered to me. I loved my mother and could never imagine doing something to her like what Heather did to her mother. Nevertheless, I knew I was lucky in that regard and others weren't so lucky. Heather apparently fell into that latter category.

"We can get to that later," I said. "I'm so sorry, I didn't know I was on this case until about an hour ago. I haven't had the chance to look at your file or anything else. I'll be completely honest – the only thing I know about your case was learned by glancing at the headlines in the newspaper." I looked at my watch, which read 1:15. There was just enough time to get out of that jail and high-tail it across the street to the courtroom in time to watch the gavel fall. I also knew Heather would have to be transported, which would take some time as well.

We both would be late to court. *This is off to a great start.*

"Well, Harper, I guess you're in a hurry. Can you at least do something about my bond?" She made a face. "Orange is not my color, I'm afraid. It makes my skin look totally sallow. It's such a hideous color of orange, too. They couldn't have gone with more of a burnt sienna or even a nice salmon? It's like they deliberately want to make us look our very worst. So I need to get out of here as soon as I can. I hope you can arrange that."

"Yeah, about that. I'll do what I can to get you a 10% bond at the very least."

"10% bond. What's that?"

"You'd only have to come up with 10% to get out. In your case, you'd be able to make bond if you put up $25,000. Bear in mind, though, that if you jump, you'd be on the hook for the entire $250,000. That's how it works."

Heather nodded. "I guess somebody in my life can come up with $25,000. He'll get it back, won't he?"

"Of course. As long as you show up to all your court appearances, your surety will get the money back. I'm assuming you'll get that money from the same person who paid my fee?"

"Yeah. He's good for it. I'll just have to make sure I make

him very happy in bed." She raised an eyebrow. "Do you know about that, Harper? Making your man happy?"

I groaned. "If I had a man, I'd know about it. But let's not get so personal just yet. Anything else you need to know?"

Heather shrugged. "I guess not. Please try to get me that 10% bond. We can maybe get a cocktail and I'll tell you all about why I did what I did. It's a good story, I can assure you."

"Okay, but no cocktail." I took a deep breath. I was on the wagon, and would stay there. I now had Heather's life literally in my hands. I couldn't screw this up.

Maybe I could still make amends for my role in Gina's death.

FIVE

"Harper Ross," the prosecutor, Vince Malloy, said to me as I made my way into the packed courtroom. The place wasn't packed because of my case, but, rather, it was just how it was for these initial appearances. Every defendant was granted an initial appearance and there were always a lot of people committing crimes in the jurisdiction, which meant these dockets were always extremely busy. "And the dead shall rise. Seriously, where've you been? I keep seeing your law partner covering for you, and, I'm sorry, but she doesn't know her ass from a hole in the ground around these parts. I'm pretty sure she's damned happy you're back. And you *are* back, right?"

I always thought Vince might have a slight crush on me, and the way he was acting at the moment didn't exactly dissuade me from that thought. He was a handsome enough guy, with his jet black hair, blue eyes and dimples and, at 6'3", he was tall enough for me to date. Being a woman who was 5'9" meant my prospects were somewhat limited if I didn't want to tower over my date.

But I never wanted to mess where I sleep and dating the

lead prosecutor on many of my cases would be a definite no-no in that regard. "I'm back," I said. "And feeling like crap, so go easy on me, k? Listen, I'll be asking for a bond reduction for my client, and if Judge Wilson here doesn't allow it, I'll make a motion for the trial judge, whomever that may be, to hopefully reduce the bond. Please don't make me beg. My client is trans and in detention with men. I don't think I need to tell you how dangerous that is for her."

Vince shook his head. "You know what happened, don't you? On this case?"

I stiffened my spine. No, I actually didn't know what had happened on this case. I only knew my client killed her own mother, apparently by slicing her jugular vein with a sharp knife. That was what I gathered from the newspaper articles about the case, as well as a quick cursory glance at the statement of information, which I speed-read right before I got into court.

"Of course I know what happened," I said to Vince. "Don't mansplain me. You only need to know that my client isn't a flight risk and has no priors. There's not a reason for the bond to be as enormous as it is."

"Not a reason? Killing her mother in cold blood, there's your reason right there. No, I won't concur on a bond reduction. You'll just have to try to get that over my strenuous objection."

"But-"

"You know better than that. Our office is considering the death penalty on this one, so, no, Harper, I don't foresee your client getting out on some kind of 10% bond if that's what you're thinking of asking for."

"The death penalty? What kind of aggravating circumstances were there?" I demanded, knowing I was showing my hand by asking that question. If I would've read through the

Statement of Information more thoroughly, I probably would've already known what aggravating circumstances were present and would've anticipated the prosecutor would make it a capital crime.

"We're going to show she killed her mother to get ahold of her life insurance policy," Vince said. "And it was a big one, too. $250,000."

I bit my tongue wanting to ask the next question, but I really didn't want Vince to know how little I knew about this case. But I needed to know what happened to my client's father. If the father was still alive, then the life insurance policy would go to him, not Heather. That would negate the prosecutor's aggravating circumstance right there.

"What else you got?" I asked him. "That sounds pretty flimsy on its face. I mean, come on. If my client wanted to murder her mother for her life insurance policy, I'd think she'd do a better job of covering up the murder."

I wanted to say more about the circumstances of the case, but I wasn't sure of certain things. Like who called the police? Did my client try to flee the scene? Did she try to finger somebody else? Did she lie about what happened when interrogated? I didn't know the answers to those questions, but if my client did little to cover up what had happened, it would be extremely easy to show the jury she didn't commit the murder for money. It would be rather idiotic for my client to kill her mother for her life insurance policy and not even attempt to cover up that she committed the murder. Duh.

Then again, I hadn't even had the chance to really speak with my client and get her story. Maybe she'd tell me she didn't kill her mother at all. Some other dude did it, or the SODDI defense, was one I often used and it sometimes worked.

"The murder was especially depraved," Vince said.

"In what way? Because there was a lot of blood squirting

out her neck? That's going to happen when you hit the jugular vein, for your information." I crossed my arms and tapped my foot. "You're grandstanding, Vince. You're standing on whipped cream here by asking for the death penalty. I think you know this."

At that point, the judge came in and called everyone to order. Vince and I rose and sat down, and Vince immediately went up to the bench to give his recommendations on everyone who appeared.

I wouldn't get the chance to talk to Vince about the death penalty business further, but I'd certainly call him and find out what the hell was going on. I knew Vince was using the death penalty thing as a bargaining chip. If I were an inexperienced litigator, I might get scared about the death penalty and urge my client to take any offer that came down the pike, just so my client could avoid the needle.

I knew that game and wouldn't play it. Vince would have to show me exactly why he was asking for the death penalty. Thus far, it seemed he had nothing. He knew it and I knew it.

While Vince stood at the bench making his recommendations, I did a better read-through of the Statement of Information. My heart sunk as I read. My client didn't call the police. In fact, she ran and hid out with her drug-dealer boyfriend. She was picked up for questioning three days after the incident, after an eyewitness told the police she heard a loud fight between Heather and her mother, and called the police the next day when she couldn't get in touch with Connie Morrison, who was Heather's mother. Heather never told the police she committed the murder and the weapon wasn't recovered at the scene.

Well, there's good news and bad news. The good news is, there's still a possibility of a SODDI defense. The bad news is, there's still the possibility the prosecutor can show Heather killed her mother for money. I shook my head. Nothing was ever cut and dried in this business, unfortunately. As much as you try for a slam-dunk every time, you usually get a lay-up instead. Still, I'd work with what I had. That was all I could do and all my client could ask.

I looked up and saw the in-custody people brought out and seated in the jury box. Everybody was hooked together in a line, each prisoner being attached to the one next to him by a handcuff. They were dressed in light blue jumpsuits because the prisoners usually switched from the hideous orange into the baby blue for court appearances. I had to admit, my client looked much better in the blue than in the orange. She was right – that orange color did nothing for her but the baby blue really did.

I smiled as I realized I was getting my gallows humor back, for whatever that was worth.

I cringed, though, when I looked at Heather. She looked like a girl and was hooked together with a guy with a face full of tattoos and a mouth full of gold teeth on her left and a huge angry-looking guy on her right. They both towered over her. She looked completely out of place in that lineup.

Out of place, but not frightened. In fact, she looked rather bored with the whole thing. Her dark hair was pulled back into a low pony and she kept smacking her lips. She never made eye contact with me but was eyeing Vince appreciatively.

The judge called up her line and she went to the bench with the others. Each of the others attached to her had an attorney there and they each pled not guilty and got a new court date. Some got court dates for a preliminary hearing, where the prosecutor would present evidence to the court to show probable cause for the defendant to be bound over for trial, while others got the same court date, but their case would go to a Grand Jury.

My client would be grand juried, of course. That was how it was done in the Jackson County Circuit Court. Murder, arson, kidnapping, robbery - basically any kind of major crime got the Grand Jury treatment. I hated that, because I knew it meant Heather would be bound over for trial. It was a rare Grand Jury that didn't return an indictment, so rare that the Defense Bar still got stunned when it happened.

Judge Wilson read Heather her charges and asked how she pled.

"Not guilty your honor," I said on her behalf. "And I'd like to request a bond reduction from $250,000 cash to $250,000/10%."

"Denied," the judge said without even looking at the prosecutor. "Your case will be remanded to Division 33 for trial, date to be set by Judge Reiner."

Well, Tammy sure called that one. The Rocket Docket it was.

"Your honor," I said. "I'd like to at least request a bond review hearing. As you can see, my client is transgendered. She's basically a female living in detention with all males. It's detrimental to her mental health to be in such a situation, so I'd like for her to go home to await trial."

Judge Wilson was a good ol' boy. He hunted on the weekends and would spit tobacco into a cup while he talked to lawyers and clients. He wore blue jeans and cowboy boots underneath his robe. He was a typical rural Missouri boy who made good and I never could relate to him. I found his tobacco habit beyond disgusting, and the fact that he found sport and happiness out of killing defenseless animals made my skin crawl. There were rumors he often used the "n word" with like-minded attorneys, although that could never be substantiated, which was why he still had his job. I didn't exactly know how he felt about LGBT, but it probably wasn't good.

"Mr. Morrison," he said, addressing Heather directly. "Is what your lawyer saying true? You identify with being a female and not a male?"

Heather batted her long eyelashes and looked coyly at the judge. "Yes, your honor. That's true. I haven't had a reassignment surgery yet, because I haven't the money, but, yes, I identify as female."

I braced myself, expecting the judge to call her a freak and tell her to get out of his sight. Judge Wilson wasn't one to mince words.

To my surprise, he actually seemed to sympathize. "Okay, Ms. Ross. $250,000/10% will be your client's new bond. If she can't make that, I'll see what I can do to get her sent to the ladies' side of the jail. No promises though."

You could've knocked me over with a feather after I heard what the judge said. He not only reduced Heather's bond, but called Heather by the feminine pronoun and said Heather could be remanded on the women's side of the jail if she couldn't make bond. I wasn't expecting that from him, and I knew that sometimes people can surprise you in the greatest of ways.

Vince looked at me, smiled and shook his head. "Your honor, I object to lowering Mr. Morrison's bond. There's no reason for it. He's accused of a brutal murder and he's living with a drug dealer who has the means to spirit him away. $250,000 cash is an appropriate amount, if not a little low, considering what he allegedly did to his own mother."

The judge simply shook his head. "This kid is trans. She stays in the men's detention much longer and she won't live to see trial. But she still has men's parts, so she doesn't really belong in the ladies' side of the detention area, either. I won't be responsible for her having the crap beaten out of her because of how she looks and who she is. That won't be on my watch.

$250,000/10% is her bond. You want to take it up with Judge Reiner, go right ahead. I won't have blood on my hands, though."

At that, he called the next case and I walked away from the bench, feeling absolutely stunned. Just goes to show – never judge somebody by their prior actions and thoughts on other issues. Considering Judge Wilson as a whole, I never thought he'd be sympathetic to my client.

Who knew?

SIX

The next day, I had to meet with Heather. She posted bail and was currently staying at a halfway house. She couldn't go home to her drug-dealer boyfriend because the conditions of her bail precluded that. The judge specifically stated she couldn't be around drugs or people into drugs, nor was she to fraternize with felons. Her drug-dealer boyfriend flunked on all of these fronts, so, even though said boyfriend actually posted the bond, he wasn't allowed to enjoy the fruits of his labor and Heather had to have someplace to live.

It occurred to me that perhaps I could have Heather live with me. I knew a halfway house wasn't the right place for her because she'd be around bad influences there, as well. And, after losing Rina and Abby to the system, my big house was feeling...empty. Cold. Drafty. Scary. There wasn't much in my house except furniture, plants, appliances and televisions, and I really needed more lifeblood in it.

I made the decision to petition the court to allow her to stay with me for the duration of the trial. There would be no reason not to and a thousand reasons why that would be a good decision for her. The biggest reason was that I'd been to this particular halfway house and didn't think it was a healthy place for anyone. It was on the wrong side of the tracks, where condoms and trash were strewn around, stray dogs ran freely and homeless people were living in small communities nearby.

I drove up to the home, in the middle of a neighborhood standard for this part of town. The houses were all old, most probably dating from the turn of the 20th Century. Trash completely littered the street. Smashed liquor bottles, cigarettes, condoms, fast food sacks and wrappers, and more than one plastic pop bottle filled with urine. I presumed the urine-filled pop bottles were a product of the homeless population, as they needed to do their business somewhere, but, then again, I never quite understood why they just didn't pee in the bushes or against trees. Why pee in a bottle? Perhaps it was somebody driving along who would do the deed and throw it out the window.

I came up to the home, opening up the front gate, and walked up to the enormous wooden door. I was greeted by a slight blonde woman who looked friendly enough.

"Hello," she said pleasantly. "Can I help you?"

"Yes. I have a client living there. Her name is Heather Morrison, but you might have her listed as Heath Morrison."

"May I ask who is calling?"

"My name is Harper Ross. I'm Ms. Morrison's attorney." I showed the woman my bar card and she got out a pair of glasses and looked at it. She didn't look convinced, so I showed her my driver's license as well. I didn't usually get too much scrutiny, mainly because the jail and the courthouses knew who I was, but I was new to this halfway house. I was actually happy she was so thorough. It wouldn't be good for just anybody to come and see the current residents.

"Wait for her just over there," she said, pointing to a room in the front of the house. It had hardwood floors that looked new, with a red leather couch, a coffee table, a colorful throw rug and a plant in the corner. "I'll get Ms. Morrison."

I looked around, thinking this was a nice room and happy the state provided a little something nice for the people who had to stay here.

About five minutes after I arrived, Heather came into the room. She was dressed down, in a way, in that she was wearing skinny jeans and a Grim Bunny t-shirt that featured a cute little bunny dressed as the Grim Reaper, complete with a hood and a sickle, and words that said "hippity hoppity death is on its way." Her long brown hair was held back by a glittery red headband and her nails were painted jet black. She was in full makeup and she wore a lot of it – dark black eyeliner, full foundation, red lips and mascara. On her ears were enormous hoop earrings, such as worn in the 1970s, and, on her feet were a pair of high-heeled boots. She also wore a tea green scarf that was doubled around her neck.

She looked effortlessly fashionable. She was so thin and little and had the kind of frame that would make a potato sack look *haute couture*.

I stood up and Heather wrapped her arms around me. "Harper, I can't tell you how happy I am to see you. I was sure I was doomed to wear that hideous orange number until my trial. As you can see, I look much better on the outside." She twirled around and smiled. "I even have a semi-private bathroom here." She rolled her eyes. "Of course, I have to share the bathroom with the boys, because this is a men's hellhouse. I mean halfway house. Freudian slip."

I smiled back. "You look happier than you did the other day. To say the very least."

"Oh, you don't know. Anyhow, I can't really leave this

place but we can talk in private. They have little rooms where lawyers can talk to their clients with nobody around."

We walked through the house and I noticed her ankle bracelet. That was another condition of her bail, of course – she had an electronic monitor. Not that she was a flight risk, but she was commanded to not leave the halfway house at the moment.

She walked with a sashay, as if she was announcing to the world that she was the most fabulous person in the room and you better know it. I wondered if her demeanor – the fact that she didn't show much fear in the courtroom, the fact that she seemed to be in good humor, and the way she was so light and joking – was her mask. Just like I had a mask that showed the world I was a confident attorney who had it all – a beautiful home in Brookside, a new Beemer and a successful practice, but, inside, I was sometimes a depressed mess – I wondered if there were layers to Heather as well.

I'd soon find out the answer to that question.

SEVEN

"Okay," Heather said. "I want to talk to you and tell you about my case. I know you have questions, so go right ahead."

We were sitting in a small room that didn't have much in it besides a metal desk, a black office chair and a smallish red chair with wooden arms. This room didn't have nearly as nice a vibe as the room I was in before, the cute and cozy room where I waited for Heather to show. This room did have a poster in a frame – it was an old movie poster for some kind of 1950s schlocky sci-fi film, but, other than that, it was a cold, oppressive place.

I shuddered and shook my shoulders. I took a deep breath and tried to quell the roiling feeling of anxiety. I had to have all my mental faculties firing on all cylinders if I wanted to win this.

And, after meeting Heather, I knew I'd have to win it. There was simply no other option. If I lost, God forbid, she'd possibly get the death penalty. At any rate, she'd be spending the rest of her life in a prison. A men's prison. Being tiny and transgendered, there was no way she'd make it in such a place. She'd be beaten to death within a year.

No, I had to win this case. So I had to be mentally healthy.

Heather smiled, and, as if she was reading my mind, she addressed my concerns. "I'm not going to prison, Harper, but if I did, I think I can make it." She raised her eyebrows. "You'd be surprised to know this, but straight boys love getting with me. They can get their freak on and never admit they really like boys. Why do you think chicks with dicks are so popular on the porn scene?"

I opened my mouth but didn't really have an answer for that. I felt hopelessly square, because I really didn't know that "chicks with dicks" was a thing, much less a popular thing. "I, um."

Heather laughed. "Oh, my lawyer is speechless." She touched my arm with her black-nail-polished hand. "You didn't know that straight boys like girls like me, did you? Well, they do. Trust me, I'm very popular at parties. It's because of this." She stuck out her tongue and I saw it was pierced. "They love that. So, if I'm in prison, I can get by."

I cleared my throat, finally seeing what Heather's game was. "Heather," I said. "You don't have to try to shock me. Trust me, I've seen it all. And I know lots of straight guys like girls like you. But all of this is neither here nor there. I need to know what happened, in your own words. And then I can start to build a defense."

Heather sneered, her bright red lips puckering and her nose scrunching. She glared, thinking she'd intimidate me, but I was determined not to let her. She was the client, I was the lawyer, and I would be in control.

"Okay," she finally said. "I've been trying to think this whole thing over. What I'm going to tell you. Because I've seen *Law and Order.* I know if I tell you I offed that old bag that you can't put me on the stand." She made a face that briefly reminded me of a parakeet I used to have – the bird saw himself in the mirror and thought it was another bird. He would flirt with that image all day long, just staring at it and cocking his head. Somehow, Heather reminded me of that bird at that moment.

I got out a yellow pad and pen. "Heather," I said. "That's true what you say. If we're going with the SODDI defense – some other dude did it – then don't tell me you murdered your mother." I struggled with this, ethically. I needed to know the truth, but, yet, I needed to give her the best defense. I didn't know how I'd do this if I knew she was guilty.

"SODDI defense," she said with delight. "Some other dude did it. I like that." Then she nodded. "Except some other dude didn't do it. I did it."

EIGHT

I groaned. There went my defense. At least one of them. I wrote down on the paper *the client confessed* and felt the despair creeping back into my bones. I cracked my neck, looked up the ceiling and took a deep, cleansing breath. Perhaps it wasn't such a good idea, taking Heather into my home. I certainly didn't want to get attached to her, not when she would most likely spend the rest of her natural life in prison. And her "natural life" would probably be very short.

But perhaps all wasn't lost. "Okay," I said in a brusque tone that belied the emotional churning I was feeling inside. "You killed your mother. Now we have to look at mitigating circumstances. Perhaps I can show it was a heat of passion, in that you didn't plan it out for even one second. That would be a basis for a manslaughter charge. I can, alternatively, have you psychologically evaluated for an insanity defense."

Heather shook her head. "It was a murder but not a crime," she said with a smile. "I always loved that line in *Chicago*. Never thought I'd be saying it one day, but here we are."

I tapped my pen to my forehead as I contemplated her.

That was something else I could ask her. The one thing, outside of jury nullification, that could possibly get her off completely. And that was self-defense.

"And what do you mean by that? A murder but not a crime?"

"Just what I say. I killed her but only because she was about to kill me first." She flipped her head back to and fro, and, just for one second, I saw the depth of pain in her eyes. It was like I was looking, for a split second, at a heartbroken and devastated person. I'd seen that look in clients' eyes too many times – it wasn't a blank look, but, rather, it was like looking at a deep well that plunged miles into the earth and ended in blackness.

With Heather, that look came and went so quickly that an ordinary person wouldn't have necessarily even caught it at all. If I hadn't seen it in numerous desperate people over the years, I wouldn't have seen it either.

I scribbled on my pad. "Go on," I said. "What do you mean?"

Heather sat back in her chair, slumping with her feet on the floor in front of her. "Well, my mother, she was...well, she was and she wasn't. I mean, let's start from the beginning. She hated me from the start. She always dressed me up in boys' clothes and cut my hair short, but I always knew that wasn't right. Always. Always always always. Since I was four years old, I knew I wasn't supposed to be dressed in boys' clothes and have my hair cut short. I knew I wasn't supposed to have this...thing...between my legs. Do you know what it's like, Harper, to feel like you want to crawl outside your own body, just so you'd have the chance to crawl into somebody else's? I know that sounds sexual, but I don't mean it that way."

Heather was suddenly becoming more serious than before. No more joking around about straight boys getting their freak on with her. She seemed to know it was time to be straight with me, and I appreciated her decision to do so.

"Actually, I do," I said to her, thinking about the times, when my depression was at its most acute, and I wanted to somehow turn my skin inside out. I imagined Heather felt that way her whole life. "But go on."

"You do." That was a statement, not a question, and I wondered if she somehow knew about my darkness. "She never understood me. I'd scream, absolutely scream, when she would drag me into the barber shop to get my hair cut because I so wanted long hair like my little cousin, Cathy. On Easter Sunday, when all the little girls were in their pretty little dresses, and I was in my little three-piece suit, I felt like everyone was staring at me because I looked out of place. In my mind, I wasn't supposed to wear that little suit, I was supposed to wear a dress, so I just assumed I looked like a freak. Of course, in reality, I'd be a freak if I wore the dress, but I didn't know that. I was only 6 years old."

She shook her head. "When I was ten, I started to demand that my mom and everyone else call me Heather. I refused to answer to the name Heath. Well, you can imagine what happened next. It was always 'Heath, do your homework. Heath, do the dishes. Heath, pick up dog poop. Heath this, Heath that.' I flat-out told her I wouldn't answer to the name Heath and if she wanted me to do something, she had to address me by my proper name, Heather."

She sighed. "If only she'd named me Cameron. Or some other boy-girl name like Terry or Dana or Kelly or Stacey or Tracy or even Blair. There wouldn't have been a problem, because I could simply pretend my name was a girl's name, not a boy's, and I wouldn't have been beaten all the time."

I continued to scribble and wrote down the words *possible abuse?* Not that abuse would get Heather off for murder. In

Missouri, evidence of abuse can be used for a spouse or partner, but not for a child. I thought that was a hideous miscarriage of the law – if a spouse can use the defense, why can't a child – but I didn't make the law. Still, I could possibly get evidence of abuse in front of a jury to at least mitigate the case to a manslaughter.

But even manslaughter would be too much for Heather. I had to find a way that she didn't serve even a single day in prison.

Heather tapped her black nails on the plywood desk and looked at me. "So, yeah, my mom wasn't exactly happy with me, to say the least. My father, neither, but he got himself killed by a drunk driver when I was 13 years old. Stupid fool was wearing all black, it was at night, and he just dashed in front of this wasted dude. My father's fault, but, since the guy was drunk behind the wheel, he spent 10 years behind bars." Heather rolled her eyes. "The justice system totally reeks sometimes."

I knew that better than anybody – how much the justice system reeked. But I didn't want to tell her that.

"After my father bit it, that was all she wrote for me. Which all would've been just fine, except Mom became all Jesusy on me. Started quoting Leviticus and shit." Heather shook her head as she looked up at the ceiling. "Started telling me I was bound straight for hell. Do not Pass Go, do not collect 200 dollars. I didn't know where she was coming up with this shit."

"Did the abuse get worse after your father died and your mother started getting religious on you?"

Heather looked at me as if she didn't hear a word I said. "Good lord, I don't know where she came up with all that bull crap. She never went to church, not once, when I was growing up, and all of a sudden, she starts coming at me with this 'man shall not lie with another man' crap. I wasn't having her Flying

Spaghetti Monster bullshit. At all." She shook her head and crossed her arms in front of her. "I told her I wasn't a man lying with another man, but a girl lying with a man, and, frankly, I don't think I ever 'lied' with anyone. That ain't what I do if you know what I mean."

I knew what she meant but didn't want to encourage her.

"She not only ranted about my going to hell but also threatened me. She'd say shit like she thought I had the Devil in me and that Satan was working through me to corrupt the world. Shit like that. I started to get scared and wanted out of her house but had no place to go. I finally agreed to go to conversion therapy because she insisted on it. As I said, I didn't want to do any of that crap, but where was I gonna go? I was 17 at the time and I didn't know Charlie or anybody else who could take me in. I certainly wasn't as fabulous as I am currently. I was just a scared kid."

"Tell me about the conversion therapy."

"I had to go to this clinic that treated being gay and transgendered as some kind of a serious mental illness. At first, it wasn't that bad – I had to see some weird dude who tried some kind of cognitive behavioral therapy or some shit. Every time I had a sexual thought about a man or a thought that I was supposed to be a woman, I was supposed to stop the thought and immediately think about something else." Heather shrugged. "That wasn't so bad. Of course, it didn't work, mainly because I didn't try. I really don't care what people think about me and my lifestyle and wasn't about to change. I just went to those conversion therapy sessions so my mom would get off my ass."

My mind started to turn as Heather spoke. I wondered if her mother was a latent schizophrenic, who didn't show signs until she was older, or perhaps always had schizophrenia and it got worse after Heather's father died. I knew that was a possibility – sometimes a person had mental illness tendencies but the mental illness didn't manifest until there was some kind of extremely stressful incident, such as the sudden death of a spouse.

"At some point, the weird dude decided his therapy wasn't taking. I don't know why he thought that, but he did. I mean, I lied and said I was all cured - I didn't think of men or boys sexually no more and accepted I was a boy. I even told him I was dating a girl and that things were going awesome with her." Heather shook her head. "I guess the guy was trained to know when people were bullshitting, because he decided to go to the next level, or so he called it."

"The next level," I said, scribbling on my paper. I didn't know if the gay conversion thing was relevant to Heather's defense, but something told me it was a piece of the overall puzzle. That was how I saw these cases – as puzzles for me to solve. Each moving part was pertinent in slowly building a case. "What was the next level?"

"It was called aversion therapy, and it was pretty sick." Heather shook her head. "Basically, they'd show me pictures of things that would get me off and then would show me something disgusting. Like showing a mound of crap or an overflowing toilet. They found out through a questionnaire what I found disgusting and they'd show me that. Big spiders, animals that had been slaughtered and hanging up on a tree, that kind of thing. They even showed me erotic images and then proceeded to force me out on the balcony of the building. The office was on the 12th floor and they made me look down. They did that because I made the mistake of telling them I was afraid of heights."

Heather sighed. "I need a smoke. I hope you don't mind. Just remembering this stuff is giving me a serious case of the shakes."

I looked at her hand and saw she was literally shaking, so I nodded.

"Thanks. I can't smoke here, so I have to go outside on the front porch. You're welcome to join me. They have a porch swing out there and stuff, if you'd like to talk some more out there."

We went out on the porch, and Heather lit up a cigarette, her hands shaking the entire time. She sucked on the end of the cigarette and put her face up to the sky. "So, yeah. There was all kinds of bullshit going on in that place. I don't know why or how my mom even heard of this place or even started thinking about it or what. But I told her, after the day I was forced out on that balcony, in the freezing cold, mind you, I was done with the conversion therapy. I told her I wouldn't go through no more therapy and I was just fine the way I was."

We rocked on the swing as we talked. Heather's hand was gripping the metal chains holding the swing, her high heels scraping the wood of the porch.

"What happened when you confronted her?"

Heather shrugged her shoulders. "She didn't throw me out of the house like I thought she would. I was all prepared to live on the streets if I had to because I had no desire to go through the foster care system or wherever kids go when their bat-shit cray mom kicks them out of the house. In fact, she didn't say nothing to me at all. Which actually freaked me out all the more. I was prepared for her to start yelling at me again about going to hell, but she didn't."

I made some notes, thinking that, although it sounded like things calmed down a bit between Heather and her mother, I knew the storm was coming. It always did in situations like this. I'd done enough criminal cases that involved domestic violence of some sort to know that peaceful lulls never lasted.

Heather rolled her eyes and smacked her lips. She brought

out a tube of lipstick out of her pocket and carefully applied it without a mirror. She was an expert at this, as her lips were perfectly outlined in cherry red, with no smudges nor any of the color getting on her teeth. I wished I could do as well.

She shook her head. "That didn't last. In fact, one night, I was sleeping in bed and woke up in the middle of the night to see her standing over me with a damn pillow in her hands. She was staring at me and saying some kind of shit in Latin. Turns out she thought I was possessed by a demon and was chanting some kind of spell. I remembered some of the words she was saying to me, even though I couldn't really spell them or understand them, and Googled them. They were words people say in an exorcism. Cray shit."

"She had a pillow in her hands?"

"Yeah. She did. And this look in her eyes...she looked like she was in some kind of a trance or some shit like that. I thought she wanted to kill me by smothering me with that pillow."

"Did you ever go to the police after that?"

"No. I should've, but I didn't. I didn't want them getting involved because I told myself my mom was crazy as a bat, but wasn't violent and maybe didn't mean anything by holding the pillow over me like that. I told myself the whole thing was a fluke. Mainly, I didn't want the cops involved because I might've been taken out of the home. That was the last thing I wanted. No way did I want to go into the foster care system. Heard too many horror stories about that and I was 17 – who'd want me? And transgendered. I had more chance of hitting the Powerball than getting into a decent home. I wanted to stay with my mom until I finished high school and then hopefully got into a good college about a million miles away from her and her bullshit."

"Did you tell anyone about the pillow incident? Any of your friends, your teachers, anyone at all?"

Heather shook her head. "I should've, but I didn't. I was afraid they'd call the police for me. Teachers are required to report that shit. And my friends might've called the police, too, 'cause that's some trifling shit right there. I just wanted the pillow thing to be a secret. I was desperate not to have to leave the home under any circumstances. Besides, I was almost 18 when the pillow thing happened. If I could make it to my 18th birthday, I could be sure the foster care system wouldn't get involved if any more shit went down. I was a few months out at the time. I thought I could just roll with her cray for awhile. I'd applied to several colleges and was accepted by a few. Got some scholarships, some grants, some student loans. I was all set to get out of that hell-hole. I needed to make it just a few more months."

"So what happened next?"

Heather shrugged. "Nothing much, not for several more months. Then I turned 18, so I knew the foster care system wouldn't come and get me if something happened, so, I don't know, I started to relax a little. And then we had this big fight one night, right after my 18th birthday. She again told me I was possessed by a demon and wanted me to see some kind of priest who'd get that demon out of me. Throw some holy water on me and maybe make my head turn all the way around, like in that movie. Or some shit, I don't know what they do in an exorcism. I only know what they did in that movie. I wanted no part of that. I screamed at her, she screamed at me, and then..."

"And then what?"

She shuddered and sucked on her cigarette again. She looked into the distance, as if remembering a painful memory. She wrapped her arms around herself, as if she were trying to hug herself, and shook her head.

"She came at me with a butcher knife. We were standing in the kitchen and she opened up the drawer and came at me with this knife. Scared the crap out of me, but thank God I had a pocket knife on me. I always carried it around with me, because I always got the crap beaten out of me in school, so I needed to have it on me at all times in case I needed to defend myself at a moment's notice."

I was quiet, trying to get the incident out of her without freaking her out too much. She looked like she would break down at any moment. This was a painful memory for her. I knew that, so I was sensitive about this.

She finally sighed. "She lunged at me with the butcher knife and I plunged my knife into her neck. I didn't even have time to think about it. I just was on auto-pilot. I just put that knife in her and blood started to squirt everywhere. It was every-fucking-where. And I ran. I ran out of the house and went and stayed with Charlie."

I nodded. "Charlie. When did you meet him?"

"At a party. I didn't really know him all that well. He gave me his number after the party, asking me to call him, but I didn't want to. I don't like to play that. I like to keep my options open at all times and didn't want to get tied down with nobody. That's why I never tried to stay with him before. But after that happened with my mom, I needed a place to go and went to stay with him. He lives in the Bottoms in a converted loft. I felt safe there, but somehow the cops found me anyhow. I think one of Charlie's buddies snitched on me because my face was in the paper after my mom was found. And somehow the whole thing blew up. I don't know why, but the papers got on it and blew it up, like I was a public enemy or something like that."

I opened up my file that had the criminal statement of information and read through it again. I was looking for any kind of evidence that a butcher knife was found at the scene. It sounded like Heather fled the scene right after she killed her mother, so the butcher knife would've been found. There wasn't any reason why it wouldn't be there.

Yet, as I read through the Statement of Information, I couldn't find the words "butcher knife" anywhere in there. I shook my head, wondering if I could trust my client's recount of events. I had to look at all angles, because the prosecution sure as hell would. No way would the court let her get away with saying her mother had a butcher knife if one wasn't recovered at the scene.

I didn't want to confront her with that pertinent piece of information, though, until I could do some independent investigation of my own. I didn't want her to get defensive with me because then she would just shut down.

Just then, I looked at my phone and saw Tammy was texting me 911.

"Excuse me," I said to Heather. "I need to take this."

Heather just shrugged her shoulders. "Okay. Just make sure you come on back as soon as you can. And keep me posted on what's going on. I hope you believe my story."

I didn't believe her story. Not entirely. It sounded good, but the problem with self-defense was that it was difficult enough to prove. Defendants often claimed that he or she had to kill because the victim would kill him or her. But actually proving that was the case...there was the rub.

"I have some more questions," I said. "But I need to issue some subpoenas so I can get some independent verification on what you're saying. I'll schedule depositions for the people you saw at the gay conversion therapy center, so I need to know all the doctors and therapists you saw and the name of the clinic where you went. And I'd also like to subpoena your mother's computer. I have a feeling that, when I go through her history, I'll find the information I'll need to build a good defense. There's something you're missing and that's what caused her to suddenly become so aggressive with you when she wasn't before. Once I find that out, the pieces of the puzzle might come together better."

"Okay," Heather said, putting her forefinger in her hair and twirling it around and around. She swung her legs to and from, swinging back and forth, while she smacked her lips. "You take that call. I have to get back to my room. I hope to see you back here once you get the information you need. And my therapists were called Dr. Schultz, fucking Nazi, and Dr. Woods. The name of the conversion therapy place was called – get this – Rainbow International. How fucking ironic is that? The official word is they call it that because they want their clients to have hope and a rainbow is the symbol of hope. Or some shit." She started to laugh. "I have no idea if they know what the rainbow means to us queer folk. If they don't, well, what rock have they been under?"

I nodded, distracted by the text message from Tammy. What was going on? Was it bad or good? I had no idea, no clue.

I only knew that there was some kind of emergency.

NINE

I called Tammy and she picked up immediately. "You need to get down here right away," she said. "Rina and Abby are here. They apparently ran away from their new foster family. They need to talk to you."

I groaned, but, at the same time, I was happy. I desperately wanted them back in my life. I really bonded with them when they were at my house. They were happy I'd taken an interest in them. Apparently, nobody else in their lives did the same.

"Keep them right there," I said. "I'll be at the office in a half hour."

I went and found Heather in her room. She was bunking with three men, two of whom were currently in the room with her. One guy was completely bald with tattoos all over his face and his bald head. He looked like he might've been halfway good-looking at one point, before he apparently started doing steroids and getting completely inked. His eyes were piercing blue, he had long dark eyelashes and a straight Roman nose. The other guy was an overweight African-American man with extremely dark skin. Both men were over 6 feet tall. The third guy wasn't in the room, although I saw his bed and, next to his bed, was a mound of clothes.

I wondered if these guys were okay with bunking with somebody who was essentially a woman. Here was Heather, in her high heels, sparkly headband and full makeup, bunking with these guys who were obviously guys. She didn't belong there at all. She was a woman, for all intents and purposes. A woman, not a man.

"Hello," Heather said, looking at her nails. Her two roommates were playing cards and weren't paying attention to me or Heather. I wondered if that was always the case. "I know, you have to leave, don't you?"

"Yes. But I'll be back. Listen, I'd like to petition the court for you to stay with me until you have your trial." I looked around the room. "I think you might be more comfortable at my house."

Heather nodded but I saw tears come to her eyes. "That would be nice. It would be nice to have somebody in my life who's older and not a total phobe. Not that you're older, but you know what I mean."

I did know what she meant. I was 35 and Heather was currently 18, so, technically, I was old enough to be her mother. She desperately needed somebody who cared about her and wouldn't judge her. From what she was telling me earlier, it sounded as if she never had that in her life.

"Ta ta," she said, waving her hand. "Don't be long." She pursed her lips, making a kissing motion to me and I laughed.

"I won't be."

I ARRIVED in the office to find Rina and Abby waiting in the lobby of my office suite. Rina came up to me when I came in and immediately gave me a hug. "Harper," she said. "You made it."

"I did. What's going on? Why aren't you at your foster family's home?"

Abby looked at me and then cast her eyes downward. "We hate it there. The mom and the dad fight all the time, and the dad beats on the mom. And…" Abby started to look extremely nervous.

"Go on," Rina said. "Tell her. Tell her and maybe she can try again to take us in. She can give the court reason to get us out of there and back with her. So just tell her."

"The court won't believe us. They'll make us go back there no matter what we do," Abby said and then she started to cry. "They're going to have a status hearing on Monday. We need to tell our Guardian Ad Litem about what's going on so she can hopefully recommend we come back to Harper's home."

In Missouri, minor children got their own attorney when they were involved in the system or any time abuse or neglect was alleged. Rina and Abby's Guardian was named Alexis Winters and she annoyed me because she was the one who advised the Family Court not to allow me to adopt the two girls.

I wanted to take the girls in, but I knew that taking in Heather would destroy my chance. I promised Heather I'd take her in and needed to keep that promise. Her reaction to my offer to take her in sealed the deal. That proud young girl, who tried to show the world she was fierce and not scared of anybody or anything and could whip anybody's ass, let her guard down and showed me her emotions. That meant the world to me.

"Tell me what happened," I said to Abby. "Tell me and I'll do all I can to make sure you won't go back there. I'll call Alexis right now and tell her you can't go back and I'll file an emergency hearing to get temporary custody of the two of you. But you have to tell me what's going on."

Abby sighed. "They have this son who's 18 and living with them. He's very weird. He has all these outbursts all the time, where he starts to scream at the top of his lungs and punches walls. There's holes everywhere in the walls from him. The mother, who's the only sane person in that house, told me the son, his name is Pete, has something called Intermittent Explosiveness Disorder and can't control these outbursts. So, we have the dad who also seems to have the same disorder, because he acts the same way, and the son both becoming violent all the time."

Rina looked over at Abby, who shook her head.

"Okay, if you're not going to tell her, I will," Rina said. "Pete molested Abby tonight. The parents weren't home – I think they were at some kind of a fundraising event or something like that, and he attacked her. I had no idea what was going on because I was in the living room at the time, watching TV. He gagged her with a sock so she couldn't scream. Harper, you have to get us out of there. He did that to Abby, and told her I was next, because we're identical twins so he quote wants to have us both unquote." Rina looked disgusted and Abby started to cry. Rina put her arm around her and put her head on her shoulder. "Shhh, Abby, don't cry. Harper will help us out. Won't you, Harper?"

"Of course," I said without hesitation. "You just come and stay with me tonight and I'll give a quick call to Alexis tomorrow. Then I'll file an emergency motion with the court and hopefully we can see the judge within the next few days. That's a very serious charge, Abby, so Alexis will be on board with, at the very least, the two of you leaving your current home."

Abby and Rina looked at one another. "I told you," Rina said to Abby.

"I know," Abby said, her head hanging.

"You know what? You told her what?" I asked Rina and Abby.

"I told her you probably wouldn't take us in again." Rina's voice was accusing and her body language was just as accusing. She had her arms crossed in front of her and her eyebrows were raised.

I was devastated by her words and more devastated by their predicament. I was responsible for where they were at the moment. If it weren't for me, they'd be with their mother right now.

"Let me call Alexis," I said, looking at the clock. It read 9:20. I didn't know what time Alexis went to bed but I'd call her anyhow. I needed to get some kind of reassurance that she would, at the very least, not object to me getting the girls temporarily.

I got on the phone with Alexis. She picked up on the second ring. "Hello," she said. "Alexis Winters."

"Alexis, this is Harper Ross," I said. "I'm sorry to bother you this late, but it can't be helped. I have Rina and Abby Caldwell here in my office and they had to leave their foster home."

"Why did they leave that home? The social worker gave that home an A and that family is one of the most prominent in the city. If I were you, I'd take them back there tonight."

I sighed. I hated it when people talked like that – as if, just because somebody was wealthy and connected, they were automatically considered to be a good home.

"Alexis, I'm not going to advise those two girls to go back to that house after what they told me. They said the father is abusive and rageful and so is the son. And the son sexually attacked Abby." I felt the bile rise in my throat and blinked back tears. The haunting I felt ever since I found out about Gina got hotter and hotter until I felt like it was about to overwhelm me.

Alexis sighed. "Do you actually believe that? There have been other foster children who have stayed with the Browns and there has never been a reported problem. They're playing you, Harper, because they want to stay with you. You and I both know that's not a good idea."

I looked over at Rina and Abby, wondering what the truth was. They certainly looked freaked out, but maybe they were really good actors. If what Alexis was saying was true – the Browns have had foster kids before, with no bad reports, what was the chance they suddenly had these kinds of problems when they didn't before? As a lawyer, I was cynical. People lied all the time.

Yet I really wanted the girls back with me. A part of me wanted this whole awful story to be true. Not that I wanted them to have gone through such trauma, but I really wanted them to come home with me and stay for good. It wasn't just my guilt feelings at this point, although, I admit, that was my initial motivation for taking them. Once I found there wasn't any friend or relative who could care for them and they would be going into the system, I knew I had to save them. After having them under my roof, though, I bonded with them and enjoyed having them around.

"No, you and I both don't think my having them is a bad idea. Only you think that."

"Yes, I think that, because I'm an attorney too, and I know how hard it is to juggle everything. And, I hate to be frank with you, but I find it hard to juggle everything and I'm not a recovering alcoholic. Nor am I dealing with two traumatized girls who just lost their mother in a brutal way. It all adds up to you not being right for them. They need to be in a nuclear home and the Browns are the best family I could find for them. Tell them to go home."

I could feel my blood boiling with every word Alexis said. She was being completely unfair in her assessment of me and my supposed fitness to be a mother to the two young girls. How dare she judge me like that? She should know there are always intangibles that go into every situation, and, yes, I looked terrible on paper. But she didn't know I did all I could to make sure those two girls had an incredible home. They'd be much better off with me than with a father and son who had temper problems and they certainly would be better with me than with a pervert boy.

I looked over at the two girls who were now huddled together on the leather couch in my office lobby. Literally huddled together. Rina was speaking softly to Abby and I could hear various words. I gathered that she was comforting her and telling her everything would be okay. I heard something about how I'd fix the problem.

No, I wouldn't fix the problem. Not if I wanted to keep my law license because if I took those girls to my home, I'd be guilty of kidnapping. Getting a felony slapped on me would tend to make the Missouri Bar to not look on me so kindly, to say the very least.

"You can't talk to me like that. Just because you have problems making everything work doesn't mean I do too. I told you before that I hired help to stay with those two girls when I had to work late. I also had them come to my office during some really late nights. And, yes, I've had a problem with alcohol in the past, but that's all in the past."

"I know what you're saying, and I agree, you were doing a good job with them. But the answer is still no. Those girls need to be in a home where there's a mother and father and they need to be with somebody who has time for them. No offense, but that somebody isn't you. Now please send them back. Within the next few minutes. I'll be getting a phone call from the Browns any second now and I want to to tell them the girls are on their way home."

"Don't they get a say? At all? I mean, they made their way over to my office and want to stay with me. They don't want to stay with the Browns. Doesn't that mean anything at all to you? They're old enough to decide, or they should be. They're very mature. They should have a say."

"They do. But, of course, their wishes are but one piece of the puzzle for me. Just one factor out of many. And it's the only factor favoring you."

I looked over at them again, dreading what I would have to tell them. It needed to be done, however. If I didn't want to get charged with kidnapping, it would have to be done.

"I'll be filing a motion for temporary custody tomorrow morning," I said to Alexis.

"You do that. I'll oppose it, of course. Now, take them back to the Browns. File your motion with the court but don't expect anything to happen. There's no reason for them not to be there. In fact, if they file a petition to adopt them, I won't oppose that. At least, not right now. I'll have to get the results of the home study in, but it looks good right now. Besides, you know I have no say on what you can do with the kids tonight. Neither does Rick." Rick Haverford was the attorney for the Browns and would have to sign off on my taking the kids anywhere but back to the Browns that evening.

I sighed, looking over at the kids, and thinking hard. I didn't want to take them back, not after what happened over at the Browns that night. I had no idea if they were telling me the truth, but if they were, that was really serious.

"Fine," I said. "Listen, I didn't want to do this. I really didn't, because I know it's going to open up a whole can of big fat worms. But I think I'll have to call the police. What these girls have told me warrants that."

I hated getting the cops involved. That would inevitably escalate anything going on in the home and would put a lot of undue pressure on two traumatized girls. But Alexis was leaving me no choice.

Alexis sighed. "Don't do that. You'll cause a huge mess over there when it probably isn't warranted. Kids say things to implicate their foster families. It's what they do. It's what Rina and Abby are probably doing."

"Probably doing. Probably. And what if they're telling the truth. What then?"

"Take them back and file your motion. I won't go round and round with you tonight. Now, if you'll excuse me, I really have to go to bed. It's late." At that, she hung up on me.

I swallowed hard as I looked at the phone in my hand.

"What?" Rina asked. "What did she say?"

I straightened my spine. "I have to take you back to your home. To the Browns."

At that, Abby started to cry. It was as if she was holding back before because she had a glimmer of hope that she wouldn't have to go back there, but when I told her I'd have to take her back, the dam just burst.

"You can't do that. You can't make us go back there." Rina was adamant.

"I'll call the police," I said to Rina. "I'll call them right now. They'll investigate and probably take you to a safe place tonight. Back to the home you went to after your mother died. And then I can-"

"No. Don't call the police. We won't talk to them," Rina said.

"Why won't you?" I asked her. "That's the only way you

can prevent being taken back there. If I kept you at my house, the Browns would have me arrested for kidnapping."

"We won't talk to them because Abby has promised me not to call them. She said Pete threatened her. He told her that he would kill us both if she went to the cops and the cops would never believe her anyhow, because the Browns are like the biggest contributors to all the charities the cops are involved with. Just because they're rich, the cops won't hassle them. They'll hassle us."

"Well, then, I can't take you to my home tonight and I can't take you anywhere else, because that would be kidnapping."

"How can it be kidnapping? We came to you. You didn't forcibly take us," Rina said.

"Kidnapping doesn't have to be forcible. The Browns are your legal guardian and if I kept you away from them, I would be guilty of kidnapping in the state of Missouri. I'm sorry, I just can't..." My voice trailed off. I just couldn't what? Risk my law license and my freedom? And why shouldn't I? After all, these girls would have their mother with them if it weren't for me. They wouldn't be in the position where the freak of a father and an even bigger freak of a son were tormenting them.

"You can't what?" Abby was finally speaking and I looked into those big brown eyes and knew she was telling me the truth. She was genuinely terrified. "You can't what?"

I opened my mouth and shut it again. "I can't let you go back there. You'll come home with me tonight and I'll file a motion with the court in the morning to have you stay with me for good."

Rina and Abby both jumped up off the couch and hugged me. "I knew it. I knew it," Abby said. "Rina told me you wouldn't do this for us, but I knew you would. Thank you, Aunt Harper. Thank you."

I sighed as I hugged them back. I was opening up a can of

worms that would lead to me going to jail myself. I didn't need this hanging over me when I was working on a possible capital murder trial.

I didn't need the hassle but I needed to protect these girls.

I couldn't protect their mother, but I'd be damned if I couldn't protect them.

TEN

Of course, after I took Rina and Abby home, I knew there would be hell to pay. I looked at Rina sitting next to me in my car. "I don't know what I'm doing," I said. "If we go home, the cops will meet us there. I can almost guarantee that. Alexis knows what I'm up to, and as soon as your foster parents come home and see you're not there, they'll call the police on me."

I gripped the wheel, my mind spinning. What was I doing? Still trying to assuage my guilt, for one, but, for another, I genuinely cared about these two girls. But my priority still had to be on Heather's case and getting arrested would make doing that extremely tough.

"Where are we going to go?" Abby asked me from the back seat. "We can't go to your home, so where can we go?"

"I'm thinking." My mind started to race. What was my next move? Hide these girls? How would that work out? It wouldn't. It couldn't.

I finally sighed. I promised the girls I wouldn't take them back to the Browns yet I couldn't possibly think of an alternative that would work for any period of time. Even if I hid them, the jig would eventually be up and they'd be returned to the Browns, who would be good and angry at both of them. And I'd be put in jail immediately. And possibly prison at some point. Nobody would win in that situation.

"Girls, I-"

"Don't say it, Aunt Harper," Abby said. "Please don't say it."

"I'll file a motion with the court as soon as possible, I promise, to get custody."

"Didn't you say Alexis isn't for that?" Rina was wise beyond her years and understood perfectly the dynamics of her and Abby's case.

"Yes, but that doesn't mean I can't file a petition with the court to get you back."

"But the judge will side with Alexis, won't she?"

"Not necessarily. Really, we should get the police involved."

"No police," Rina said firmly. "Pete is dangerous. We're both afraid of what will happen once the cops get involved."

I felt like I was in the ultimate no-win situation. The girls would have to return to a place where there was physical and sexual abuse and there wasn't a thing I could do about it. I gripped the steering wheel with frustration, angry that Alexis refused to listen to me and angry that there was little that could be done in this situation to help them.

Most of all, I was angry, furious, with myself.

I looked at Abby in my rear-view mirror. She was cowering in the backseat, literally shaking. Her eyes were huge and she had silent tears streaking down her cheeks. Her breathing was labored and heavy – I could see her chest heaving up and down, up and down. She bit her lower lip and looked out the window.

Rina looked behind her at her twin. "Don't cry, Abby,

please don't cry. Aunt Harper will get this straight. She will. She loves us, and won't make us go back there. Come on, Abby, please. Please."

I sighed, trying to figure a way out of this for the two girls. If something happened to either of them, and I could possibly have stopped it...I couldn't live with myself. Yet, what could I do? Alexis wasn't listening to me and the judge would have my balls in a jar, if I had balls to put into a jar. There was just nothing I could do.

"Rina, don't tell her that. Don't tell her I'm not going to take her back to the Browns's, because I have to."

"No, you don't," Rina said.

I opened my mouth and then shut it again. "Okay, here's what we'll do. I'll call Sophia and have her take you to a hotel tonight. It wouldn't do to take you to my house because the only thing that'll happen is that the cops will show up and take you guys back to the Browns. Then tomorrow I'll file a motion with the court to get temporary custody. I'm sorry, that's the only thing I can do tonight. I'll definitely have to get Alexis on our side for this and I have to figure that one out. This is the best I can do."

Rina looked back at Abby, who said nothing, but nodded. "Okay. If that's what you have to do, then do it. It's better than going back there."

My hands gripped the steering wheel, as I wondered what kind of blowback I'd get for this. Was I still technically guilty of kidnapping? I wasn't their guardian and was keeping them away from their guardians without permission. The Browns were wealthy and could afford a high-dollar attorney to come after me.

I'd have to cross that bridge when I came to it. My first priority was that the girls were safe.

In the back of my mind, however, I was worried about what my actions with the girls would do to Heather. I'd be distracted and possibly in jail myself. Perhaps facing criminal charges.

I hoped none of these things would happen. But if they did, I had to be ready. And so did Heather.

ELEVEN

The next day, I got to work on Heather's case, while bracing myself for what would happen with Rina and Abby. I decided to get some subpoenas ready to go so I could see the computer of Heather's mom. I knew there was something on there that would lead me to why Heather's mom was acting so strangely. Heather told me her mom wasn't overly religious while she was growing up, and then the mom ended up getting "Jesusy" as Heather put it. Why was this? I needed to see her e-mails and the websites she frequented, in order to get the answer to that question.

Plus, I'd have to see if she'd seen any doctors prior to her death – doctors who might be able to testify to her mental fitness. I'd have to find a way around the doctor-patient privilege for that, which would be tricky, to say the very least.

I'd also have to depose the friends of the mother and, of course, I'd have to depose the "therapists" at that abhorrent Rainbow International clinic. In short, I'd have to put together a case for the jury that showed that Heather's mother was, more likely than not, crazy enough to come at her daughter with a butcher knife.

At the same time, I had to somehow explain why a butcher knife was never recovered from the scene. That detail nagged at me and would be fatal to the case. If I couldn't explain that one away, all bets were off – Heather would lose her self-defense case and there would be very little I could do for her, except plead her out.

Because one thing was for sure – Heather killed her mother. There would be no SODDI defense, no pointing fingers at somebody else. Heather told me she did it, so that took away SODDI right there. Some other dude didn't do it – she did it. Self-defense was literally my only card to play. Without that, I might as well plead her. And, if I pleaded her, I'd be sentencing her to an almost certain death.

The pressure was ramped up because of the limited options I had. I had to paint the mother as a crazy lunatic, and that meant I had to investigate that mother eight ways to Sunday.

Tammy knocked on my open door. "Hey," she said. "Can I come in?"

I nodded, looking over my subpoena. "Give this to Pearl," I said, handing Tammy the subpoena. "To type this up. I need to get ahold of the computer of Heather's mother and I need to subpoena some people for a deposition. And-"

"I'll give these to Pearl," she said. "But I wanted to find out what happened with Rina and Abby?"

I sighed and sat back in my chair. "That's become a nightmare. Those girls were being abused, mentally and sexually. At least one of the girls has been abused sexually, and the other one is in grave danger of that. I don't think there's physical abuse just yet, but they told me that both the father and the brother have explosive tempers and they seem terrified of both of them. I called

Alexis, and she doesn't want to believe me. So, I took the girls to a hotel last night instead of taking them back to the Browns. I've..." I trailed off. "I just couldn't take them back there."

"You opened a can of worms," Tammy said. "But that's a tough one. Why didn't you call the police?"

"They begged me not to," I said. "Listen, I have to get these subpoenas out the door, just in case the cops show up here to take me down. I fully expect that to happen."

Tammy sighed and made a temple with her fingers as she examined me. "You're still beating yourself up, aren't you?"

"Yes. Yes, I am. Let me. But it's more than that – I genuinely love those two little girls. They're a part of me. I don't care that the adoption wasn't approved. When they hurt, I hurt. They don't have their mother because of me. There's no way I can let them suffer because of what I did. I know what you're thinking and I know what you're going to say. Please don't bother with telling me how I'm screwing up, because believe me, I know I am. I know."

"Well, at least you know." She raised her eyebrows and her voice got really small. "Alexis has been calling all morning. I think you might be right about the cops thing. She's pissed and she's really upset that she doesn't know where they are. I think everybody will end up in court about this mess either today or tomorrow."

"I know. She's been blowing up my cell phone too. I've been ignoring it. I have to get going on Heather's case because she's been assigned to the rocket docket. There won't be a ton of time to get everything done that needs to be done."

"Get the subpoenas out and then talk to Alexis. You can't ignore her forever. That'll only piss her off. She can possibly prevent you from going to jail for what you did. Call her. And, while you're at it, tell her where the children are."

I shook my head. One disaster at a time. "Let me give this to

Pearl," I said, going out to our suite's lobby where Pearl, our secretary and receptionist, sat.

I approached Pearl, who was my African-American secretary. She was slim and pretty, with café au lait skin, braids and a gap between her teeth. She was talking to somebody on the phone and I saw her roll her eyes and purse her lips. "Ms. Winters, I-" She paused, looking at me and shaking her head. "I told you, Ms. Ross is busy. Busy. She'll call you when she's out of court...how do you know she's not in court...traffic court... she's not answering her cell phone because she's in traffic court...I will."

She hung up the phone and looked at me. "Girl, you really pissed off Alexis Winters. Are you going to tell me what you did?"

"I will," I said. "I'll give you the 90 second version, because I'm late for traffic court. Anyhow, Rina and Abby are being abused in their foster home, and I called Alexis last night to ask if I could keep them and file a motion for temporary custody. She said no, so I took the girls over to a hotel and my nanny is watching them right now. The nanny has no clue that I essentially kidnapped those kids, so if the shit hits the fan, she won't be implicated."

"Don't be ridiculous," Tammy said. "You didn't essentially kidnap those kids, you kidnapped them. And the nanny will be dragged through the mud, too. You have to get those kids back to their foster parents. Do things right."

"I won't. If you would've seen Abby last night in the car, you wouldn't take them back, either. She was genuinely terrified. There's no way I'll let either of them be subjected to what's going on over at the Browns. No way." I took a deep breath, knowing the chances were great that I wouldn't make it back from court. I completely anticipated being arrested the second I stepped into that courtroom. If I made it that far.

Pearl gave me a head-roll and raised her right eyebrow. "I know that's right. If someone is abusing a kid, you don't take them back there. I've seen too many kids end up dead in those situation. You doing the right thing, Harper." She nodded approvingly.

"Thanks. I knew you'd understand." I shot a look over at Tammy. "Now, please, Pearl, execute these subpoenas. I really need to get Heather's case off the ground before the shit hits the fan, which it inevitably will."

SURE ENOUGH, when I got to the courtroom, cops were waiting for me. Of course, I didn't necessarily know the cops were there for me, exactly, as there were always a ton of cops in these traffic courts. Yet, when I walked in, and I saw them look at me and point, I knew.

I glanced over and saw the Browns there, as well.

I went over to the cop who pointed at me when I first came in. "Okay, Harry, I know you're here to cuff me. But I have a traffic client. Can you wait until I get my deal with the prosecutor for him?"

The cop looked over at Seth Brown, who was the father in the Brown household. "I will, but you need to talk to Mr. Brown over there. Maybe cuffing you won't be necessary."

"I'm pretty sure it will. Because I won't do what those people want me to do. But I'll go and talk to him."

I went over to Seth Brown, who looked like he wanted to charge me. In fact, if he weren't in a courtroom, with bailiffs and cops all around, he probably would've decked me. As for Marina Brown, she looked terrified. I looked at her face and saw she was heavily made-up, but you could see, right under the shit-ton of foundation she had on, the outline of a faint bruise.

I shook my head. Abusers usually were smarter than to hit their victims in the face, where everybody could see the marks. Either Mr. Brown wasn't that smart, or he simply couldn't control himself.

"Hello, Mr. Brown," I said, extending my hand.

"Don't hello Mr. Brown me," he said. "Your ass is mine." He clenched his fist and took a deep breath. He was apparently using all his energy in restraining himself from wailing on me with his fists. "You need to bring those kids back, and I mean yesterday." He started to raise his voice, and Marina's eyes got wide. She took his arm and tugged it and looked at me.

"Please, Ms. Ross," she said to me. "Please bring those girls back to our house."

"Don't you plead with her," Seth said. "That little bitch doesn't deserve your respect and she certainly doesn't deserve your pleas. The only thing she'll understand is when those cops over there take her into custody for kidnapping." He turned to me. "Now, Ms. Ross, this is your last chance. You call the person who's watching those girls, have her bring them into this courtroom within the hour, and I'll call off the cops. Otherwise, you're going to jail today. Right now."

I nodded. "I understand." I turned away and went over to the prosecutor, who was offering plea deals for all the traffic clients who were in the courtroom. As I spoke with the prosecutor, whose name was Mitch Gross, I glanced over at the Browns. Marina was literally holding Seth back – she had his arms behind his back and he was struggling to free himself while she talked to him, presumably about his not flying across the room and belting me.

"I'll reduce the speeding ticket to a defective equipment ticket," the prosecutor said. "And I'll go ahead and give it to the judge. You have bigger things to worry about right now." He gestured to the cops who already had their handcuffs out.

"I guess I do. And thanks." I went over to the cop with the handcuffs out. "Okay, Harry," I said, putting my wrists out. "I'm ready."

"I don't want to do this to you, Harper," he said, putting the cuffs on me. I looked around and saw my colleagues whispering amongst themselves. I inwardly was amused by their faces. One thing was for sure – I'd be the talk of the town after this.

I followed the cops out to their car and they put me in the back, taking off my cuffs. "I only put those cuffs on you for Mr. Brown. That man wants you tarred and feathered and run out on a rail."

I nodded as I sat in the back of the squad car. "Can I make my phone call now? Tammy, my law partner, will have to know what's going on. I have three court appearances this afternoon that she'll have to cover." Thank God Tammy rarely went to court herself. As an estate planner, she basically did her work in the office. I was lucky in that regard.

"Will she bond you out?"

"I don't know what the bond will be, but I'd imagine she'll post it for me." I sighed, knowing that wouldn't be the end of it. The next thing would be my being held in contempt of court. There would be no bonding out of that one.

"Tammy," I said into the phone. "I was arrested, just like I thought. Could you appear for me tomorrow morning and then bond me out? And cover for me for the rest of the day?"

Tammy sighed. "Harper..."

"Please." I knew Tammy was at the end of her rope. I didn't blame her. I basically took a month off and left her holding the bag, and now this. "Tammy, it has to be this way."

"You're in the middle of a high-profile case and now you're being arrested. How will that look in the media?"

"I don't know. If Heather wants to fire me, then she can..." My voice trailed off. How irresponsible was that of me? I entered my appearance on Heather's case, her life was literally in my hands, and I would be in jail. Yet there wasn't any way around it for me. I had to protect Rina and Abby. I'd just have to figure out a schedule that would allow me to do what I needed to do to represent Heather, while being in jail, assuming the Family Court judge ordered me to bring the girls back and I refused, which I planned to do. I'd then be in contempt of an order, and I wouldn't get out of jail until I complied with the order. That would be the twelfth of never, and that's a long, long time.

"She can what? You committed to her and she wants you. Only you. She's adamant about that."

"I wonder why she wants only me on her case?"

"I don't know. She said something about an article you wrote while you were in law school. She apparently did some research on her case and she came across you and your *Law Review* article. What did you write about, anyhow?"

"I wrote about self-defense cases and how the victim's character can be used in court when building a case. But the arguments I made weren't necessarily new. However, I included a case where the victim was brainwashed and that caused her to become violent towards the assailant. I wonder if that was Heather's angle. That sounds pretty similar to her case, so maybe that was why she wanted me to be her attorney so much."

Was that what happened? Heather's mother was brainwashed? Did Heather believe her mother was brainwashed? That was an avenue worth pursuing.

"Well, it sounds like that's why she chose you. At any rate, you need to resolve the issue with the girls pronto. You can't leave her high and dry, which you will, if you're in jail."

I sighed. "I can't. I just can't. I have to protect them. No matter what happens, I have to protect them."

"So what do you want me to do?"

"Call Heather and tell her what happened. I'll be out on bond by tomorrow, and I should be out of jail until the judge calls a hearing on the Rina and Abby matter, at which point he'll probably put me in jail for contempt of court. But I'll cross that bridge when I come to it."

"Well, you better get as much done as you can, because Pearl scheduled an emergency hearing on the Rina and Abby matter for Friday at 4."

"Okay, then I have three days to get something done on the case." I nodded. "Let's expedite the subpoena for the mother's computer. Heather has her password, so it won't be a problem getting into it."

"Pearl will get it done. It's already with the process server. As long as the prosecutor doesn't quash the subpoena, you'll have her computer within a day or so. You'll have to work quickly, though. I don't see how you can conduct depositions if you're behind bars."

"I'll cross that bridge when I come to it. In the meantime..." I looked up and saw the jail coming into view. "In the meantime, I need to get that computer and see if I need to do any depositions or investigation."

I sighed as Harry opened up the door. "I never thought I'd be arresting you," he said. "I know you know your Miranda rights like the back of your hand, but I need to read them to you anyhow."

I smiled. "Maybe this is karma, huh? After all, you and I have been in opposition on more cases than I care to think about."

Harry laughed. "Yeah, but that was all business. I always knew that. Now, you have the right to remain silent..."

My mind wandered as he went through the rest of the Miranda rights. I couldn't think past today, however. I refused to think about the possibility that I'd go to prison for a long time for this. Kidnapping was a serious charge, to say the very least. Not to mention, I'd soon be in contempt of an order. Thank God it was summertime, and the kids were out of school. Otherwise, there would be one more crime that I would be guilty of, and that was truancy.

Everything was piling up, and all I wanted was a drink. I tried to tamp down that urge. I had to, anyhow, because I couldn't get alcohol where I was going. Drugs, yeah. Apparently, according to my clients, there were more drugs behind bars than there were on the outside. But alcohol – no, I wouldn't have access to that. That made me crazy, yet it also cheered me, because there was no way I'd go back to that anyhow.

I went into the jail, where they fingerprinted and mug-shot me. Everyone was joking around with me, because I knew all the cops. I'd worked against them many times, and had cross-examined more than a few of them. Yet they never seemed to hold that against me. They had a job to do, and so did I.

After I was processed in, and I handed in my clothes, bag, shoes and jewelry and was issued an orange jumpsuit to change into, I was led into a cell. It was tiny, with a metal toilet and bunk beds that were really cots. The floor was cement and, even though it was in the middle of June, the cell was pretty drafty. I wasn't quite sure why that was – maybe the air conditioner was up too high – but I was in need of at least a little blanket.

I lay down on the cot and pulled my thin blanket over me. I didn't have a cell-mate just yet, although I knew that was coming.

All at once, the adrenaline coursing through my veins prior to this seemed to have settled, which left me feeling empty. I swallowed hard, knowing depression would roll in again. I closed my eyes, trying to will it away, plus will away the anxiety that inevitably accompanied it.

I was in an absolute low place, laying there on that cot. I'd made so many messes with my life. The girls were in an abusive situation and I didn't do the right thing by hiding them in that hotel room. I didn't see any way out, however. I had to do that. And Heather....I was behind bars. How could I give her a good defense?

I knew the depression could get really bad, because I didn't have access to my anti-depressants or the anti-anxiety pills I took when things got bad. I knew the jail would provide me with my prescription anti-depressants if I had to stay here long enough, but I wasn't as confident that my Ativan, which I took for anxiety, would also be provided, because I took that particular pill as needed.

I stewed with my thoughts until nightfall, which filled me with dread even more. It was completely dark and surprisingly silent. I closed my eyes, trying to sleep, but knew it was hopeless.

This cell might be my home. I couldn't chase that thought away, no matter how hard I tried.

TWELVE

The next day, I was led, along with the other inmates, to court for my initial appearance. I was linked together with everyone else, and I dreaded this. It was bad enough that I was in jail for something serious, but I knew everyone in that courtroom would be absolutely shocked to see me. The gossiping would soon begin. I didn't want to deal with humiliation on top of everything else, but I would just have to keep my chin up and try to ignore the staring.

I sat down in the jury box, along with all the people who were hooked onto me. I hung my head, not wanting to see the eyes that were no doubt boring into me. I didn't want to hear the whispers, either. I wanted to scream that I was charged with kidnapping because I was protecting two little girls, not that I was really a criminal.

Then again, I technically *was* a criminal. There wasn't any getting around that. It didn't really matter that I had a justification – kidnapping was kidnapping was kidnapping. Unlike with Heather, who, if she could prove self-defense, would be judged not guilty, there wasn't the same kind of defense available for me.

Tammy came up to me. "Okay, I'm here," she said. "Your bond will only be $25,000/10%. That's a good sign, huh?"

"Yeah," I said. "A very good sign. Somebody must think I'm not so bad." I looked at Tammy, trying to studiously avoid looking around that courtroom. "Is everyone talking?"

"Of course. They're all asking me why you're here. I just told them you're here because you're standing up for what's right. They all think you got arrested doing some kind of protest or something. You're okay."

"They're going to soon find out I wasn't arrested for protesting. I'm being charged with kidnapping. In what world is kidnapping a part of a protest?"

Tammy shrugged. "I don't know. Listen, I registered all my objections to you about what you're doing, but you seem determined, so I'm on your side 100%. Plus, I saw Marina Brown, and you're right. There's a bruise on her face bigger than Dallas. She covers it up with a ton of makeup, probably Chanel makeup, but nothing can cover that up. She seemed pretty terrified, too."

My ears perked up. "Marina Brown? When did you see her?"

"She came into our office. She wanted to impress upon me the importance of you bringing back those two girls. She didn't say as much, but I got the impression she wanted the girls to come back because the stress with the girls being gone was making her husband that much more of a monster. She said it was very important that the girls come back. She seemed desperate to make that happen."

I raised an eyebrow. "I wonder about that. Why didn't Seth come, I wonder?"

"I got the impression that Seth didn't know she was coming

to see me. At any rate, I'm sure your initial impression about that is right – I think Seth is abusive. You're doing the right thing."

I sighed. "What about Heather? Did you explain to her that I'm in jail and I might be there for a long time?"

"I did. She said she still wants you to represent her. I hope you can resolve this as soon as possible."

I sighed. "Me too."

The judge called my case, and I went up there. It was Judge Wilson again. He was the Associate Circuit Judge, so he was usually the one who ended up getting the initial appearances in the Jackson County Circuit.

He shook his head when I was brought up. "Harper Ross, I guess you got yourself into a pickle," he said as he studied the paper in front of him. "Charged with kidnapping." He read through the statement, which was unusual. He usually just read the charges to the defendants and sent them on their way. "Well, okay, then. Harper Ross, you've been charged by the State of Missouri with kidnapping in the first degree. How do you plead?"

"Not guilty, your honor."

He nodded. "I'm going to assign you a signature bond," he said. "Is there any objection from the prosecutor?"

I furrowed my brow, wondering what was getting into the cantankerous judge. First, he let Heather bond out and acknowledged her as a female, and now he was letting me out on my own recognizance?

The prosecutor, Ron Temple, just smiled. "I think Ms. Ross isn't a flight risk. She has too many cases to deal with around these parts. I don't have any objection to a signature bond, with the condition that she has no contact with the victims."

I had to stop myself from rolling my eyes. *Victims.* Those two girls were victims, alright, but they weren't my victims.

They were the victims of the Browns. Specifically Seth and Peter Brown. Marina seemed decent. She was probably a victim, too.

Just then, though, Seth stood up and raised his voice. "Your honor, you can't let this bitch out of jail. She has to stay in jail. I want her to think long and hard about what she did and she won't change her mind about bringing those two girls back unless she suffers."

The prosecutor looked over, and so did the judge. "Sit down, sir," Judge Wilson said to the clearly enraged man.

I looked at Seth, and, once again, it looked like he wanted to haul off and hit me. His fists were clenched, his eyes were bugging out, and I could see a vein coming out of his forehead. His body was coiled, as if he was a Cobra ready to strike.

"I won't. I won't sit down until you agree not to let that cunt out on bond."

At that, Judge Wilson banged his gavel, because everybody in the courtroom started to talk at once. Nobody could quite believe this man was screaming the "c" word.

"Bailiff, please take this gentleman out of this courtroom." Then the judge leaned down and spoke in a low voice. "I used the term *gentleman* lightly, of course."

I nodded. "Of course. Thank you, your honor, for the signature bond."

"You're one of us," he said with a wink. "And I think I know why you did what you did. Good luck with that, though. Judge Michaels won't give you any quarter, I know that. You better get your ducks in a row, because she don't take much shit."

Judge Michaels was the Family Court judge who was overseeing the girls' case. She'd hold me in contempt if I didn't bring back the girls. I was prepared for that.

"Thanks."

The bailiff led me away and I looked back at Tammy. She was standing by the bench, talking to the prosecutor. Then she came over to me. "Well, looks like you'll back in the office today. And none too soon, either. We have the mother's computer."

I smiled. Things were going well on that front, at least.

"Good deal. I'll have to get to it tonight. That computer will unlock a lot of key information."

At that, I was led out of the courtroom and into the van that would take me back to the jail. I would get my stuff, sign my name promising to appear for every court date, and get to work on Heather's case.

Something told me the computer would hold something major.

THIRTEEN

When I got back to the office that evening, I called Heather. "Heather," I said, "This is Harper."

"I know. I got caller ID, you know. How are things?"

"Good. I have your mom's computer."

Heather didn't say anything.

"Is there anything wrong?"

"Yeah. I got a friend, or I had a friend. Name's George. He was a gay boy, not trans. He helped me when I transitioned. Well, not totally transitioned, but you know what I mean. He was there."

My heart sunk. Just the way Heather was talking, I surmised that this George person had died. I wondered if he died of AIDS, then I immediately felt bad that I jumped to conclusions. Just because a young gay person dies doesn't mean that it was AIDS. "You said you had a friend. What happened to him?"

She sighed. "I've been trying to get in touch with him for a few weeks now. You know, 'hey it's me, call me back,' that kind of thing. He didn't call. Then today I found out why. If you got a newspaper, look at it."

I had a newspaper, right in front of me. I opened it up and scanned it, but didn't see anything. "Okay, you got me. What are you talking about?"

"The Metro section. You know, where they talk about this person being found or that person getting into a car accident. This one's not big enough to be in the front section."

I flipped through to the Metro section where, on the front page, there was a headline. "Body of young man found floating in the Missouri River."

"I found it," I said, scanning the article. It was a standard piece that talked about how George Donnelly was reported missing by his mother two weeks prior, and the authorities found his body washed ashore of the Missouri River. "Heather, I'm so sorry. This was a dear friend?"

"He was." She was silent for a few seconds. "Anyhow," she said, her voice cracking, "you're out of jail?"

"I am. For now."

"What do you mean, for now?"

"Well, I have a hearing on the girls' case on Thursday. The Family Court Judge will probably order me to bring the girls back to the Browns, and I won't do it. So, I'll be jailed until I comply, which will be the twelfth of never. Especially after I've gotten a look at the father, Seth Brown. That man needs anger control, at a minimum. I won't subject those two girls to him and his psycho son."

"I admire your conviction, but I hope you can do my case justice. My life is in your hands, you know. Literally, I guess."

I sighed. "I know. I wish I could figure out a way around all of this, but..."

"Okay." She sounded defeated, dejected. Certainly not the Heather I'd grown to know.

"You okay?"

"No. But I will be. As soon as...."

I heard her sobbing. "Heather...I'll come and visit you. We'll look at your mother's computer together. I can even bring you some of your favorite food, whatever that is. What is it?"

"Church's Chicken," she said. "I'm not even kidding. There's one in Mid-Town, on the way. Original recipe, mac and cheese and cole slaw. And a large iced tea."

I laughed. "I like a girl who knows what she wants. I'll be there in about an hour."

ABOUT AN HOUR LATER, I arrived at the halfway house, Church's chicken in hand. I picked up a two-piece for myself with mashed potatoes and mac and cheese. Heather came out and met me, and we took our food to the enclosed porch at the back of the house.

"Um hm," she said, looking me up and down as I got the food out of the bags and put it on paper plates. "Where do you put all that junk? You're as skinny as a ferret."

I laughed. "I could ask the same about you."

"I actually hit the gym five days a week. Don't laugh. It's the perfect place to eye cute boys while getting my ass as high as it can. Course, I haven't been doing that lately. Been just watching TV in my room this whole time." She slapped her butt. "Gotta get this working again soon. Hope they'll give me passes out of here. You still going to try to get me to stay at your house?"

"I am," I said. "If I don't-"

"Go to jail. I know." Heather rolled her eyes. "Anyhoo, let's look at the old bag's computer. What are you looking for?"

"I'm going to start with her browsing history. See what sites she frequents."

"I'm sure it won't be good. Something was making her all Jesusy and freaky. Hope this computer can explain that."

I booted up, and, since the computer was ancient, it seemed to take forever. "You okay?" I asked Heather while we waited and waited and waited for the computer to come online. "I mean, losing a friend is rough."

"Yeah, it is. It really is." Heather shook her head. "Harper, it's still so hard to be different. To be trans, to be gay. It's like there's no more groups to openly hate except for us. And trans is even more hated than gays. But the gays are hated enough. You'd think people would learn to live and let live by now, wouldn't you?"

We ate our chicken and I listened to the sounds outside the enclosed porch. It was a warm night, as it always was in June in Kansas City, and the cicadas were sounding off in the huge oak tree growing in the yard in the back of the house. The bugs were buzzing by the thousands, teeming in the trees. I always wondered why I never saw any of these bugs, but I could always hear them, especially at dusk. The people next door were laughing and talking. I couldn't see them, because the wooden fence was over seven feet tall, but I could hear snippets of conversation and laughter.

I watched the fireflies buzzing through the air, their lights flickering off and on. The fireflies on the ground were blinking their lights at the ones in the air, the females calling to the males silently with their glow.

"I don't know," I finally said. "I can never figure out why people like to hate on defenseless others who aren't like them, just because they're different. Society always has to find some kind of a scapegoat. Somebody who we can point to and say our problems are all because of them. Muslims, undocumented workers and LGBT – these groups seem to be the scapegoats of the moment. Unfortunately, LGBT seems to be the perennial scapegoats."

I put my arm around Heather, and she lay her head on my shoulder. "What do you think happened to your friend?"

Heather shrugged. "I don't know. Probably had the shit beat out of him by some hateful people. Or some shit like that."

"Well," I said, carefully removing my arm from around Heather's shoulders. "Let's get to work. The sooner we find out what your mother was up to, the sooner we can get the show on the road. And time is really of the essence now. After all, I might be returning to jail in just a few days. We gotta get something figured out by then."

"Okay. Here's the password," Heather said, writing down the word *Langston*. "Believe it or not, that was her favorite author at one time. Langston Hughes. Before she got all weird on me and shit, she actually was kinda sane. Liked great literature, appreciated the arts and classical music. She used to be able to stand the sight of me, too. When I was her little boy." She shuddered. "Her little boy. I was miserable as her little boy. When I became her little girl, it was like I suddenly felt good for the first time in my life."

I typed in the word *Langston* and the computer came online. The little icons popped up, and they were the first things I looked at. I wanted to see what kind of apps she'd downloaded.

That didn't bear much fruit, but I didn't think it would. She pretty much only had common apps such as Netflix and Hulu and things like that. Not that I thought I'd hit the jackpot right off the bat, but it would've been nice.

"Okay, let's take a look at her browsing history." I went into her history, which she never cleared. She probably didn't think she'd have reason to clear it, because she obviously wasn't anticipating her own daughter murdering her, and she certainly couldn't foresee that her computer would become so pertinent to the investigation.

I smiled when I saw *X-Hamster* pop up in her history. X-Hamster was a porn hub, where people could access porn clips and movies for free or for a fee. "Typical hypocrite," I muttered. "Do as I say not as I do, huh?" As much as I wanted to access the exact movies she'd downloaded, I didn't want to go that far just yet. It wasn't my business, it wasn't pertinent and it was really an invasion of her privacy.

Heather had a smirk on her face when the X-Hamster thing popped up on the history. "So Mom got her freak on. Who knew?"

"Well, a girl gets lonely," I said and Heather smiled and then laughed out loud.

"True that."

"Hmmm," I said, looking at some more of her browsing history. "What's this?" It was a website for a church, called *The Church of the Living Breath*. She'd logged onto the website several times a day. Perhaps that was the website she'd logged onto the most. "You said your mother was never religious?"

"Not until recently when she became Jesusy. Why? Does she have some church pop up on her history a bunch?"

"You might say that," I said, going to the Church website. I read the mission statement for the church, which read like a pretty generic statement. "We at the Church of the Living Breath aim to provide Christ-centered principles to your everyday issues. Please join us for services at 9 and 11 AM Sundays and 7 PM Saturdays."

I raised my eyebrow and made notes. So far, there wasn't anything out of the ordinary about this particular church, even though I'd never heard of it. I didn't even know what denomination it was. It wasn't like it said the denomination on the website.

Then I started to look at the articles the website hosted, and one in particular caught my eye. It was an article about how to handle sons and daughters who had come out as LGBT.

Has your son or daughter come out to you as gay or trans? As you know, the Bible states that homosexuality is a sin and the wages of sin is death. If you are afraid that your child is bound for hell because of his or her lifestyle, The Church of the Living Breath states that you are correct. Your child will be condemned to an eternity in hell unless you take affirmative action to make sure this does not happen.

We can help. We can offer counseling and a referral to therapists who can reverse your child's perverted desires. If you are truly interested in saving your child from certain damnation, please pay us a visit and ask for Louisa Garrison. Thank you.

Heather was sitting next to me and reading every word of the article. "What a load of crap," she said. "Going to hell. I'll tell you who's going to hell – that Louisa Garrison, whoever that bitch is."

"Well, this message isn't really that much out of the mainstream," I said. "Unfortunately, this seems pretty in-line with a lot of right-wing religions. The message is a bit more out there than other churches, but, other than that…"

Still, it was a place to start. For one, it seemed that the church gave the mother the idea of forcing Heather into conversion therapy. I wondered where she found this place, or why she ended up going there. This was my answer.

"If that's what mainstream churches preach, hate, then I want no part of that nonsense."

"Well, I didn't say it was mainstream. I said it wasn't that far out of the mainstream. Many churches are based upon love and non-judgment and they don't even mention things like homosexuality. Others seem to stand on judgment, as this one does. So far, though, this message on the website doesn't actually seem all that different to me than some of the more extreme churches out there."

"So, are you going to talk to this bitch or what?"

"That's a place to start."

"Start there, I bet you'll find out a whole lot from these weirdoes."

We ate the rest of the chicken as I listened to the sounds of the cicadas in the trees and the distant sound of a barking dog. "Heather," I said. "Why did you choose me as your attorney?"

"I knew you'd understand me," she said. "Your *Law Review* article was something I read after I was put into jail," she said. "And I came across the case you cited that talked about how evidence of brainwashing of the victim can be used to show self-defense." When she said the word victim, she used air quotes.

"So you had the feeling your mother was being brainwashed?"

Heather shrugged her shoulders. "I guess. It seemed she was. She certainly wasn't acting like she used to."

I read some more of the Church's literature, and I couldn't escape the feeling I got when reading the articles hosted on the site. Anti-gay articles, articles about how women need to accept their husband's behavior no matter what, even pro-slavery articles were on this website.

I had the feeling Heather's mother wasn't a part of a church at all.

She was a part of a cult.

FOURTEEN

The next day, I was prepared for two different things – one, I was prepared to go down to this "church" and talk to this Louisa person and find out what this church was all about. Perhaps I needed to go to a service first, though. I needed to see for myself what this cult was teaching their followers. These people might call themselves a church, but I knew the difference between a church and a cult, and, based on the odd articles they hosted on their website, I immediately thought it was a cult.

I was also prepared to go to jail within a few days. Specifically, the day of the hearing, when I'd be taken into custody for contempt and would have to stay in jail until I bowed to the judge's order. I wouldn't do that anytime soon.

I wanted to talk to Rina and Abby, but, as a condition of my bond, I couldn't have contact with them. I did talk to Sophia, the nanny who was staying with them, and she said that they were doing fine, but bored. They couldn't risk leaving the hotel room, so they had to stay cooped up there. It was a nice hotel room, though, so it wasn't all that bad. In fact, it was a suite, complete with a jacuzzi tub, a dining room table, satellite TV with every channel imaginable, and a video game console. Sophia bought them some video games with the credit card I gave her, and she said they were busying themselves with that.

"But Harper," she said, "what are you going to do? What's your long-term plan?"

I didn't know. Maybe hire my own undercover agent to find out what was going on in that house, which would hopefully force Alexis to change her mind about advocating on behalf of the Browns. I didn't know if that would work – Alexis seemed to have her mind made up.

I got to the church, which was behind an enormous gate. I shook my head, thinking how weird this whole thing was. It certainly didn't look like a church – it looked more like a compound.

I drove up to the guy who was minding the gate. "Where are you going?" he asked me, a clipboard in his hand.

"I'm here to see Louisa Garrison," I said to him. "This is a professional visit."

"A professional visit?" he asked. "What is the nature of this?"

"I'm an attorney," I said, showing him my Bar Card. That usually did the trick– nobody wanted to mess with an attorney. That card got me in just about anywhere.

"Could you please take that card out?" he asked.

I took the card out, and the guy looked at it closely. "Could you please show me another piece of ID, please? One with your picture on it?"

I nodded, thinking this security guard was probably one of the most suspicious I'd ever encountered. Nevertheless, I took out my driver's license and handed it to the guy. "Here you go," I said.

He carefully examined each piece of ID, and then handed them back to me. "What does this visit concern?"

I sighed. I couldn't very well tell him I was there to ambush Louisa to find out what kind of operations she was running here. I couldn't tell him my suspicion that Louisa was brainwashing people, including Heather's mother. "It's confidential," I said.

He narrowed his eyes, and I could see his cheek start to quiver beneath his left eye. I could almost see the wheels turning – maybe he was thinking he shouldn't let me in, but, if he didn't let me in, I could end up sending the authorities in there.

Finally, he made his decision. "Okay," he said. "Louisa's office is the first building on your left when you go in. Next time, please make an appointment."

I nodded and drove through the gate.

The buildings behind the gate were cute enough – there were a series of smallish structures built of stone and wood, much like small cabins with wood porches. The words "ski lodges" popped into my head, because these little homes looked like miniature ski chalets, with their pitched roofs and homey looks.

I took a deep breath and gathered my thoughts as I knocked on the door.

And knocked again.

Finally, a woman answered. She was a petite woman, with blonde hair held back tightly by a bun. She had on a ton of makeup - blue eye shadow, caked-on foundation, false eyelashes and red lipstick. Under the makeup, I could see deep wrinkles, so I could only surmise this woman was trying to cover up her age. As was usually the case, all she managed to do was make herself look older and pretty ridiculous.

As for her clothing, she was wearing a rather dated navy

blue suit, with big gold buttons on the jacket. Her shirt was ironed and pressed and buttoned up to her neck. On her feet were a pair of flat blue shoes.

"Can I help you?" she asked. Her voice was high-pitched and Southern. She probably grew up in Alabama or Georgia or someplace else in the Deep South.

"Yes," I said. "My name is Harper Ross, and I'm an attorney. I need to ask you some questions."

She cocked her head slightly. "I can answer a few questions," she said in her high-pitched voice. She drew out her words, so that it took her twice as long to get a phrase out as somebody who didn't grow up in the South.

"Thank you," I said. "May I come in?"

"You may." She nodded. "Come in, please," she said.

I followed her into a smallish office that was decorated sparsely. The walls were white and the desk was plain. The floor was carpeted, but it was the kind of carpet that looked like it was five dollars a yard and was a light color of taupe.

The only decoration she had on the wall was a picture of Jesus, who was looking into the distance with light surrounding his head.

"What is your visit regarding?" she asked me. Her blue eyes got wide, and she looked almost like she was in a trance. Spellbound.

I narrowed my eyes, thinking this woman looked somewhat like a mannequin. Her affect was flat and, aside from the fact that her right hand had a tremor, I'd have thought I was speaking to a talking doll.

"My visit is regarding a..." I struggled for the word. Parishioner? Congregant? The term I wanted to use was "cult member," but I figured that if I used that term, the visit would end right then and there.

I finally settled on the word "parishioner." "My visit is

regarding a parishioner. Her name was Connie Morrison. As you probably know, she's deceased."

She blinked her eyes rapidly, and, just like the guard, her cheek, just below her left eye, started to twitch. Other than these apparently involuntary tics, however, her demeanor didn't really change. "Yes."

I took a deep breath. "Are you aware that her daughter-"

"She didn't have a daughter. She had a son." Her eyes got huge when she said that. "A son, not a daughter."

"Her daughter," I said, looking her right in the eye, "noticed that-"

"Her son was perverted and was sinning in the eyes of God."

I took a deep breath and closed my eyes. "Ms. Garrison, with all due respect, I don't believe Heather Morrison is sinning in the eyes of God. Jesus himself wouldn't think so, either. After all, Jesus was all about lifting up the down-trodden and *judge not, lest thou be judged*. Those without sin casting the first stone and all of that. And I believe God made my client transgendered, because I don't believe God makes mistakes. And I believe He loves my client as much as He loves anybody else. So, how can you judge-"

She stood up at that point. "I won't be condescended to," she said. "By somebody who is evidently a heretic."

I shuddered. "A heretic. That's a word I haven't heard in awhile. Isn't that what they called the people burned at the stake for believing in something different than what other people believed?"

I wasn't going to get anywhere just yet, but that was okay. This visit was really my way of trying to suss out what kind of person I was dealing with, and this woman was quite the doozy.

She was now shaking, from head to toe, and her bony fingers were gripping the side of the desk. "You do not know about the good book. You are a secularist, and you need to leave this office right now."

I raised an eyebrow, suddenly knowing this woman would be quite easy to crack on the stand. She didn't exactly have a poker face.

I didn't quite get the answers I was seeking, but it was all starting to make sense.

FIFTEEN

The next day was the hearing for the girls in the Family Court. I hated going to the Family Court – the waiting room was always packed with people and the court rarely ran on time. I could never forget one time when I had an assigned case in the Family Court, and it was scheduled for 1:30. At 5 PM, my case still wasn't called, and then I was informed by the bailiff that my case would be postponed for another week. So, yeah, I spent over four hours wasting my time in the waiting room of the court, only to be told I needed to go home. And the whole place smelled like kids.

When I got there, though, Alexis came up to me to tell me the hearing would be on time. "Rick Haverford is here," she said. "And he's pissed. So are the parents. Well, Seth Brown is. Marina, the mother, seems to be kinda quiet about it all."

"I wonder why?" I crossed my arms in front of me and raised my eyebrows. "Maybe she's afraid to say anything."

"I don't want to hear about that, okay? You need to do what's right."

"I *am* doing what's right. I'm keeping the girls away from an abusive situation."

Alexis rolled her eyes as I was approached by Rick Haverford, who was the attorney for the parents. "Here," he said, giving me a copy of the contempt order he drafted. "This is a copy of the order I'm going to have Judge Michaels sign."

I nodded as I examined the order. It was pretty standard – the language on it was that I, Harper Ross, was ordered to bring the girls back to the home of the Browns within 24 hours. "Thanks for that."

Rick shook his head. I got along with him about fifty percent of the time. The other fifty percent of the time, I found him to be an arrogant boor. He was kinda nebbish, with his bald head, glasses, ill-fitting suits and pot belly, and he wasn't very tall – he was probably only about 5'5", and I towered over him, especially when I wore high heels. "What are you doing, Harper?" he asked me. "Why are you risking your career and your freedom like this? You know that when this judge orders you to bring back those girls, and you refuse, you'll be put jail until you comply. You won't get out of this. I don't understand your motivation for doing this."

"I'm standing up for what's right," I said. "Your client's son, Peter, is a pervert. Your client, Seth, is abusive. I won't let those girls be subjected to that for even one second."

"Do things right," he said. "If you think that's happening, then send the girls back and open up an investigation with Alexis and the social worker who's doing the home study. Go through the proper channels. This grandstanding will get you nowhere."

"You didn't hear me. I said I'm not going to let those girls be subjected to that household for even a second. Not even a millisecond. I mean, what will happen if I send them back there and go through the proper channels, as you say, which will take months, by the way, and they're abused sexually and physically in the meantime? What then? Maybe they'll even end up dead. What then? Sometimes you can't go through the proper channels. Sometimes the proper channels just grind too slowly and you need a faster solution."

"Dammit," Rick said. "You've done domestic cases. Not a lot of them, but you've done them. What do you do whenever one of the parents keeps the kids away from the other parent? The parents make stuff up and so do the kids. Two sides to every story. If your client is the mother and the father is keeping the kids away, you'd rightfully file every motion in the world to prevent that. And you know the judge in that case would use the father's obstruction against him having the kids in the future. You know that. Yet, you're using the same sort of tactics that underhanded parents use. You're digging your own grave."

"So be it."

The case was called and we all took a seat around a table in the courtroom. Seth Brown was there, giving me dirty looks the whole time, but he kept quiet. Rick no doubt talked to him and told him he needed to control himself, but he still looked like he was about to explode. Alexis was there. Marina, for her part, sat quietly next to Rick. I shook my head as I looked at her. She looked terrified, and it looked like there was yet another new bruise, this one on her upper arm. She was wearing short sleeves, so she didn't even try to cover it up. I wondered if that was her way of crying for help.

"All rise," the bailiff called out.

The judge came out and we all stood up and sat back down.

"The court calls the case of Brown v. Ross," she said. "Mr. Haverford, please call your witness."

"The plaintiff calls Seth Brown," he said.

Seth got up and was sworn in, and he sat down behind the witness stand.

"Please state your name," Rick said.

"Seth Brown."

"Mr. Brown, you are the foster parent of two girls, Abby and Rina Caldwell, is that true?"

"Yes."

"Are those two girls currently under your roof? Are you currently caring for them?"

"No."

"And why is this?"

Seth took a deep breath and hung his head. I could tell he was trying hard not to pop off and come over the stand and throttle me. "Because that woman there, Harper Ross, took them from me. She refuses to bring them back."

Rick paced around the floor a little, and took off his glasses and bit the spectacle's handle. That was his little trick, his way of looking like he was being thoughtful and ponderous. I wondered if he did it deliberately, or if it was something unconscious, but it was something he did a lot. "She refuses to bring them back. Does she have any reason to refuse?"

"No. But she wants to adopt those girls, and that could be why..."

"Objection," I said, standing on my feet. "The witness is speculating."

"Sustained," the judge said. "Mr. Brown, please refrain from speculating on why Ms. Ross would refuse to bring back the children, and stick to what conditions, if any, in your home might be the reason why Ms. Ross would refuse."

"Well, then, no. I don't know why Ms. Ross would refuse to bring back the girls. Our home is a peaceful home, and we've taken very good care of those girls."

I rolled my eyes. *Yeah, your home is so peaceful. It's so*

peaceful that there are holes in your walls and your son is forcing Abby to jack him off.

"Your witness," he said to me.

I nodded. "Mr. Brown," I said, pointing to Marina Brown. "I notice your wife has a bruise on her upper arm. I also notice she has a faint bruise on her face. Do you know anything about that?"

Seth's eyes got wild, and he looked like he wanted to kill me. I saw him take a huge breath and count to 10, and then he answered me. "What are you getting at?"

"I'd just like to know where she got those bruises. I'm going to call her to stand, too, even if Mr. Haverford doesn't, and I'm going to ask her about the bruises. I'd just like to hear it from you."

He looked over at Marina, whose eyes didn't meet his. She was staring at the ceiling, and the judge was questioningly looking over at the poor woman.

"I don't know. My wife is clumsy. She got hit on the face with a door, and then, the other day, she fell off the bed."

"I see. Isn't it true that your house has holes in the walls because you and your son have punched the walls on more than one occasion?"

"No." He crossed his arms in front of him. "That's not true."

I knew he wouldn't admit to this, but I wanted this fact out there in front of the judge. I also knew that, with the body language he was displaying as I asked him these questions, the judge probably knew he was lying.

I got an idea as I looked at Seth. I knew the next question would be objectionable, but, as with the question about the holes in the wall, I wanted the judge to know this accusation was "out there."

"Mr. Brown, did you know your son forced Abby Caldwell,

age 11, to masturbate him?"

"Objection," Rick said, rising to his feet. "This calls for speculation and is frankly offensive."

"Sustained," Judge Michaels said, pointing at me. "You know better than that, Ms. Ross."

"I apologize your honor. I have nothing further for this witness."

"Ms. Winters, do you have any questions for this witness?"

"No, your honor."

"Mr. Brown, you may step down. Mr. Haverford, please call your next witness."

"I have no further witnesses, your honor."

"Okay. Ms. Ross, please call your witnesses."

"I'd like to call Marina Brown to the stand," I said.

Marina looked at me questioningly. She probably wasn't prepared to take the stand. She looked at the judge and then at me and then back again.

"Ms. Brown, please take the stand and raise your right hand to be sworn in," Judge Michaels said.

Marina tentatively got out of her seat and then walked to the witness stand, was sworn in, and then sat down.

"Ms. Brown," I said, deciding just to jump on ahead to ask her what I really wanted to know. "I notice you have a bruise on your upper arm. Can you please tell the court how you got that bruise?"

She looked desperately at her husband, and I turned around and saw that Seth was staring daggers at her. "I was playing softball with my son, and he accidentally hit me with the ball."

I nodded, knowing Marina apparently didn't hear her husband say she got the bruise when she fell out of bed. I wasn't surprised – she didn't seem to be paying much attention to what her husband was saying on the stand. "I see. Your husband's testimony was that you got that bruise when you fell out of bed." I stated that as a fact. "But you're now saying you got the bruise playing softball. So, which is it?"

Her eyes got wide as she looked over at Seth, a look of apology on her face. I turned around and saw Seth's arms were crossed and he was shaking his head as he glared at her. I then looked at the judge, and she was watching Seth very carefully, her eyes peering over her glasses. She then made notes, and I felt encouraged.

"Softball," she said in a quiet voice. She looked down at the stand, looking like she wanted the floor to swallow her whole.

"And the bruise on your face? How did you get that?"

"That same softball game," she said. "My son doesn't have a good aim." She laughed nervously. "To say the least."

"You didn't get it when you ran into a door? Because that's what your husband testified to."

Once again, she looked at Seth with a look of apology, and Seth looked as if he would blow a gasket. His eyes were wide, his arms were crossed, and he had a sneer on his lips as he looked at his wife. The judge was observing all of this, and scribbling notes on a pad of paper.

"No," she said. "He was mistaken about that."

"How did he get the idea that you ran into a door?"

"I'm not sure. I guess he didn't know how I got this bruise and he was just speculating."

"He was just speculating? So, he sees you with large bruises on your face and arm, and he didn't bother to ask you how you got them? Is that what you're telling the court?"

She looked uncomfortable. "My husband is a busy man," she said in a tiny voice. "And not always observant."

"Are there holes in your wall?"

"No," she said uncertainly.

"I'd like to remind you that you're under oath, and anything false you say to this court will be considered perjury. Are you sure you don't have holes in your walls?"

"No."

"Have you ever had holes in your walls?"

She looked at her husband desperately, and he was slicing his neck with his hand and glaring at her. The judge was watching it all.

"Yes," she finally said. "There were holes in the walls."

"How did those holes get there?"

She swallowed hard and didn't answer for several minutes. She wasn't looking at her husband, probably because she was afraid to.

"My son," she said after a few minutes of silence. "He punched the walls."

"I have nothing further," I said.

I looked over at Alexis, who was also making notes.

"Ms. Winters," Judge Michaels said. "Do you have any questions for Mrs. Brown?"

"No, your honor," Alexis said.

"Okay. I'd like to hear closing statements, and then I'll make my ruling."

Rick stood up and cleared his throat. "Ms. Ross took the children, Abby and Rina Caldwell, and she didn't have just cause to do so. She's hiding the children in an undisclosed location. She was arrested for kidnapping these children, spent the night in jail and was formally charged with kidnapping in court the next day. She didn't have a reason for taking the children. Therefore, I ask that this court order her to bring the children back to my clients immediately."

He sat down, and I stood up. "If it please the court," I said, and Judge Michaels nodded. "Your honor, Mr. Haverford just told the court I didn't have a reason not to take the girls back to the Browns. I beg to differ. The girls told me..."

"Objection, hearsay," Rick said. "If Ms. Ross wants to use the girls' statements, then she needs to bring the girls in to testify. But she won't, because she's hiding the girls from my client."

"Sustained," Judge Michaels said. "Ms. Ross, please refrain from using any statements the two girls might have given you about the Brown's care of them."

I nodded. "Your honor, I apologize. I'd like to point out the evidence that Mr. Brown has been abusing Mrs. Brown. Mrs. Brown has one story on how she got her bruises, and Mr. Brown has a different story. Mrs. Brown also admitted on the stand that her son, Peter, has punched walls. I'd submit to you that the Brown's home is dangerous for Rina and Abby, who are two 11-year-old girls who recently lost their mother in a violent way. Your honor, it's dangerous for those two girls to go back to the Browns' for even one minute, which is why I decided to keep them away from the Browns."

I sat down and Alexis stood up. "In lieu of a closing statement, I'd like to reiterate my recommendations to the court. I recommend that Ms. Ross brings the girls back to the Browns, and let the process go through. I agree that more investigation of the home is probably needed, and I intend to do this investigation thoroughly. I also recommend that the family be ordered to go to family counseling. But Ms. Ross cannot unilaterally make a decision to keep those children. It's not her call."

Alexis sat down, and the judge made some notes. "Okay," Judge Michaels said. "Here's what I'm going to do. Ms. Ross, you are ordered to bring the children back to Mr. and Mrs. Brown within the next 24 hours. I'm going to order that the social worker, Danny O'Hare, who is not present, follow up on the allegations of abuse. Ms. Winters, you also must follow up on these allegations. I'd like a full report on my desk in three weeks. I also order that the entire family, Mr. and Mrs. Brown,

Peter Brown, and Rina and Abby Caldwell, submit to family counseling. Mr. and Mrs. Brown, your attorney will provide you a copy of the approved list of family counselors, and you must submit to your counselor once a week. I will call a status hearing in one month, and I will make further rulings then."

She then banged her gavel. "It is so ordered."

I sighed. This outcome wasn't unexpected, so I wasn't upset that the judge ruled this way. Judges have to be as balanced as possible. If I were the judge in this case, I'd do the same.

"So," Alexis said to me. "You're now ordered to bring back the children. When can we expect the children to be delivered to the Browns?"

"The twelfth of never," I said, picking up my briefcase. "You can quote me on that."

Alexis sighed. "You're going to jail again if you don't bring the kids back in 24 hours."

"So be it. But I'm not bringing them anywhere near the Brown's house. Not in 24 hours and not ever. Sorry, but it's dangerous over there, and I cannot let them be in that environment."

Alexis put her hand on my shoulder. "I understand your position. I really do. I admit, those bruises on Marina are suspicious. But there's a legal process, and you have to honor that. You know this better than anybody."

"I do. And I'm not going to honor it. Put me in jail indefinitely if you have to, but I'll protect those girls at all costs."

"You have 24 hours," Rick said, pointing at me. "If you don't bring the girls back in 24 hours, you'll be jailed for contempt of court."

"I understand."

At that, I took my briefcase and walked out of the courtroom.

SIXTEEN

"How did it go?" Pearl asked me when I got back to the office.

"Like I thought it would," I said. "The judge ordered me to bring back the girls, and she gave me 24 hours to do it. Which means, in 24 hours, I'll be in contempt of the order and probably will go back to jail. But, on the bright side, I saw Louisa Garrison, and she's just as crazy as I thought she would be. I definitely need to keep her in mind when I go through my witness list. She'll be right at the top."

Pearl looked concerned. "How are you going to try Heather's case if you're behind bars? Not to mention all the other cases you got going?"

"I don't know just yet. I haven't yet figured that one out. All I know is that those two girls won't go anywhere near that house of horrors. Now, can you please do me a favor and set me up with a meeting with that Rainbow International place? Dr. Schultz and Dr. Woods are the two 'counselors' that Heather saw, and I do use the term 'counselors' lightly."

"Already on it," she said. "You go and see them today at 4. Sorry for the late notice, but that was the only time both of them could see you. Don't worry, I have your afternoon appointments covered. I rescheduled them all for tomorrow."

I looked at my watch, and saw that the time was 3:15. "Ah, crap. Well, I guess it can't be helped. Thanks, Pearl, you're a doll. What would I ever do without you?"

Pearl shrugged her shoulders. "Sink, I'd guess," she said with a smile. "Now, go."

I ARRIVED AT THE "CLINIC" right at 4 PM. It was really just two offices in a high-rise building that featured balconies. It was unusual that a high-rise would have balconies, but this one did. I looked up at one of the balconies and felt an internal shudder. I remembered Heather saying she was forced out on the balcony in the cold, because she told them she was afraid of heights. I wondered if this place did this on a regular basis.

I soon got my answer as I looked up at the building. I saw a dark-headed kid, with curly hair, who couldn't have been more than 17 years old, on the balcony looking down. He looked terrified and there was an older guy right behind him. I couldn't hear what they were saying, because they were too far up, but I saw the kid rapidly shaking his head, as if he were crying. The older man stood squarely behind him, blocking his entrance back into the office suite. The young boy put his hands over his eyes, and the older man swung him around, took the boy's hands and put them behind his back, and then turned him around to face the outside of the balcony again.

I bit my lip, not wanting to see this, yet knowing it was significant. The boy looked terrified, and this was exactly what Heather was talking about when she told me about the aversion therapy. That they would couple terrifying or disgusting stimuli with sexual imagery, in an effort for the person to think of the terrifying or disgusting thing every time they were aroused sexually by something deemed "wrong" by the therapist.

The boy was finally allowed to go back into the suite, and the older man behind him led him back, with his arm around the boy.

I took the elevator to the 20th floor, which was where this clinic was, and, sure enough, in the waiting room was the boy I'd seen from down below. He was shaking all over, and I could see from his face that he'd been crying. The man next to him was talking to him. "You did well, Hans, very well," he said. "We'll be seeing you tomorrow so we can continue with our therapy, but you did excellent."

The boy, apparently named Hans, nodded, unable to speak. "My mom is downstairs," he finally managed to say.

"She'll be very proud of you," the man said. Neither the boy nor the man seemed to notice I was there. If they did, they didn't acknowledge me. "You're very brave. You should be cured in no time."

The boy finally noticed me, for he looked right at me. His eyes were blue and framed by dark eyelashes. He was slight, couldn't have weighed much more than 160 lbs, even though he was over six feet tall, and his hair was curly and somewhat unruly. I looked into his eyes and saw he was haunted. That was the only word I could possibly use at that moment – haunted.

He passed by me without a word, and the older man finally noticed me too. "Hello," he said, extending his hand. "You must be Harper Ross," he said. "Your assistant called me today. She told me you were interested in our services. I understand you have a young son who you're concerned about."

I nodded, surprised that Pearl was able to lie with such ease. I knew she needed to, because if she ever told this place what I was really up to, they wouldn't want to see me. I could subpoena them, but I doubted that I could get good information about it.

"Yes," I said. "I have a son, his name is Patrick," I said, thinking of a name quickly. I assumed that Pearl didn't give the guy the name of my non-existent son, because if she did, surely she would've told me.

"Patrick." He looked at me. "And what is the problem with Patrick?"

"He's gay," I said. "And I don't want him to be. I want him to be normal." I almost bit my tongue in disgust having to say that. I felt dirty being here, and I'd feel dirty talking about gay kids as if they were defective and needed to be fixed. That went against everything I'd believed in my entire life.

"Well, you've come to the right place," he said. "Come on in. My name is Dr. Schultz, and my partner's name is Dr. Woods. My specialty is behavioral modification, and Dr. Woods' specialty is aversion therapy. It's a more extreme kind of behavioral modification," he said, leading me into his office.

I brought out a paper and pen and started to write. "Thanks for seeing me on such short notice. Now, tell me about your therapy. What goes into it?"

"Well, we operate on the belief that homosexuality and transgenderism is a type of disease of the mind, one that can be cured. Much like other kinds of diseases of the mind that can be cured– like alcoholism or drug addiction or gambling addiction. It's a compulsion, and, really, all that most homosexuals and transgender folks need is some good old-fashioned therapy to cure them."

"What does this good old-fashioned therapy consist of?"

"Well, we start with cognitive behavioral therapy. Are you aware of that?"

"Somewhat." I wrote down what the man was saying in my notebook. "Tell me about that."

"We identify maladaptive thoughts – such as when a man thinks sexually about another man. That would be a maladaptive thought. That kind of thought is harmful. I simply train them to replace that maladaptive thought with something more positive. Such as thinking about a woman in such a sexual way. I even give my clients pictures of women to take with them in their wallets, and, every time they see a man and feel sexual longings, they are to look at the picture of the woman. They can retrain their brains to think about that woman in the same way that they previously thought about the man."

I had to suppress my laughter as this guy was talking. It was extremely difficult to do so, however. I couldn't believe people were so naïve to think a gay person could just change their brains in that manner just because this man was telling him to. If it were really so easy, I thought, all those anti-gay folks wouldn't have any gay children, because they could just change them by giving them pictures of a hot girl to carry around.

I bit my lower lip to keep the laughter in, and I had to compose myself enough to ask the next question. That took a Herculean effort, because the laughter was right there, and I knew that if I said something it would come spilling out. I looked up at the lights and took a deep breath. *Compose yourself. Compose yourself. Think of Heather.*

"Okay," I finally said, amazed that I could talk to this guy with a straight face. "Cognitive behavioral therapy," I said, "what other kinds of therapy do you offer?"

"Well, psychoanalytic," he said. "We are of a firm belief that homosexuality is the result of a blockage in one of the psychosexual developmental steps that were outlined by Sigmund Freud. We use extensive talk therapy to try to root out the causes of the homosexuality or transgenderism, and try to uncover the exact moment in childhood where the person experienced the frustration that led him or her to the perversion of their current state."

I nodded. I didn't feel like laughing this time, because this therapy seemed a bit more serious. There was just something about the last therapy, where the gay male was supposed to carry around a picture of a hot woman, to take his mind off men, that made me want to laugh hysterically. But psychoanalysis was more serious.

"Once you find out the moment that the person was frustrated in childhood, how do you use that information?"

"Well, we feel that bringing that out is beneficial to the patient, because it gives him or her a chance to examine why they feel the way they do. It gives them the tools to understand him or herself. Sometimes just understanding the compulsive behavior and the roots of it is enough."

I kept writing frantically. "And if it's not enough?"

Dr. Schultz nodded. "Well, when psychoanalysis and behavioral modification do not work, we go onto aversion therapy. We prefer not to do this, but this is a last-ditch effort to change the person's ways. Let my colleague, Dr. Woods, explain this process to you better." At that, he punched a speaker phone on his desk. "Dr. Woods, we have a potential client who'd like to know more about the aversion therapy."

Dr. Schultz smiled warmly at me. "Dr. Woods will be right with you."

Sure enough, in a matter of minutes, a tall and skinny man with wild brown hair and glasses entered the room. He was dressed in a sweater vest and khaki pants, and his shoes were scuffed and wing-tipped. He extended his hand for me to shake.

"Harper Ross," Dr. Schultz said to Dr. Woods. "This is Dr. Woods."

"Hello," I said.

"Hello." He looked at me sternly. "I understand that you have a gay son and you're interested in changing him."

"Yes," I said. "That's right."

"You've come to the right place. Dr. Schultz gave you a brief overview on some of the methods we use to change the mindset and patterns of gay individuals. I also have a method, and I find it quite effective."

I raised my eyebrow. *Effective my ass. There's not a study around that shows that anything that you two quacks do is "effective." Thank God.*

"Okay, tell me about what you do."

"It's very important to understand something. Changing a person's mindset and beliefs involve both a carrot and a stick. Rewards and punishment. Dr. Schultz focuses on the positive aspects – the reward that comes from thinking about something good when they're faced with something bad. The reward of thinking of a woman sexually instead of thinking of a man sexually. That gets us halfway there. What I specialize in is the punishment aspect – the stick, so to speak."

"The punishment aspect?"

"Yes. We've found that it's not enough that our patients are encouraged to think of women sexually when they think impure thoughts about men. Or, in the case of lesbians, the opposite. It's not enough to uncover their deepest feelings from childhood, the exact moment they became frustrated in their development, which led them to their perversion. We also have to associate those sexual thoughts with something negative."

"Go on."

"Yes. It's called aversion therapy. Basically, we'll find out what your son is afraid of. What disgusts him the most. It could be that he's terrified of spiders or heights or enclosed spaces. We also find out what his greatest sexual fantasies involve. Maybe it's simply that he wants to kiss an older man. Or it might be something more explicit. Whatever the fantasy is, we show him a film that features the fantasy. Then, in the case of the boy who is terrified of spiders, we immediately show him a film featuring hundreds of spiders. We even have a tarantula right here in the office, and we bring out the tarantula and show the boy the live spider. We have the tarantula, because a fear of spiders is very common."

I nodded, wanting to throttle this arrogant son-of-a-bitch. "Okay. I get it."

"Yes. We link the intense fear of something with the sexual longings. The goal is for the patient to think of the spiders whenever he thinks of kissing an older man."

"Is that what you were doing with that boy on the balcony?"

"Yes. Dr. Schultz has just begun training with the aversion therapy, so he did that with the boy. It's very effective. We cannot divulge too much about that boy's therapy, of course, but, yes, making him go out on the balcony is extremely effective. It always is with individuals who have a fear of heights."

"And the disgust? What does that entail?"

"Disgust is another effective stimuli in aversion therapy. People are disgusted by all different kinds of things. Most people are disgusted by the sight of human feces, so we juxtapose pictures of feces with sexual imagery. Sometimes we show pictures of people with their legs amputated, or a video of a complicated surgery involving a lot of blood, and we use those images to go with the sexual imagery. That really works well with people who are afraid of the sight of blood. Sometimes people get very freaked out about horror movies, such as *Saw*. They can't handle the sight of people being tortured on screen. That's a very effective movie for us to use in that case – we show some of the most graphic scenes from that movie and juxtapose that with sexual imagery."

I blinked. I had the unmistakable feeling that this man, this Dr. Woods, was a sadist. He was talking about his aversion therapy as if he was remembering a really good dream. He was smiling the entire time he described these heinous ways that he and Dr. Schultz tried to get gay kids to stop being gay.

"What about snuff films?" I asked him calmly.

"Snuff films?"

"Yeah. You know, films where the person is actually tortured and killed on-screen. Those kinds of films. Surely you have access to them."

"Snuff films..." He looked like he'd actually consider them. "Those aren't legal, unfortunately. But if they were, they'd be the ultimate in aversion therapy."

Those aren't legal, unfortunately. Unfortunately. Unfortunately. UNFORTUNATELY! This guy was for real. If there was any doubt in my mind that this man was a sadist, he just removed it completely.

"What about killing a gay kid?" I blurted out. "Since these kids are so damaged?"

He furrowed his brows. "I'm sorry?"

"Just wondering."

He narrowed his eyes. "Ms. Ross, why do I have the feeling you don't have a child who is gay?"

I straightened my spine, cursing myself. I should've kept my big mouth shut.

"No, I do. Have a gay child."

"Well, surely you aren't insinuating we advocate murder in this clinic?" Dr. Woods looked genuinely confused.

"No, I don't. I'm so sorry. I don't know where that came from."

"Okay." Dr. Woods shook his head. "Well, please, if you'd like to make an appointment for your boy, then please do. It's now after-hours, so we don't have our receptionist here, but you can make an appointment with Dr. Schultz or myself. Would you like that?"

"I'll be in touch," I said. "Thank you very much for your time in meeting with me. What's the fee for this office visit?"

"We charge $150 for the initial consultation. You can put it on a credit card."

I got out my debit card and Dr. Schultz ran it.

"Thanks," I said as Dr. Schultz gave me back my card. "I'll just show myself out."

"Please come back," Dr. Schultz said. "We really do good work here."

"I'm sure you do."

As I left, I realized I needed a hot shower. Being in there made me feel really dirty.

I GOT HOME and booted up my email. I immediately saw one from Alexis, and I clicked on it. "Please call me whenever you get this." That was all it said.

I called her. "Alexis, this is Harper. I got your email. What's going on?"

"Something happened," she said. "You need to come and see me tonight."

SEVENTEEN

I headed over to Alexis' office immediately. I had no clue on what was going on. I only knew something happened. Something big. Huge, maybe.

Alexis' office was downtown. She was a partner in a large law firm, and when she worked as a Guardian Ad Litem, she did it on a *pro bono* basis, as she had to complete so many *pro bono* hours for her firm every year.

Washington, Park and Huffington was the largest firm in the city – some 600 attorneys worked for the Kansas City branch of the firm, doing mainly defense work for large corporations. When there was a merger with two behemoths, Washington Park was sure to be one of the firms guiding the merger. When there was a products liability class action case, Washington Park was the firm defending the corporation. That was what they did, and the lawyers all got paid top dollar for doing it.

I personally felt these lawyers were selling their souls for a buck, and what they did disgusted me. There were many law school colleagues who dreamed of doing environmental law, and they got a job with Washington Park where they did environmental law, all right – defending the polluters. It was their job to hire the big guns – the high-dollar expert witnesses – that were, in turn, used to squash the little guy who had been wronged. Plus, their lawyers didn't see the inside of a courtroom for a decade after they got out of school. Most of the attorneys did little but legal research for their bosses, maybe write a motion and a petition or two. Yet they all worked 70+ hours per week. I could think of nothing more soulless and stressful than working for Washington Park or any other big firm.

As for Alexis, her main job was in the pharmaceutical division. If there was a class-action lawsuit regarding a drug, she was one of the ones working on it.

Washington Park occupied the top three levels of a 50-story high-rise, one of the tallest buildings in the city. The building was all blue glass and steel, and the bottom level of the building was basically a shopping mall. There was a food court on the bottom level, along with about fifty shops.

I got to the elevator and pushed it. This elevator only went to the top 25 floors, so it rapidly bypassed the bottom 25 floors and, before I knew it, I was on the 49th floor. I walked through the enormous double-glass doors, with the logo of the firm etched in the doors in gold, and stopped at the round desk in the lobby. A bored-looking blonde woman, dressed in a simple white blouse and black skirt, with a headset on, looked at me. "Can I help you?" She asked.

"Yes, I'm here to see Alexis Winters, please."

"Are you Harper Ross?" she asked. "She said Harper Ross is to go to her office right away. No matter who she has back there. But she's in a meeting right now, so it'll be just a minute or two before she's finished."

I nodded. This sounded important. Whatever she would tell me was something that was extremely critical. I just had that feeling. "Thank you. By the way, who are the clients in her office right now?"

She shrugged. "Two representatives from Bayer. She's working up a defense for a major class-action lawsuit against them." She touched the phone, said a few words to Alexis, and then looked at me. "She'll be right out."

I sat down and flipped through a magazine. My mind was racing on what was going on. Perhaps this whole thing was a trap. Alexis gets me here and ambushes me somehow. I couldn't imagine how, though. I was already out on bail. If she wanted me to be arrested, that wouldn't work.

Been there, done that.

After a few minutes, Alexis appeared in the lobby. "Harper," she said. "Come with me. Thank you for coming in so soon."

I nodded and followed her back through the maze of offices and cubicles. I marveled when I looked into some of the offices, which were enormous and had the most unbelievable view of the city I'd ever seen.

Alexis' office was one of the larger ones. It was an almost perfect meld of old and new. Her desk was curved and made of green glass with steel legs. On one of the walls of the enormous room were modern cubist paintings and on the other wall was a floor-to-ceiling bookcase with every law book imaginable. The office was also bordered by a wall of windows.

I sat down in the plush red chair across from her desk and waited for her to tell me what was going on. She looked extremely pale and her hands were shaking. "Harper," she finally said, as she lifted a glass of water to her lips. "Something happened with the Browns."

"What happened?"

"Seth Brown killed Marina last night. He turned himself in this morning. I just got word not two hours ago."

My heart suddenly sunk, and I nodded. "I, I, I..." I lost my words and shook my head, but I wasn't surprised. The erratic way Seth acted told me he was a ticking time bomb that would go off at any second.

"I know. I'm sure you're not surprised. He also beat his son so badly that he's currently in the hospital in critical condition. He's not expected to make it through the night."

I breathed in through my nose and out through my mouth. "I don't know what to say."

"I do." She laid her hand on mine, both of our hands on her desk. "You're a hero for doing what you did. I've had to reevaluate just about everything I've ever learned and held dear for so long. I try to do the best job that I can for these kids. But I'm blinded, just like everyone else, to certain things. I figured the Browns were respectable members of society. They're active in their church, they give to charity. I didn't listen to you about what was going on over there, and for that, I'm very sorry."

I bit my bottom lip. "So..."

"It goes without saying that I'll going to talk to the prosecutor on your case and encourage him to drop the kidnapping charges. That won't be a problem. And it goes without saying that the Family Court Judge won't hold you in contempt for hiding the girls. And I also want you to know that if you want to renew your effort to adopt the girls, I won't stand in your way. You showed you have their best interests at heart much more than I did, I'm afraid to say."

As her words settled in, I couldn't help but feel mixed. I was beyond happy to get a chance to adopt the girls. Plus, I wasn't going to jail.

But a woman was dead.

I closed my eyes and saw her terrified face and I shuddered. I didn't even want to think about how much she'd suffered while living with that monster. How anguished she must've been, seeing her son following in his father's footsteps. I could feel her despair in my bones, and my blood chilled just thinking about her.

I opened my eyes and smiled at Alexis. "Thank you, Alexis, for that."

"You're willing to go to jail to protect them. You probably were even ready to go to prison for them. That means something. You're not perfect, nobody is, but I'd like to ask you one thing. If you ever go off the wagon, I want you to call me. I won't keep the kids with you if you do that. I believe you'll be open with me about that. You're good people, Harper. And those girls love you. I know that. When I took them from your house, you were all they talked about. It's obvious they look up to you. So, please, Harper, get those kids out of hiding and file a petition with the court. I'll recommend the adoption go through."

"Thank you. I don't know what to say."

"Just say you'll get that petition together today, and get into court at the first available date. You'll have another home study, of course, so be ready for that."

I stood up to leave. "I'll do that, and thanks. I'd say you've made my day, but a woman is dead. A boy is near death. I can't be entirely happy that things turned out this way."

Alexis nodded. "Well, I have a deposition I need to get ready for," she said. "Good luck."

I left her office and, when I got into my car, I couldn't decide how to feel. I was happy beyond belief, but the sacrifice that had to happen for this whole thing to go through was unacceptably high.

This was the very definition of a Pyrrhic victory.

EIGHTEEN

Louisa Garrison sat up straighter in her chair and thought about her life before she found this church. Before she found God, she was unclean. She let women do things to her that were filthy, disgusting. Sometimes women she didn't even know. At one time, she actually enjoyed it. Sex. Doing bad things. With bad people.

Thank God she found this place. The Reverend John took her in, as filthy and disgusting as she was, and gave her a home. Made her a part of things. He showed her around, showed her how things really could be. How she'd be seated at the right hand of the Father when she finally went to her just reward. She gave up all the women and all the drugs after finding this church. The Church of the Living Breath became her everything from the moment she set foot on the grounds.

Some of the principles she learned at the church weren't exactly principles she thought she'd adopt. The church taught her that, as a woman, she needed to be subservient to men. That was a hard one for her. The church forbade her to do anything but say yes to whatever a man wanted from her. Even when she got into an abusive relationship with Arnold, who was her current husband, the church counseled her that she not only couldn't leave him, but she had to take the beatings. She didn't quite know why that would be, but she knew that the church knew best, so she acquiesced without question. If she didn't, she might've fallen out of favor of the reverend, and she couldn't handle that, so she always did as she was told.

She also knew that quite a few of the church members had slaves at their homes. These were domestic slaves mostly, although some of the men took the slaves into their beds. Nobody really knew that slavery still existed, but it did – it was just kept extremely quiet. These slaves were generally people from other countries and in this country illegally. They were desperate not to be found out by the authorities, so they allowed themselves to become slaves. They would take care of the house, do all the cooking and cleaning and child care, and not earn a single dime. In fact, many of them were homeless. They only did the slave work because the masters would feed them, and they were desperate for food.

The church encouraged this. Slavery was Biblical, after all. If it was in the Good Book, then it was something in the church's teachings.

She shook her head, trying to dispel the doubts that sometimes quelled within her. She did the right thing at all times. The right thing was defined by the reverend, and she never questioned any of it. That was demanded of her, and that was what she gave. 100%. At all times.

Even when the reverend handed down to Louisa and all the counselors at the Church what he deemed his own Final Solution. He explained that Hitler had a Final Solution, and that it was wrong, because it targeted the wrong group of people. The Reverend had no love for the Jews, but he didn't think the Jews were destroying society. The people who were destroying society, explained the reverend, were the perverts. The queers. The fags. The trannies. All those people made society less pure. They were always flaunting their lifestyle – they had their own parades, and they had their own television programs. Society was tolerating them, and then society celebrated them.

When they got the ability to be married, the reverend knew he had to put an end to all of it. He alone knew there was only one way to handle this type of invasion. And that's what it was – an invasion. He explained that every society that began to tolerate perverts fell. He knew America would fall as well, unless something was done about the problem.

Of course, the reverend had his share of young boys who he "trained." It was an open secret, really, but nobody really cared. He explained that his own proclivities were pure and just. He had only the boys' best interests at heart. He wasn't a pervert or disgusting or any of that. He wasn't like those queers who flaunt their degenerate lifestyle for the whole world to see. What the Reverend did with these young boys was private and secretive. He couldn't possibly corrupt the rest of the world if the rest of the world didn't know about what he was doing.

If this was sick logic, Louisa didn't see it as such. She could only see that the reverend had answers for her life. She didn't question him. She only took orders from him. He knew what he was doing. He knew what was best.

Louisa drummed her fingers on her desk and contemplated what the Reverend asked her to do. Deep down, she didn't like it. Deep down, she knew a church should never ask her what the reverend was asking. A church was supposed to be about sustaining life, spreading love and guiding people to walk in the service of the Lord.

That's what a church was supposed to be.

This church wasn't about that.
Louisa just accepted it and didn't question any of it.

NINETEEN

I got home and I was immediately greeted by Rina and Abby.

"Aunt Harper," Rina shrieked the second I walked through the door. "Oh my God, I can't tell you how happy we are to be out of that hellhole."

Abby nudged Rina. "Rina, it wasn't a hellhole. It was a beautiful hotel suite. We couldn't have asked for a better place to be hidden."

Rina shook her head. "It might have been a gorgeous suite, but, come on. We were cooped up in there for like a hundred years." She rolled her eyes. "I thought I'd never get out of there."

I smiled. "I'm happy to see you girls, too."

Happy actually wasn't the word. Ecstatic. The girls gave me purpose. I felt that way, occasionally, whenever I got an innocent person off. As I firmly believed Heather to be. But usually, I felt I was complicit in a system that rewarded winning above all else. Above morality. Morality, unfortunately, didn't usually enter into the equation on what I was doing.

But these girls made me feel that, perhaps, I had a purpose on this earth. They were brought to me under the worst of circumstances. The very worst. Yet they could maybe help me with my constant search for redemption for my myriad of sins.

Rina started to dance around the room. "Aunt Harper, tell me," she said. "Tell me why we're in your home now. Why now? Why did we suddenly get sprung from that prison?"

I took a deep breath, not knowing if I wanted to tell the girls the truth about all of that. "Well, uh…"

Abby chimed in. "Rina, don't you remember? I gave you that newspaper article." She turned to me. "I gave her the article about what happened. I guess she didn't read it, though."

"So you know."

"I do." Abby hung her head. "It's horrible."

"It is." That was all I could say.

Abby started to cry. "Marina was a nice person. She really was. But she was with this monster. She didn't deserve…"

Rina came over. "I didn't forget about that article. But I want us to not look back. That was an awful part of our lives. No use dwelling on it."

"Dwelling on it?" Abby was incredulous. "It just happened."

"I know." Rina shook her head. "I realize that, Abby." She looked at me with a panicked expression. "Aunt Harper, how can I make her stop crying? She's been crying ever since she found out. She's been crying ever since that damned asshole Peter did that to her."

I didn't know if I should've corrected her cussing. I personally wasn't opposed to anybody cussing. I figured that they were just words, and, as a lawyer, I dealt with words all day long. Words can never hurt anyone. Actions hurt. Words didn't. At least, they didn't hurt me.

But, at the same time, I was the adult, and she was the

child. A young child. If a teacher heard her say those things, she probably would be thrown out of school. "I know how you feel, but I'd ask you not to cuss in this house."

"I understand," she said. "I just get so damned mad. Damned is okay, isn't it? I hear my teachers say that word all the time."

"I guess." I sighed. Having two young girls under my roof, for good, would be an adjustment. They stayed with me before, but that was different. Now, I would be their mother, and I had to try to navigate it the best I could. "But I don't want you sent out of class for saying bad words."

Abby shrugged. "Aunt Harper, you don't know my school. It's a private school, but everyone my age is saying bad words, and a lot of kids are already drinking and smoking. I think smoking is disgusting, but…"

"And drinking is too." I drew a breath. God knew, this child didn't need to be getting into alcohol. Not at at the age of 11. It was bad enough I started at age 14.

Then I had to remind myself that not everyone who drank, even at a young age, would end up with a problem. I did because I was self-medicating, plus I seemed to have had a bad gene somewhere along the line. The girls wouldn't drink, not until they were of age. I would have to make sure of that.

"I guess. I've tried wine. My mom…" Rina trailed off. "Who cares what Mom did? She met that…man…" She seemed to be choosing her words carefully. "That man, he beat her, yet she stayed with him. He killed her."

Just then, she looked over at Abby, who was cowering on the couch, a wad of Kleenex in her tiny hand. "Abby," she said softly. "Is that it? What happened to Marina is what happened to Mom. Is that why you're crying?"

I was amazed at how sensitive Rina could be to her sister's moods. I also figured Abby was crying not just for Marina, but for their mother, who died much the same way Marina did. "Yes," she said, and then started to wail. "Neither of them deserved what, what, what..." She couldn't finish her sentence. Her sobbing reached a crescendo, and then tapered off, and then crescendoed again.

I sat down next to both of them on the couch. I couldn't take away their pain. It would lessen with time, but would never entirely go away. These were two very young girls who would be growing up without their mother.

The only thing I could possibly do would be to make things better for them.

They could never be whole. But they could possibly be better.

TWENTY

Agent Springer shook his head as he examined the body that had washed up on shore. It was the fifth one this week. The media hadn't yet been alerted that there seemed to be a serial killer haunting the city. He was used to seeing this type of thing in the inner cities. Drug deals gone wrong were often the cause behind most of the murders in the city. But this was something different.

He'd done the investigative work on the other victims, and none of them seemed to fit the profile of drug dealers or people involved in the drug trade. None of them even seemed to fit the profile of prostitutes, another group Agent Springer had seen way too much of in his 20 years on the Kansas City police force. These victims all came from "good" solid Midwest families. Christian families. Families where the parents attended church every Sunday. He had asked around the neighborhood about these families, and everyone said the same thing – they were solid God-fearing salt-of-the-earth people.

The neighborhoods where these kids, the victims, grew up were not the same type of neighborhoods he was used to seeing murder victims come from. The neighborhoods that "produced" murder victims at a rate like a factory were the poor ones. They were the 'hoods where the houses were run-down, where the weeds grew tall and the homeless slept nearby underneath highway overpasses. Where the cars were as loud as shotguns, both because they were in disrepair and sometimes souped up that way.

But these kids came from neighborhoods that weren't like the troubled ones that he was used to investigating. These were kids who grew up in the Brookside area. The Loose Park area. The Country Club Plaza area. The houses where these kids grew up were all $400,000 and up, which was high for Kansas City. Some of the kids were in private schools. In fact, most of them were, as the Kansas City school district was known for having a multitude of problems.

Kansas City was also known for having a murder problem. Last year, there were 210 murders, which worked out to one every day and a half or so. People were shot in cars, they were killed in parking lots, murdered on the streets. Most of them, however, were known criminals themselves.

If it was all an isolated incident, Agent Springer might have let it go. One suburban kid found murdered was probably a runaway incident. Agent Springer wasn't naïve enough to think suburban families didn't have their own problems, and their kids ran away just like any other kid might do if their parents were having issues. Once the kids ran away and lived on the streets, they were basically sitting prey for the dregs of the city to pick off.

Two suburban kids in a short span of time might've been a coincidence. He didn't like to believe in coincidences, but, at the same time, it could very well happen. The kids got tired of the parents being so strict with them, as Christian parents sometimes were, and they rebelled and left the home.

But five kids? In the span of one month? All of them from upper-middle-class neighborhoods? Agent Springer shook his head. No. This wasn't a coincidence. Somebody was killing these kids. It might be one person, a serial killer. In fact, he believed this was the case.

There was one other thing these kids had in common. They were all apparently members of the LGBT community. That would apparently make them all targets. Society had not yet fully accepted that some kids were just who they were – they loved members of the same sex, and some of them believed themselves to be members of the opposite sex. It was what it was. Agent Springer's sister Lucy was a lesbian, and, at first, he had a hard time accepting that Lucy had a wife. But he soon got to know Lucy's wife, whose name was Susan, and, before he knew it, he was having them over for dinner. His ex-wife, Neila, had no qualms in accepting both of them. In fact, she was excited, because she wanted to add a gay couple to her circle of friends.

But society at large was still grappling with kids being different. He'd seen his share of kids who were bullied, harassed, stalked and beaten because of who they were. He had even seen a murder or two of a gay man or a lesbian woman who were apparently killed just because they were different.

He had never seen something like this, though. Not so many in such a short period of time.

There was a connection between the murders. He knew this. The connection went beyond the fact that all the murdered kids were gay, or that all the murdered kids were from well-to-do communities, or that all the kids came from Christian families.

There was some other connection, and he was determined to find it.

TWENTY-ONE

"Okay, Pearl," I said to my secretary. "What do you have for me?" It was the day after I got the girls back in my home, and I came in early to pick Pearl's brain about the reports she'd been studying about Heather's case.

"I got in touch with the investigator," she said, as I admired anew her fashion sense. She was wearing skinny black pants and a high-necked sweater with pearls and boots. Her hair was newly braided, and her café au lait skin was unadorned, without makeup. She still looked beautiful. "And we have the initial report on Heather and the mother." She shook her head. "Girl, all I can say is that the mother over there had a serious problem with the cray."

I nodded, feeling more confident that maybe Heather's story would check out after all. I still had the nagging thought that there wasn't a butcher knife recovered at the scene, which would have to be explained away. But if Pearl read the report and found the mother was crazy, this would go a long way towards proving to the jury that the mother did, indeed, strike first.

I went into my office and opened up the file. "Pearl," I said. "Come in here. I need to bounce some ideas off you. You read the report, so maybe you and I can brainstorm this." This was something Pearl and I often did. Because Pearl wasn't a lawyer, she was the perfect person to poke holes into any theory I could come up with. I found out early on that other lawyers would be blind to certain things. We knew the law, so we assumed our brains thought the same as a lay-persons.

I found out differently on one of my earliest cases. It was a personal injury case that fell into my lap, because a lawyer friend witnessed an accident, so couldn't take it himself, as it was a conflict of interest. He couldn't be both a witness and the lawyer, so he gave it to me.

The accident involved a fire truck and a car. The car had the green light, and the fire truck was barreling through the intersection and hit the car. At first, I thought this was a dead-dog loser of a case. Then I started to get into it and realized the fire truck didn't have its sirens blazing at the time it came through the intersection, but it had its lights flashing. I thought I might have a shot.

The jury came back in five minutes, finding for the defendant, against my client. I came home, feeling dejected, and I ran it by my sister Albany.

"Oh my God," she said. "I can't believe you took that dog of a case."

"Why was it a dog?"

"Because the fire truck had its lights going. Anybody knows that when that happens, you stop immediately. And your girl proceeded through the intersection, even though she saw that rig barreling towards her. What were you thinking, Harper, taking that?"

What was I thinking, indeed? It was then that I knew that I needed to get a lay person's perspective of any case, because the jury would think just like them. The jury wouldn't think like lawyers. They would think like people on the street, which is what they were.

Pearl sat down across from me. She had a little ball in her hand, which she enjoyed tossing up in the air when she and I did our brainstorming sessions. "Okay," she said. "Let's go."

"The mother was-" This was our word-association game that warmed us up. I would give her a phrase and she had to complete it without thinking about it. She just had to shout the first thing that came to her mind.

"Religious."

"Heather is-"

"A lesbian." Then she shook her head. "No, sorry, a trans woman."

"Why did you say lesbian? Why did that come to your head first?"

She blinked. "I was thinking of something else. The mother. She was religious but also a lesbian."

I perked up when she said that. "Why do you say that?"

"The investigator dug up some information on Connie from one of her friends. He found out that Connie was always hanging out with some girl named Louisa. He got the impression the relationship between the two was an open secret."

I bit my lower lip. I had to either trust my gut or try to analyze the situation intellectually. Was Heather's mother hanging out with Louisa Garrison because they were friends, and Louisa was brainwashing her, or were they actually lovers? I had a feeling that Louisa's job was to do just that – brainwash the followers into doing whatever the reverend wanted.

"So?" I asked Pearl. "Isn't it possible they were just friends?" I didn't want to say more about who Louisa was. I wanted Pearl to have as little information as possible. She probably already knew, but I wouldn't direct her any more than I had to.

"Come on. She spent the night with her. Heather didn't tell you there were nights her mother didn't come home?"

"No, she didn't. I wonder why…"

Now I was going off on this tangent. Connie was a lesbian? Louisa too? Not that any of this surprised me. The most anti-gay people in the world were often the ones who were gay themselves. Struggling with being gay. It was self-loathing at its finest, really. Just like there was always talk that Adolf Hitler was part Jewish, the people who wanted the gays to be wiped off the face of the earth really hated themselves.

I looked out the window at the Country Club Plaza, looking forward to the time when the beautiful buildings would be lit up brilliantly in every color of the rainbow. It was summertime, so that wouldn't be happening for quite awhile, but the Christmas season was my favorite time of the year. "This could be something I could use on the stand."

"I think you can. What's the next term you want me to tell you about?"

"Butcher knife."

Pearl raised her eyebrow. "Not sure what you mean?"

"Exactly. That's what keeps me up at night. Heather said her mother came at her with a butcher knife. Heather then picked up a knife and stabbed her mom in the neck, then ran out of the house. Yet the butcher knife wasn't recovered at the scene. Why?"

Pearl looked distant. "Somebody removed it from the scene? That's the only thing that makes sense. Unless…."

"Unless what?"

"Unless the cops at the scene didn't list it for some reason."

"That would be tampering with a crime scene. It's not

unheard of, but why would they go through all this trouble on this particular case?"

I wrote this down on a piece of paper. *Butcher knife missing from scene. Cops took it? Somebody else came in to clean up the scene before the cops got there? Or Heather is lying?*

"We have to figure this out," I said to Pearl. "If I can't get straight on this one element, the entire thing falls apart."

I bit my lower lip. "Get Fred on this. He needs to find out more about the cops on the scene." There were two cops on the scene to begin with, and then, when it was clear there was a body in the kitchen, six more showed up. The first two cops were the ones I was most interested in. They both would have to be compromised in order for them to tamper with the crime scene.

Pearl wrote down some notes. "K. What do you want to find out about these cops?"

I had a hunch. I didn't know where it might lead, but it was something I needed to know. "Find out if they're religious. And if they are, find out what church they belong to."

"Why does that matter?"

"The mother was a part of a church that's more like a cult. I need to do my own investigation on that place. So far, what I've found out makes the Westboro Baptist Church look like Unity." Unity was a liberal church I sometimes attended. It made no judgments whatsoever, and was focused on the goodness about Christ's teachings. The Westboro Baptist Church, on the other hand, made their name by protesting funerals with hateful messages like *God Hates Fags*.

"That bad?"

"Yeah. Let's just say they advocate slavery and advise women to be completely subservient to their man and to stay with their man even if they are being beaten."

Pearl shook her head. "I thought that bullshit went out in

the Victorian age. I wonder if they also encourage women to give all their property to their man. That's how they did it in the Victorian age – women weren't allowed to even own property."

"That's part of being subservient – the man owns all the property. Even if a woman comes into the marriage with property, it soon is signed completely over to him. That's good thinking on your part. Maybe I'll investigate that angle too. It can bolster our case of brainwashing, because only a brainwashed woman would do something like that."

Pearl made some more notes. "Are you going to some of the services to see what's going on there?"

"If they allow me. We need to check if this church is tax-exempt, because if it is, they can't ban me. If they're not, they can tell me to take a hike if I go in there. I might just send Fred to the service if they won't let me come back. He can tell me what kind of nonsense is being preached there."

Pearl nodded and made more notes. "Okay. What is the next term you want to cover with me?"

I made a temple with my fingers and swiveled in my chair. "LGBT."

She shook her head. "Murdered."

"Murdered?" I didn't quite know what she was talking about.

"Yeah. There's been five murders of gay youth in just the past few weeks. I've read about it in the paper."

My eyes got wide. "There have been? I guess I've been out of touch, what with all the issues with the girls and Heather's case. I haven't had the time to read the paper or watch the news. Tell me about this."

She shrugged. "They think a serial killer is working the area. The kids were all from good homes, all kinda rich. Not really rich, but they all had money. They weren't the usual gangbangers from the East side."

I wrote down this new piece of information. *Gay kids being murdered.* "Have Fred find out more about these kids. What were their families like." I furrowed my brows. "I wonder if..."

"I know what you're thinking, but I wouldn't go there just yet. There's a big difference between hating on gay people and actually telling people to murder them."

"I understand that, but it wouldn't be beyond the purview of a cult. It might be a doomsday cult. But you're right. That's a stretch. Maybe I can get a better handle on what's going on if I go to a service."

"Okay, then, go to a service and report back."

"I will. I'll get to the bottom of this. I have a feeling that church is rotten to the core."

I was getting closer to the truth. I knew that, and I also knew this church would play a huge role in Heather's case. I didn't know how I knew that.

I just did.

THAT NIGHT, after I put the two girls to bed, over their protests – they both wanted to stay up and watch some movie on HBO, but I told them that I'd DVR it and show it tomorrow, which seemed to satisfy them – I decided to go back to Connie Morrison's computer. I didn't know if her email had the same password as her computer, but I hoped it would. Heather didn't know the answer to that, either, when I'd asked her about it.

I went into my sunroom, where I had my home office. On sunny days, when I wasn't suffering from depression, this room gave me a sense of peace and solace. It faced the backyard. There was a bird-feeder back there, along with two bird houses. I learned how to attract birds to the house, so I usually had a resident in there building a nest. My backyard was carefully laid out to give a sense of tranquility. There was a Japanese garden, with a statue of a Japanese house and a Buddha fountain. There was a Koi pond that ran on rocks underneath a small wooden bridge. I could hear that fountain when I sat in my sun room, lightly gurgling. It was always a sound I found soothing.

Tonight, as it was summertime, I could hear nothing but crickets and the fountain. I closed my eyes, trying to soak in these sounds. I had a nervousness bubbling up inside of me, an anxiousness that I couldn't quite put my finger on. I didn't know if the feeling was associated with Heather or all the other cases I had on my plate. Or it might've just been my brain chemicals going haywire, as they had all my life. Clinical depression and anxiety were terrible bears to wrestle, and the worst thing about these two illnesses was I could never tell when they would pop up again and bite me square on the ass.

I shook my head, squared my shoulders, and got to work. That was one thing that always helped me – getting busy on a project. And this was a very important project indeed. Heather's very life depended on what I could find about her mother, and I couldn't screw this up.

I figured out that Connie Morrison had a Yahoo account, for she had a shortcut for that on her desktop. I got into that app, and was heartened to see her user name was already on there. The user name wasn't creative – it was just her name, conniemorrison@yahoo.com.

I cracked my knuckles and put in the word "langston" as her password. I immediately got the message that this wasn't the right password. I sighed, and tried Langston with a capital "L", and then tried it with different numbers after the word.

At some point, I got the message informing me that if I kept putting in the wrong password, I'd be locked out for 24 hours. I sat back in my chair and closed my eyes. I had five more tries to get in, otherwise I'd have to wait 'til tomorrow. I had no desire to wait until the next day. I wanted to get in there now. I felt every second I wasn't working on this case was a second wasted.

I raised my eyebrow, wondering if perhaps there was something else I could try. Just out of a hunch I had, I typed in the name "Louisa." Nothing came up. Then "Louisa1."

To my surprise, that was the right password. Connie's e-mail came up, and I let out a breath. I nodded and got up to get a glass of water and a snack. I came back to my desk and sipped my water and ate my little brownie. A part of me felt guilty for being in there. Like it was an invasion of her privacy. I tried to quell that feeling, and, after a few minutes, I knew I had to forge ahead.

As soon as I started looking at the subject lines of the e-mails, I knew I found the treasure trove. There were hundreds of e-mails from the church, but also seemingly hundreds of emails to and from Louisa herself.

I was about to click on one of the emails when I heard an enormous crash. It sounded like it was close by, so I got up and ran out the door.

"What the hell?" The entire side of my car was bashed in. I looked down the street, and saw nobody. It was as if it were a ghost that came and destroyed my car. Whoever did this did it and ran – and my car was in the driveway, so it wasn't just an accident. Somebody did this deliberately.

I sighed as I saw a scrap of paper on my windshield. *Next time you will be in the car.*

I shook my head, feeling threatened and pissed-off at the same time. The first thing that came to mind was that John Robinson was behind this bullshit. He was still pissed at me because I didn't take his second murder case. I couldn't believe he had the gall to ask me to take him on. I really couldn't believe he would get pissed when I refused it, but he did. He was presently in prison for Gina's murder, but he had people on the outside who might threaten me.

Well, it would just be a matter of getting a handwriting sample from him and comparing it to the note on the car. I looked around, hoping there was somebody, anybody who saw what just happened. I found that, in my neighborhood, there often was a person around somewhere on the street. People would walk their dogs, or sometimes just be out jogging, taking advantage of the cooler temperatures the nighttime provided.

There was nobody around.

I'd have to look at my file to get a sample of John's handwriting. I had his signature on my intake sheet.

I might also need a gun. That was something I'd been meaning to do for years and never did. I didn't like having guns around. I didn't know how to use one, and I was against them on principle. But, then again, I also had two young girls to protect now. It was no longer just about me. I had to worry about them.

I went back inside and shut down the computer, no longer in the mood to think about this case. My mind started to race 100 miles per hour, and I could feel a hint of rage bubbling up. I'd dealt with a lot of asshats in my life, and had defended quite a few of them as well. I once again started to question my chosen profession. Now I was possibly putting my life on the line, as well as the lives of my two girls.

If it weren't for Heather, I probably would've turned my back on my practice for good.

TWENTY-TWO

I couldn't get my car fixed until the garage opened on Monday, so I had to rent a car for the weekend. That really burned me, but I had to do it, so I just bit the bullet.

On Sunday, I made plans to take the girls to services at Our Lady of Sorrows, an old church in Midtown, right by the Crown Center.

"We don't have to go," Rina said. "In fact, I don't want to go."

"Rina," Abby said. "We have to go. We always go. Why don't you want to go?"

"It's boring." She raised an eyebrow. "And Aunt Harper has enough on her plate right now. She needs to go to that weird church today and find out what's going on over there. I'd rather do that with her." She grinned wickedly. "I'd like to find out what kind of crazy stuff happens in a cult. What kind of stuff they talk about."

I had no idea how Rina knew so much about the church, and I really didn't want her exposed to all that. I had no idea what that Reverend would be saying at the pulpit, and I was quite sure it would go against everything Our Lady of Sorrows impressed upon the girls. Their church was all about love thy neighbor and take in the stranger. The Living Breath Church's message would be quite different from that.

"Rina," I said. "I don't think..." I trailed off. Her big brown eyes were looking at me, trying to plead with me.

"Aunt Harper," she said. "Here's the thing. I'd like to do what you do one day. Maybe not defending people, but I'd like to become a prosecutor. After what happened to my mom, I'd like to get the bad guys. I need to know what I'll be facing one day."

I had to smile a little when she said that. "Rina, you're only 11. How are you so sure about what you're going to do? You have your whole life in front of you. Believe me, criminal law of any kind isn't for everyone." I understood where she was coming from, though. Her mother was murdered. If that happened to me, I probably would have done the same – go into the field of prosecuting criminals.

I finally just shook my head. "No, I'm sorry, Rina. I can't take you to this cult service. I don't know what will happen in there, and you're too young to be doing something like this."

Rina threw her arms in front of her and crossed them, but said nothing. "I hate you," she said to Harper.

Harper tried to suppress a smile when Rina professed her alleged hatred. How many times did she say the same thing to her own mother? Too many times to count.

"I love you," Harper said to her. "Now, Abby, I think you have a little party to go to after services? Why don't you let your sister tag along?"

Rina shook her head. "Really, Aunt Harper? Do you know how lame Abby's friends are? Are you really going to make me go over to Eva's house?"

"It's either that or Sophia will come and watch you. Your choice."

"I want to go with you."

"You can't. Now, Sophia watches you after services or you go with Abby over to Eva's house. Your choice."

Rina snarled and then mumbled. "I'll go and see lame Eva," she said. "But I'm not happy."

"Noted," I said.

AFTER SERVICES I dropped off the girls, and I approached the grounds of the church. The cars slowly moved through the gate, and I came to the guard's station.

The guard looked at me closely. "I'm very sorry, but you cannot go in there."

"Why?"

"Because I know who you are. I've been told to look out for you and if you show up, you can't come in. I'm sorry. I have my orders."

I was prepared for this. "Mr. Mulvaney," I said, looking at his name tag. "I *will* go through."

"I have my orders. You can't come on church grounds. We know who you are and why you're here."

I raised my eyebrows. "This is a church?"

"Yes."

"As such, it doesn't pay taxes. Correct?"

His cheek started to quiver right under his left eye. It was a stress tic, one I was familiar with. "I don't know about that."

"If this is a church," I began with a measured voice. It was difficult to not go off on this guy, but I somehow managed. "It's tax exempt. If it's tax exempt, you cannot turn anybody away. It's not private, so you can't exclude people. Now, if you'd like to exclude me, I'll sue to take away the church's tax exempt status, because that would necessarily mean the church is acting like a private entity. That will undoubtedly cost your church millions. Now, are you going to exclude me?"

He blinked his eyes rapidly, and I thought he was about to cry. "I have my orders," he said in a much smaller voice.

I looked in my rear view mirror and saw the cars lining up behind me. They were probably losing patience. I knew I would be if I were in that queue. "Listen, I don't have all day. Call your boss, tell them I'm coming in, and if he tells you I can't, tell him to expect a lawsuit this week."

His hand was shaking as he dialed the phone from his guard's station. He was speaking rapidly behind the glass, and I couldn't understand what he was saying, but I figured it wasn't good.

Not good for him, anyhow.

He hung up the phone and looked at me. "Go on through," he said, his voice quivering.

I nodded and drove on through the gate.

I came up to a large building to the West with a vaulted roof and a cross on top. "That would be the church, I would imagine," I said to myself.

I parked in the parking lot, and felt a bit nervous. I didn't know what would be preached in there. I walked through the doors of the church, and was greeted by two older ladies who handed me a flier. They smiled, nodded and shook my hand.

"Are you here as a guest?" one of the ladies asked me.

"I am."

"Right this way," she said, opening the enormous wooden door.

I walked through and noted that not much about the church's interior looked out of place, except there were no paintings on the walls. I was used to seeing portraits on church walls – pictures of Jesus and Mary and the saints. Some churches had pictures of Jesus that were just his head and shoulders. Others had the whole Stations of the Cross depicted. Still others had paintings of Jesus as a baby. This place, however, didn't have any of that.

"That's a clue," I said to myself. "I have a funny feeling this isn't a Christian Church at all. Jesus never said a word about homosexuality, he certainly wasn't in favor of slavery, and I doubt he wanted women to be completely subservient. These are all big tenets of this church."

I had a feeling this church was about to go Old Testament on me.

TWENTY-THREE

It wasn't long before the Reverend Scott made his appearance. He very tall, probably around 6'6". Yet he probably didn't weigh much more than 150 pounds. I once had a doll named "Stretch Armstrong," who was short and fat and could stretch out to be really long and thin. Reverend Scott looked like that. He had a large bald spot on the top of his head, although on the sides of his head he had thick dark hair growing. He was dressed in street clothes – a button-down blue shirt and blue jeans paired with cowboy boots. And, even though he was indoors, he was wearing dark sunglasses. I wondered what he was hiding.

One thing was for sure – he didn't look like any priests or reverends I'd ever seen.

Well, maybe Jim Jones. Reverend Scott reminded me of a very tall and very skinny Jim Jones, the infamous doomsday cult leader of The Peoples Temple. He became infamous in the late 1970s because of the Guyana Tragedy, where almost a thousand of his followers, and Jim Jones himself, killed themselves and murdered hundreds of children.

After everyone took their seat, the Reverend Scott stood there for several minutes. He just looked out into the crowd. He stood very still, his bony hands clasped in front of him, his expression impassive and just scanning every face of his followers. I looked around and saw everyone staring at him in rapt attention. They almost looked like they were in trances.

I furrowed my brows, wondering what was going on.

This went on for several minutes. The room was so silent you could've heard a pin drop. Not one person was speaking. Nobody was looking around. Everyone, and I mean everyone, had their eyes trained towards the tall skinny man in the blue jeans and cowboy boots.

And then he started to speak.

His voice was sonorous and deep. His tones were clear. Yet he spoke extremely softly.

"Welcome," he said, as he paced back and forth across the floor. "To all my acolytes and guests."

Acolytes...an interesting thing he called his followers. I had never heard that term used in a religious context before.

"I would like to begin by telling you a story. A very important story. This is a story about a pervert and an innocent young boy." He raised his fingers to the ceiling and then pointed at every person in the front row. "The pervert's name is Sam." He raised his voice and his head started shaking as his pacing grew more and more frantic. "I want you to remember that name, Sam. Say it with me!"

At that, everyone in the audience said the word "Sam."

"That's right, Sam! Sam is a disgusting pervert who corrupted, CORRUPTED, an innocent young boy named Jake." He shook his head sorrowfully. "An innocent boy named Jake," he said in a voice that was just above a whisper.

Everyone whispered the name Jake.

"You see, Jake is only 10 years old. 10 years old. And this man, Sam, took Jake's innocence last week."

Everybody gasped as Reverend Scott paused and let that last phrase sink in. He was back to his staring mode, his sunglassed eyes scanning the crowd darkly.

Reverend Scott shook his head. "Took his innocence. Stole it as easily and with as little regard as somebody might shoplift a strawberry from the corner market."

Everybody started to shake their head. A few people had tears in their eyes.

Then the reverend brought out a picture. "Here is a picture of Jake," he said, and then a screen was filled with a picture of the young boy. I had to admit, Jake was a beautiful young boy. Blonde curly hair, big blue eyes, a tiny little nose and rosebud lips. He had the creamy skin of a boy who rarely saw the sun without wearing a good sunscreen, and his white skin contrasted with the red of his lips. He was wearing some kind of Superman pajamas and he was smiling big, his two front teeth conspicuously missing.

The tears of the followers started in earnest.

"You might think this Sam is just a sick person. Born a pervert." He shook his head and rapidly paced back and forth across the floor. "You might think he's simply a monster, an outlier, something rare. But he's not."

He shook his head and paced some more. "He's not. He's a pervert and a sodomite and nothing but a product of the sodomite lifestyle. He's not unusual – he's typical of sodomites everywhere! This is who they are! Every sodomite, every man who lies with another man, every woman who lies with another woman, every queer who thinks they're a man born in a woman's body or a woman born in a man's body – this is who they are. They are products of Satan, every last one of them.

Products of Satan. Some of them are Satan himself, in a clever disguise."

Once again, his voice got quiet. "This is who they are."

I bit my lower lip and clenched my fist. This guy made me want to get up and strangle him with my bare hands. The Reverend was now pacing back and forth like a jungle cat trapped in a small cage.

He put his hands in front of him and clenched and unclenched his fists. "Leviticus 20:13 states that men who lie with other men shall be put to death. *Shall* be put to death. Not may be put to death. Not some are put to death and others are spared. No, Leviticus is clear – the perverts are not to live. They are not to live. You see, the ancient peoples knew something this society seems to have forgotten – if you let the perverts live, they will take over society. They already have!"

Everybody started to shake their head rapidly, as if everyone started to become agitated all at once.

"They already have. They're out there, literally parading around. In fact, just next weekend, they're having a pervert parade. A pervert parade. They'll be flaunting their asses in little pink tutus on the streets, throwing their disgusting body and soul in your face. And they can be married. Imagine, they're getting married, just like you and me. Married. Taking our most sacred ritual, the very bedrock of this society, and perverting it. Sullying it. Your marriage means nothing now. NOTHING!" He was now shouting, his face red, his long body coiled, his breathing coming faster and faster.

Everyone's head started to rapidly shake and one guy stood up. "Those perverts can't get away with it. They can't destroy us from within like this. They can't!"

The reverend's head just nodded. "Right. You're right! We don't have the death penalty for the queers, but *The Bible* calls for it. It calls for it!"

He clasped his hands in front of him.

I narrowed my eyes, the wheels turning in my head. I tried to quell my fury at this guy and what he was doing, and simply turned on the analytical part of my brain. I couldn't let my emotions cloud my judgment on what this guy was up to. One thing was for sure - he had a charisma about him, much like Adolph Hitler and others who got masses of people to follow them. Evil men could attract a huge following because they knew how to mesmerize people. Almost hypnotize them.

The reverend rapidly changed the subject. His next subject was apparently women. He used the same tactic as before – bringing in individual case studies to illustrate his point. In this case, he started talking about a woman who emasculated a man, so the man committed suicide because he was so humiliated. He then thundered about how this story illustrated why women needed to let their men control them completely.

"And remember, a woman cannot own property! When she owns property, she becomes uncontrollable! She must not become uncontrollable, because when she does, her man literally loses his balls!"

By the time the "service" was over, I like I needed a hot shower.

Everybody stood up to leave, and I did the same.

As I turned to leave, I felt a cold hand on my shoulder.

I slowly turned around. I somehow knew just who was summoning me, and I felt chilled.

I looked up at the Reverend Scott's face, and saw he was no longer wearing the sunglasses. I looked into his penetrating eyes and felt an unmistakable shudder. Like I was in the presence of pure, unadulterated evil.

His eyes were pale, so pale that the irises might appear white to somebody who was looking at him from a slight distance. That was probably why he wore his sunglasses – he probably knew his odd eyes freaked people out.

I swallowed hard, wanting to get the hell out of there. This guy was skeeving me out like I'd never been skeeved out before. "Can I help you?"

He narrowed those pale eyes and nodded. "I know who you are. And I'm watching you."

At that, he simply turned on his heels and walked away.

TWENTY-FOUR

When I drove home from that...place...I felt chilled, even though it was 90 degrees outside and sunny. I picked up the girls and took them home. Rina, for her part, still looked angry that she had to spend time with Abby and her friends, instead of coming with me.

"Did you guys have fun?" I asked as I buckled up after making sure the girls did the same.

"We did," Abby said. "We ate pizza and played board games."

Rina rolled her eyes. "It was the lamest day I've ever had. I really wanted to see those weirdos with you, Aunt Harper. Why can't I? When you go back there, I want to go back there, too."

I shook my head. "No. Trust me, you don't want to be anywhere near that place. It's harmful to even be in the presence of that Reverend Scott guy, and I won't put you through that."

"Whatever. I'm not a baby."

"No, that's true," I said. "You may not be a baby, but there are some things you're not ready for. You're too young."

"I'm going to find out about that kind of stuff anyhow," Rina said. "You can't keep me at home, you know. I need to know what kind of freaks are out there so I can be ready for them."

I took a breath. "Later. Much, much later."

THAT NIGHT, I finally decided to get into Connie Morrison's computer. I'd been so distracted by the car accident and the cryptic note, combined with going to the "church" that morning, so I didn't really have time to get into the computer.

I booted it up and got right into the e-mail. I immediately zeroed in on the email chain between Connie and Louisa Garrison.

I searched the top of the page to find when the earliest email was. To my surprise, the emails between the two women went back three years. I started reading the chain from the very beginning, up to the current date, even though there seemed to be hundreds of emails between the two.

KITTYDARLING@YAHOO.COM

To conniemorrison@gmail.com

June 17, 2020

HEY THERE YOU! I REALLY ENJOYED MEETING YOU TODAY. I'M REALLY EXCITED YOU'RE LOOKING FOR ANSWERS FOR YOUR SON, AND I KNOW HOW MUCH YOU LOVE HIM. I KNOW HOW WORRIED YOU ARE THAT HE WON'T BE WITH YOU IN THE AFTERLIFE, AND YOU'RE RIGHT TO WORRY. I HOPE YOU WILL VISIT ME AT MY CHURCH. WE HAVE ANSWERS FOR YOU. YOU'RE NOT ALONE.

. . .

CONNIEMORRISON@GMAIL.COM
    Kittydarling@yahoo.com
    June 17, 2020

    THANK THE LORD I MET YOU TODAY. I DON'T WANT YOU TO THINK I DO THAT KIND OF THING ALL THE TIME, THOUGH. I DON'T MEET PEOPLE ON PINKCUPID ALL THE TIME, AND I'M REALLY EMBARRASSED. I THINK WE CAN HAVE A FRIENDSHIP, ALTHOUGH I HAVE TO ADMIT, YOU CERTAINLY DO KNOW HOW TO USE YOUR TONGUE. MY GOD...I'M BLUSHING NOW. I CAN'T WAIT TO SEE YOU AGAIN.

I NODDED. I had the feeling something was going on between these two. So that was how Connie found that cult. She found Louisa Garrison on PinkCupid, the lesbian answer to Grindr. Apparently they hooked up right away.

    I got out a yellow pad of paper and jotted down some notes on what I was reading. Louisa Garrison would be an indispensable witness. I just didn't know how much.

    I kept reading the email exchange between the two. They emailed each other back and forth several times a day. It started out friendly and flirty, and, for some odd reason, for the first year or so, it looked like Connie was resisting going to Louisa's church.

    For instance, there was an e-mail from Connie to Louisa, about six months in, where Louisa was angry that Connie hadn't yet come to the church:

KITTYDARLING@YAHOO.COM
    Conniemorrison@gmail.com

December 24, 2020

Christmas Eve is here, and I can't believe you STILL won't come to my church. You need to find out our message, and I'm telling you, we have answers for your life and your sick son. I think I'll have to re-think our relationship. I love you. I love being with you. I think about you all the time. Constantly. But you don't seem to want to share my life with me, and that hurts like nothing you could ever imagine.

Please reconsider your decision not to come with me to our Christmas Eve service. If you don't, then I'm sorry, I just can't be with you.

CONNIEMORRISON@GMAIL.COM
Kittydarling@yahoo.com
December 24, 2020
Okay, okay, I'll come with you. See you tonight.

I WONDERED why Connie didn't want to go to church with Louisa. I anticipated finding the answer through the email chains. There weren't anything in the emails that came before the Christmas Eve ones that gave me that answer.

I kept on reading the emails, looking for some indication on when Connie became radicalized and why. I soon came across it:

KITTYDARLING@YAHOO.COM
Conniemorrison@gmail.com
October 19, 2021

I KNOW THAT YOU KNOW I'M RIGHT THAT YOUR SON NEEDS HELP. AS YOU KNOW, AS THE REVEREND SCOTT HAS TOLD YOU, YOUR SON IS GOING TO HELL. IF HE STAYS THE WAY HE IS, HE IS IN VIOLATION OF NATURE AND GOD'S LAW. GOD MADE US PERFECT, IN HIS IMAGE, AND YOUR SON NEEDS TO MAKE SURE HE DOESN'T DO ANYTHING TO GO AGAINST THAT. HE IS ALSO WICKED BECAUSE HE IS LYING WITH OTHER MEN, AND YOU KNOW WHAT LEVITICUS SAYS ABOUT THAT. YOU NEED TO MAKE SURE YOUR SON CHANGES HIS WAYS AND THAT RAINBOW INTERNATIONAL CLINIC IS JUST THE PLACE FOR HIM. PLEASE RECONSIDER. I KNOW YOU DON'T HAVE THE MONEY FOR THIS PLACE, BUT I'LL LEND YOU THE MONEY. PLEASE. YOUR SON'S AFTERLIFE DEPENDS ON IT.

CONNIEMORRISON@GMAIL.COM
   Kittydarling@yahoo.com
   October 19, 2021
   I'LL THINK ABOUT IT.

I TOOK a breath as I realized this was the last email between the two women. I had no idea what happened after that.

Obviously, Connie decided to send Heather to that clinic. Why was she acting like she didn't want to do it? Like she didn't want to go to the church at all? And why did the two women quit e-mailing one another?

It seemed like every time I was getting closer to the truth, something happened that made it all seem so far away. Again.

There was something I wasn't seeing. I just didn't know what it might be.

TWENTY-FIVE

The next day, I went to work, after dropping off Rina and Abby at their new private school. I also went to the body shop to get my car worked on. I didn't know for sure that John Robinson was behind the car vandalism, although I suspected he was. The only problem was that his handwriting in my file didn't match the handwriting on the car note. No matter, I knew it had to be him. As if I didn't have enough problems in my life without a psychotic murderer harassing me.

"Hey," I said to Pearl. "How are things going with the investigation?"

"Good," she said. "I tracked down the guy who's investigating all the gay kids being killed. And I just got the order from the court that Heather was indicted by the Grand Jury." She handed me the order. "I guess the case really begins now, huh?"

"I guess so. Now, tell me about that Detective. Can I talk to him?"

"Sure. Do you think he'll tell you something relevant?"

"I do. I think. We'll see." I was being unusually flighty and non-committal. "I'll talk to him, anyhow."

"Good." She looked embarrassed. "Because he's coming in. At 10."

I nodded. "Great. Thanks for the extra-long notice." I had a donut in my hand, which was my breakfast that morning, and a newspaper I was planning on reading. "Well, as you know, since you keep my schedule, I have hearings all this afternoon. I also have motions to write and I need to get a petition together for the Family Court for the girls' adoption. I really wish you could've warned me this guy was coming in."

"Well, he wanted to talk to you. He has some information for you that might be helpful."

"Okay. Well, send him in when he gets here."

"I will."

ABOUT A HALF HOUR LATER, Agent Springer showed up. He was in his early forties, and was taller than me – he stood about 6'2", and his face was slightly craggy and very masculine. His temples were greying slightly, but he had a full head of hair that was jet black and slightly wavy. His eyes were blue and steely, his cheeks were broad and his lips were puffy. He was dressed in blue jeans and a tight black t-shirt that showed he'd kept himself in pretty good shape over the years.

I blinked my eyes and lost my breath. There was something about this man that was incredibly sexy. *Down girl.* I hadn't been attracted to a man in so long, I couldn't even remember the last time I was. But this guy – the way he looked, his posture, and the fact that he looked like he worked out every day of his life – made my stomach do flip-flops.

I stood up to greet him. "Agent Springer," I said, hoping I

wasn't coming off as some love-struck school-girl, "you wanted to see me."

"Yes," he said. His voice was deep, with an Australian accent. I died right there, because I *loved* Australian accents. "I think I might have some helpful information." He raised his eyebrows, and I was wondering what he was looking for.

I shook my head, realizing how rude I was being. "I'm terribly sorry, you're just standing there, and I haven't asked you to take a seat. But please do."

He smiled, his lips going slightly crooked, and he raised his eyebrows again. "Thanks, Ms. Ross," he said. "I'm an old-fashioned guy, and I never presume a lady wants me to sit down."

I chuckled. "Old-fashioned. I like that. Anyhow, what do you have for me?"

He sat back in his chair, his left leg crossing over his right knee. His casual stance was something else throwing me. He just seemed so laid-back, which I couldn't say the same about myself. I was always so Type-A, which was probably the reason, in the end, for my on-going bouts with depression – I was always at war with myself. I beat myself up on a regular basis and usually fell short of where I wanted to be.

"You're working the Heather Morrison case, I know. I've seen that case in the paper a lot."

"I am."

"Well, then, you'll want to know what I've been working on." He leaned forward, and I could smell the faint scent of a woodsy cologne. I bit my lower lip and put my hand on my leg. I wanted to put my hand on his leg instead.

Just then, the phone was ringing. Pearl had put it through, even though I told her to hold my calls, so I glared at her through my window. She turned and looked at me and mouthed the words *you need to take this*.

"I'm so sorry, Agent Springer," I said. "But I have to take this. I won't be long."

"Please, call me Axel," he said.

I smiled. I happened to love the name Axel. I thought it was the coolest name ever, and it really suited him. "Hello," I said, "This is Harper Ross."

"Harper, this is your neighbor Ally."

"Oh, hey Ally. How are things?"

"Not good." She paused. "I didn't want to bother you, but..."

"But what?" Alarm started to rise in my gut, and it threatened overtake me.

"I don't want you to get too alarmed, but, well, there was a fire."

I blinked. "A fire?"

"Yes. Well, yes. A fire. Your kitchen caught fire. I called the fire department right away, and it didn't seem to spread that far. But I think your kitchen is gone."

A fire. Did I leave anything on? Like the stove or oven? I racked my brain. "Thanks for calling me."

I hung up the phone. "Um, Agent Springer," I began.

"Axel." He smiled. "Do you have to go?"

"I do. I'm so sorry." I looked at my watch. I needed to go home and see about my kitchen, because, otherwise, I'd obsess about it all day. I couldn't afford to do that, because I had court appearances that entire day and needed to have my head in the game. "I appreciate you coming in, though. I'm so sorry to cut this short. Can we meet another time?"

He raised his left eyebrow. "How about we meet over some tacos and tequila? It's Tuesday, after all. I have a lot to discuss with you that you probably will be interested in."

I swallowed hard. "Tacos, yes, tequila..." I shook my head and brought out my AA chip.

He smiled again and nodded. "I got you, mate. Tacos and iced tea, then."

"Tacos and iced tea. Manny's on the Boulevard?"

He looked at the clock, which was behind my head. "Okay, I'll see you at...7?"

"7." I nodded. "I'll call my nanny, Sophia. She'll have to pick up my girls."

"You got kids? How many?"

"It's a long story, but I have two at home." I smiled, realizing I enjoyed saying I had two girls. "You have any kids?"

"Yeah. My son just started college." He dipped his head slightly and grinned. "I feel so old saying that, but I just turned 40. I was a young pup when Boyd was born." He cracked his knuckles, which made me inwardly smile, because I did that whenever I was nervous. "Well, anyhow, you better, uh, get to your, uh..."

"Fire." I was remarkably sanguine about it. I felt like I'd seen it all, which I probably had over my life. "My kitchen apparently caught fire while I was sitting here in this office, which is strange, to say the very least. Plus, my car was bashed in. Maybe you can look into all that." I wondered if I was batting my eyelashes. I felt awkward for the first time in a long time.

He furled his eyebrows. "Your car was bashed in. A hit and run? It was on the street, I assume."

"No, it was in my driveway. I have this psychotic former client who hates me. I'm sure he was the one who got somebody to bash in my car. To intimidate me."

"Huh. You certainly seem calm about all this."

"How am I supposed to seem?" I smiled. "Axel, if you knew the things I've seen. The clients I've defended. If there was some way for me to make my mortgage, and send my two girls to college, that didn't involve doing this, I'd get out tomorrow."

I didn't really feel that way. I felt this was my calling. A passion. But I didn't want the cop to know that. After all, he was, by definition, on the opposing side. It wouldn't do for this handsome man to know that I secretly loved my job. Aside from that crisis that happened after Gina Caldwell, which still made me shudder and kept me awake nights, I felt my cases made me feel alive. Especially Heather's case.

"I know what you mean. I've probably seen all the same things. I'm on the other side, though, of you."

"Yes. Well, I have to-"

"I know. I'll see you at 7."

Axel left, and I looked around for my purse and keys. "Pearl," I said, "I have to get home. I've had an emergency."

"I know," she said. "Girl, what's going on? That lady on the phone told me she had to talk to you right away."

"Well, my kitchen burned down. I guess that's emergency enough."

Pearl grimaced and pursed her lips while she looked at me. "You leave your stove on?"

"No. But it's an old house. Old wiring. Probably something happened where something shorted out or something."

"Have your fridge looked at. I hear that's sometimes a problem. I hear people have had their house burned down because of a bad fridge."

"A bad fridge? How does that catch fire?"

She shrugged. "I didn't say I knew how they catch fire, I only heard they sometimes do. Like it's a spontaneous combustion or something."

"Hm, that's weird. Really weird."

"When can they find out what happened?"

"I don't know, probably a week. Why?"

"You should watch yourself. I worry about you. You're always meeting these tough dudes who get pissed-off at you.

One of these days, one of those guys might get you. I don't want to see that happen."

"Thanks for looking out for me."

At that, I left the office and got into my car and headed to my house.

WHEN I GOT HOME, there were still fire trucks and police cars outside my house. I shook my head and got out of the car.

"A bit of an overkill, isn't it guys? Bringing out two fire trucks and three police cars?" I smiled at one of the firefighters, who was standing outside my house and making notes on a pad of paper.

"We can't be too careful," he said to me with a smile back.

"Ha. I know the truth. You guys hang around the fire house bored to tears, just itching for something to do. Along comes a little kitchen that burns down, and it's excitement time. Admit it. You just love the thrill."

His slight smile when I said that showed I hit the nail on the head. "We're investigating the cause of the fire," he said. "So, I'm sorry, you can't go into your kitchen just yet. There's a yellow crime scene tape cordoning off the kitchen."

"A crime scene tape? Is that necessary?"

"It's a suspicious fire," he said. "We checked to make sure all your appliances were turned off, and they were. Until we find out the cause of the fire, we have to investigate it."

I sighed. "I have this psychotic client. My car was bashed in, now this. I'd imagine he's behind it. I mean, not him, exactly, because he's in prison, but he has buddies on the outside."

A cop came over, one that I didn't know. "Hello, ma'am, I heard you speaking with Tom here about a client of yours. Could you tell me more about him?"

I told him the story about John, and about he was angry

with me, as the cop, whose name was Officer Heaney, rapidly wrote down what I told him.

"Is there anybody else who might be behind this?" Officer Heaney asked.

"I'm a criminal defense attorney. Take your pick."

"We'll investigate this John," he said. "But I need to know who else might be threatening you."

"Well, there is this one guy. He leads a cult. He's extremely odd. His name is Reverend John Scott. He's upset with me because I've been snooping around his cult."

"Reverend John Scott," he said. "That name sounds familiar."

"Yeah? Maybe you're investigating him for something else? If you're not, you probably should be."

He shook his head. "The KCPD is a large organization. If one of the divisions is investigating him, I wouldn't necessarily know about it. No, I've heard his name in another context."

He was furrowing his brow and shaking his head while he wrote some notes on a yellow sheet of paper. *Where have I heard that name,* he was mumbling to himself.

Then he snapped his fingers and looked at me. "My sister was talking about him."

I wondered if this was significant. "Does your sister happen to have somebody who is LGBT in her family?"

"My nephew. He's deceased now, though."

I narrowed my eyes. "Deceased? Can I ask you what happened to him?"

Officer Heaney looked uncomfortable. He scratched his neck and looked down at the ground. "He committed suicide," he said. "Hanged himself."

I drew a breath. "I'm so sorry to hear that."

He shrugged. "It happens. My sister never accepted him,

neither did her husband. The poor kid had a hard time." He let out a mighty sigh. "Anyhow, that's neither here nor there."

I would have to ask him something sensitive, but necessary, under the circumstances. "Can I ask you something?"

"Sure."

"Did your nephew leave a suicide note?"

"No."

"Was there an autopsy?"

I crinkled his brows. "No. Why would there be an autopsy? He hanged himself, that's that."

I was striking a nerve, but I had to press on. "Is anybody sure he died from the hanging? Or maybe he was dead before he was hanged?"

Now Officer Heaney was looking annoyed. "That's the stupidest thing I've ever heard. Of course he died by his hanging. What kind of a question is that?"

"I'm an attorney. It's my job to ask the tough questions. Anyhow, I'm sorry if I've offended you."

Officer Heaney shuddered slightly and shook his head. "Well, I'll do the investigations of those two people," he said. "I'm sorry, but you can't use your kitchen until our investigation is through."

"I'll live." I checked my watch. "In the meantime, I need to get to court. I'm late for a hearing."

I got into my car and turned on the radio, but my mind was 1,000 miles away. The puzzle pieces were starting to fit.

But could I prove it in a court of law?

TWENTY-SIX

I met Agent Springer at Manny's on the Boulevard. It was a two-story Mexican restaurant right in the middle of the area that Kansas Citians refer to as "Little Mexico." There were plenty of Mexican restaurants around the area, along with different shops that sold Mexican items. The restaurant was on the corner and marked by an orange and green vertical sign on the side of the building.

Manny's was one of my favorite places to get greasy Mexican food. It was always jammed, it seemed, even though it was two-stories and could probably seat 500 people.

I walked in and there was Agent Springer. He stood up when I came in, and I thought I saw a look of hope in his eyes. Or maybe it was just my wishful thinking.

"Harper," he said. "You made it."

"I did. I'm sorry about earlier. My kitchen caught fire."

"I know," he said with a smile. "I remember. You told me."

"That's right, I did." I suddenly felt self-conscious.

"That's okay. I repeat myself all the time."

Just then, the hostess came over. "How many is in your party?" she asked us.

"Just two."

She led the way through the darkened room, and we took our seat at a two-top table. Our waiter came over to us almost immediately, gave us chips and salsa, and took our drink orders.

"Just water for me," I said. I was somehow embarrassed to be only ordering water, because it made me seem cheap. But I didn't like pop and I couldn't drink tea because I had a hard time processing caffeine, so I usually stuck with water.

"Me too," Axel said.

"You can get some tequila," I said, nudging him from across the table.

"Nope. I have an aunt in a 12-step," he said. "I know what it's like to want a drink and have your companion drinking." He raised his fist. "Solidarity."

I raised my chip. "Solidarity."

The waiter left and I leaned in closer to Axel. "So, I don't want to beat around the bush. What do you have for me?"

"You're an impatient one, mate," he said with a smile. "But I'll tell you. I'm investigating the murders of five LGBT youth in the past month. I was confused before about what, if any, connection there was between them, but I think I found it."

The waiter came back and gave us our waters and I took a sip. "I'm on pins and needles," I said. "What did you come up with?"

"Well, all these blokes' families had one thing in common. And the reason why I'm involving you is because you have a client who also has this one thing in common. All their families, their mothers and/or fathers, went to-"

"The Church of the Living Breath," I said excitedly. My eyes got wide. "That's it. That's…" I didn't want to jump the gun, but, at the same time, I could see the puzzle piece fitting nicely in. Finally. I was suddenly excited, so excited I had to see my client right that second, and contact the DA to see if I could possibly get the case dismissed.

"That's what?"

"Don't you see? It's a cult. A cult where the leader is a very charismatic and strange person. He holds his people in something like a trance. He's virulently anti-gay. He must be convincing his people, brainwashing them, and telling them they have to kill their gay and trans kids. Oh, he says the parents first must try to change their LGBT sons and daughters, but, when they don't change, he tells them to kill their kids."

Axel's eyes looked skeptical. "I actually wasn't thinking that, but it's, uh, an interesting theory. One that I've never heard of before. Who's going to kill their kids just because a cult leader tells them to?"

"You don't seem to know much about cults," I said. "I've studied them a little bit, and I can tell you that the followers will do anything their leaders tell them. Not within reason, but whatever they're told to do. Now here are these gay kids, and all of them have family in that church? I think you have your answer right there."

He shook his head. "Maybe. I'll have to do some more investigating, but it's an interesting theory."

"What's your theory?" I asked him as I dipped a chip into the salsa. The salsa was light and fresh and aromatic. It was heavy on the cilantro, just as I liked it.

"I was looking into the possibility that there was a serial killer who was targeting specifically the gay and trans kids in that church. I figured it was somebody who knew these kids, came across them, from the kids going to this church, and that made these kids a target. Somebody unhinged, who feels the kids are spoiling this church with their very presence. I've investigated serial killers before, and it sounds like the most logical explanation. A more logical explanation than that parents are killing their own kids just because a charismatic leader tells them to."

I raised my eyebrow. "Never underestimate people. And never underestimate the power an authoritarian figure can have on weak-minded people. Our history has been full of such figures getting people to do worse things than killing their kids."

Axel leaned back and nodded. "Look who you're talking to," he said. "I've been on the police force for twenty years. I've seen everything. But I haven't run across the situation you're talking about."

My mind started to turn and I found I wasn't even focusing on what Axel was saying to me. I only knew I'd have to subpoena Louisa and the Reverend Scott, and that I suddenly knew my case was looking better than it ever had before.

I bit my lower lip. There still was the issue of the missing butcher knife. And exactly why Connie Morrison and Louisa Garrison stopped talking to one another over the e-mail. I knew Louisa would be an indispensable witness, and I was excited to make her crack, as I knew I would. The Reverend Scott was a different story. He seemed like he would be a hard nut.

I wondered if I could subpoena some of the other parents who were in the church, too.

I suddenly knew the case was opening up, and I couldn't have been more excited about it.

TWENTY-SEVEN

"Hey girly," Heather said when I went to see her the next day at her halfway house. "What's up? What's going on with your plan to let me stay with you?"

"I filed a motion with the judge," I told her. "I expect to get an answer on it this week. The one thing that might be standing in the way would be Alexis Winters. She's fine with me having Rina and Abby, but she might balk if you come in. We'll have to see."

Heather's face fell, and I felt awful. She shrugged. "It's okay, I guess. I don't mind staying here. My roommates harass me, but I told them all I was about to cut a bitch, and they've backed off, surprisingly enough. I guess they're not interested in catching another case. And they *will* catch another case if they fuck with me too much. I'll squeal like a stuck pig if they get too much up in my grill. I can hold my own." She sat up in her chair, squaring her shoulders, and she leveled her heavily made-up eyes toward me. "Anyhow, what you got for me?"

"Well, I've been investigating that church your mother

went to. What can you tell me about her relationship with Louisa Garrison?"

Heather shrugged. "I don't know who that is."

I cocked my head. "Did your mother stay out at night? Like overnight ever?"

"Yeah," she said. "She stayed out a lot, actually. Why do you ask?"

"Your mother was having a lesbian affair with Louisa Garrison, who is in a position of authority over at the Church of the Living Breath. That's significant, because Louisa might be the point woman for the reverend. I think she's the woman who carries out his dirty work. But I have to ask you about the butcher knife. Why wasn't it recovered at the scene?"

"It wasn't?" Heather genuinely looked perplexed. "I don't know about that. All I know is that I ran out of the house after I killed her, so I have no idea what could have happened to it."

I bit my lower lip. Things were looking good, as far as my working on a theory on what happened at Heather's house. But could that theory be trusted here? What if Axel Springer was right – what if a serial killer was targeting gay and trans kids at the church? That theory really made much more sense to me. Like Axel, I really couldn't imagine parents could ever be brainwashed into killing their own flesh and blood. If it was a serial killer, I was at square one, because it would never explain why Connie was on the verge of killing Heather.

I stood up and started to pace around the room. "I'm going to have to figure this out," I said. "If I can't answer the DA's questions about what happened to that butcher knife, this case goes out the window. We need to figure that out."

Heather shrugged. "How am I supposed to know? I told you what I know, and that's that the old bag had a butcher knife in her hand when I killed her. I can't tell you what happened to it. You'll have to figure that out. You're the lawyer."

"There's another thing bothering me," I said to Heather. "When did you read my article? My *Law Review* article?" That detail was nagging at me suddenly. I simply couldn't imagine that Heather, who was on the run after killing her mother, would have the presence of mind to sit down and do legal research. For one, finding *Law Review* articles isn't that easy. You can use Google to find what you want, but to actually read the article, you typically needed some kind of legal software, like Lexis/Nexis or Westlaw. Would her drug-dealer boyfriend have access to these databases? Maybe, since he was a drug-dealer, and he might actually use case law to try to figure out the limits of what he could get away with.

Maybe, but I doubted that.

"Why does that matter?" Heather looked at me suspiciously. "Why do I have the feeling you're not believing me all of a sudden?"

"I'm just trying to get things out of the way. I have a working theory, but I need to clear the bugs out of it if I'm going to sell it to the jury. That's all."

"I'm not buying that," Heather said, crossing her arms in front of her. "The DA won't ask me about my reading that article. He doesn't even know I read that article. He probably doesn't even know the article exists. You're asking me because you think I'm lying. That I looked at the article because I wanted to know if I could have a defense before I killed my mom. Aren't you?"

I had to admit, Heather was sharp. She had my number.

"Well, is that the truth? When did you read the article?"

Heather sneered and suddenly stood up. "If you don't believe my story, maybe I should find another attorney who will. You can give me back my retainer, what's left of it, anyhow." She looked genuinely hurt.

"Where did that come from? I'm simply asking a question.

That's all. I need to know, because I don't want to be blind-sided." The way Heather was acting, right at that moment, was raising my suspicions about her and I didn't want to feel that way. Not about my client – I needed to believe in her if I would give this case my all. God forbid it turned out to be another John Robinson case.

"I'm not blind-siding you. I told you what happened, and that's that."

I crossed my arms, and I suddenly started to question everything I knew about this case. "I know you told me, but you're acting weird about this article, and I need to know why. Why, Heather? I have the feeling you read it long before you killed your mother, and, if you did, why did you?"

"I need for you to leave," she said. "You're going back on your word about taking me in, and now you're acting like you don't believe my story. I don't need your shit, Harper. I've taken my share of crap from all kinds of flying monkeys through the years, and I don't need it from the one person who's supposed to be in my corner."

I knew she would try to fire me, but I wouldn't let that happen. She had to know I had her back, even if I didn't entirely believe her. I couldn't let this case go. I was connected to the girl, really connected, and I had to see the case through.

But first, I needed to give her some tough love.

"Heather," I said. "You can fire me if you wish. But you have to know one thing – if you lie to your next attorney, that attorney can't do your case justice. You have to come clean with me. Come clean with me, Heather, and we can do this together. I'll figure out a theory on what happened to the butcher knife, and hopefully I can get evidence about it. That's a major deal, but it can be explained away. But I need to know what you're hiding from me. And you *are* hiding something from me, Heather. I know you are. You might as well tell me, right here, and right now. I surely don't want something coming up to bite me in the ass later on."

Heather's lips pursed and her long eyelashes fluttered. She tapped her high-heeled foot on the wooden floor as she crossed and uncrossed her arms.

I let out a tendril of breath as she said "Okay. I'll tell you."

TWENTY-EIGHT

"I need a smoke," Heather said, looking down at the floor. "Let's go out on the porch."

We went out on the porch, sat on the swing, and Heather got out her cigarettes. "Hey, Ace," she said, calling to a homeless guy walking along the sidewalk pushing a shopping cart. "What's up?"

Ace waved to her and motioned to the shopping cart. "I'm picking up cans and bottles. You got any for me?"

"You know I do." Heather nudged me. "There's a box in the kitchen with all the recyclable bottles and shit. Bring that out here. Ace has room in his shopping cart for it."

"You're stalling." I was disapproving of her dancing around the question of the article, and it was just making me all the more suspicious.

"I'm not. Now go. I'll be sitting right here. Where am I going to go? I got this goddamn ankle bracelet on. I was hoping to stay in a nice house with a nice bed and have some good meals, but *that* looks like it's not going to happen." She glared at me. "Thanks for getting my hopes up and letting them crash down."

I sighed and went into the kitchen. It was an old kitchen, with appliances that looked like they were from the 1940s – a white stove that had two different compartments inside, a refrigerator with a metal handle, and no microwave. Heather told me that very little cooking went on in the house, because she and the other people living in the house were fed mainly frozen foods heated up in the oven. There was even a litter box in there, because there was a cat living in the house, although I'd never seen it.

I found the box and went out to the porch, where Heather was smoking her cigarette. She was wearing ripped jeans and her usual high-heeled boots, topped with a black tank top that showed off her surprisingly muscular arms. Around her neck was a floral pink and black scarf. She was nervously sucking on the cigarette, and was rapidly rocking back and forth on the swing.

"I have the cans and bottles," I said to Heather.

"Ace is waiting," she said, pointing to the homeless guy just on the other side of the front-yard fence.

I went down to the guy and dumped the cans and bottles into Ace's shopping cart.

"Thanks, ma'am," he said politely. He then started to push the shopping cart on up the street, looking carefully throughout the sidewalk for more recyclables.

"Okay," I said, walking back up the worn concrete steps that led to the wooden porch. "Now, the time for beating around the bush is officially over," I said, sitting next to her on the swing. "What's going on?"

She sighed. "I read the article before my mom came after me," she said. "I didn't tell you before because I knew it looked bad. Like I planned this whole thing from the start." She shook her head and sucked on her cigarette some more. "All right? You happy? I read your article before my mom attacked me. Now I suppose you think I'm guilty, and you're going to want off my case. So go ahead, withdraw. Why don't you fucking leave me, just like everyone else has?"

I looked at her and saw she was on the verge of crying. She turned her head away and sucked harder on her cigarette, and she blew it out with an enormous breath. Her right hand, which was holding onto her cigarette, was shaking hard. She bit her lower lip and continued to turn her face away from me.

I was, at last, getting beneath the layers. Seeing the scared kid behind the mask. The kid who had known nothing but rejection from the adults in her life. Her mother tried to kill her, it sounded like her father rejected her too, and now she was positive I would do the same.

I put my arm around her, and I felt her shoulders stiffen beneath my touch. "Heather," I said. "I'll go ahead and petition the court to have you stay with me. I'll run it by the guardian ad litem for the girls, though. If she's okay with it, then I'll do it. I don't know that she will be, though, and I'm at a really precarious place with them."

She nodded and I saw a single tear slide down her cheek. She blinked hard, trying to stem the tide no doubt threatening to come, but she didn't say a word.

"But Heather, I won't withdraw. Not unless I think you're lying to me. Now, I have to admit, there are two things that give me pause, and we need to get to the bottom of it. Because if we don't, the prosecutor will. The butcher knife is a mystery, and now you need to tell me why you read my *Law Review* article before you killed your mother." I crossed my arms in front of me. I suddenly felt like my case wasn't nearly as strong as I thought it was.

"You won't believe me anyway. You have your mind made up I'm lying to you. I can see it in your eyes."

"Heather, don't prejudge what I'm thinking. I'll admit, I need to answer these nagging questions before we go forward. You need to help me with this. You need to come clean."

She narrowed her eyes and kept on swinging. "I've changed my mind. I won't tell you. I don't think you'll believe me."

I sighed. "Heather, don't do this to me. Don't shut down. I need you to tell me everything. Everything. The prosecutor will find out about you reading my article, and then he'll use that information to hang you. Don't think he won't somehow get access to your computer, and if that article is in your history, well, then, you're history. It looks bad, Heather, really bad, that you're reading about self-defense before your mother attacked you."

I looked at Heather and saw she wasn't going to talk to me about this issue. Her body language was completely closed, and her face had the hard mask on it again. "You can withdraw." She looked away. "I don't want you to, though. But if you want to, I understand."

I sighed. "I won't withdraw." I looked at my watch. "I need to go. I told the girls I'd be home by 7. I try to have dinner with them every evening, and they're showing a great deal of patience with me in waiting until 7 to eat."

I looked at Heather, who looked once again that she was about to cry, and my heart went out to her. "Heather, I won't withdraw. But I won't be blindsided. I won't be. I'm on your side, but you have to cooperate with me. Now, I'm going to tell you this not because I don't believe you, but because I have to cover all my bases. But if you killed your mother for some reason other than self-defense, I need to know this. Maybe we can get mitigating circumstances in front of the-"

I was about to say the word "jury," but that word never

made it out of my mouth, because Heather hauled off and punched me before I could finish my sentence.

Sigh. Here we go again.

TWENTY-NINE

I got home and Rina and Abby were waiting for me with Sophia. "Aunt Harper," Rina said, coming up to give me a hug. "Why didn't you tell us you had a boyfriend?"

Boyfriend? What was she talking about? "Because I don't," I said. "Why do you think I do?"

Rina shrugged, and Abby came over to tattle. "She was reading your e-mails, Aunt Harper." After she said that, Rina slugged her hard on the arm. "Ow!" Abby hit her back, and I had to get in the middle of the two.

"Come on," I said. "I know the two of you are starving, so you're irritable. I made a casserole last night and I think Sophia has baked it up, because I smell it." Even though I was technically not supposed to use my kitchen, I defied that order and I used my oven, which, surprisingly enough, was still workable. I had created "funeral potatoes," which was one of my favorite recipes. It was basically hash browns, sour cream and cream of mushroom soup, mixed with onions and garlic. I even threw in some turkey sausage.

"We're starving," Rina said. "But tell us about Axel."

I shook my head. "Sit down. No, wait, get the plates out, and then sit down."

The two girls obediently got out three plates, three forks and three glasses and set the table. I got out a pitcher of water and poured everyone a glass, and then went to the oven and brought out the casserole and set it on the Lazy Susan in the middle of the table.

"Okay," I said, as I spooned some of the casserole on each of their plates. "Now, what are you talking about again? You read my emails? How did that happen?"

Rina shrugged her shoulders. "I'm snoopy, you had your computer on and your email page was up and I read that email from Axel Springer." She smiled. "I guess you guys had a date the other night?"

I cleared my throat, not sure about how to feel about Rina grilling me about this. I didn't know how I was feeling about Axel, and I didn't know how to explain it to them. I was certainly attracted to him, wildly so, but I had so much on my plate, I wasn't at all sure where he would fit in. If he would fit into my life at all.

The girls dug into the casserole and Abby smiled, big. "I love this," she said. "Mom made casseroles for us. She used to make this awesome casserole with chicken and green chilies and sour cream and mushroom soup. She crunched up some taco chips on the top." She rubbed her tummy. "That was probably my favorite, but she made this exact thing too. She called it pot luck potatoes."

Rina didn't mention the food because she was still apparently going to keep on me about Axel. "Tell me about Axel," she whined. "I've never known you to like a dude."

"I don't like a dude," I said. "He's a friend. He's helping me on my murder case."

"The transgender case," Rina said, nodding her approval. "I need to meet this chick."

"Do you know about transgender?" I asked the girls, secretly relieved that the topic had been changed off Axel and onto something more comfortable to talk about.

"Of course," Abby said. "We have two transgendered kids in our class." She shrugged. "It's no big deal. I know this girl, her name is Cameron, and she used to be a boy also named Cameron, and I knew her when she was a boy, too. Nobody really cares. The adults make a big deal out of it, for some reason, but none of my friends care. She uses our bathroom, too, and that's not a big deal, either."

"Cameron is one of my best friends," Rina said. "In fact, I'd love to have her for a sleepover this weekend. She'd like to go to the cult. I told her all about it. She likes weird things, just like I do."

"We'll talk about that," I said. "I'm happy you girls know about trans people and don't have any prejudices about it." I took a deep breath. "I'd like to do something, and I need to run it by the two of you. Then I'll run it by Alexis. But I need to talk to you two first."

"Okay," Rina said. "But we won't let you get off the hook about Axel. We're dying to know about him."

Abby rolled her eyes. "I'm not dying to know. You need your privacy, Aunt Harper. It's none of our business."

"Thank you, Abby. Now, I have a client, whose name is Heather Morrison. She's accused of murdering her mother. She says it's self-defense. I'd like to take her in for now, just until her trial. She's currently staying at a halfway house, and I don't think it's the healthiest place for her. Plus, I kinda said I'd take her, and she thinks I'm turning my back on her now because I'm hesitating. Would you girls care if she lived here?"

Rina's eyes got huge. "No way. That would be totally rad." She nodded. "It would be righteous."

Abby smiled. "I would like that, Aunt Harper. It sounds like she doesn't have anybody, and you would be a good influence on her."

"That's what I was thinking," I said. "She has nobody. Her mother didn't accept her, and, if Heather's story is believed, her mother tried to kill her. She's an orphan, and she's only 18. She's having a tough time right now. Plus, she's living with three other guys who have committed crimes, and they're in the halfway house because they're out on parole, or they're awaiting trial. She says she holds her own, but I worry about her."

"What will Alexis say?" Abby asked.

"Well, that's the thing. I doubt she'll be in favor of it. There's still the off-chance that Heather is a cold-blooded killer. I don't really know at this point. She has a good story, but there are holes in it. I need to get answers from her. I'm of a mixed mind about this, to be honest with you."

"Hey, it's okay," Rina said. "Just because she killed her mother doesn't mean she's a killer in general. If she killed her mom, she probably had her reasons."

I smiled. "You're going to make a great attorney," I said to her.

"You know it." Rina smiled.

AFTER DINNER WAS OVER, the girls did their homework and watched a movie, and they were sent to their rooms to go to bed, I finally got the chance to get on my email to find out what Rina was talking about. She seemed to finally forget about bugging me about Axel, and I was so relieved about that that I resisted the temptation to get on my email when she was awake.

I didn't want to talk to the girls just yet about Axel, because I wasn't even sure if I wanted to date him.

I hadn't really dated anybody for a long time. I was always so busy with my career, but that wasn't necessarily why I resisted getting involved with anybody. The main thing was that, when I was drinking, I didn't feel good enough for anybody. My self-esteem was constantly in the toilet because I couldn't stand to look at myself in the mirror. When I looked at myself, all I saw was a wasted person who couldn't stay sober.

Well, I was sober finally. I knew I'd stay that way, because I had to for the girls. So, maybe I could dip my toes into the dating waters.

I took a deep breath and looked at my emails. I immediately saw the one from Axel.

HARPER, *I JUST WANTED TO LET YOU KNOW I HAD A GREAT TIME WITH YOU AT MANNY'S, AND I'D LOVE TO DO IT AGAIN SOMETIME. IF YOU LIKE JAZZ, THERE'S A GREAT TRIO PLAYING AT THE PHOENIX THIS WEEKEND. THEIR FOOD'S PRETTY GOOD, TOO. LET ME KNOW. IF YOU DON'T LIKE JAZZ, THEN WE CAN'T GO ON. :) NO, REALLY, I'LL SURVIVE. JUST LET ME KNOW WHAT YOU'D LIKE TO DO.*

AXEL

I PUT my fingers to my temple and tried to concentrate. Axel got me feeling tingly in all the right places, tingly in places I hadn't thought about for way too long. But he also made me nervous. Was I ready to start dating? I was learning in AA that getting into a relationship wasn't such a good idea for the first year in recovery. In my case, my recovery was barely in my rearview mirror.

I bit my bottom lip and started to type.

AXEL, I'D LOVE TO GO TO THE PHOENIX THIS WEEKEND. I ENJOY LIVE MUSIC, AND I DON'T KNOW MUCH ABOUT JAZZ, BUT I'D LOVED TO FIND OUT MORE ABOUT IT. WHAT TIME WOULD YOU LIKE TO MEET?
HARPER.

MY CURSOR HOVERED over the send button, trying to figure out if that was the direction I wanted to go. I tapped my fingertips on the desk, and then got up and paced around the room. *Come on, Harper, it's only a date. You remember dating, don't you? It's when two people go out and see a jazz act or get tacos. It's when two people like each other and have fun together. Axel is sexy as hell and he seems like a nice guy. What is your problem?*

I scratched my head absent-mindedly and finally sat down to my computer again.

And I erased my previous message.

In its place, I wrote another one:

AXEL, I'D LOVE TO GO TO THE PHOENIX, BUT I HAVE A DEATH PENALTY CASE I HAVE TO GET READY FOR. I CAN'T GET INVOLVED RIGHT NOW. I'M SO SORRY.

Once again, my cursor hovered over the send button.

I was being indecisive. I didn't know where I wanted to go with this.

I finally decided just to go to bed without answering him.

THIRTY

The next morning, I had a pre-trial conference on Heather's case, and, as usual, I was running late. I had a hard time being on time for court appearances and meetings before I had two pre-teens under my roof, and I was having a hard time getting adjusted to their schedules, so I really started to run late for things.

"Rina," I yelled while I frantically tried to pour cold cereal for everybody, "you need to get down here." Abby was already sitting at the table, obediently eating her cereal and drinking her orange juice. Rina, thus far, hadn't yet emerged from her room.

She came out of her room, her hair not yet brushed, and still in her pajamas. I rolled my eyes. "Rina, you know better than this. I told you last night that everybody is to be here at the breakfast table right at 7. That means you have to be dressed and with your hair combed and ready to go. Now go back up and get dressed, comb your hair and be down here in ten minutes. Your cereal will be soggy by then, so you might as well live with it."

"Why do you pour my cereal and milk before I get down here? That's stupid."

"I do that to train you to be on time next time. And you'll eat every cluster of your Honey Bunches of Oats. Every cluster."

Rina rolled her eyes and I bit my tongue and sat down across from Abby.

"She does this," Abby said quietly. "She hates waking up in the morning."

"Don't we all. I did the same thing when I was her age. I hated getting up for school. I used every trick in the book to stay home." I chuckled. "One time, my mom was taking my temperature and she left the room. I put the thermometer on a light bulb, and I really freaked my mother out because she thought I had a fever of 110."

"What happened?" Abby asked, her eyes wide.

"Well, my mom dragged me to the ER, where they took my temperature and it was normal. The doctor informed her that having a temperature of 110 was impossible, because I would be dead if that were the case. I found out later, years later, that my mother wasn't a fool. She knew I was faking it, and she made a big production of taking me to the hospital to teach me a lesson." I shook my head. "Lesson learned."

"Don't tell Rina about that," she said. "You'll give her ideas."

Rina finally appeared, her hair combed and wearing her school uniform. "You happy?" she asked, sitting down to the table.

"I am, but I'm not happy with your attitude." I looked at her sternly. "I suspect you're staying up late watching TV or playing on the internet, so if you don't want me to take those things away, I suggest you go to sleep at a decent hour so you can get up at a decent hour."

Rina mouthed my words mockingly and silently, and I took a deep breath. I didn't need her brattiness. I looked up at the ceiling and counted to 10 and then looked at her. "Finish your cereal, and get your backpack. I have an early pre-trial conference at 8, so there's no time to dilly-dally." Actually, my pre-trial conference was at 8:15, but I needed to light a fire under Rina.

"I'm not dilly-dallying, I'm eating my cereal." She was eating extremely slowly. First one corn flake went into her mouth, and then another, and then a cluster went in, and then another.

I drew a breath as Abby nudged her. "Come on," she whispered. "We have to go."

Rina snarled at me, and then started taking huge clumps of cereal and shoveling them into her mouth. Her cheeks were full of cereal, and she gulped huge amounts of orange juice to wash it all down.

I rolled my eyes at the show Rina was giving me and, once again, I counted to ten.

Finally, everybody had their backpacks and we all headed into my SUV.

"What's your pre-trial conference about, Aunt Harper?" Abby asked me while Rina stared out the window, silent and sullen. They both were sitting in the back, which was a habit of theirs, for some reason. I guessed they actually enjoyed sitting together. I didn't mind it, because it cut down on fights on who would get to sit in the front seat. I remembered those fights all too well, for they happened often with my siblings and me.

"It's on that murder case," I said. "It's a meeting with the judge and the prosecutor to see where the case is at. We have to give deadlines for discovery and witness lists and things like that. And the judge generally wants to know if there is any chance of a plea bargain, which there's not. Not right now, anyway."

"What do you mean, not right now?" Rina asked, suddenly paying attention to what I was saying. "You're not thinking of pleading your client, are you?"

"No, not at the moment. I need to figure a few things out before I make a decision, though. I don't think she's lying, but there are a few nagging details."

We arrived at their school, and the two girls got out. "Sophia will be picking you up," I said to them. I never could get free at 3:30 PM, which was when the girls got out of school. "I'll be seeing you hopefully by 6."

Rina and Abby nodded, and then ran off to join the other kids who were rushing through the door of their school.

I GOT to the court right at 8:15, and let out a sigh of relief. I was often late to court, but that wasn't always a big deal if there was a large docket. I would just call the court clerk and explain what was happening, and I could get my client put on the end of the docket. But pre-trial conferences were a different thing. The judge typically would schedule pre-trial conferences in 15 minute slots, and if you were late, you missed your slot.

And Judge Reiner was known for going off on attorneys who wasted his time. If I would've been late for the pre-trial conference, I would've been called on the carpet for doing just that.

"Hey Harper," Vince said as I bolted through the door of the courtroom. "And not a moment to spare. Let's go on back."

I nodded, unable to speak, because I had literally ran from my car and up the five flights of stairs to the courtroom. I didn't wait for the elevator, because the elevator was notoriously slow.

We went back to the judge's chambers, where Judge Reiner

was waiting for us. He was smoking a cigar, and he put it out in an ashtray when we approached. His chamber was a typical chamber – dark walls, a large cherry-wood desk, and leather chairs held together with gold studs up and down the seat. Behind him was a large library that had every law book imaginable.

"Harper, Vince," he said. "Have a seat."

We both sat down.

"Where are we with this case?" He asked us. "And why isn't it settled yet? Trial's in two months. Time's a wasting."

"Your honor," I began. "I have yet to get an offer from the prosecutor. So far, all I've heard is that he's seeking the death penalty. I can't very well consider an offer when there's no offer to consider."

Judge Reiner leaned forward and looked Vince right in the eye. "That true?" He pointed at me. "How is she supposed to accept a plea deal when you won't even give her one?" He then looked at both of us. "I'd like this case off my docket. The press will be all over this one. Flies on shit comes to mind. I'm in no mood for cameras in the courtroom. The last media-ready case I had ended in a mistrial." He glared at me. "As you know, Harper."

I didn't know why he was bringing me into it. My John Robinson case wasn't in front of him. It was a media shit-storm, as my client was a Kansas City Chief's linebacker, but it was in front of a different judge. "Your honor?" I asked questioningly. "I don't understand?"

"Your media-crazy case ended in a mistrial and the prosecutors didn't want to deal with it anymore. And then he went out and killed again." He shook his head. "I won't deal with that. That happened in my courtroom, too, except so far, my guy hasn't killed somebody else, thank God. But I want this case gone. You two need to work it out."

I looked over at Vince, and so did Judge Reiner.

"Vince, why don't you make Harper a reasonable offer? Give her an LWOP sentence, and everybody's happy."

"LWOP" was slang for "Life Without Parole," which was unacceptable to me, of course.

"Your honor, with all due respect, I wouldn't be happy with an LWOP sentence."

"It's better than the needle, Harper," Judge Reiner said.

"In the case of my client, it would be the same as the death penalty. She's trans."

"So?" Judge Reiner shrugged. "Your client's made her bed by acting like a woman, how is that supposed to affect her sentence?"

"Your honor," I said. "That's not an acceptable sentence. At this point, nothing will be acceptable. We're going with self-defense."

Vince snorted. "Self-defense? That's really where you're going? What proof do you have? The victim in this case was a God-fearing woman who nobody had a bad word about. You should think twice before you go with yet another self-defense case after John Robinson went so wrong."

Low blow. But I had to admit he had a point. For all I knew, Heather *was* pulling the wool over my eyes. "You'll just have to find out, Vince, what proof we have. Go through the discovery process. We won't hide anything from you, of course. But I won't volunteer anything right now."

Judge Reiner just shook his head. "Okay, you two work things out. I don't want this case in front of me, though, Harper. I'm just warning you."

"Why are you directing that statement at me? Vince is the one who won't make me an offer I can even consider."

"Give her something," he said to Vince. "And let's get the show on the road."

Judge Reiner gave us both a deadline of September 21 for the close of discovery, and the trial was to start one week later. "That deadline isn't a suggestion," Judge Reiner said. "You two have to have everything into each other by then, and that includes your witness list. No other witnesses may be called except the ones on your lists. You got that?" He pointed at both of us. "No games, no surprises. No eleventh hour witnesses. I won't put up with shenanigans in my courtroom. Now, go." He made a shooing motion with his arms. "Make a deal. Please."

Vince and I exited the chambers. "Do you want to sit down and make a deal?" Vince asked me.

"No. I told you, I'm going with self-defense. No offer you give me will be accepted."

"What the hell? The way you were talking in there, it sounded like you were just waiting for an offer. Were you lying in there?"

"No, of course not. I never once said I'd accept an offer from you. I simply said you haven't given me anything. Plus, I did tell the judge I'm going for self-defense."

Vince sighed. "On what grounds? We can show your client and the victim went through some serious fights, and I'll bring in witnesses to testify that your client told others she wanted her mother dead. She used those words – I want my mother to die."

I would have to ask Heather about that. "Those are just words. Everyone says things like that – I could kill you. I wish you were dead. I mean, I've never said such things, because I'm superstitious, and I would be afraid my words would somehow make it happen. But people say stuff when they're angry. And my client and her mother didn't exactly see eye to eye, and there were plenty of fights."

"Listen, Harper, I can't believe you're getting sucked in by yet another client. After John Robinson, I'd think you would be gun-shy, no pun intended."

"That's a low blow."

"It's not a low blow. It's truth. Wake up, Harper. Your client is playing you, just like John Robinson played you. This case will explode in your face, just like the John Robinson one did. Your client is a psychopath just like John Robinson. She killed her mother in cold blood. Now, I'd be happy to give her LWOP, which would save her from the needle. If you don't take that, it's malpractice."

"You're acting like you're doing me this amazing favor, giving me an offer for life without parole. That's bullshit, and you know it. Even if you gave me an offer for a year in prison, I still wouldn't take it, because my client won't survive the year."

"You're not being reasonable." Vince shook his head. "I don't want to try this bitch, and I'd be surprised if you do. I'll tell you what I'll do. I'll give you an offer for twenty years without a possibility of parole. If you don't take that, you're certifiably insane."

I crossed my arms in front of me and stared at Vince. Now he was talking, really. LWOP would never be something I'd consider, but twenty years...that was infinitely better than the death penalty.

I was suddenly questioning my stance. What if he was right? What if Heather was lying through her teeth? What if I went ahead and tried it, the case fell apart, and the jury gave her the death penalty? I had the chance to possibly see her out of prison before she was forty years old. Would it be malpractice if I didn't encourage her to take it?

Then I reminded myself that Heather was trans, and she wouldn't last in prison.

Still, she was a tough one. She could possibly find herself a protector in prison, and maybe she would be okay. She couldn't wear her shit-ton of makeup and her high-heeled boots, but she'd live. And maybe get her life together when she got out of prison.

"I'll think about it," I said, hoping I sounded more confident than I felt.

"You'd better. That offer will expire in 24 hours, so I suggest you start applying pressure on Ms. Morrison."

I sighed as I exited the courtroom and walked down the stairs.

This case just got that much more complicated. Before, I didn't have a decent offer, so I would try it, come hell or high water.

Now, I didn't know what to do.

THIRTY-ONE

Louisa Garrison was scheduled to meet with the reverend at 6 PM, and she was nervous, to say the least. She had fallen off the wagon, in a way, because she'd cheated on her husband with a woman. Again. She'd tried to keep it secret, but the word got around anyhow, and now the reverend wanted to see her in his office.

She lived in terror that he would fire her. Or worse – banish her. Excommunicate her. That would be like death. The church was her lifeblood. It was her air, her water, her food, her everything. If she was asked to leave the church, she would literally die.

She'd tried to stop meeting women behind her husband's back. Her marriage with her husband was loveless and lifeless, and he beat her often, but she was married to him, 'til death do they part. She gave God her word that she would forsake all others, and she meant it at the time.

Truth be told, her husband was her first, as far as men went. She was 28 years old when she met Tom, and, before she met him, she was nothing but sinful. She had one relationship after another with women, and she was happy in lesbian relationships. But she also learned, from an early age, that same-sex sexual relationships were sinful in the eyes of God, and she had learned, from an early age, that her same-sex desires would send her straight to hell.

She still remembered their wedding night. She'd never seen a man naked, and, as she looked at him, with that thing between his legs, she felt sick. He felt alien to her, and, thank God, he didn't last very long. It was about thirty seconds of his thrusting and then he fell asleep. Since then, she tried to find every excuse she could not to have sex with him, and he thankfully was a man with a low sex drive, so their relations happened annually, if that.

They'd been married for five years, and she fought her every desire for women that whole time. Then she met Connie Morrison, and fell madly in love. Connie had a son in school, and had been left a lot of money by her husband, who had died in a car accident years before. Connie didn't work, and she didn't want her son to know that she was seeing Louisa, so the two only met during the day when her son Heath was in school. That was best for Louisa, too, for she didn't want her husband to know what she was doing. Connie occasionally spent the night with Louisa, whenever Louisa's husband was out of town.

They met like that for years, and then Louisa got her job at the church. Her husband, Harry, made her go to work, saying he was tired of providing for her and, since they didn't have any children together, there wasn't a reason for her not working. Louisa hated that, because she and Connie had spent many blissful days in Louisa's bed, and occasionally they even dared to venture out. They would go to the Farmer's Market on Saturday afternoons when Louisa's husband was out of town. Connie would tell her son she was at a church function, and the two of them would go and look at the fruits and vegetables and would get lunch at The Farmhouse, which served fresh farm to table food. They would go to the zoo sometimes, and even dared to see live music once in a great while.

Connie was the love of Louisa's life, so, when Connie was murdered, Louisa was beyond inconsolable. She was different, and had been different, ever since Connie was found.

Louisa was the one who had found her lying in her own blood, a butcher knife in her hand. Louisa immediately knew what had happened. She knew that it was coming. Connie had been urged by the Reverend Scott to take care of her son, one way or another. Heath had been sent through therapy, and that didn't take, and Connie was desperate. Reverend Scott told Connie only one thing could be done, and that would be to kill her son. It had to be done, because her son was corrupting Connie. Louisa knew Heath was a corrupting influence for Connie and had expressed her concern to the reverend about this. Connie sometimes told Louisa that she wanted to leave her son be, and sometimes said she was ready to accept that her son had become her daughter.

That couldn't happen. Louisa was fearful that Connie's soul would also end up in hell if she accepted her son. She had the reverend talk to Connie, to convince her that she needed to do what was necessary to ensure her son didn't corrupt her further.

So, when Louisa went to see Connie, and saw her lying in her own blood, a butcher knife in her hand, Louisa did what she had to. She took that butcher knife and tried to scrub Connie's computer as much as she could, deleting as many emails as possible. She didn't get all the emails, because she heard somebody else coming into the house and had to hide. She couldn't be seen tampering with a crime scene. That would be very bad.

She didn't know who called the cops, but the cops were

soon on the scene while Louisa cowered in the closet. They never saw her, even though they searched the house, guns drawn. She didn't know why they didn't find her, but she was lucky to not be detected.

The cops finally left, and Louisa was afraid of being seen, so she had gingerly let herself out through the bedroom window.

She still had the butcher knife. She had it in her closet at home. She was scared to go to the police to tell them what she had done. She didn't even know why she felt it so important to take that butcher knife. Connie apparently tried to kill her son with that knife. That was what Louisa discerned from the state of things.

A huge part of Louisa wanted to go to the cops and give them the butcher knife. Tell them the knife was important to the case. Louisa didn't want Heath to serve time in prison, not if he was only defending himself from his mother's attack. She wanted Heath dead before, but now she felt guilty, like she was an accomplice to all of it. Like she was ultimately responsible for Connie dying and Heath being charged with her murder.

Yet she was frightened of doing so. She'd seen an attorney about it, and that attorney told her that she could be charged with a felony for taking the knife. She didn't even tell him that she also scrubbed the emails clean as much as she could. That attorney told her that she could face up to five years in prison for doing what she did with the butcher knife.

She even went to the reverend and told him what she did. The reverend convinced her not to tell anybody about the knife. He told her Heath belonged in prison. If he was in prison, he couldn't corrupt the outside world with his perversion. He would have to keep his perversion within the prison walls, and, since the other prisoners were already corrupted and bound for hell, Heath couldn't possibly do any damage behind bars.

The reverend said that Connie did the right thing when she tried to kill Heath. Louisa didn't want to hear that. She'd heard it before from the reverend, but she wasn't in the mood to hear it about Connie. All Louisa knew was that the only person she'd ever loved, Connie Morrison, was dead. She apparently died because she listened to the reverend, who apparently urged Connie to kill her son.

Louisa secretly hated the reverend because she ultimately blamed him for the death of Connie. Yet, at the same time, she needed the church all the more. She had nothing else. Her husband was distant and abusive. The one person she loved was dead. She had no children. No pets. There was nothing in her life that made it worth living, except for the church.

But she still wrestled with her desire to do what was right. Even if she had to go to prison for tampering with a crime scene. Then she would chicken out.

She still had the butcher knife.

But nobody would ever know it.

THIRTY-TWO

You have 24 hours to get your client to take my offer. Those words rang through my ears as I drove along to my home. I needed clarification on what to do. 20 years wasn't bad if Heather was good for the case. In fact, it would be a godsend, assuming that Heather could stay alive behind bars.

I had to first get answers from Heather, though. I needed a firm answer on why Heather read my article before she killed her mother. That looked bad to me. And the butcher knife...I had to figure that out.

The butcher knife issue would sink the case faster than anything. I imagined putting Heather on the stand and having her tell the jury what happened, and then see the prosecutor read the police report to the jury and point out that no butcher knife was found at the scene. The jury would return a guilty verdict for sure.

If I couldn't figure that one out...I shook my head. Perhaps one of the cops on the scene took the knife, but I couldn't imagine why they would do that. My investigator, Fred, found that neither of the first responder cops was associated with the Church of the

Living Breath. I couldn't imagine the cops tampering with a crime scene if there wasn't a reason for it. If they were part of the church and somehow brainwashed, they might tamper with the scene because they would be interested in seeing Heather go to prison.

I paid a visit to Heather at the halfway house. Perhaps she was in a better mood and wouldn't be so defensive. I could talk to her about taking the plea deal.

I got to her halfway house and went in. "Hello," I said to the receptionist. "I need to see Heather Morrison."

The receptionist looked at her list and squinted. "This is a man's halfway house," she said.

"Sorry, they list her as Heath Morrison." I always forgot to clarify that point.

"Heath Morrison," she said. "Let me call him and let him know you're here."

Heather soon appeared, wearing ripped jeans and a silk blue tank top. She also wore her trademark sparkly red headband and a pair of red leather pumps on her feet. "What do you want?" she asked demanded.

"I need to talk to you."

She bobbed her head back and forth in defiance and crossed her arms in front of her. "I've got nothing to say to you."

I sighed, and my hopes that she'd be ready to talk to me were dashed. She clearly was in a defiant, defensive mood.

"Heather, we need to talk. I got an offer from the prosecutor, and I'm bound to give you all offers."

"An offer? An offer? What the fuck are you talking about? You know I don't want no offer. You know where you can put your offer."

"Heather," I said, trying to sound measured. "The offer is for 20 years in prison. Parole isn't an option with this offer. You killed your mother, and the previous offer was the death penalty. 20 years is pretty good compared to where it was before."

"No." She shook her head. "No way. I did nothing wrong. All I did was defend myself."

"Okay. Here's the scenario. We go to trial. You tell your story. The prosecutor points out that there wasn't a butcher knife recovered from the scene, and it's game over. The judge won't give you 20 years for a cold-blooded murder one. I also doubt he'll give you the death penalty. You'll probably end up with life in prison without parole. LWOP, we call it. With the prosecutor's offer, you'll be out before you're forty and might pick up the pieces."

"Where is this coming from?" Heather's body language was closed–her arms were crossed, and her posture was ramrod straight. "You were on my side, and now you're not."

"Tell me about the article," I said. "About why you read the article. And I need to know what the hell happened to that butcher knife."

Heather sneered. "Okay, I'll tell you about the goddamned article." She rolled her eyes. "And I don't know about the butcher knife. Somebody must have taken it."

"We'll have to figure out who took it, and then we have to figure out how to prove that somebody tampered with the crime scene. That one aspect will be the death of this case, though. But, please, tell me about the *Law Review* article."

She sighed. "I was scared, all right? When my mom stood over me with a pillow in her hands, it freaked me out. And I thought I might have to kill her." She continued to cross her arms and look away. "That's it. That's all. After the pillow incident, I went to the law library and looked up everything I could about self-defense. I probably know more about it than you do by now. And your article caught my eye because you specifically talked about brainwashing and how you can bring in the issue to show the murdered person was violent."

"Is that it? That's all? Why the big secret?"

"It looks bad, all right? I mean, if I knew my mom would try to kill me, why didn't I just get out of the house? I should've done something else to stop her cray. I knew she'd end up trying to kill me, yet I stayed in the house and let it happen. All right? You happy? Go ahead, tell me how stupid I was for sticking around when I knew what would happen. Go ahead. I've heard it all before."

I shook my head. "No, Heather, I won't tell you that. We probably won't have to explain that aspect to the jury unless the prosecutor gets smart and gets ahold of your computer and finds it. Then all bets are off."

"Can they do that? Look at my computer?"

"If they subpoena it, they can. They can look at your history and your downloads and everything. I can try to quash the subpoena, but as long as they can show the judge they're not on a fishing expedition, the judge will allow it."

"Fishing expedition?"

"Yeah. They must show the judge why the computer will lead them to relevant evidence. That's not a high bar to meet. Is that article on your hard drive?"

"It is. Can you erase it?"

"I can't. That would tamper with evidence, and I can't do that."

"What the hell? It wouldn't be hard for you to do at all."

I sighed. "I can't do that. It would get me disbarred if I did that and somebody found out. Now we must figure out what's going on with the butcher knife. I'm most concerned about that."

"Somebody took it. Figure out who."

"Thanks for that." I rolled my eyes. "Finding out who has

that butcher knife will be worse than finding a needle in a haystack. Anybody who took it won't tell me they did. That would be tampering with a crime scene, which is a felony. I can ask Louisa Garrison and the Reverend Scott, who seem the most likely suspects for cleaning up the crime scene, but unless they come clean, I won't get anywhere. I can't try to get a search warrant for their apartments and offices because I don't have grounds for that."

"Figure it out," she said. "I'm not taking that fucking offer."

"You're gambling," I said. "And we will lose. Unless we find that butcher knife, we will lose."

"So fucking be it."

I sighed. This case was going south. It was always an uphill climb, but I had nothing to work with before. The only offer on the table was the death penalty.

Now I had a 20-year offer and suddenly felt the walls closing in on me.

If I lost this case, I'd feel like I lost everything.

THIRTY-THREE

Two things happened the next day. One was that the kitchen fire investigators came back with findings. "It was definitely arson, ma'am," the chief investigator said. "But we don't have a clue who did it."

"Thanks for that," I said, hanging up the phone. I bought a brand-new fridge and stove and had people put in all new walls, cabinets and floors. Remodeling the stupid kitchen cost me a mint, and I was pissed. Pissed at John Robinson or...the Reverend Scott? It might've been him. He could have climbed through the window and done it. I only wished somebody had been around to see the culprit.

The other thing was that I finally gave Axel a chance, so I tentatively sent the email about not knowing much about jazz but being willing to learn, and I promptly got an answer in return.

SEE YOU AT 7? DON'T WORRY ABOUT NOT KNOWING ABOUT JAZZ. I'LL TEACH YOU EVERYTHING YOU NEED TO KNOW. IT SOUNDS LIKE A LOT OF NOISE AT FIRST, BUT WHEN YOU LEARN THE GENRE, YOU'LL SEE IT'S VERY POETIC.

So, I arranged for Sophia to stay with the girls that Friday night and put on a little black dress, strappy gold shoes, diamond earrings and a gold choker, put my hair up and got out my little Michael Kors gold clutch.

I went down the stairs and saw the girls lying in front of the television, and Sophia was sitting on the couch. "Woo hoo, Aunt Harper," Rina said with a huge smile. She was back to being her bubbly self after her inexplicable crappy mood the other morning. "You're looking hot!" She winked. "But remember, no glove, no love."

Abby nudged her twin. "Don't say that. That's rude." She smiled at me. "You look beautiful, though, Aunt Harper. You clean up very well."

"Well, this isn't really a date," I said, even though I was dressed for a date, no doubt. "I need to pick his brain about Heather's case. He might give me some idea on how to approach it."

I assumed the prosecutor's twenty-year offer was off the table, although I had yet to hear if that was the case. Something told me that if Heather decided to take 20 years, Vince would gladly give it to me. He didn't want to try this case any more than I did.

And Axel was a seasoned investigator. He probably had seen it all, just like I had. He could be an invaluable sounding board.

"Not a date," Rina said. "If this is how you dress for something that's not a date, what do you wear on a date?"

"It's a jazz club. I can't go in there looking like a bum." I looked in the mirror and saw my cheeks were redder than normal. I realized I was blushing.

"So why are you wearing perfume, then?" Rina said. "Is that required for a jazz club, too?"

"Oh, be quiet," I said, not wanting to answer that question.

"This isn't a date." I turned to Sophia, who looked at me appreciatively with a smile. "Now, Sophia, make sure the girls are in bed no later than 11. They can have a small bedtime snack–I have some cheese and fruit in small containers in the new fridge."

"Don't worry, I know the drill," Sophia said. "The girls will watch a movie on Netflix, and then I'll put them to bed."

"Thank you." I took a deep breath and looked in the mirror once more. "Okay, Harper, here goes."

I got in my SUV and headed downtown to The Phoenix.

I GOT THERE, and Axel was standing in front of the club, his hands in his pockets. He cleaned up well. He was dressed in black slacks and a blue silk shirt, his salt-and-pepper hair slightly shorter than the other evening. He saw me and smiled big.

"Harper," he said. "So good to see you."

"Axel," I said, nodding to him slightly. "Um, it's good to see you, too."

He put his arm around me, and I could feel his muscles, which were surprisingly bulging. I guessed he needed to keep in shape because he was a cop.

We entered the dark club, where a jazz trio was playing. A guy was playing an upright bass, a guy was on a saxophone, and a guy was on the piano.

The server came around and took our order. I ordered sparkling water, and Axel ordered the same. "Please," I said to Axel. "Order a real drink. I'll feel self-conscious if I'm keeping you from ordering what you want."

"Are you sure?" Axel said.

"Positive."

"Okay. Then I'd like a Moscow Mule," he said, ordering the drink that, unfortunately, was my go-to back when I was drinking. It was made with vodka, ginger beer and lime juice. "And we'll be ordering food as well."

I watched the jazz trio for a while, catching Axel's eyes trained on me every so once in a while. "What?" I said. "You're staring at me."

"You're beautiful," he said. "Has anybody told you that?"

I took a deep breath. Truth be told, I had been told that by more than a few guys. They always made me feel uncomfortable, though. Yet Axel didn't make me feel uncomfortable. It was the opposite–I was feeling very comfortable. I had butterflies leaping around my insides, but I still felt comfortable.

"Thanks," I said, looking down at the floor.

The server came around and gave us our drinks, and I told Axel I wanted the chicken fried chicken, and he ordered the steak. My mouth was watering, I was so hungry.

"So," Axel said, his voice loud over the live music. "What's been going on?"

I shrugged, not wanting to talk to him about Heather's case just yet. For one, the music was loud. Plus, it wasn't necessarily a good dinner conversation. "Not much." I sipped my water. "Tell me about this trio."

"Well, they're an old-school jazz trio, which is what I prefer. They're more in the style of Thelonious Monk and Miles Davis than Gregory Porter and Esperanza Spalding, who have innovated jazz and are doing different things."

I nodded. I kind of knew the difference, but I had a lot to learn. "This all sounds like a lot of noise."

Axel smiled. "It does at first, doesn't it? Discordant notes are a hallmark of this genre, but once you listen, you see it as a conversation, like one person trying to talk over another and everyone doing their own thing, except in harmony. You're probably used to music that is much more...harmonious. Even rock music has a tempo and a structure you can follow. Old-school jazz, not so much."

I nodded and tapped my foot to the music. I remembered my father playing some old Dizzy Gillespie records and thought about how I never understood jazz then. I still didn't understand it, but I hoped Axel would help me with that. I could see the potential of coming to enjoy the jazz genre.

"I like it," I said. "I can feel it. That's how I process music – I know little about stanzas, notes, keys, or any of that, but I go by how it makes me feel. This is very upbeat, and I really enjoy it."

Our food came, and I dug in, realizing I was starving. I tried not to eat rapidly, but I sometimes had issues with my blood sugar, and I hadn't eaten since breakfast, so I was feeling woozy.

"Oh, this is delicious," I said, putting a small piece of chicken on his plate. He did the same with his steak, and I tried that, too. "Yum."

"Yeah, this place has some excellent food and drink. I love this place," he said, swaying a bit to the music.

I looked around, seeing that everyone looked fairly mature and classic and that this place was hip and stylish. I knew I'd grow to love this place, too, just like the jazz music was gradually growing on me.

LATER, we walked around The Plaza, getting ice cream from Cold Stone along the way. We sat down by the fountain in the middle of The Plaza, with the four horses representing the world's four great rivers. There was the horse that represented the Mississippi, which was fending off an alligator; the Volga, which was fighting off a bear; and the Seine and the Rhine.

Axel put his arm around me. "So," he said. "We can talk better now. Tell me about the case you're working on. The case with the religious person killed by her own daughter."

"Well...Are you sure you really want to hear about this?"

"Of course. It's fascinating to me. Of course, I see things from a different perspective, but I can help you see things through fresh eyes."

"I need fresh eyes," I said. "This case suddenly became more high-stakes than before. See, before, I didn't have an offer, so I would try it, come hell or high water. Now I have an offer for 20 years, and I don't know what to do. It's a self-defense case, and my client insists her mother was coming at her with a butcher knife, yet none was found at the scene. It's made me question whether she's telling me the truth. And if I can't figure that out, I can't win this case."

Axel blinked and looked into the distance. "Yeah," he said. "That's a tough one." He nodded and snapped his fingers. "Lean on Heather's mother's lover, whoever that might be."

"I was thinking the same thing. Why do you suspect that?"

"Okay, here's what I think. I can get into the minds of killers or potential killers and the people who love them, who are often as warped as the killers. But let's say you're in love with a killer. You didn't know that person was a killer, though. But you suspect something is off about the person."

I closed my eyes, trying to imagine that. "Okay, go on."

"You walk into your lover's home. You haven't heard from him for a while and you're concerned. You see him dead on the floor with a butcher knife nearby. You don't want to believe he did anything to cause his death. It's obvious, though, that because he had a butcher knife in his hand when he was killed, he probably struck first. You don't want to see him dragged through the mud at trial because self-defense will probably be the defense of your lover's killer. You know that to prove self-defense, your lover's background, proclivities, and everything else will come out because the defense attorney has to show your lover was violent. You don't want that. So, what do you do? You remove the one item that shows your lover struck first. You might do that without thinking."

I nodded slowly, seeing that Axel had a point. "I see. Is the lover the only person who would risk tampering with the crime scene?"

"I think so. Who else would stick their neck out and do something like that?

"You have a point." I sighed. "Now, how do I prove it? I suspect that Connie Morrison was carrying on an affair with Louisa Garrison, who works at the crazy church you're looking into. By the way, have you gotten any more leads on those gay kids dying? Do you still think a serial killer's at work?"

"No," he said. "I'm investigating an attack on a gay kid from the church. He's in foster care right now. I wanted to talk to you about this earlier because it's important."

"What happened?"

"I went and talked to the kid. He told me his mother forced him to go to conversion therapy, and when he refused, she tried to kill him. She attempted to strangle him, and he got a pair of scissors and stabbed her in the leg. He immediately ran out of the house and went to the police. The case is being investigated right now. The mother is a part of that church." He shook his head. "You might be right. There might not be a serial killer in that church. The parents might be brainwashed to kill their kids, just like you said."

I ate my ice cream as I thought about what he was saying. It was all clear, but how would I prove it? I couldn't call this kid in to testify because it would be difficult to show relevance. I could see the thread, but would the prosecutor? Would the judge? It was difficult to get evidence in unless it was directly related to the case, and this kid's story wasn't directly related.

Perhaps I could get the entire scenario into the court, show the judge the pattern of gay kids dying, gay kids whose parents are a part of the church, and show Heather's mom was a part of the church. Therefore, Heather's mom probably was violent and wanted to kill her.

"What are you thinking about?" Axel asked me.

"I'm just trying to game out how to use what you told me. What I think is now clear." I dug into my ice cream. "And how I can show Heather was a victim of this when there's no damned knife."

"What do you mean? It sounds pretty cut and dried to me. Your client's mother is a part of this church. Gay kids keep dying in the church, and now there's a gay kid who told me his mother attacked him. It's a clear through-line. It shows your client's mother was brainwashed just as these other parents were."

"Ah, if only it were that easy to get evidence in. Unfortunately, it's not. I can only show prior acts Heather's mom did that showed she was violent. Brainwashing goes to her character, so I might show the church brainwashed her into doing this. But I can't show somebody else being attacked by his mother to show my client's mother did the same thing."

"That doesn't seem right."

"Law never is." I sighed. Everything was clear, but how would I show it to the jury? How would I convince the judge to let this evidence in? It wasn't even clear I could use the evidence of the church's brainwashing to show Connie Morrison was violent, and I certainly couldn't use the evidence of the other dead gay kids and this gay boy whose mother attacked him.

I had to tie everything I knew all together to show Connie was a violent person. There must be something else, something I still wasn't seeing.

I slowly ate my ice cream, suddenly lost in thought. There was the issue of when my client found her mother standing over her, pillow in hand. I could use that if the jury would believe my client that it happened.

I could get the reverend on the stand, but no way would he admit to what he was doing. Encouraging mothers and fathers to kill their kids...brainwashing them into doing that...he'd be found an accessory to murder, so there was no way he'd ever admit to doing what he was clearly doing. He could even be found guilty of murder, like Charles Manson. After all, Charlie Manson was near none of those murder scenes, yet was found guilty because he brainwashed his followers to commit the crimes. Just like what Reverend Scott was doing. It was like stochastic terrorism, which meant inciting violence by demonizing a group.

Even if I could pick off a parent or two who could testify about what the reverend was doing, that wouldn't be admissible in court. I'd have to show that Connie, in particular, was instructed to kill Heather. Other parents who heard the reverend preaching his hate and his instructions to parents to kill their kids wouldn't be admissible. The law was clear – only evidence showing the victim in a self-defense case was violent could be used.

"Hey," he said. He had my chin in his hand. "Let's think about this later."

I closed my eyes and felt his lips on mine. A slow burn that became a conflagration coursed throughout my body. I never knew a kiss could be like this, for I felt it in every cell of my body.

"Oh my God," I said quietly.

"Yeah," he said. "We definitely need to do this more."

"Uh-huh," I said as we kissed again.

For one hot second, Heather's case was forgotten. All that mattered was Axel kissing me.

And the feeling he gave me was one I had never felt.

THIRTY-FOUR

"Okay," I said to Heather. I went to visit her the Monday after my date with Axel. "I have a hearing today on whether you can stay with me. So far, Alexis seems to be on board with it, surprisingly enough. I think she feels so guilty about how she treated me before that she won't question my judgment again on this."

I got the hearing date that morning. It was happening soon because I motioned to the court that Heather was in a bad place, considering she was trans and in a man's halfway house. I wanted Judge Wilson as our judge because he seemed sympathetic to Heather's plight. On the other hand, Judge Reiner didn't have Judge Wilson's sympathy. But that was okay – he didn't have to sympathize with Heather. He only needed to decide that I was appropriate to watch Heather while she awaited trial. This was irregular but not completely unheard of.

Heather smirked. "I'm not holding my breath."

"You don't have to. I'll let you know later on today what the judge says."

"You believe me now? Again?"

"I do. I believe you 100%, Heather. I've found out that the church that your mother went to has a crazy Reverend who apparently encourages the parents of gay kids in that church to kill these kids. That's all fitting together. It's all circumstantial evidence, but it's enough that I know this is going on. But that still doesn't mean that your case is a slam dunk."

"Why not?"

I sighed. "It's just difficult getting evidence in. I can't bring in evidence this is happening at the church, and I can't even get in evidence about this one gay kid who was attacked by his mother who went to that church. I need to find the butcher knife. And I'll have to figure out a back-door way of getting all this stuff in front of a jury."

Heather smirked. "You said back door." She then started doing a Beavis and Butthead laugh.

"Haha. I have to really think about all this, Heather. This will be complicated."

"What's so complicated? That church has a cray rev, cray parents, and a bunch of dead gay boys and girls. It seems cut-and-dried to me."

"It might be," I said. "But probably not."

I GOT to the hearing on Heather's staying with me, and Vince was waiting for me. "You're nuts," he said, shaking his head. "Although I don't see any reason to oppose your motion to take in your crazy client."

"Good. Since there's no opposition, I assume the motion will go through."

"Yes, I would assume so. She has on an ankle bracelet, so she's not a flight risk at the moment, but Harper, I suggest you make sure there's an adult in your home at all times. You'll have to ensure this adult knows that he or she will be responsible if Heather jumps."

"I have one. Her name is Sophia. She stays with my two girls while I'm working. I've already spoken with her about her new responsibility, and she's okay with it."

"Okay, then. Let's go back and see the judge and see what he wants to do."

Vince and I went back into Judge Reiner's chambers. He was waiting for us and shook his head when he saw me. "Harper Ross," he said, "sit down." He pointed at Vince. "You too. I want to get to the bottom of this here motion."

We both sat down, and Judge Reiner stared at me for a few minutes. Then he shook his head again. "What is this fool thing you're doing, Harper? Taking in your client?" He opened a drawer in his desk and brought out a vial of Tums. He then put the entire plastic vial up to his mouth. About five Tums cascaded into his jaw. "Are you crazy?"

"No," I told him. "I'm not. She's in a man's halfway house, which isn't the best place for her."

"She'll be in a man's big house, Harper. I can almost guarantee that. She better get used to being around a lot of big hairy men who want to make her their bitch, and the sooner she accepts that reality, the better. You're setting her up for a fall."

I took a deep breath. "With all due respect, your honor, I do not plan to lose this case, so I don't plan for her to go to prison. Right now, it's a fragile time."

"Harper," Judge Reiner said, leaning forward. "You've been a defense attorney for long enough to know that most cases go south. You should be prepared that this one will go that way as well. You're doing nothing for your client in trying to shelter her from reality."

"It's not reality," I said helplessly, knowing he was probably right. Heather's case was *still* a long shot, which was the most frustrating thing in the world. I had all the evidence I needed to show what happened, but getting that evidence in front of the jury would be impossible. "I'll win this case."

Judge Reiner rolled his eyes. "What about you, Vince? You okay with this?"

"I haven't any objections. I told Harper that she has to be sure there's a responsible adult at all times watching the defendant, and she assured me that would be the case."

Judge Reiner shook his head. "Motion denied. Sorry, Harper, I know you're a do-gooder and everything, but your client needs to know, sooner or later, what's she in for. Maybe you're right, maybe you'll win the case, but I doubt it. I've read the file, Harper, and I don't want to prejudge it, but I'm just going by statistics. You're statistically unlikely to win this case."

"Judge Reiner, with all due respect, it sounds like you *are* prejudging this case."

"I told you, I'm not. I'm simply being realistic. It would do well if you were too." He turned away from us. "Now, if you would excuse me, I have to get on my exercise machine before my next docket." He was referring to the elliptical trainer in the office's corner.

I left the chambers feeling defeated. Heather would be upset, but I was just as upset.

Was Judge Reiner right? Did I deny reality? Did I really not have a chance?

If that happened, it would be a huge miscarriage of justice.

But it wouldn't be the first time, and it wouldn't be the last.

I decided to pursue the Louisa angle. If Axel was correct, she was the one who would've taken the butcher knife. There had to be some way to get that out of her. I didn't know how, but I'd have to figure that out.

I headed back to the church, calling Heather on the way from my car. "Heather," I said when she picked up. "I'm so sorry. I just filed a motion with the court to allow you to stay with me, and he refused. I tried, though."

Heather was silent on the other end.

"Heather?"

"I gotta go," she said, her voice breaking.

At that, the line went dead.

I felt awful for getting her hopes up. I knew she hung up on me because she was crying. I made a mental note to visit her after I finished seeing Louisa.

I got to the compound and saw the guy at the guard's station. He recognized me, of course, but he didn't give me a hard time. "Go on in," he said, sweeping his hand towards the grounds.

"Thanks." The reverend must've gotten the memo that I'd be allowed on the grounds. After all, they didn't want a lawsuit.

I got to Louisa's building and went on in.

"Can I help you?" asked the receptionist as I entered.

"Yes," I said. "Is Louisa Garrison around?"

I looked up and saw Louisa standing there with a cup of coffee in her hand. She lowered her head and motioned me to come into her office.

She looked softer than the last time I saw her – she was wearing less makeup and slacks instead of a skirt. Her hair wasn't up, and it wasn't as blonde as before. Before, it was more platinum, and now it was more of a honey blonde, with darker blonde and red highlights. Because she toned everything down, she looked younger than before and much prettier. I could see where, when she was a younger woman, she must've been quite a stunner.

I followed her into her office.

"Sit down," she said, motioning to a chair.

I sat down, wondering what was going on. Why was she suddenly being so accommodating?

"Ms. Garrison," I began. "I wanted to apologize for how I acted before when I was here. That wasn't called for, and I hope you accept my apologies."

"That's okay," she said. "Would you like a cup of coffee?"

"Thank you," I said, trying to be polite. I wasn't a fan of coffee, for the most part, because I disliked how caffeine made me feel, but I knew enough about social interactions to know it was best not to refuse.

She poured the coffee. "I was expecting you," she said. "Sooner or later."

"You were." That phrase came out more like a statement than a question. She knew what I was after.

"I was. And I've been thinking, ever since you came to see me, what I would say to you." She breathed hard. "Ms. Ross, have you ever felt like you were in a box with no air? Like you had restrictions around your soul? Like your body was surrounded by a rope strangling you, and you didn't know what to do?" She narrowed her eyes as she looked at me and nodded. "Yes. I think you do."

She hit the nail on the head. Yes, I'd been there. Where she was, how she was feeling - I'd been there more times than I'd cared to think about. For months at a time, I had exactly those feelings – the restrictions, the box with no air or light, the rope strangling me. Yes, I could relate more than she could ever imagine.

"I broke free," she said. "When I decided to..." She looked down at her desk. "Leave this church. This church saved me, but I've concluded it's dark. Oppressive. It's not where I want to be. Not where I need to be. I don't know why I allowed it to control my life for far too long. I'm happy you're here because I know why you want to talk to me. If you didn't come and talk to me, I would've talked to you." Her hand was shaking. "I have what you need."

I nodded, wondering if she was talking about what I thought she was talking about.

"You do?"

"Yes," she said in a low voice. "I've been thinking about this for the past few months. Agonizing over it. I know what I did was wrong, and I want to make it right."

Just then, the reverend appeared at her door. "Ms. Garrison," he said. "I need to see you. In my office. Right now." He glared at me, and I felt the familiar chill run down my spine. I looked at my arm and saw goosebumps roiling up and down.

"I have to go," she said. "I'll be in touch."

"Do you have my number?" I asked.

"I do," she whispered. "I'll be in touch."

At that, she left her office.

I wondered when I would see her again. I also wondered if she was talking about the butcher knife.

I could suddenly see this case opening up, and I couldn't be happier about it.

THIRTY-FIVE

"Okay, Heather," I said to her when I visited her right after I came from Louisa's office. "I think things might be turning around in your case."

We were in her room, her roommates gone for the evening, as they all recently got a job working nights. They were slobs and I was surprised the halfway house director put up with it. Nobody's bed was made, and there were clothes everywhere on the floor. The room also had a peculiar smell to it – almost like rotten onions, but I knew the smell came from body odor.

"In what way?" Heather looked disinterested. I knew she wasn't; she was defeated. I saw her spirit slipping away with every visit I made to her, and it was concerning. I needed her to be mentally tough, but she was getting weaker with every passing day.

Even her appearance was lackluster. She didn't bother to put on makeup that morning, and her feet were bare, which was jarring to me, because I always associated Heather with her high-heeled shit-kicking boots. She was wearing sweat pants and a t-shirt and her long hair wasn't combed. She was giving up.

"I got in touch with Louisa Garrison, and she holds the key to the case. She didn't say as much, because we got interrupted by the creepy reverend, but I have a feeling she knows where the butcher knife is. If we can get that, and show she took it from the scene, that will go a long way towards proving to the jury that your mother was attacking you."

Heather rolled her eyes. "She ain't gonna give it up," she said. "Surely you know that."

"No, I don't know that. I don't know that at all. Listen, I met with her today, and she seemed very different than the first time I talked to her. It was almost like she'd been living with a huge burden and she was finally free. I know what that feels like and it's liberating. I know we can count on her to do the right thing."

"Why?"

"Why what?"

"Why do you persist in not seeing the truth about people? Why can't you see that people are cruel, they're heartless, and they don't do the right thing? Not ever. And they certainly won't do the right thing if that right thing means their ass will be be fried, which hers will be if she cooperates with you. If she took that knife, she committed a crime. She'll be sent up the river if she confesses. Bitch knows it. She ain't gonna confess. She's gonna lie and scheme and continue on with her trifling ways. Ain't nothing to do about it."

"You don't know that." I knew, deep down, Heather was right. Louisa's self-interest would be in continuing to hide the knife, assuming she took it. I still thought her self-interest might be overridden by her sense of doing what's right. However, I knew most people wouldn't do that. Most people would continue to hide and obfuscate, because they didn't want to put their neck on the line.

I hoped Louisa's sense of decency would out.

"I know that. I do. Now stop trying to get me to be positive about this case, when there's nothing positive about it. Nothing. You can't get things into evidence that should be in evidence. That church is queer as a three-dollar bill and just as fraudulent. That church is evil, it made my mother go bat-shit, and you can't put that as evidence to a jury. That's bullshit." She bowed her head. "That's bullshit. And it's bullshit you promised I could live with you and that you could take care of me. Yet I'm still here. I'm still here, and you're there, living with your two little girls and probably have a man around, and I'm here. Nobody has ever loved me, nobody has ever accepted me, and nobody ever will. Life isn't fair, Harper. It never has been and it never will be."

I blinked my eyes. "Where is this coming from?"

"What do you mean, where is this coming from? It's coming from a lifetime of rejection. I've got no family and I'm gonna spend the rest of my life in prison. Ain't nobody gonna see me as anything but the freak I am."

"Heather, I-"

"Get out of here, Harper. You can't help me. Nobody can. I might as well straight-up take that goddamned twenty-year deal, because you're not gonna win this case." She glared at me, her right hand shaking, her left hand nervously stroking her long hair.

"Heather, you don't want to take that deal. Not when I'm getting so close."

"You ain't close to nothing. Tell that prosecutor I'll take that goddamned deal."

"I won't. Not until I talk to Louisa again and see what I can get out of her. She's the key to this, I promise you. Just wait until I talk to her. Please."

"Okay. I'll give you 24 hours. I hope the prosecutor's offer is still good. But I want this mother-fucking thing put to bed. Yesterday."

"Heather, what changed? You seem like you've just given up."

"I've finally faced reality, that's all. Just finally faced reality."

I left, determined to go and see Louisa. I wouldn't lose this case.

I wouldn't lose Heather.

UNFORTUNATELY, something happened I didn't foresee, although I probably should've.

I went to the church the next day to see Louisa.

I got there and her office was cleaned out. Completely.

"Where is Ms. Garrison?" I asked the receptionist.

"She doesn't work here anymore."

My heart plunged about thirty miles. "She doesn't work here anymore. Can you please tell me where she went? Or how I can get ahold of her?"

"I can't tell you that," she said. "That information is confidential."

My case was suddenly getting complicated again.

To say the least.

THIRTY-SIX

"Aunt Harper," Rina said, coming into my room. "What's going on? Why is Sophia still here? Why aren't we having dinner together?"

"I'm so sorry," I said to Rina. "I really need to concentrate tonight. Something happened on Heather's case. If I don't figure it out in 24 hours, a full-blown disaster will happen."

"Why? What happened?"

"There's a witness I need. The key to the case. I'm pretty sure she is, anyhow. And she's gone. I don't know where she is." I snapped my fingers. "I got it. I'll subpoena that crazy reverend, put his ass under a deposition and make him tell me where she is."

Would that work? I doubted it. I'd have to show the reverend had information that would lead to hard evidence on my case, and, at the moment, I only had a hunch about Louisa being the key to my case. I didn't know that for sure. Yes, I had her emails to...

"I got it," I said. "Why didn't I think about this before?"

I booted up Connie's email, and promptly sent an email to

Louisa. "Louisa," my email read, "This is Harper Ross. I guess you're not working for the church anymore. I need to talk to you ASAP. Please contact me at Harperross@att.net. Or call me at 816-555-3940. Thank you."

I sent the email.

And then groaned when I got the message telling me the email didn't go through.

"What the hell?" I put my head on the desk. "I guess she doesn't have that email anymore."

I looked up, and Rina was still standing there, staring at me.

"Can I help you?" I asked her.

"No. I just wanted to help. I'd like to at least watch you, Aunt Harper. I want to learn everything you do."

I sighed. "Rina, I..." I shook my head. "All right, have a seat." I patted the chair next to me.

She beamed and sat next to me. "Thanks Aunt Harper."

"It's okay. Where's Abby?"

"Watching TV with Sophia. She doesn't cares about this, but I do. Tell me what's going on."

I sighed. "I'm close, Rina. Very close to cracking this case. Louisa Garrison, who has a job at that church, I think she knows where the butcher knife is. I went back to talk to her, but she's not working there anymore. They won't tell me where she's gone, either. I could hope she calls me. She said she has my phone number, but why do I feel she doesn't? And I also feel her leaving the church wasn't coincidental. I think the crazy, murderous reverend probably sent her to outer Siberia once he figured out she was ready to jump."

"Ready to jump?"

"Yeah. That woman knows a lot about that church. A lot. And when I was talking to her, it sounded like she was ready to spill what she knows." I shuddered. "I hope she's okay."

"What do you mean?"

I tousled her hair, knowing she was only 11, and she probably wasn't ready to hear my theory - that a Reverend with no qualms about brainwashing parents into killing their kids probably also didn't have qualms about murdering somebody like Louisa. Especially if he knew Louisa might be on the verge of turning him and his murderous operations into the police.

"Nothing, Ladybug," I said.

"Come on, Aunt Harper," she said. "Tell me what you meant."

"Rina," I said. "Please forget I said something like that. I was just thinking aloud, like I usually do. Now, if you're going to hang out with me, please stop asking questions. I'll tell you stuff as you need to know."

Rina crossed her arms and stuck out her lower lip.

"Oh, all right," I said. "Louisa looked like she was sick when I saw her. She might've gone to the hospital." That was a satisfying lie, I thought, but, when I looked at Rina, I could see she didn't believe it.

"That's not what you meant."

"Isn't it your bedtime?" I looked at the clock, and it read 9 PM.

"You've been letting us go to bed at 10. Even on school nights."

"Right. Well, you're a teenager and you need lots of sleep. 6:30 comes early. Maybe you should go to bed now." I raised my eyebrow at her, and she shook her head, as she apparently got my drift.

"I'll be quiet."

"Good." I still had authority over Rina, and she better know that.

I got back on the internet. I looked to see if she had a Facebook page. Nothing. Twitter. Nothing. Instagram, Pinterest and Linked-in. Nothing. Nothing. Nothing. Tik Tok. Nothing.

I even Googled her name. Nothing, except the information about her working at the church.

I felt tears coming to my eyes. "I'll just subpoena crazy rev," I said. "But he'll quash it if he has decent legal counsel." I put my head down on the desk, knowing Heather would demand I give it up and plead her out.

"What does quash mean?" Rina asked.

"It means he'll try to make it not take effect. Do you know what a subpoena is, Ladybug?" Rina was "Ladybug," and Abby was "Buttercup." They both loved those nicknames, so I used them whenever I could.

Rina shook her head.

"Well, a subpoena is when a person is ordered to do something. It has the effect of a legal order, even though it's not issued by a judge. So, if I subpoena a person, I'm ordering that person to appear somewhere at a certain time. I can also subpoena records, or other things, which means I can have access to them. If somebody quashes the subpoena, it doesn't take effect."

Rina nodded in understanding. "So if somebody subpoenas me, I have to appear somewhere for them?"

"Yes." I tousled her hair again. She'd be an amazing lawyer one day. Of that, I was sure. "So, I can subpoena crazy rev, put him under oath, and ask him where Louisa went. If he lies, he's guilty of perjury."

"Why could he quash the subpoena?"

I sighed. "Because I haven't yet shown Louisa will be an indispensable witness. To be honest, I don't know what she knows. I don't know for sure she has the knife. It's all conjecture at the moment. For that matter, I can't even show crazy rev will be indispensable or even valuable. That's what's so frustrating – I know what happened with Heather's mom. But I can't prove it in court. Not yet."

"What happened with Heather's mom?" Rina's eyes were wide.

I shook my head, inwardly cursing myself for spilling too much to my extremely young foster child. She was only 11 – how do I tell her there's a church apparently instructing parents to kill their kids?

I sighed. "Rina, I should just tell you my suspicions. I believe, and I have evidence that backs this up, the church is evil. I believe the reverend in that church has been brainwashing his congregants to kill their gay and trans children."

Rina's eyes got even wider. "Oh my God, Aunt Harper. Are there actually people like that?"

"Unfortunately, there are. Just look at the Nazis and what they did. There will always be people who can convince others to do their dirty work. There will always be those who believe society is sick because of this group or that, and, if they have access to impressionable people, they can be extremely dangerous. Extremely dangerous."

"But their own kids?"

I cleared my throat. "Heather, my client, told me her mother started accusing her of having the Devil inside her. If a parent believes that and they're told their kids are bound for hell unless they do something about it, I don't think it's farfetched that they would kill their own children." I took a deep breath. "I hate that you have to learn about this stuff at such a young age, but it can't be helped. You're going to learn about it sooner or later."

"Well don't tell Abby. I don't think she can handle it."

"You're probably right, Ladybug." I looked at the clock. "And now, for sure, it's your bedtime. Go upstairs, get your jammies on and brush your teeth. Grab Abby while you're at it and have her do the same. I'll be up in a few to tuck you guys in."

Rina groaned and rolled her eyes, but she got up and went downstairs. I heard her telling Abby to get her little butt into the bathroom, too, to brush her teeth, and I smiled. Rina was such a little boss. She reminded me so much of myself at that age.

Poor thing.

THIRTY-SEVEN

"Well?" Heather asked when I went to see her the next day. "What did you find out?"

"Nothing yet. I have a subpoena for the reverend. If it goes through, I'll get him under oath and find out where Louisa is. I don't have anything to go on just yet. I don't know where she went."

"Plead me," Heather said. "I'm sick of this shit. Plead me and get it done."

"Heather," I said. "If I plead you, that's it. There's no appealing it. No changing your mind. Once it's done, it's done. I don't want to slam the door on this case until I turn over every rock."

"And if you go on much longer, that offer won't be good." She crossed her arms in front of her. "I've been talking with these dudes in here. They've been around the block a few times. And they tell me that once a prosecutor starts working up their case, they won't want to deal. They tell me that once you cross a certain point, all offers go away. They also tell me 20 years is a good deal for murder."

"All those things are true, but, Heather, we'll win this."

"We can't. Not if you can't get that Louisa woman to tell you what she did with the knife. That's if she has the fucking knife. If she doesn't, what then? Who else you gonna shake that knife out of? You got any other ideas on that, Harper?"

I had to admit, I didn't. Perhaps the reverend took the knife. Perhaps one of the cops on the scene took it, although I doubted that. They didn't have motive to do that. The reverend would, however.

"I don't. We'll just have to proceed without it." I shook my head. What was I saying? Proceed without finding the knife? Really? The prosecutor would slam-dunk this case without effort.

Heather raised one of her eyebrows. "Proceed without it? Who you trying to fool, Harper? Seriously."

"Give me a chance to talk to the reverend. If I subpoena him, he has to answer questions. Give me that chance."

Heather rolled her eyes. "Schedule a plea bargain, Harper. Schedule it, and if you find out where Louisa is, cancel it. But you need to do what I'm telling you. I'm the boss, and what I say goes. That's another thing I learned in this joint. You work for me, so I call the shots."

I CALLED Vince when I got back to the office. My heart was racing as I dialed his number. This was the wrong thing. I knew it. Yet, Heather was right – without that knife, we would lose. And she certainly wouldn't get 20 years if we lost. That was for sure.

"Vince Malloy," he said in answering the phone.

"Vince, it's Harper Ross." I took a deep breath. "Is that 20-year offer on the Heather Morrison case still on the table?"

"It is. I haven't started discovery on this case yet, so, yeah. 20 years is still the offer."

"Put it on the docket," I said. "For next week." I figured a week would be a good time to put it on. By then, I'd know whether or not I could depose the reverend about Louisa's whereabouts.

"I'll schedule it and send you a copy of the docket," he said. "You're doing the right thing, Harper."

"Thanks."

I hung up and sighed, looking at my picture on the wall of my office. It was a black and white photo of John F. Kennedy. He was in profile, and was quite young and handsome. *One person can make a difference and every person should try.* That was the quote on this poster.

I also had a picture of the great Supreme Court justice, Thurgood Marshall, on my wall. *To protest against injustice is the foundation of all our American democracy* was this quote.

Heather would go to prison if she took this deal. For a long time. How was this justice being done? She did nothing wrong. She simply defended herself when her mother tried to kill her. Yet the possibility of proving this, at this point, seemed remote. I was getting somewhere when Louisa seemed to be accommodating when I saw her. Yet that, like everything else in this case, was a blind alley.

I had a slinky toy tucked in my desk. I got it out whenever I was feeling stressed. I was definitely feeling stressed, so I got it out and started folding it in and out, just like an accordion.

"Hey you," Tammy said, popping her head in. "You want to talk?"

"No," I said. I didn't feel like talking about this. If I did, I'd lose my shit. "I'll talk about stuff, just not about this case."

"Heather's case? I'm sorry I stuck you with it."

"Don't be. It's going south, but you never know."

"Well..." She put a letter on my desk. "This is from another lawyer. A lawyer for John Scott. It's a motion to quash your subpoena."

"That's good. At least I can get this out of the way. When is the hearing on this?"

"Two days from now."

"Good. I'll know before I plead Heather what the status will be on this." I continued to look at my slinky toy. "Do you know who invented the Slinky?"

"No, who?"

"Some random guy named Richard James. He left the company to be a missionary in Bolivia." I kept folding the toy in and out. "So, what's happening with you?"

"Nothing. I just wanted to check in."

"I wish I had good news to tell you. I really do. But I don't."

TWO DAYS LATER, I had the hearing on the subpoena for the crazy reverend. He wasn't in court – only his attorney was. Judge Reiner was at the bench, electing to hear arguments in court as opposed to the two of us going back into chambers and arguing informally. He wanted this on the record.

"Ms. Ross," Judge Reiner said, calling me up to the bench. "And Mr. Marshall. Come on up."

Blake Marshall, a lawyer I didn't know, was the attorney for the reverend. His motion simply said I didn't have a reason to subpoena Reverend John Scott. I couldn't show he'd lead to evidence regarding my trial.

"Okay, Mr. Marshall. I've read your motion, and you're saying this subpoena is unduly burdensome and the application for the subpoena was not made in good faith because Ms. Ross is on a fishing expedition. Ms. Ross, are you fishing?"

"No, your honor. I'm not fishing."

"Then tell me, Ms. Ross, what the subpoena for Mr. Scott will lead you to?"

"He knows where Louisa Garrison is. Louisa Garrison will be an indispensable witness for my case."

"In what way?" Judge Reiner asked.

"Your honor, there is an issue in this case that Ms. Garrison should have information on. Specifically, there's a butcher knife that has gone missing, and I believe Ms. Garrison knows where this knife is. Since finding the whereabouts of this knife is crucial in this case, I need to speak with Ms. Garrison to find out what she knows."

"And what leads you to believe Ms. Garrison knows where the knife is?"

I swallowed hard, feeling embarrassed. I didn't know why I thought that – it was only a hunch. Plus, Axel gave me the idea that Louisa probably knew. "I have evidence, your honor, that Ms. Garrison and the victim in this case, Connie Morrison, were having an affair. That gives Ms. Garrison motive for cleaning up the crime scene, if she happened upon it before the police got there."

"In what way?" Judge Reiner asked. "Why should she have motive to clean up the crime scene, just because she was romantically involved with your client's mother?"

"The theory is she wanted to protect the memory of her lover, Connie Morrison, so she took the knife from the crime scene. She didn't want her lover to be seen as a violent person, and, if her lover was found dead with a knife in her hand, that would mean her lover was, in fact, violent." Even as I was talking, I knew I sounded like an idiot.

Indeed, Blake Marshall was suppressing laughter as he listened to me spin my wild-ass theory.

"Ms. Ross," Mr. Marshall said. "I've read this statement of information, and the two cops on the scene were the first responders. That means nobody else had been to the scene before they got there. There was no indication that Ms. Garrison or anybody else had been there. And, quite frankly, your theory is just that – a theory. You have no hard evidence to show Ms. Garrison will be valuable to your case."

I sighed. He was absolutely right. I could put forth the theory that Louisa was important because she could testify the church was into brainwashing parents to kill their gay children, but that theory, too, would be laughed out of court.

Judge Reiner shook his head. "Motion to quash is granted," he said. "If you get something more for this court to chew on, Ms. Ross, file your subpoena again. Until then, please don't clog my dockets with your nonsense. I say that with all due respect, of course."

I nodded. "Of course."

I walked out of the courtroom and called Heather with the bad news. "We've reached another dead end," I said. "I'm so sorry."

"That's fine," she said, her voice sounding monotone. No life. "I guess I'll be pleading to twenty years soon."

I fought back tears. "I guess so."

I was defeated.

And so was Heather.

THIRTY-EIGHT

Louisa Garrison put her thumb out, trying to get yet another ride to the West Coast. She'd gotten in touch with her mother, who was living in San Diego. Her mother said Louisa could stay with her for the time being. Just until Louisa found another job.

The reverend fired her, of course. She knew he would. He had an uncanny way of knowing when people were ready to get out and, possibly, ready to go to the authorities about him and what he was doing. He was very good at getting rid of threats before they could become full-blown. The final straw for him was her talking to that Harper Ross. He knew who Harper Ross was, and Harper Ross threatened him. Harper Ross was an intelligent woman, and, if she got to the bottom of what was happening at the Church, it would be game over.

The reverend had even been doing things to spook Harper, although Louisa doubted Harper knew it was him doing these things. He hit Harper's car and left a threatening note, and then he climbed through Harper's window and set her kitchen on fire. He did all these things so she would back off. But

Harper wasn't backing off. She was on the case and she was getting close.

Of course, before Reverend Scott fired Louisa, he also threatened her. He told her he'd call her mother and tell her the truth about her lesbian relationships. That would mean her mother would never let her in the house. He also told her, in no uncertain terms, that he would kill her if she spoke a word about the church.

Before she left her house, she took a backpack of her belongings. Things she'd need on the road. She had several changes of underwear and clothes, a toothbrush, some makeup, a hairbrush. She also packed her pocket Bible, which, for her, was indispensable. She read it when she was in times of need, and it gave her comfort.

She also took that butcher knife. She was close to giving it to Harper. She would give it to her. She didn't want to go to prison, which she would surely do if she told anybody what she'd done, but, yet, she didn't want Heath Morrison to go to prison, either. She agonized over it, and then she made a decision. Give the knife to Harper, and come clean. Come clean on what she had done.

Then the reverend fired her, and threatened her, and she was terrified to talk to Harper now. The reverend would surely find out if she talked to Harper, and then he would kill her. She knew the reverend well enough to know his words weren't idle threats. He was directly responsible for the deaths of at least eleven kids whose parents were congregants of the church. He was responsible because he gave a direct order to the parents whose children were gay – they were to try to change their kids, through conversion therapy, and if they couldn't, they were to kill them. Only five of those kids were active homicide cases, and, as far as Louisa knew, there wasn't a lead on any of them. The others were "suicides," or they were listed as such, but

Louisa knew better. She'd been in the room with him, every time he issued those orders.

A truck pulled up alongside the road, and Louisa hopped in. "Where to?" the trucker asked.

"I'm going to California," she said. "Where are we now?" She knew she was somewhere in the Rocky Mountains, but she hadn't paid attention to the cities as they passed on by. She slept a lot when she was given rides, because these rides were the only chance she had to fall asleep. She noticed the terrain was looking slightly different than before – there were more buttes and fewer mountains. Either way, the scenery was gorgeous - mountains that went on for miles, covered with green grass and tall pine trees. Now she was seeing the red buttes, some that seemed to form natural arches, but most of them flat on top. Some of them were in formations that almost looked like a modern artist sculpted them, and these fascinated Louisa to no end.

"We're in Utah. Just passed Moab awhile back."

Moab was a Biblical name Louisa knew well. He was born of incest, the incest between Lot and his oldest daughter. She closed her eyes, not wanting to think about Moab and how he was born. It reminded her too much of her own father and the child he fathered with her. The child she didn't ever get to know, because she gave him up for adoption some 18 years earlier. She had to do it, of course – she was carrying her father's child. She'd never tell her father's secret, either. He didn't even have to threaten her to make her keep the secret – she kept the secret because she loved him still.

Louisa was presently thirty-eight, but knew she looked much older than her age. Years of drinking, drugging and sleeping around aged her tremendously. She spent her entire life trying to forget what her father used to do to her, trying to forget that dirty secret, that dirty seed he'd planted in her. Even now, when she saw him, she put what he did to her right out of her mind. All that she could see was a handsome man, in his late fifties, with slightly greying hair and a still-fit body. She didn't see him as the man who deflowered her, when she was only 12, and who continued to do unspeakable things to her until the day she left the house at age 22, for her first job at a veterinary office.

"Where'd you say you were goin'?" the trucker asked me.

"San Diego, California," she said.

"You on the run?"

"No," she said, wondering why he was thinking that. "Why do you ask that?"

He shrugged. "Mind if I smoke?"

"Of course not. I'm at your mercy, I won't say nothing about what you want to do." Louisa wasn't about to protest anything. This guy was doing her a solid. Hopefully she could ride all the way to California with him.

"I'm going to Vegas," he said. "Lost Wages. Not to gamble, but I gotta drop off this shipment at a furniture store there. After that, I gotta be in Texas. So, I can take you as far as Vegas, then I gotta let you go."

Louisa nodded. Vegas was good enough. She could surely find somebody in Vegas who could take her the rest of the way. "Thanks for letting me ride with you," she said. "I won't be a bother, I promise."

The trucker shrugged his shoulders. "I don't care. I could use the company, to be honest. I pick up hitchhikers a lot for that reason. It gets goddamn boring driving by yourself all the damned time. So, you're not on the run, yet you're hitchhiking. What's your story?"

Was she running? She was sort of on the run from Reverend John, but, really, she'd been on the run her entire life. Always running from her past. From her feelings. From her insecurities, inadequacies and her inability to get away from her perverted feelings about women. There was just no running from those things, though.

The old saying was true – wherever you go, there you are.

"No story." She looked out the window, fascinated with the red buttes. "No story at all."

That was a lie. But she wasn't about to tell the truth to this stranger.

She couldn't even admit the truth to herself.

THIRTY-NINE

Heather's plea bargain was set for 9 AM, and I ate breakfast that morning slowly and deliberately. Axel had been over the night before, and I made dinner for him and the girls. Everybody had a great time. He even said he wanted to spend the night, but no way was I ready for that, especially when I had the two girls there, so he left at 10 last night.

Rina and Abby ate their breakfast with me. The two girls were quiet, because they could see I was lost in thought.

"Aunt Harper," Abby said. "I like Axel. He's cute and seems very nice."

"Mm hm," I mumbled, looking at my bowl of oatmeal. I had a pit in my stomach, a huge pit the size of a softball. Heather would plead to 20 years, and that was the worst possible outcome.

Maybe this was my karma for John Robinson. I got him off, and now I was suffering by seeing an innocent person go to prison. Then I immediately felt guilty for thinking that. *It's not about you, Harper. Her going to prison isn't about you.* It wasn't, of course. She was innocent, yet she would go to prison anyhow. Happened all the time. It didn't make things any easier, though. To know your client is innocent without the ability to save her – that was a fate worse than death for me.

"What's going on, Aunt Harper?" Rina asked me.

"Nothing," I said. I could feel the dark pincers of depression squeeze my insides, and I felt slightly panicky. I couldn't get down again. Not when I had two girls relying on me to be mentally healthy. Not when I had a full docket of other clients also relying on me. I wouldn't have Heather's case to worry about after today, but I had a dozen other criminal cases on my roster, and I had to keep going for them. For the girls and for the people who relied on me, I had to keep going.

Rina sighed. "Well, we're ready for school." They picked up their backpacks and I looked up.

"Good," I said without enthusiasm. I tried to fight back tears, mainly because I didn't want the girls to be concerned about me. They were both so sensitive to my moods, I guessed because they were always looking out and making sure I wouldn't lose my shit the way like the Browns did.

Rina bowed her head. "Let's go, then," she said. "We're going to be late."

"Okay." I picked up my car keys, leaving the half-eaten oatmeal on the table. "Sophia can get that."

We all headed to my SUV.

I dropped them off at their school, and headed to court.

I felt like I was heading to my own execution.

I GOT TO COURT, and immediately saw Heather. She was sitting behind the court area, looking at her black nails. She was back to wearing her high-heeled boots, but she was also wearing a pair of black dress slacks and a button-down blue shirt. Her long hair was piled up in a bun, and her makeup was relatively toned down. She still had on deep-red lipstick, however.

She saw me come in, looked at me briefly, and then looked away.

I sat down next to her and put my arm around her. "You ready for this?"

She shrugged. "As ready as I'll ever be."

"I haven't had the chance to go over with you how this works," I began.

"What's there to know? I go up there, say I want to plead guilty, and that's that. Right?"

"Well, no," I said. "There's more to it than that."

She shrugged and looked at the wall.

"Heather," I said. "I'm going ask you to state the facts to the judge about the case. You have to admit to the court you killed your mother, and didn't have a defense for it. You'll have to tell the court how you killed your mother, and what day you did it. That's what's called laying down a factual basis for your plea."

Heather didn't react. She continued to look at the wall.

"Heather," I said. "Did you hear me?"

She shrugged.

I sighed and looked around. "Vince will be here any moment. Are you ready for this?"

She shrugged.

"I don't like this, either. I feel like I let you down. I feel like..."

"Don't give me that bullshit. After today, you'll go on. You have your two girls, your home, your television, your hot shower, your soft bed, your computer, your phone and everything else. I'm gonna have nothing. Nothing but a tiny little cage, cold showers with large men, and crappy food. I'm probably gonna have the living shit beaten out of me every single fucking day in there, because I weigh a buck ten, and everybody else will be a lot bigger than me. I'm gonna have nothing."

She crossed her arms and looked at the wall again, her face turned away from me.

I tried to put my arm around her again, but she shrugged it off.

Vince came in, his file in his hand. "Okay," he said, "Let's get this show on the road."

I nodded. "Heather," I said. "It's time."

We both stood up, and Heather stiffened her back so that she pranced to the front of the court. She was going out by showing the prosecutor she wasn't afraid. She wouldn't ever give him the satisfaction of knowing he beat her.

Judge Reiner was on the bench. "All rise," the bailiff said, even though the three of us were the only ones in the courtroom, and we were all already standing. "The court calls the case of State v. Morrison."

"You may be seated," Judge Reiner said, and all of us sat down at the tables in front of the bench. "As I understand it, the parties have reached an agreement on this case. Am I correct about this?"

I sighed, my heart heavy. It was heavier than it had ever been. "Yes, you're honor," I said. "We have."

"Okay, then," he said. "Make your record."

I nudged Heather. "Go ahead and have a seat up there," I said, pointing to the seat next to the judge's bench.

Heather went up and sat down. The bailiff swore her in.

I approached. "Please state your name for the record."

"My name is Heather Morrison," she said.

"Ms. Morrison," Judge Reiner said, "your given name is what's required, please."

Heather rolled her eyes. "Heath Morrison. My name is Heath Morrison."

"Ms. Morrison," I said. "Do you understand you are accepting a plea agreement from the state?"

"Yes."

"You understand that if you accept this plea agreement that your case is final? In other words, you would not be entitled to an appeal?"

"Yes."

"Has anybody coerced you into taking this plea agreement?"

"No."

"Are you of sound mind and body?"

"Yes."

"Are you currently under the influence of alcohol or drugs?"

"No." Heather shifted in her seat.

"You're currently 18 years old, is that correct?"

"Yes."

"Okay. Take me back to the night of June 19 of this year." I read from the statement of information. "Isn't it true that you and your mother had a fight that night?"

"Yes," she said, looking down at the table in front of her. She clasped her hands in front of her.

"Did you kill your mother that night?"

"Yes." She sighed and rolled her eyes. She pursed her lips and looked up at the ceiling.

"How did you kill your mother?"

"I took out a pocket knife and stabbed her in the neck."

I paced back and forth in front of Heather. I took a deep breath. "And you had no affirmative defense, is that correct?"

She furrowed her brows. "I'm sorry?"

"You have no affirmative defense for killing your mother, is that correct?"

"Affirmative defense?"

"Yes. You had no legal justification for killing her?"

"She was coming at me with a butcher knife and she would kill me first. I had to do it, or I'd be chopped hamburger on the floor." She crossed her arms and rolled her eyes, and I smiled.

"Ms. Ross," Judge Reiner said. "Please approach. You too, Vince."

Inwardly, I was doing cartwheels. Heather just blew up her plea. She couldn't make the factual basis in front of the judge, and that meant the plea deal couldn't go through.

"Ms. Ross," Judge Reiner said. "Did you explain to your client that she would have to make a factual basis for this plea deal?"

"Yes, your honor."

"You know I can't take this plea now. Not when the record shows Ms. Morrison has an affirmative defense to the homicide."

"Your honor," Vince said, "she made the elements on the record. That should be good enough to allow the plea deal to go through."

"I'm sorry," Judge Reiner. "I know what you're saying, but if she has a self-defense claim, and she puts that on the record, I can't take the plea. You'll have to try it."

Vince narrowed his eyes and stepped on my foot. Hard. I pursed my lips and looked away.

"Okay," he said, facing me. "I guess we're trying this case. You'll be getting my discovery requests next week. Since we're on an accelerated schedule, I suggest we ask the judge right now to expedite the dates we have to get everything into each other."

"That sounds good," I said.

"Thanks a lot," he said sarcastically and under his breath. "You did that on purpose."

"Maybe I did and maybe I didn't," I said. "You'll never know."

"That's enough," Judge Reiner said. "We'll try this case in less than two months, so the two of you will have to get your discovery into one another in three weeks. That means you both have to get a move on."

"Thank you, your honor," I said. "I anticipate getting Vince's witness list by next week, so I can begin scheduling depositions. I'll do the same for him."

I went over to Heather, who was still sitting at the witness stand, not understanding what was happening. "Come on," I said.

"What's going on?" she asked. "Is that bailiff going to put the cuffs on me and take me away? Or do I get sentenced later on? What's going on?"

"The plea deal collapsed," I said. "When you told the judge you had a self-defense claim. He can't accept the plea deal if you put that on the record."

"What?" Her eyes got wide. "What the fuck?"

I looked over at the judge, who was smiling and shaking his head. He could've put Heather into contempt for using foul language in his courtroom. He must've been in a decent mood, because I'd seen him put people in jail for less.

"Come with me," I said.

"No." She crossed her arms in front of her and glared at me. "I'm not going nowhere until you tell me what the fuck is going on."

"Heather," I said. "There will be no plea deal."

"Oh, hell no," she said, looking over at Judge Reiner, who was gathering his files in preparation for going back into his chambers. "Hell, no. I want that plea deal."

"You won't get it," I said. "We're going to try this case."

"No. We're not going to try it. We're going to lose this

fucking case, and you won't be who's going to spend the rest of her life in fucking prison. It's going to be me. My ass will die in prison. I'll probably live to be 100 fucking years old, staring at those crazy-ass walls for 24 fucking hours a day. Goddamn it, you promised me. You promised me I could get out of prison before I'm forty, and now you're saying I'm going to grow old and die behind those prison walls."

"We're going to try it," I said. "We have no choice now. That judge won't take your plea. We have to go forward with a trial." I smiled and winked. "Buckle up, Buttercup."

I didn't know why I was suddenly feeling so light and free. I only knew that I felt, deep in my heart, that pleading Heather was the exact wrong thing to do. I knew that as much as I knew anything in my life. And Vince was right – I didn't have to ask Heather if she had an affirmative defense for killing her mother. I only needed Heather to say on the record that she killed her mother. If I would've stopped there, the plea deal would've went through. Heather would be headed to prison right now.

But I didn't stop there. I went forward, knowing that Heather was, more likely than not, going to blow up her plea because she would tell the truth.

Vince was right.

I did that on purpose.

FORTY

"What do you mean, you blew up Heather's plea?" Axel and I were sitting by a fountain in Loose Park, having met there after he and I both got off work. I had a peanut butter and jelly sandwich in a brown bag, along with a yogurt and a granola bar. I brought Axel the same thing I was eating, and we sat and ate the food while we watched the ducks and geese swimming around in the lake.

I walked over to the ducks and got some bread crumbs out of a bag and threw the crumbs on the ground. The ducks swarmed to me, their little fat bodies waddling over to me by the hundreds. They looked like a battalion of tiny green and blue soldiers ambling slowly over to me. The geese were more aggressive, their long necks craning, their bills pointed towards the sky.

"I blew it up," I said. "Heather was adamant to take the plea, and I didn't want her to. I didn't mean to blow it up, but maybe I did. At any rate, Heather's case will go to trial, and there's not much either of us can do about it at this point."

"What exactly happens when a plea blows up?"

"The judge won't accept it. He can never accept any plea agreement unless the defendant can make a factual basis on the record." I continued to throw out bread crumbs, and the little ducks were quacking with delight. They were fighting over the crumbs, entertaining me to no end.

"You really like doing this, don't you?" Axel asked me. He had his own handful of bread crumbs, which he was scattering along the ground next to me.

"I do. Sometimes I watch the ducks, just swimming around, without a care in the world. I start to think that in my next life, maybe I'd like to come back as a duck. I mean, all they have to worry about is, well, nothing. They have all the food they need here at the lake, they have all their buddies around, and they just look so relaxed."

Axel smiled. "They don't have anything to worry about until they get blown out of the sky," he said. "Or eaten by a hawk."

I shrugged. "These ducks don't have to worry about being shot. They're smart if they just continue to hang around here. Or at the zoo." I laughed. "You ever see those random ducks swimming at the zoo? For some odd reason, I find that hilarious."

Axel nodded. "I have, and I find them funny too."

I ran out of bread crumbs, so the two of us walked back over to some of the fountains. I got on the ledge of the fountain, and Axel took my hand. "Jump," he said. "I'll catch you."

I jumped down, and Axel put his strong hands on my sides. I looked down at the ground, suddenly feeling self-conscious. "We better go. I know it's Saturday, but I have a hellacious day ahead of me. I'm pretty much going to be working 24/7 until the Heather trial goes through."

Axel smiled. "You'll fit me in. I'll make sure of it." He kissed my forehead and I sighed.

He was right. I'd fit him in.

No matter what.

I DECIDED to find out everything I could about Connie Morrison. I didn't have the knife, and I didn't have a good witness, although I'd try to find other church members who might talk to me off the record about the reverend and the craziness he was imparting on them. Not that any of them would – they were probably either completely brainwashed or were being threatened. Nonetheless, there might be somebody who would talk.

I'd put the Reverend on my witness list. It certainly couldn't hurt, even though I knew he'd lie on the stand. Plus, I doubted he'd be approved as a witness, unless he was willing to get on the stand and admit he brainwashed Connie and Connie tried to kill her daughter because of it. I had a better chance of being struck by lightning or winning the lottery than to see that happen.

I called in my computer whiz, whose name was Anna Smythe. She could get any record I wanted, because she could hack into any records database I needed her to. "Anna," I said. "Could you come in and help me today? I'm working from home." Anna was available pretty much seven days a week, because she clearly loved what she did, and she didn't have a life outside her computer hacking.

"Sure," she said. "I'm just sitting home playing video games right now. When do you need me?"

"Whenever you can get here. I need to get records on my client's mother. There might be some kind of criminal history or mental health records we can shake out." The problem was, always, getting these records in front of the jury, especially the mental health ones. But if Connie had a criminal record, that would be a cinch to get in front of the jury. I crossed my fingers and prayed I could find something. Maybe she assaulted somebody, or a lot of people, and I could show these assaults showed her character as a violent person.

Maybe, but I doubted it. Still, it was worth throwing it against the wall to see if it stuck.

ANNA ARRIVED ABOUT AN HOUR LATER. "I'm here," she said. Anna was young, only 23, and gorgeous in a tough-girl badass way. She had short black hair and brown eyes and her entire right shoulder and back was covered in tattoos. She was small, compact and muscular and typically dressed in a A-shirts, torn jeans and high-topped tennis shoes.

"Cool," I said, feeling I was anything but cool, especially next to her. "Here's my girl," I said, giving her Connie's information – her date of birth and social security number. Heather supplied both of those things for me, which was extremely helpful.

She nodded and sat down, cracking her knuckles. "I'll have a preliminary report for you in an hour," she said, plopping her laptop down on one of the desks in my office. "If you want to, go and do whatever you're doing today. Go play with those two little girls I saw when I came in."

"Thanks," I said. "I do need to spend some time with them."

I went out to talk to Rina and Abby, who were playing music in the living room and dancing around wildly. "Hey girls," I said. "Let's watch a movie, and then you need to do at least an hour of homework."

Rina rolled her eyes. "Yuck," she said. "I hate doing homework on a Saturday."

"Well, we'll watch a movie, then you guys can do one hour of homework, and then I'll take us all to the drive-in."

The two girls cheered wildly. Like me, they loved going to the drive-in. "Can we invite some girls?" they asked.

"Sure, sure. The SUV is big enough for two more. We'll pick up some chicken, pop some popcorn and have a good time."

"Okay," they said in unison.

"I don't mind studying on a Saturday," Abby said. "But Rina does."

We all sat down and watched a movie, one the girls picked out, while Anna worked in the other room.

After the movie, I got up. "I need to go and check on Anna," I said. "To find out what she found out about Connie. Can I get you girls anything while I'm up?"

"Another pop," Rina said.

"I'll get you a water," I said. "Or juice. You know you can't have more than one pop in a day."

"Whatever," Rina said, rolling her eyes. "Okay, a glass of grape juice."

"Abby?"

"I'm good."

I went into the kitchen and got a glass of grape juice and went back into the living and handed it to Rina.

"Thanks," she said. "Come on, Abby, let's go and study."

At that, the two girls went to their rooms, and I went in to check in on Anna.

Anna was sitting in front of her computer, a rope of red licorice hanging out of her mouth. She seemed lost in thought, so lost in thought she didn't notice me when I walked in the door.

"Oh, hey," she said finally, looking up at me. "What's up?"

"I could ask the same. What did you find out?"

She shrugged. "No mental health records, clean arrest record. I'm sorry, I wish I could find some kind of dirt on this chick, but she seemed to be pretty clean."

I sighed and nodded. "I was afraid of that. Another blind alley."

"I guess. Did you know Heather was adopted, though?"

I cocked my head. "Adopted? No, I didn't know that." I tapped my pencil on the desk. "I don't even know if Heather knows she's adopted, either. Can you find out who her mother is?"

She grimaced. "No, that's apparently not a matter of record, at least not on the internet. The records might only be available at the courthouse, if at all. It was a closed adoption, that much I can tell you."

I sighed. Was this another dead end, or was it significant? And if it was significant, why would it be? Heather was adopted. So what?

Still, I had a feeling I'd need to find out who the birth mother was. "What was the jurisdiction," I asked. "Where the adoption went through?"

"Savannah, Georgia," she said. "Chatham County."

I nodded. "Thanks, Anna," I said. "What do I owe you?"

"Two hundred dollars," she said. And then she smiled. "And maybe a drive-in movie? I heard you talking to your girls."

I laughed. "You got it. Meet me here at 7, and we'll go."

OVER THE NEXT month or so, I did all the digging I could. I talked to Heather's friends, Connie's friends and was even able to talk to a couple of church-goers willing to be honest with me.

"Reverend Scott is crazy," one lady, whose name was Haley Matthews told me. I met with her in her house, a beautiful Victorian mansion in the Gladstone District, which was known for turn-of-last-century Queen Ann homes, which were generally made of stone, three stories tall, with circular cupolas, turrets and pointed roofs. "Would you like some tea?"

I nodded as I sat down in her sun room with her. "Thank you."

She sat down with me, each of us sipping our tea. "Now, what would you like me to tell you specifically?"

"You say he's crazy, can you elaborate?"

She sighed. "I've never been in the proximity of such hate. Such virulent, nausea-inducing hate."

"How long were you a part of that church?"

"For a year. I know, I know, why did I keep going? Well, my husband was a part of the church, and he demanded I go with him. So, I did. And it eventually destroyed us, because I finally decided I had enough. I heard rumors…"

I nodded. "Rumors…"

"Yes, rumors. Rumors that the reverend told parents to kill their children if the children were LGBT. And I could believe it, because the reverend told the congregants, week after week, about how the LGBT community is destroying this country."

"Can I get you to testify in court?"

She shook her head. "I'd rather not. I'm scared of that man. I think he's capable of anything."

Nevertheless, I thought I should probably subpoena her. I put her on my possible witness list right then, even though I knew her testimony probably couldn't come into court, anyhow.

One other woman, a Sally Toby, said virtually the same thing, and, like Haley, said she wouldn't testify. She, too, was scared, but I still made a note to subpoena her as well. You never know…

As for Heather and Connie's friends – they were no help. In fact, all of them told me that Connie and Heather fought constantly, and that Heather said lots of incendiary things about her hatred for her mother. Still, it gave me a heads-up on what I could expect from the witnesses in trial. I would have to cross-examine them and hope to get some kind of positive testimony out of them.

After doing my research, and talking to the witnesses, the case didn't seem any more promising than before.

In fact, it seemed even worse.

FORTY-ONE
ONE MONTH LATER

The day of Heather's trial was finally here, and I had a pit in my stomach like I'd never had before. Nothing had worked out for me in my discovery process, unfortunately. I never was able to track down Louisa, even though I sent my investigator out after her. Anna wasn't able to find out any information about her, either. She tried, but, for some odd reason, Louisa was like a ghost. Of course, it would've helped if I had something to go on with Louisa – her date of birth, for instance, or her prior address. I didn't have access to any of those records, and the church where she worked apparently expunged her contact information when she left that place.

There wasn't anything on-line that would help me find Louisa, and that was frustrating.

I also tried to find out who Heather's birth mother was, and was getting close to finding that out. I didn't know why that was important, except that I wanted Heather to possibly have a family who might want to know who she was. She didn't have anybody – her mother and father were both gone, and they both were only children, so she didn't have any extended family around, either. I wanted to find out her birth mother because I wanted her to have family.

Not that Heather cared about that. Every time I went to see her, after her plea deal blew up, it was the same – she'd apparently given up. She didn't even bother to dress for me when I saw her, because she was usually in her pajamas and had even cut off her hair. It was short, because Heather told me she didn't want to bother with making it look pretty anymore.

"Why should I care about doing my hair?" she asked. "I'm going to have to get used to not having access to my blow-dryer and flat iron, and my hair is so curly, I just don't want to mess with it anymore." It was a little surprising that Heather's hair was curly, because, before, when she was caring about her appearance, it was always straight. "I used a straight iron every day," she explained. "I'm just gonna go *au naturel*, because it's gonna look like this when I'm in that fucking cage, where I'm going to be for the rest of my fucking life."

She never bothered putting on makeup, either, so she looked very different than the first time I met her. She didn't exactly look like a man, but she was no longer trying to look like a woman, either, so I could almost tell what she looked like before she decided to transition.

I WENT to pick her up for our trial at 7 in the morning. I was happy to see that she'd bothered to dress appropriately for the occasion. She was wearing a dark blue dress, with a lighter blue sweater over it, tan pumps and hose. Her curly hair was tied back with a colorful scarf, and she carried a tan bag. She was wearing makeup, but it was subtle, so subtle that I probably wouldn't have known she was wearing makeup if I wasn't up close.

"What?" she asked when I picked her up. She brought out

a mirror and looked into it, rubbing her teeth to get the lipstick off. "You looked at me funny. I know you probably wanted me to look like Heath Morrison for this occasion, but fuck 'em. The jury might as well know the truth about me, don't you think? So, I'm sorry I'm not in a suit and all, but I want to feel I look good."

"I wasn't thinking that," I said. "Honestly. I was thinking you looked beautiful."

"Huh." Heather raised her eyebrow. "Whatever." She looked ahead, her small hands clutching her purse at her feet. "Is the media gonna be there?"

"I'd imagine," I said. "This is my first murder trial since John Robinson, so they've been interested in this case. They were interested, anyhow, at the beginning." I sighed. "I wanted to tell you what will happen today. We won't actually be picking a jury until the afternoon. This morning is just me and the prosecutor arguing pre-trial motions. I presented him with a list of witnesses from that church, and the prosecutor is objecting to them on the grounds of relevance. I basically have to tell the judge what these witnesses will testify to, and the judge will decide if they're relevant or not. If he says they aren't relevant, then-"

"We're fucked. What else is new?" Heather studied me, her fingers, with pale pink polish replacing the black, tapping her forehead.

"I don't want you to think we have a good chance with this case," I said. I hadn't been able to locate that butcher knife, and that was still the real problem. That would still mean the prosecutor could slam-dunk this case. But at least we were going down swinging. "But you never know. If the judge allows the testimony of the church people, we just might make a good case."

"What are the chances of that happening? That the judge lets you talk to these people on the stand?"

"10%," I said. "To be perfectly honest. It'll be difficult to show relevance unless the Reverend is willing to testify to brainwashing Connie, in particular, which he won't do. But you never know. The problem is, even if, by some miracle, the judge allows these people to testify, the prosecutor might have grounds to appeal that decision, because it would be so out of the realm of what he's supposed to do. But, best-case scenario, he allows the testimony and the prosecutor doesn't bother to appeal if he loses."

Heather rolled her eyes. "None of this is sounding appealing to me. What else we got?"

"Your testimony," I said. "We got nothing else, so you gotta be convincing."

"Of course I'm gonna to be convincing," she said. "I'm telling the truth, so I'm gonna be convincing."

Heather and I had gone over her testimony, in depth, the night before. I not only peppered her with my own questions, but I also played the part of the prosecutor, and I came at her with all my firepower. I couldn't shake her, so I was encouraged by that.

In the end, that was all we had – Heather and the truth. The truth and Heather. The prosecutor would try to nail her on the butcher knife, and she'd have to admit she had no idea what happened to it. That was where our case would fall apart, no doubt. But I had long ago decided that this case would be a long shot. I could only hope that, if we lost, I could win over the judge on sentencing. Maybe the prosecutor might be able to prove, beyond a reasonable doubt, that Heather killed her mother and didn't have justification for doing so, but the judge had wide discretion on sentencing and maybe, just maybe, I could put enough doubt in the judge's mind about what really happened, and that would mean he'd go easy on Heather in sentencing her.

That was another reason why I wanted the judge to at least be aware of my theory on what happened. Even if the jury couldn't hear the testimony of the church-goers who were willing to talk on the record, or of the reverend, perhaps I could put the seed in the mind of the judge that this was happening.

Heather looked down at her hands. "I got my nails done," she said. "Professionally."

"They look very nice."

"I guess." She looked out the window of the car. "It'll be fall soon," she said. "My favorite time of year." Her voice cracked, and I knew what she was thinking.

"You'll get to enjoy autumn," I said. "We'll win this." I didn't know why I was being so positive with Heather, because, usually, I was realistic. And realism would dictate I tell her she had less than a 10% chance of actually enjoying autumn.

"You think?" Her face looked hopeful, perhaps for the first time in months, and it broke my heart.

"I do." I put my hand on her shoulder. "We're here," I said. "At the courthouse."

"So we are."

We got out of the car, and I noticed the irony of the beauty of the weather, which was contrasted with the overall feeling of doom Heather and I shared. September was, in general, one of my favorite times of the year in Kansas City. Aside from the days that were considered to be "Indian Summer," which was marked by super hot days for long stretches, the weather was beautiful and marked by temperatures in the 70s and 80s. I yearned for the next month, October, when the leaves started to change into their brilliant red and orange and yellow hues and the crisp air would smell of leaves and bonfires.

Heather walked slowly, very slowly, up the sidewalk with

me. It was almost as if she were trying to delay the inevitable, which I assumed she was. I put my arm around her and she hung her head. She looked at me and I could see tears forming.

"It's going to be okay," I whispered. "Somehow, we're going to pull a rabbit out of the hat. If anybody can do that, it would be me. Remember that. I've won unwinnable cases before, and I can do it again. Trust me."

In a way, I was kicking myself for giving her false hopes. On the other hand, I needed her to hold her head high and show her sparkling personality to the jury. She was all I had in this case thus far, so I had to keep her spirits up enough that she could show the jury she was an honest person. I couldn't allow her to show the jury her snarly, bratty side. That would be death for sure.

I knew the snarkiness was simply her defense, her armor, her mask. She had been through so much in her life, and nobody had ever shown her any kindness. She was very hurt underneath all the bravado. The bravado was what would kill her on the stand, so I had to break through that.

We went through the doors and found the elevator. The courthouse in downtown Kansas City was in the Art Deco style so popular in the 1930s. It was around 20 stories tall and was built in stone. The floors were marble, and, because it was early, the foyer wasn't completely packed, but there were a fair number of lawyers and their clients standing around the elevators. There were lawyers with files so large they had to haul them on wheels, and others who were carrying briefcases.

In my case, because Heather's murder trial didn't turn on complex issues, I merely carried her file in my leather satchel. I had some witness statements in the file, but that was about it. The people I found from the church weren't willing to testify on the record, and I didn't have enough to show they were relevant enough for a subpoena, so I simply interviewed them and put them on the witness list. If the judge miraculously admitted their testimony in front of the jury, I could go ahead and subpoena them for trial. I wasn't expecting much there, however.

We got on the elevator and it slowly climbed to the fifth floor, which was where our courtroom was. I grabbed Heather's wrist, because I could see her shaking and I nodded to her. "Take a deep breath," I said. "Just remember – you have to get on the stand and tell the truth. Just tell the truth, and we have a chance."

The door dinged and we got out and walked into the courtroom. Vince was there, along with his second chair, a female DA named Rachel Morgan. She was a very pretty blonde with bright blue eyes and seemed to stay in top shape. She was wearing a light purple suit with matching pumps and her hair was up in a bun. I didn't know what role she would take – the second chair typically doesn't do much, but sometimes they take some of the witnesses. Rachel would be an attractive person to the jury. She was pretty, but not stunningly so, which made her accessible. She also had a soft southern voice, as she was from South Carolina, which also appealed to the jury, especially around these parts. I found that people in Kansas City tended to be conservative, and Rachel would appeal to them much more than Heather would.

As for Vince, it was more hit or miss with him. He was aggressive and tall and spoke with authority. He had a tendency to grandstand, which was persuasive for some, a turn-off for others. Personally, I found his demeanor in court to be off-putting. He came across like a bully, and I thought Vince might've lost winnable cases because of this.

I sat down at the table, putting my briefcase down, and motioned to Heather. "Go ahead and take your seat," I said.

"Now, Harper," Vince said. "Are you still trying to

convince the judge to let evidence in about your cock-eyed theory about the murdering reverend?"

"You know I am," I said. "It's all I got. And it's not cock-eyed. For your information, Agent Axel Springer has been investigating this church himself."

"I'm aware of that. From what I understand, they're ready to make some arrests there. But you know the rules of evidence as well as I do, and you won't get this defense in front of a jury. What are we even doing here? Let's just pick a jury and get the show on the road. Let's not go through this motion *in limine* nonsense. We should just stipulate you won't use that church as your defense and get moving on this."

I crossed my arms in front of me. "Nice try. I have to at least ask the judge if he'll let me use the church as a defense. You're not giving me anything to give it up." I raised my eyebrow. "Give me something in exchange for my stipulation, and I'll ask my client about it. Otherwise, we're going forward."

Vince shook his head. "Your position isn't strong enough for me to give you anything. Sorry, Harper. I just thought I'd appeal to your desire to have an expedited trial, along with your acknowledgement of reality, which is that your case is a dead dog loser, and we'd go on."

"You thought wrong." Truth be told, if Vince gave me something in exchange for my stipulation, I probably would've gone forward. I knew he was right – the judge would rule against me. But I wouldn't give it up for nothing. He should know that.

"Can we at least stipulate your client killed Ms. Morrison?" he asked. "Or will you make me work for that as well?"

"What do you think? Again, if you're willing to give me something, I might stipulate to that. Otherwise, forget it. At this point, you'll have to show the jury my client did it." That was one strategy I had up my sleeve – make the prosecutor work to show my client was the one who killed her mother. Then, if I saw he didn't do a good job in showing this, I'd gamble on not putting Heather on the stand at all. That would be a huge gamble, but that would present a better chance for her acquittal than trying to argue self-defense in a case where there isn't a butcher knife to show her mother was trying to kill her.

Vince sighed. "You're going to make me work for it. You're still going to do SODDI possibly?"

"All options are on the table. Give me something and I'll maybe change my mind. And it's gotta be good. Really good, or it's a no-go."

He narrowed his eyes and then shook his head. "No. This case is too air-tight for me. I'll put on my case and you put on yours."

"I knew you'd say that."

At that, the judge came into the room. "Remain seated," he said as he took his own seat. "Okay, Vince and Harper, come on up."

We walked up to the bench, my heart pounding out of my chest. Trials always made me nervous. Always, always, always. There was so much at stake in any trial, so they were necessarily nerve-wracking. But today's trial had me freaked out. I couldn't lose, yet it looked inevitable.

"Where are we?" Judge Reiner asked as he put a stick of gum in his mouth. "I'm trying to quit smoking," he explained with a grin. "And chewing."

I nodded and looked at my shaking hand. Ordinarily, I kinda liked the banter with the different judges. But at the moment, I was completely in my head.

"We still need to do our motions *in limine*," Vince said. "Specifically, Harper needs to determine if her witnesses will be admissible."

"Okay then," the judge said. "Let's do it and get this show

on the road." He examined the motion I made with regards to the witnesses I'd lined up from the church. They were all subpoenaed and were all terrified of testifying. I didn't blame them, but I knew it was necessary. I only had two people willing to put their necks on the line, both former church members who'd left because they didn't like the message being put out by the reverend. Unfortunately, they didn't have first-hand knowledge of the reverend ordering church members to kill their children – they only heard this from other people. It was a mere rumor. For that reason alone, I was limited on to how much I could ask them on the stand, but I wanted to at least get the information out there.

"Ms. Ross," Judge Reiner said. "I've read your motion before, I just wanted to review it. Now, as I understand it, you're trying to get in evidence about a church where the victim went. Your theory of the case, as I understand it, is that the reverend in this church has been encouraging or ordering parents in his church to kill their gay and trans children. You want to put witnesses on the stand who will testify to this, and you've also subpoenaed the reverend of this church, and this reverend is supposed to testify he's been doing this. Do I have this right?"

"You do. They're all on my witness list. I can give you a list of the questions I'll ask these potential witnesses if you like."

Judge Reiner sighed. "There's no way I can possibly allow this. I might possibly allow the testimony of the reverend, but only if that testimony goes to whether or not the reverend personally influenced Ms. Morrison. You'd have to extract testimony from him that would demonstrate to me and the jury that he told Ms. Morrison to kill your client." He narrowed his eyes and stared at me. "And something tells me he won't do that. As to your other witnesses on this list, if they can't testify they personally asked Ms. Morrison to kill your client, their testimony isn't relevant. I don't care if that reverend asked them to personally kill their own children, it's not relevant to your case."

He leaned back and crossed his arms. "So there you have it. You may call the reverend, but the only testimony I'll deem relevant from him is that he personally told Ms. Morrison she must kill her child. You cannot elicit testimony from him that he's anti-gay or anti-trans, or that he has a philosophy that gay or trans kids must be killed, which, I notice, is a large part of your rationale here in calling the reverend. He must testify that he personally told Ms. Morrison to kill your client. I won't tolerate a fishing expedition on this, so you'll be walking a very fine line. If you go outside those parameters, I'll call a mistrial, and I won't be happy. Fair warning."

I looked back at Heather, who was listening to every word.

"I understand," I said. "Thank you, your honor." This was better than nothing, but not really. I had about a snowball's chance in hell that the reverend would admit to telling Connie to kill Heather. That would set him up for criminal charges for sure, and, with Axel investigating him and his church, that would send him to prison for life.

"Is there anything else I need to know about ahead of trial?" the judge asked.

"No, your honor, but I reserve the right to ask for a future Motion *in limine* if something else comes up."

"Mr. Malloy, do you have any Motion *in limines* for me?"

"No, your honor, but, as with Ms. Ross, I reserve the right to ask for a future one if something else comes up."

"Okay, then," he said. "Let's take a break until 1:30, I'll bring in the panel, and we'll pick a jury." At that, Judge Reiner got up and went back to his chambers.

"You gonna call that reverend?" Vince asked me as he looked over the witness list I had provided him.

"I will," I said. "He's under subpoena."

Vince shook his head. "If that's all you got..." He looked pityingly at me. "Why are we even here?"

"You know why."

"Yeah, the plea blew up. Listen, I don't want to tell you how to do your job, but, come on. This was a dog case for you from the word go. You're wasting everyone's time and the taxpayer's money on this."

I raised my eyebrow at him. "You don't tell me how to do my job and I won't tell you how to do yours. Sorry the taxpayers have to pay for you to do your job, but that's just the way it goes sometimes, isn't it?"

I went over to Heather. "We're free until the afternoon. Let's go across the street and get a bite."

She stood up and glared at Vince. "What's his problem?"

"He's lazy and doesn't like to try cases. He likes to plea them all out because it takes him five minutes, and trials take hours and days to prepare and days in court. They're stressful, too." I gathered my briefcase and beckoned Heather. "Come on, we're going to need some sustenance for this."

I didn't mind picking a jury, although that was pretty stressful as well. I knew the importance of getting the right jury – in law school, I was shown a film portraying two different juries hearing the exact same case. Same set of facts, same lawyers arguing the case, everything just the same. It was a civil case, and one of the juries found for the plaintiff and awarded the plaintiff $9 million. The other jury found for the defendant, and the plaintiff got bupkis. Nada. Nothing at all.

We headed across the street to the little bar and grill that everyone frequented during the day. It was early yet, only 10:30, so it wasn't all that crowded. I flagged down a waitress and ordered scrambled eggs and hashbrowns. "And what would you like?" I asked Heather, who was staring at her menu.

She shrugged. "Just a cup of coffee."

I raised my eyebrow. "You need to eat," I said. "And I'm buying."

"Some biscuits and gravy." She handed the menu back to the waitress. "This is a cute place," she said, looking around.

"It is, and they have pretty good food here, too."

The coffee came and Heather slowly sipped it. It was like she was savoring it, like this would be her last cup of coffee. I could tell that's what she was thinking – she'd never drink coffee again after today. Which was wrong, even if we lost – the trial would last at least two days. Vince had a full roster of witnesses ready to go – the cops on the scene, the person who heard the fight, yet didn't report anything amiss until the next day. He also had a forensic expert who would testify the knife recovered from Heather's possession had only her fingerprints on it. And, for good measure, he was bringing in witnesses from Connie's past, witnesses who were going to testify that Heather and Connie didn't get along, and somebody who would testify that Connie had taken out a life insurance policy.

As for me, well, I had Heather herself and, possibly, the crazy reverend. I was still debating whether to call him, but I thought he might be a good witness for me. If nothing else, he might start spouting off his nonsense about how gays and trans are a product of the Devil, and that might engender some sympathy for my client.

I still had one more witness on my list, a witness that I was prepared to call, if I could miraculously find her.

That other witness was Louisa.

FORTY-TWO

Jury selection took the rest of day one. The next day was time for opening statements. Heather was dressed in another conservative suit, this one in navy with white piping and matching pumps – her pumps were off-white and navy blue, which was the opposite of her suit, which was mainly navy with white accents. She also wore a turtle neck and pearls, and a colorful scarf held back her hair, which was growing out and carefully straightened with a flat-iron. Her makeup was subtle – just foundation, a bit of coral lip gloss and some neutral eye shadow and mascara.

"Ladies and gentlemen of the jury," Vince said, rising from his seat and walking over to the jury box. He walked to one side of the jury and then stopped and put his hands on the rail that separated him from the jury. "On the night of June 19, 2016, a woman died in a brutal way. Her name was Connie Morrison, and she was a mother. A very loving mother. The evidence will show that, on June 19, 2016, Ms. Morrison got into a fight with the defendant, Heath Morrison, who was the victim's son. The evidence will also show that the two had many brutal fights about Heath Morrison's desire to be known as Heather Morrison, which is why he is dressed in the manner he is dressed today. I will also provide evidence that the victim, Connie Morrison, had a life insurance policy of $250,000, and I will call witnesses that will testify that the defendant was aware of the existence of this life insurance policy. Finally, the evidence will show the defendant killed Ms. Morrison in a brutal, degrading way, by stabbing her in the neck with a pocket knife. Ms. Morrison was then left to drown in a pool of her own blood."

While Vince was speaking, he was slowly walking along the rail that separated him from the jury, and looking every juror in the eye. I had to admit, he had this whole act down.

Vince sat down, and Judge Reiner addressed me. "Ms. Ross," he said.

"I'd like to waive my opening statement," I said, standing up. This was strategy on my part, and I had explained it to Heather. I think she understood. At least, I hoped shfe did.

My rationale in not making an opening statement was that I wanted to see if Vince could make his case. His burden of proof. If he couldn't prove Heather killed her mother, then I might, just might, get an acquittal. It would be a gamble, a huge gamble, but if I thought that Vince wasn't convincing the jury that Heather was the killer, then I would simply not call Heather to the stand and hope the jury would acquit her if Vince couldn't show, beyond a reasonable doubt, that she did it. I thought this was a much better strategy than announcing to the jury I was going for self-defense, then seeing it all fall apart when the issue of the missing butcher knife inevitably came up. In fact, that might be my only shot. It was a Hail Mary for sure, but a Hail Mary was better than nothing at all.

"Call your first witness," Judge Reiner said to Vince.

I put my hand on Heather's as Vince approached the

witness stand and called the name of Officer James Hamm. Officer Hamm, along with his partner, Sam Woo, were the first officers on the scene. He was sworn in, and Vince went through the usual first questions – his name, his rank, why he was called to the scene and what he found there.

"I found the victim lying in the kitchen, in a pool of her own blood," he said.

"I would like to show the jury pictures of the crime scene," Vince said.

I stood up. "Objection. These pictures are prejudicial and do not have probative value. I think we can all agree that Connie was killed by slicing her jugular vein, so these pictures will be unduly gruesome. I would also like to object to lack of foundation." I glared at Vince, who I felt was grandstanding as usual. It would be just like him to show Connie with blood everywhere, and I, quite frankly, didn't see the point in showing the jury the pictures. I had no idea what showing the pictures would prove.

The judge seemed to contemplate my objection, and then banged his gavel. "Overruled. Mr. Malloy, you may proceed. Just make sure you properly lay the foundation."

I rolled my eyes as Vince dramatically brought out huge pictures of Connie, who was splayed on the kitchen floor. Her right arm was perfectly straight, while her left arm was on her side. Her legs were apart, and her head was turned to the left side. And, of course, there was blood everywhere. It soaked her dress, which was unfortunately white, so it showed the blood unduly well, and, all around her body, was oceans of blood. Her tongue was sticking out of her mouth and her eyes were wide open.

Vince paced the floor, looking at the jury's reactions to the photograph. He seemed pleased, because every member of the jury, save one or two, were horrified by what they saw. One girl had her hand over her mouth and was shaking her head. Another lady looked at the picture for a few seconds, and then covered her eyes. Three other women were looking at the pictures and then glanced at each other, a look of horror in their eyes. The men tried to pretend that they weren't affected, but I could see in their eyes that they, too, were sickened by what they were seeing in that picture.

"Now, Officer Hamm," he began. "Does this photograph accurately depict the scene you walked into on the day of June 19?"

"Yes."

"And you in fact took this photograph, am I correct?"

"Yes."

"Tell the jury how you developed this photograph."

"The photograph was taken with a digital camera, and was developed by the photograph was developed on-site."

"It was developed on-site? Clarify, please."

"The Kansas City Police Department maintains a photo developing lab, and the pictures were developed in this lab."

"Who else has had access to these particular series of pictures, other than yourself?"

"Just me. It's the policy of our department that only one person has custody over the photographs taken at the scene."

"So there's not a possibility that somebody else might have somehow tampered with this photograph, isn't that correct?"

"That is correct."

The foundation laid, Vince went into the heart of the matter. "I notice that, in this photograph, there's not a butcher knife in the vicinity. Is this accurate?"

"Right. There wasn't a knife anywhere near the body."

"So this photograph is accurate in that it doesn't show a butcher knife?"

"Objection," I said. "Asked and answered."

"Sustained."

I scribbled on my yellow pad, furious at how Vince was playing up these photographs. I stood up again. "I would like to renew my objections to Mr. Malloy showing these inflammatory photographs," I said. "And I would respectfully ask the court to instruct Mr. Malloy to move on." I sat back down and scribbled more on my pad.

"I agree with Ms. Ross," Judge Reiner said. "I think the jury gets the point."

Vince nodded and took the pictures off the easel and put them in a canvas folder carefully.

"Now, let's back up just a little. Who contacted your division about this incident?"

"We received a phone call from one Olivia Davidson. I notice she's on your witness list. She was worried because she had heard a loud fight that night. She was a friend of Ms. Morrison's and a neighbor. She relayed that she went to the house to check on Ms. Morrison the day after she heard the fight, and nobody answered the door. She then called our office, not using 911, but called on the regular line, to ask that we do a welfare check. We followed up on her phone call and went to check on Ms. Morrison. We knocked on her door, and she did not answer. We then got a warrant to enter her premises, and we entered."

"On what basis did you obtain a warrant to enter her premises?"

"On the basis of what Ms. Davidson said about the fight, and the fact that she tried to contact Ms. Morrison and failed. Her statement plus the fact that Ms. Morrison was non-responsive when Ms. Davidson attempted to contact her formed the basis for our search warrant."

"Thank you," Vince said. "I have nothing further."

I rose and went over to the officer on the stand. "Officer

Hamm," I began. "You stated that you entered the house because Ms. Davidson called your office and told you that she was worried about Ms. Morrison. She said that she heard the two fighting in the kitchen. Did she explain to you how she could hear the fight?"

"Yes, ma'am. She said she was walking her dog by the house, and the window was open, so she heard them fighting."

I knew there was a hole in her story right then, but I would have to wait until Olivia Davidson herself was called. She was second on the witness list, so I would have to hold my next questions until then.

"I have nothing further," I said, and then went to take my seat next to Heather.

"What the fuck," Heather whispered. "Why didn't you ask more questions?"

I shook my head and wrote down on the pad of paper. *I don't want to press him more because I want the jury to maybe "forget" there wasn't a butcher knife found at the scene. Besides, I need to press Olivia further. She's key in this.*

I knew this was a long-shot, but maybe if Olivia could be broken down, it would put some doubt in the jury's mind. I therefore looked forward to Olivia getting on the stand, so I wanted her on the stand as soon as possible. That was another reason why I didn't necessarily want to question the cop more.

"Call your next witness," Judge Reiner said, looking and sounding bored. I wondered how judges did it day after day, really – hearing boring testimony for hours on end and somehow managing not to fall asleep. When I was a baby lawyer working for the Public Defender's Office, I had to sit through depositions where I didn't do much but observe, and I was the second chair on trials where I didn't do much but take notes. I always found it almost impossible to keep my eyes open during these events. I therefore had sympathy for judges who had to listen to testimony that was boring as hell.

"I would like to call Olivia Davidson to the stand," Vince said.

Olivia Davidson was called to the stand. She was an older lady, around 70ish, with bottle-dyed red hair she kept up in a bun. She was wearing a turquoise sweater set with black pants and black boots. She also wore large glasses and little makeup.

She raised her hand and was sworn in.

"Could you please state your name for the record," Vince said.

"Olivia Davidson."

"Ms. Davidson, what relation do you have to the deceased, Connie Morrison?"

"She was my neighbor."

"Your next-door neighbor?"

"Yes." She nodded. Her words were carefully pronounced, as if she was deathly afraid to say something wrong. She also seemed as if she was determined to only answer the question asked – she wasn't one to go off on a tangent. I made notes about all of this as she spoke.

"Now, Ms. Davidson, tell the court what you were doing the evening of June 19 of this year."

"Objection," I said as I stood up. "Calls for a narrative."

"Sustained. Mr. Malloy, please narrow the scope of your question." Judge Reiner continued to look bored. He brought out a pitcher and poured himself a glass of water as he fidgeted in his seat.

I raised my eyebrow and crossed my arms in front of me as I smirked at Vince. I really didn't care that he asked such an open-ended question, but I wanted to throw him off-balance. That was one of my strategies.

"Okay. During the evening of June 19, at around 7:30 PM, what activity were you engaging in?"

"Walking my dog, Henry."

I had to suppress a smile at the fact that her dog's name was Henry. That was a human name to me, not a dog's name.

"You were walking your dog," he said. "What did you hear when you passed by Connie Morrison's house that evening?"

"I heard lots of hollering," she said. "Between Connie and her son, Heath." She glared right at Heather. "He thinks he's a woman, but we all know he's not."

"Motion to strike," I said, standing up. "Whether or not Ms. Davidson believes my client to be a man or a woman isn't relevant to the case at hand."

"Motion sustained. Ms. Davidson, please answer only the question asked and do not make comments that aren't relevant. You've been warned."

Olivia sneered, sat back in her chair and crossed her arms as she glared right at Heather.

"Okay," Vince said. "Did you hear what they were arguing about?"

"Yes. I heard Connie tell Heath that he's sick and demented and has the Devil in him. I can't say I can argue with that."

"Objection," I said.

"Sustained. Ms. Davidson, please do not add your opinions and only stick to the questions at hand. This is another warning."

She shook her head, evidently ready to explode.

"How long did you stand outside the window and hear this argument?"

"About five minutes. I heard Heath screaming and hollering, and I walked away while they were yelling at each other."

"You walked away," Vince said. "And what did you do the next day?"

"I went by there. I baked some brownies for Connie and I wanted to share them with her."

"What happened when you went by there?"

"I knocked and knocked and knocked."

"Did anybody answer the door?"

"No."

"Did you find it peculiar she wasn't at home at that time?"

"Yes."

"And why was this?"

"She didn't work. Her car was in the driveway. She didn't take walks around the block like I do. She should've been home."

"And what did you do next?"

"I called the police."

"Did you follow up with the police later on that day?"

"Yes. I called them and found out what happened." She shook her head and glared at Heather. "She was one of my best friends."

"I have nothing further."

Vince took a seat and I stood up and approached Olivia. "Ms. Davidson, you told the court you were walking your dog when you heard arguing, correct?"

"Yes," she said, glaring at me. If I could read her thoughts, I'd probably see she hated me almost as much as my client. After all, I was trying to get Heather off, so that made me the enemy too.

"You were walking your dog on the sidewalk, then, in front of the house?"

"Yes."

It was time for me to bring out a picture of my own. "Here's a picture of Ms. Morrison's house," I said, showing the jury. "As you can see, the house sits on a hill, away from the sidewalk. The sidewalk is down below, at the bottom of this bank."

"Objection," Vince said. "Lack of foundation."

"I'll put my client on the stand to testify this picture accurately depicts the house she lived in with Ms. Morrison," I said. "If need be."

The judge looked like he couldn't care less, but he did ask me to come up and let him take a look at the picture himself.

"Let's see," he said. "The street sign is in the picture here, and the picture shows the address of the house, and it seems to match up to the address of the house Ms. Morrison lived in. Lay the proper foundation, Ms. Ross, and I'll allow it."

"Thank you your honor."

"I'm terribly sorry, Ms. Davidson, but I'd like to ask if you could kindly step down for a few minutes. I need to call my client briefly to the stand."

Olivia looked perplexed, but Vince nodded, so she obediently stood up and walked out of the courtroom while I called Heather. That was another thing about the witnesses - they couldn't be present in the courtroom when there was testimony happening.

"Please state your name for the record," I said to Heather.

"Heather, I mean Heath Morrison," Heather said, her right hand raised. She looked terrified. I hoped and prayed I wouldn't have to call her to the stand for extended testimony.

"Ms. Morrison, I'd like to show you some pictures." I held up the pictures of her old house. "Is this a picture of the house you shared with your mother, the deceased Connie Morrison?"

"Yes."

"And is this picture an accurate picture of the house where your mother was found dead on or around June 20?"

"Yes."

"I have nothing further."

"Mr. Malloy," Judge Reiner said. "Do you have any questions for this witness?"

"No, your honor."

"You may step down," Judge Reiner said. "And Ms. Ross may recall Ms. Davidson to the stand."

I got the bailiff, who went out to retrieve Olivia to come back up to the witness stand, and she did, walking unsurely and looking hopelessly at Vince. It seemed as if she had no desire to come back on the stand - not that I blamed her.

"Okay," I said. "I just established that this is a picture of the house where the deceased lived with my client, Heath Morrison. Now, you were walking your dog on this sidewalk, is that correct?" I pointed to the sidewalk that was a good fifty feet away from the house and at the bottom of a steep bank.

"Yes, that's correct."

"And the windows were open, that is your testimony?"

"Right."

I narrowed my eyes. "Have you visited Connie Morrison in her home prior to June 20?"

"Yes, I have."

"And does she have central air conditioning?"

"Yes."

"Describe the day," I said. "It's June, the middle of summer. What was the weather like that day?" I would try to poke holes in whether or not the window really was open. If it was rainy, then the windows might have been open, but if it was sunny, then probably not. Not in the middle of June. In fact, I had a weather report for that day ready to be entered into evidence if Olivia couldn't remember how hot that day was. The weather report said the temperature was 101 degrees.

"I don't remember."

"What time was it that you walked your dog by the window?"

"It was around 2 PM. I usually walk my dog around that time, because it's my break time from work."

"2 PM on June 19. And the deceased had central air conditioning." I shook my head. "Your honor, I would like to enter into evidence a report on the weather on this day."

"Objection," Vince said, standing up. "Lack of foundation."

"Wait just a minute," the judge said. "If I can independently establish what the temperature was that day, then I'll allow the weather report to come in. So, let me see..." He brought out his smart phone and looked at it, scrolling through with his fingers. He finally nodded. "Okay, Ms. Ross, go ahead."

"Your honor," Vince said. "I would like to renew my objection until I have a chance to also independently verify this information."

The judge rolled his eyes. "You're not going to take my word for it, huh? Well, come on up. You too, Ms. Ross."

We both went to the bench. "Here," Judge Reiner said, handing us both his iPhone. "Here's the weather app, and, Mr. Malloy, here's what it says."

Vince took a look at the app, and then handed me the phone. As my weather report indicated, on that day it was over 100 degrees at 2 PM in Kansas City.

"That doesn't mean it was the same weather everywhere in the Kansas City area. That weather is only for downtown."

"I'll allow it," Judge Reiner said. "Ms. Ross, go ahead and enter your weather report into evidence."

I had the weather report marked "Exhibit A," and I passed it along to the jury. "As you can see, at 2 PM on June 19, it was 101 degrees," I said to them.

They all had a chance to examine it and then I went back over to Olivia. "So, your testimony, again, is that you passed by an open window in the kitchen and you heard my client fighting with Ms. Morrison. Yet you also acknowledge Ms. Morrison has central air conditioning."

"Right."

"I would like to remind you that you are under oath. Now, are you positive the kitchen window was open?"

She shifted uncomfortably in her seat. "Well, I..."

It was time to strike. "Isn't it true that you didn't hear any such fight?"

"Of course I did. I called the police, why would I call the police if I didn't hear the fight?"

"Perhaps because you went to her house the next day, saw her car was in the driveway, and she didn't answer the door. Isn't it true you didn't really hear a fight, but you made up that story to the police to sound credible?" I had no idea if this theory was correct, but it sounded like a good one.

"No, I-"

"May I remind you what the penalty is for perjury?"

"Objection, Ms. Ross is badgering the witness."

"Sustained. Move on, Ms. Ross."

"May I remind you you're under oath?" That was a slightly different way of phrasing the previous question, one that was acceptable, because it wasn't really a threat.

She finally sighed. "Yes. Okay. I didn't actually hear a fight. I was concerned the next day because Connie's car was in the driveway and she didn't answer the door when I went there with my treats. I knew she didn't take walks like I do, and I also knew she was having trouble with Heath. My mind tends to jump to conclusions."

I raised an eyebrow. "Nothing further."

I went back to my table, feeling like goddamned Perry Mason.

The case was still a long-shot, but it was looking slightly better.

Vince was glaring at me from his own table, and I knew I had scored a point. A small point, maybe, but every point counted.

"Please call your next witness, Mr. Malloy."

"I would like to call Jacob Weismann to the stand, please."

I scribbled, knowing Jacob would testify to the existence of a life insurance policy. It was fine that he put the policy into evidence, but it would be more than tricky for Vince to prove Heather knew about it. The second he tried to ask any questions about what Connie might have told Jacob, I would object to the hearsay, and hopefully, that would be that.

Vince swore in Jacob, and then asked him to state his name.

"Jacob Weismann."

"And Mr. Weismann, you are an agent with Mutual of Omaha, is that correct?"

"Yes."

"Was the deceased, Connie Morrison, a client of yours?"

"She was."

"Did you sell her a life insurance policy?"

"I did."

"I would like to show you the document I have marked Exhibit B. Can you please identify this for me?" Vince handed Jacob a document and Jacob studied it intently.

"Yes. This a copy of the life insurance policy I wrote up for Ms. Morrison."

"For how much is the life insurance policy?"

"Two hundred and fifty thousand dollars."

"And did you keep this record in the ordinary course of business?"

"I did."

"And is drawing up documents, such as this one, part of your regular routine in your business?"

"It is."

"Can you tell the court who the beneficiary of this policy is?"

"Heath Morrison."

At that, Vince started to pace around a little bit. "Heath Morrison. Are you familiar with who Heath Morrison is?"

"Yes. I guess that was her son, although I've never met him."

Vince put his hand to his mouth, as if he was contemplating something serious. "Her son. Now, to your knowledge, did Heath Morrison ever come to know there was a life insurance policy and he was the beneficiary of it?"

"Objection," I said, rising to my feet. "This question calls for hearsay." There was no way I would let Jacob answer that question, so pre-emptively objecting was the best way to keep it from coming out.

"Sounds like we need to have a talk," the judge said. "Mr. Weismann, you are temporarily excused. I'd also like to ask the jury to take a short recess. Mr. Weismann, you will be expected back on the witness stand in fifteen minutes, so please don't stray far."

The jury obediently filed out of the room, as did Jacob. When everybody was out of earshot, Judge Reiner said to Vince. "Okay, Mr. Malloy, let me have it. What questions were you going to ask your witness? If there's going to be anything on the record about any conversations Connie Morrison had with Heath Morrison, then I shouldn't have to remind you that you can't do that." Judge Reiner reached for his Tums and stuffed about five of them in his mouth and shook his head.

"Actually, your honor, I was about to ask the witness about conversations he had with the defendant."

"What conversations?" Judge Reiner asked. "He just said he's never met the defendant."

"Mr. Weismann had phone conversations with the defendant," Vince said, looking at Heather, who was shaking her head. "Explaining the terms of the life insurance policy."

I mentally kicked myself for not scheduling a deposition with this guy, and I was mentally skewering Heather. She didn't tell me anything about this. In fact, she lied to me about it. When I directly asked her if she knew Connie had a life insurance policy, she told me no. I looked over at Heather, who was now looking embarrassed.

"Did you know about this?" I whispered to her.

She shook her head, but I could see, once again, she was lying.

I bit my lower lip, suddenly infuriated at being blind-sided.

"Your honor," I said. "I'd like to have a short conference with my client. If it pleases the court, I'd like to go into one of the conference rooms."

"Make it quick," Judge Reiner said. "I got the jury standing by and Mr. Weismann cooling his jets out in the hallway. We all want to continue on down the road."

"I understand."

I stood up, and Heather reluctantly followed me.

We got into the room, and I closed the door. "Sit down," I said, feeling my anger boiling up. "Okay," I said, trying to be measured in my speech, but feeling like I was ready to explode. "What the hell is going on? Why did you lie about the life insurance policy?"

Heather got into her defensive posture. She crossed her arms, glared at me and pursed her lips.

"You need to answer me, and you need to do it quick." I counted to ten, a technique I used with Rina when she was driving me batty. I could feel the tendrils of anxiety bubbling up, and I mentally tried to fight it down. *Think happy thoughts, think happy thoughts.*

This case is over, and Heather beat it down. That was the

happiest thought I could imagine, but somehow it wasn't really coming to me. They were just words.

"I didn't tell you because I knew you would judge me. You would dump me and I couldn't have that." Heather looked out the window, her eyes refusing to meet mine.

"Is that the truth? Is it? I can't believe you lied to me." If she was lying about this, was she lying about everything else? What if I was being played all along? A sickening feeling started in my gut, a feeling that Vince might be right. I might have been representing a guy like John Robinson all along. I felt naïve, a feeling I wasn't used to, but it was inescapable. First John, now Heather. If Heather was a cold-blooded killer, and I foolishly fell into her trap, could I ever trust my judgment again? When it happened back to back, John then Heather?

No fucking butcher knife at the scene. Heather knew all along about the life insurance policy. What fresh hell would I find out with the next witness?

"Okay," I said. "Well, we can't drag this out. The judge said to make it quick, so let's get out there. I'll do my best to try to contain the damage, but goddammit, Heather. Goddammit, if I get one more blind-side, I swear to God, I'll withdraw from your case. Right in the middle of trial." That was a threat, but I knew it wasn't a good one. The judge would never allow that. But I was so angry at that point, I wanted to put that fear into Heather. Put the anxiety into her for a little while.

Heather sneered at me, stood up, and walked rapidly out of the room. I put my hands on my table and hung my head. *What have I gotten myself into?* I cursed Heather for lying to me and Tammy for foisting Heather on me without my knowledge or consent.

Most of all, though, I cursed myself. I didn't do my due diligence, and I was being blind-sided. I had it coming. I would have to soldier on.

I walked back out into the courtroom, feeling that I was needing a drink. It was the first time I had a craving like that in a long time. I closed my eyes, trying to tamp that feeling down, but I couldn't. I'd have to do something after this day of trial, something to get rid of my nervous energy and agitation. Maybe get Red Dawn out, my red road bike, and go on a group ride through town. That was what I used to do, and I had gotten out of it for quite awhile.

"Okay," Judge Reiner said when everyone was back, and Jacob was back behind the witness stand. "Thank you ladies and gentlemen of the jury for your patience. Mr. Weismann, I remind you that you're still under oath. Mr. Malloy, you may proceed."

"Thank you, your honor. Now, Mr. Weismann, the question I posed to you before the break was whether or not the defendant, Mr. Morrison, was aware of the existence of the life insurance policy?"

"Yes, he was"

"How was he made aware?"

Jacob cleared his throat. "After Ms. Connie Morrison saw me in my office, and we drew up paperwork, she asked me to call Mr Morrison to explain the terms of the life insurance policy."

"Objection, hearsay," I said.

"Sustained."

"Could you please explain to the court, without mentioning anything that Ms. Morrison might have told you, how Mr. Morrison came to know about the life insurance policy?" Vince asked.

"Yes. I called him at his home and explained that Ms. Morrison had taken out a $250,000 life insurance policy and he was the beneficiary."

"Do you have any idea why Ms. Morrison would've taken out such a large life insurance policy?" Vince asked.

"Objection, calls for speculation," I said. "And possibly calls for hearsay."

The judge seemed to consider both objections. "I'll allow it," he said. "As long as the answer does not involve anything Ms. Morrison might have told this witness and as long as the answer is not based upon speculation. You may proceed, Mr. Weismann, on those grounds."

Jacob seemed unsure on how to answer this particular question. He then seemed to hit on a good answer. "When I spoke with Mr. Morrison, he mentioned that his father was killed and didn't have life insurance. I cannot speculate that this was the reason why Ms. Morrison took out this life insurance policy, however."

"I have nothing further for this witness."

I didn't really have good questions for this witness, either. It seemed like the damage was done, so no use trying to drag it out.

"I have nothing for this witness," I said, standing up.

"Call your next witness."

Over the course of the next few hours, Vince called witness after witness who were friends of Connie. They all told of a contentious relationship between Connie and Heather, centering around Heather's need to be referred to as Heather and to be treated like a woman. All of it was tricky for Vince to get into evidence, because they couldn't say what Connie had told them, but they were around when fights would break out, so they could give the court their impressions of the two women's relationship that way. I gamely tried to poke holes in each of their stories, but it was such a deluge, that, by the end of the day, I was exhausted.

A portrait of Heather was emerging through their testimony, that of an increasingly erratic person who was losing her mind.

"In one of the fights I witnessed," one woman, Candace Burrell, relayed, "Mr. Morrison screamed at Connie and took out a pair of scissors and chopped off his hair right in front of her. He chopped off his hair and waved it around in front of her face, screaming, 'are you happy now? Are you happy now? I look like a bleeping boy, is that what you want?'"

Another woman, Selma Harris, said she witnessed Heather shoving Connie to the floor. "They were screaming at each other, right in front of me, and he just shoved her like this," she said, putting her hands in front of her in a shoving motion.

Worse still were Heather's friends.

"Heather told me many times she wished her mother was dead," said one.

"Heather said she wanted to kill the old bag, and that's an actual quote," said another.

I couldn't believe all this crazy happened in front of these women and girls, but I couldn't shake any of them on cross-examination.

But the best was yet to come.

It was the end of the day, at least it was getting to be, for it was 4 PM, when Vince announced he would call the last witness for the day.

"I would like to call Reverend John Scott."

FORTY-THREE

"Objection," I said, standing up. "Mr. Scott was on my witness list, not Mr. Malloy's. I would like to request a motion *in limine* on what Mr. Scott's testimony will be."

"Your honor," Vince said. "I have a right to call Mr. Scott, even though he doesn't appear on my witness list. I have a right to call him and treat him as hostile."

"Ms. Ross, what Mr. Malloy is saying is correct. He has a right to call one of your witnesses to the stand. Now, I don't want to go through the rigamarole of having the jury go out and come back at this late hour, so I'll just have to rule on this. Your objection is overruled, Ms. Ross."

I sat down, my heart pounding. This was vintage Vince, really, and I should've seen it coming. I should've seen that he'd do something to throw me off, and I walked right into his trap. I kicked myself inwardly as I studiously avoided Heather's face, which, I would imagine, was boring a hole into me.

I had no idea what Vince was doing with this. It was worse than any surprise witness. The only difference between what was happening with Reverend Scott and a surprise witness was that I couldn't avoid this. If Vince just sprung something on me out of the blue, some 11th hour witness, I could exclude that witness. On this, however, I'd have do the best I could.

The only thing I could think of was that Vince was cutting me off so I couldn't use this guy myself. I really didn't know how else he would be used.

I turned around, and there Reverend Scott was, looking even creepier than he did at the church, if that was even possible. He was now walking slowly with a cane and he had on a large wide-brimmed hat. He'd grown his hair out long and had pulled it into a pony-tail. He was wearing faded jeans and an even more faded button-down shirt. On his feet were Birkenstocks, which showed his long toenails. I started to feel personal revulsion just watching him, and I knew his testimony would bring up an even larger sense of disgust.

He took his seat on the witness stand, raised his right hand and was sworn in.

"Mr. Scott," Judge Reiner said. "Before you proceed, I would like to ask you to remove your hat. This is a courtroom and I demand decorum."

At that, Reverend Scott removed his hat, which didn't do much for him at all. He still looked like a crazy hippy, just slightly less-so. The ironic thing was this guy was no hippy – hippies would find his views on gays and women sickening. And as far as I knew, no hippies would be down with having gay and trans children killed just because of who they were.

"Could you please state your name for the record," Vince said.

"John Lewis Scott," he said.

"Mr. Scott, what is your profession?"

"I am a reverend. My congregation is the Church of the Living Breath."

"Was Ms. Morrison a member of your church?"

"Yes she was."

"Was she a faithful member of your church?"

"Yes she was."

Just then, I suddenly knew I had a different strategy. I could see a door opening, and I knew I could get my church witnesses on the stand after all. That was, if they were willing to come in. They were under subpoena, but my investigator was having problems locating them. They were terrified of testifying, and I knew that. But if I could find them, I could bring them in to impeach this reverend.

"What is the philosophy of your church?"

"We preach the gospel," he said. "We focus on the teachings of Christ. Our sermons focus on loving thy neighbor, turning the other cheek, and showing how the teachings of Christ can enrich our congregants' lives."

Funny, I don't remember Christ saying anything about killing gay people. I don't recall him saying anything about homosexuality at all, as a matter of fact.

"How long did Ms. Morrison attend your church?"

"She had been a member of our church for about three years."

I stood up. "I'd like to object to the relevance of this witness' testimony. Whether or not the deceased was religious is of no importance to this court." I sat down.

"Mr. Malloy, I'm inclined to agree with Ms. Ross. Where is this going?"

"Can I have a short conference?" Vince asked.

Judge Reiner rolled his eyes, but banged his gavel. "I'd like to excuse the jury for another ten-minute break. The witness may also be excused, but, please, Mr. Scott, stay close, because you might be finishing up on the stand. Thank you."

After everybody left, Judge Reiner addressed Vince. "I

should've done this first, I guess, but Ms. Ross makes a point. Where is this testimony with this reverend going?"

Vince cleared his throat. "It's a preemptive strike, your honor. Ms. Ross will attempt to show that Ms. Morrison was violent and brainwashed by this church, so I'll show the jury this church isn't about that. I've talked to this reverend, and he has assured me his church speaks the gospel and isn't about hate, unlike the portrayal Ms. Ross is planning on making."

I couldn't believe what I was hearing. And I really couldn't believe the judge would go along with this nonsense.

"Judge Reiner, I thought I made it clear to Mr. Malloy that I'll wait to see if he meets his burden of proof before I made my decision on how I wanted to proceed. If I see he didn't meet his burden that my client killed her mother, then I'll rest and not try for self-defense. That would mean I wouldn't put this reverend on the stand. I don't know why Mr. Malloy couldn't just wait to see if I called the reverend and then cross-examined him. That's how it normally goes. I've never heard of preemptive strikes like this before, and I ask that you not allow it."

Judge Reiner raised his eyebrow at me. "Ms. Ross, you're playing a game, as I see it. Everyone currently in this courtroom knows your client killed her mother, yet you're trying to play a game to see if you can prove to the jury that she didn't. That's your right, of course, because the prosecutor does have the burden of proof, but that doesn't make what you're doing any more above-board. Because you're playing a game, I'll let Mr. Malloy go ahead and play a game as well. Maybe it will force your hand. I don't know. I'll allow the questioning of this witness, but I have to warn you, Mr. Malloy, not to stray too much. My patience is wearing thin with every passing minute."

"Fine," I said. "Be careful what you wish for, Vince. That's all I'm saying."

Judge Reiner called everybody back, and the jury came back in and Reverend Scott walked slowly back to the stand.

"I'd like to remind you that you are still under oath," Judge Reiner said to the Reverend. "You may proceed, Mr. Malloy."

"Okay. Your church, Reverend Scott, preaches the gospel, right? Do your sermons ever devolve into what many would consider to be persecution against certain groups?"

"No. Our church only preaches peace and love and forgiveness. Our church believes everybody on this earth are God's children, and God loves everyone equally. Jesus was about love and forgiveness and non-judgment, and that's what our church stresses above everything else."

I watched the jury as they listened to this guy and saw them beaming and nodding along. I shook my head, seeing this reverend was spouting lies and getting away with it.

"Does your church counsel that women are lesser than men, and that they should stay with abusers if they are married to them?"

"Absolutely not. Women have full equality with men, and our church recognizes that. We would never counsel a woman to stay in an abusive situation."

"Does your church advocate that slavery is a good thing?"

"Absolutely not. Never. I told you, our church is only based upon the gospel. Christ was not in favor of slavery, he was in favor of equality, and he was in favor of loving thy neighbor and turning the other cheek. Those are the values we preach."

Vince nodded. "And Ms. Morrison was a member of your church, so she was absorbing all these lessons." Then he turned to look at me and Heather. "I have nothing further."

I scribbled on a yellow pad of paper, trying to figure out how to proceed with this guy. I could cross-examine him about all the things I heard him say in front of his congregants, but he would just lie and make me and Heather look bad. Unfortunately, he was an excellent liar. I could see on the faces of the jury that they believed his every word. If I got up there and asked him about what his church was really about, I was bound to look unhinged. The only thing I could possibly do to make this guy look like the bigot and murderer that he was was to bring in church members to testify. Trouble was, they had all gone into hiding, at least the ones I found who were willing to tell the truth.

I had a sickening feeling in my belly as I realized how Vince played me. Played everyone. He would close off my one avenue that might have made the difference, and that was showing the jury that this reverend was the head of a sick cult that commanded the killing of gay and trans children. At this point, I really had nothing at all.

This ship was going down. Hard.

And there was nothing I could do about it.

"Ms. Ross," Judge Reiner said. "Do you have anything for this witness?"

"No, your honor."

And I sat down.

FORTY-FOUR

After I left the courtroom, I had to do something to keep me from taking a drink. The first day couldn't have gone worse. All the witnesses, both friends of Connie and friends of Heather, portrayed Heather as a rather violent person who was constantly saying she wanted to kill her mother and wished her mother was dead. Heather cut off her own hair in front of witnesses and screamed about it, which made her look bat-crap nuts. Heather shoved her mother down to the ground in front of people.

And that reverend, the one person who I considered my Ace in the hole, if I decided to put Heather on the stand and make my case for self-defense, came off as saintly as Christ himself on the stand. I wished the jury could look up that church's website for themselves, but, of course, they were commanded not to do so. They weren't allowed to do any kind of independent research on anything they heard.

"Pearl," I said, calling her from my car. "Did Fred have any luck at all with finding those church witnesses?" I had only found two who were willing to tell the truth about the church, and I had subpoenaed both of them. I had exhaustively tried to talk to just about everyone I saw in that church, but none of them were willing to testify, and all of them told me that, if I called them, they would flat-out lie. They were terrified of what the reverend would do to them. Plus, there were plenty of congregants who were so brainwashed that they really didn't think there was anything wrong in that church, but they weren't willing to tell the truth, either.

The good thing was, Vince opened the door to the church-goers testimony. Their testimony wasn't relevant, really, because it wouldn't show Connie herself was brainwashed into killing Heather. It only would show the church had the message of hatred and murdering and that the congregants were fed that. But I could use them to impeach the reverend.

"Fred couldn't find them," Pearl said. "They've apparently gone into deep hiding."

I sighed. Vince was about to wrap up his evidence, anyhow, which would mean I'd have to get these witnesses on the stand tomorrow, probably. By the day after tomorrow, for sure. I didn't see that happening.

I felt sick.

And defeated.

"I need to go," I said. And then I called Sophia. "Sophia, can you please watch the girls tonight? I need to have some time to myself. I need to get out of my headspace."

As I drove along, I passed by one bar after another, and the need to go into them was strong. Not just to drink, although I craved that, too. But also to lose myself in there. To hear the music, to feel the crowds, to become anonymous. I wouldn't be the loser attorney who would blow a major case. I wouldn't be the one who would feel forever guilty, wondering if my incompetence caused an innocent client to go to prison. I would just be another bar-goer.

I hung up the phone and drove up to one of the bars.

I would go in there and not have a drink.

Which was what I always told myself before.

FORTY-FIVE

I walked into Tom's Town, which was a bar on the edge of Downtown, Kansas City, in the Crossroads Art District, on 17th and Main. When I walked in, I knew that this was the place for me. High-gloss hardwood floors, twinkling Christmas light overhead, exposed brick and a distillery. There was a lounge with leather couches, that faced walls of windows.

The bar was named for corrupt boss Tom Pendergast who ran Kansas City during prohibition. Kansas City, in general, was a hub for the mobsters during the prohibition era and had a rich history where that was concerned. Tom Pendergast ignored Prohibition, justifying by simply stating that "people were thirsty," which was Tom's Town's motto. This place was an homage to the romanticism of the 1930s, the era when jazz and spirits were kings and Kansas City was known as the "Paris of the Plains." This was emphasized by the Art Deco lettering of the logo.

The bar had a relaxed atmosphere, and the bartenders were dressed formally, so I felt like this was a place where grown-ups went.

The server came around. "What can I bring you?"

"A seltzer water," I said, my heart racing. I was tempting fate by being here, and it was taking everything I had, every bit of will-power, to not order what I really wanted, which was a shot of the best bourbon they had. But I couldn't go there. I had too much on the line.

"Would you like a twist of lime?"

"Please."

I looked around, feeling comforted by the place, yet despairing all the same. Despairing because I could feel Heather's case slipping through my fingers. Nothing was going right. I was blind-sided by the insurance agent, and both Connie and Heather's friends painted a grim picture. One thing was for sure, Vince was meeting his burden of proof, so I'd have no choice but to put Heather on the stand and try for self-defense, which was my original plan, but the absence of the butcher knife meant our self-defense claim would go down in flames.

Yet I felt a strange sense of comfort, too. I saw people all around me, laughing and drinking and having a good time, and it somehow reminded me there was still a world going on around me. There was still a chance I could become one of these happy people again. Get Heather behind me, try to move on, and perhaps really, truly, find another line of law that could make me happy.

The server came around, and I decided to tempt fate again. "Thank you," I said. "I would also like a Classic Stinger," I said, referring to a drink that made with Cognac and Crème de Menthe.

"Thank you," the server said. "I'll be right back with that."

The challenge, of course, was to order this drink and have it sit on the table without me drinking any of it at all. Just like when I used to carry around a bottle of Jack Daniels in my car, which made me prove to myself I was stronger than the drink, I'd have to prove it now, too.

I decided to call Axel on a whim. "Axel," I said. "I'm down at Tom's Town. Are you free? Can you join me?"

"I'd love to," he said. "I just got off work myself. But what are you doing in a bar?"

"Reliving old times." The server came around and put the Stinger on my table, and I just stared at it for several minutes. I closed my eyes and imagined how it would go down – smooth and bitter and sweet. All at the same time. Cognac had the bite, the crème de menthe had the smoothness and sweetness. I imagined the sensation on my tongue, and the rush it would bring to my mind.

I imagined myself forgetting everything that happened. All it would take would be downing a few of these drinks. I could smell it, and I could tell that this drink was stiff, as stiff as a shot of Kentucky bourbon, and probably just as potent.

As I sat there, the place started to fill up. This was one of hottest bars in the city, because people were attracted to the atmosphere and the crafted cocktails. Crafted cocktails were really an art form – this place was so much more than an ordinary place that used pre-made mixes in their drinks.

I closed my eyes, willing myself to not order wonderful-sounding liqueurs. That was a thing with me – I was always curious, always adventurous, always wanting to try new experiences. The drink menu at this place fascinated me to no end, and I was dying to try so many different things.

But I couldn't. I couldn't, and I wouldn't. Rina and Abby's lives depended on my staying sober.

So did Heather's.

I looked up and saw Axel walking through the door. I smiled and waved my seltzer water in the air towards him.

He sat down and gave me a kiss on the cheek. "How are

you? And what is this?" He pointed to the Stinger and raised an eyebrow at me.

"This is my temptation. My siren song. I have to periodically show myself I can be stronger than the drink, and that's what I'm doing right now. Well, that and I'm also hiding out. Today didn't go well, to say the very least."

"Oh, sorry to hear that," Axel said. "What happened?"

"I don't want to talk about it," I said. I'd always found failure difficult to talk about, and that was what today was – a big, fat, failure. "How are things going with you? Are you any closer to making an arrest in that church?"

Axel shook his head. "This church members are buttoned up, I'll tell you that. So far, I only have the testimony of that gay kid who survived his mother's attack. Nobody else will come forth and say what's going on. I know what you told me, that the reverend preaches hate from the pulpit, but apparently he hasn't openly called for killing gay kids from the pulpit, at least not according to the investigators I've sent over there to find out what's going on. I wish I had more."

"What about sending those investigators to go back and talk to the reverend one-on-one? Have them tell the reverend their kid is gay and see what he says? Have them wear a wire?"

"I've attempted that, but the reverend isn't stupid. He will only privately counsel members who have been with the church for at least a year. Apparently, it's in those private counseling sessions that the reverend lays down the law on these parents. He's a slippery one, but we'll get him."

I nodded and drank my seltzer water. The ice in my Stinger was melting, and I had to pinch myself not to take a drink. "Go ahead and order what you want," I said. "And maybe we can grab a bite later on."

"You sure?"

"Of course, I am. Truth be told, a lot of the reason why I

decided to come to this bar is that I need to live my life normally. That means I need to be able to come to a bar to meet my friends, or my sisters, or you, and be around this stuff. I won't lie. It's tough. Especially after a day like today. A day where I feel like I went 12 rounds in a boxing ring and still lost. Tomorrow is another day, though, as they say."

"Harper, you're strong," he said. "You can do this." At that, he ordered a "Pendergast," which consisted of bourbon, sweet vermouth, liqueur and bitters.

The waitress brought the drink around and the two of us lifted our glasses. "Cheers," I said.

"Cheers to you," he said. "And here's to tomorrow's day in court being better than today."

I smiled. "So, where would you like to grab something?" I asked him.

"What about Lidia's?"

Lidia's was a restaurant in the Freight House District of Kansas City, right by the Union Station. It was an enormous restaurant located in an old railroad house, so the ceilings were about fifty feet high, which gave the entire restaurant the feel of being almost open-air. The brick walls and wood beams on the ceilings made it seem intimate, however, and it was one of my favorite places to go. Lidia herself was a celebrity chef from New York City, Lidia Bastianich, who was born in Italy and had only a few restaurants around the country. Kansas City was privileged to be one of the locations where she chose to open a place.

"Well, let's finish up here," I said, suddenly realizing I was starving. I hadn't eaten since breakfast, because I was working all through lunch. That was the thing about trial work – it generally killed my appetite. "What are we waiting for?"

We both finished our drinks and agreed to meet at the restaurant.

I felt a sense of accomplishment as I walked out of the bar – I had made it through without taking even a sip of alcohol. A year ago, I certainly couldn't have done that.

Maybe I'd be okay after all.

DINNER WENT EXTREMELY WELL. I felt myself relax, more and more, as the night wore on. The restaurant was unbelievably elegant, with the white table cloths, candles and open-air atmosphere. I ordered the *Pollo al Limone,* which was basically chicken scallopine with lemons, capers and olive oil, while Axel ordered the *Bistecca,* a bone-in rib-eye, served with broccoli rabe, roasted tomatoes and garlic mashed potatoes.

I was dying for a glass of wine, too, because I hadn't ever come to this place without polishing off a bottle of wine all by myself. Yet, I resisted the temptation.

And the food was...there were no words. Magnificent. Divine. There was really nothing I liked more than good comfort food, and this place supplied it in spades.

I was kind of liking the company, too. No, that was a lie. I was falling for Axel, hard. I had to admit that to myself. Falling hard and deep. I hadn't really allowed myself to ever fall for anybody, not in my 35 years, yet I was with this guy.

The end of the evening was capped off with the two of us walking to the Union Station to check it out. This was a beautiful building, probably the most beautiful in Kansas City, and it was definitely one of the most iconic – postcards of the city usually featured the Union Station in one way or another, and was usually the only image on these postcards. The building had 95-foot ceilings and encompassed almost a million square feet. The windows to the building were enormous arches that were easily 50 feet themselves. The ceilings were painted mosaics from which 20-foot chandeliers hung. This train station was a grand old lady, and, even though trains weren't a major mode of transportation for Kansas City anymore, it did house the Amtrak station. The pictures on the walls told the story, though – at one time, this station was a major hub, and thousands of people would stream through the doors to catch one train or another.

As we walked through the station, thinking about what to do next, I felt my phone buzzing incessantly. I had turned it off when we were in the restaurant and the bar, because I didn't want to be disturbed. I wanted to turn off what had happened in court, and just relax a little bit. There really was nothing I could do to turn things around at this point, so there wasn't a reason to try to put my all into it.

"Excuse me," I said to Axel. "I need to take this. But I'll be right back."

I, shockingly, had about ten messages from Pearl, Anna and Fred. All of them told me to call them.

The first person I called was Pearl.

"Harper," she said breathlessly. "You gotta come to the office. Yesterday."

"Why? What's going on?"

"Anna found Louisa. And, girl, you're not going to believe how."

"How?"

"She's Heather's birth mother."

FORTY-SIX

"What?" I found a bench and sat down on it. "Her birth mother? I don't understand." I did understand, but it was just too weird to be believed. I mean, what were the odds? Louisa gives up a baby, the adoption is closed, so she doesn't know who adopted the baby, and she ends up having an affair with the adoptive mother? To say that was a weird coincidence would be understating it. I'd heard of weirder coincidences, but not many.

"Yeah. Heather was born in Georgia to Louisa. We don't know who the birth father was, however, because the birth certificate was left blank. She immediately put Heather up for adoption, and it was a closed adoption, so she never found out who adopted her. Connie and her husband, Frank, adopted Heather from Georgia. They were matched with her after being on the waiting list for several years."

My heart was pounding. "Okay, so where is Louisa now?"

"She's staying with her mother and father, who currently live in San Diego, California. Her family moved from Savannah, Georgia to California after her father retired. They own an almond ranch out there. 50 acres."

"How did Anna find all this out?"

"She finally figured out how to hack into the closed adoption records, which led her to Louisa's residence in Georgia. The records showed the names of her parents, and it also showed Louisa's date of birth. That gave Anna enough information to locate Louisa's parents in San Diego, and it also gave Anna enough information that she could find the phone number of Louisa's parents. She called the parents, asked for Louisa, and the parents handed the phone to her. That's how Anna finally found out where Louisa is."

I nodded. "This is good, this is very good. We need to get her on the stand. She's on my witness list." But how would I do that? How could I possibly get out there, persuade her to come in or get her under subpoena, all before tomorrow morning? I couldn't. There wasn't any way. I'd have to try for a continuance, but I knew Judge Reiner would never approve of it. Not with the jury all seated. There was no way he'd agree to a continuance.

Yet I knew I had to talk to her. I had to convince her to come in. Maybe if I told her Heather was the baby boy she gave up all those years ago, she'd testify willingly. Surely she wouldn't want to see her child go to prison. I still didn't know if she had the butcher knife, but I had a pretty good hunch she did. No doubt about it, Louisa was my last, and only, hope for an acquittal.

I couldn't do all this over the phone, though. I had to go there. If I called her, she was liable to run, and then I'd never find her again.

"Harper?" Pearl said. "Are you still there?"

"Yeah. How will I do this? I have to be back in court at 9

AM tomorrow, and I think Vince will wrap things up by early morning. He doesn't have many witnesses on tap for tomorrow. I could ask for a continuance, but no way Judge Reiner will approve of that." My heart raced faster and faster as I tried to think my way around this.

"I don't know the answer to that," Pearl said. "But you gotta think of something. You think Louisa knows about the butcher knife, right? That's your suspicion?"

"Yes. She might also know other things, too. She was high up in the church, after all, and she was having an affair with Connie. Maybe she witnessed the reverend talking to Connie, telling her to kill Heather. Maybe Connie told her the reverend wanted her to kill Heather, and maybe Connie said she'd do it. I can get a statement like that in through the admission exception to the hearsay rule."

"Well, then, we need to figure out how to get her on the stand."

"Yeah. Listen, I'll let you go for now. I have Axel here, and maybe he can give me an idea on how we can get this done before tomorrow."

"Call me back," she said. "I'll call Anna and Fred and tell them I talked to you. They've been trying to call you to tell you about this."

I hung up and looked at Axel. "Well, there's good news and bad news. The good news is, Anna finally located Louisa. She's absolutely key to this case. I have a hunch she knows a lot, and I also have a hunch she has that butcher knife."

"That sounds great," Axel said. "What's the bad news?"

"The bad news is I have to be in court tomorrow for day two of our trial. I think the prosecutor, Vince, will be wrapping up by the afternoon, which means I have to put my evidence on immediately. At this point, Heather is the only evidence I have.

Her testimony is all I have." Heather's boyfriend, Charlie, was also on my witness list, as she told Charlie what had happened. That mattered, because his testimony would be somewhat believable, as what Heather was thinking at the time she killed her mother was highly relevant. Other than that, however, I didn't have much. All Heather's friends, as well as Connie's, were already called by Vince, because their testimony was unfortunately more damning than exonerating.

I didn't want to call Charlie, however, because was he was a drug dealer and a convicted felon. That would come in, and it would make Heather look even worse in front of the jury. She fled after killing her mother and went to stay with her convicted felon boyfriend. I didn't want to get him on the stand for that reason.

I got up and started to pace around. "She's in California. Fucking California." I looked up at the clock. It was 10 PM. "Fucking California. She might as well be in Thailand."

"Won't the judge continue the case so you can bring her in?"

"No. I mean, I'll obviously ask for that, but no way will he approve a continuance. He's an impatient judge to begin with – he made us try this case just three months after we got it. The jury is sat, the jury wants to go home. I can't see him approving a continuance unless there's a major emergency."

I sat down. "The only thing I can think of is that I drag out Heather's testimony for several hours in the afternoon. God knows how I'll do that, however."

"Why do you have to drag her testimony out?"

"Well, let's just say that Vince wraps up his side of the case by lunchtime tomorrow. He has several more witnesses that he'll call, all of whom are more friends of Connie and Heather. I doubt that'll take very long. So, that would mean I'd have to put Heather up there after lunch, at 1:30, which is when the afternoon testimony would begin. I would have to drag her out until the end of the day. Otherwise, I'll have to wrap up my defense around 3 PM. That would mean the judge would make us do our closing statements tomorrow, and the case is over. But if I can drag her testimony out until the end of the day, then the case will carry over until Thursday. I could maybe, in the meantime, send Anna out to California to get Louisa, and maybe I can get Louisa on the stand Thursday morning."

Doing it this way meant some huge risks. Number one, I just couldn't see how I could drag out Heather's testimony for that long. She could testify to what happened, about why she would never kill her mother, about the pillow case incident, the rebut the witnesses who painted her as some kind of a psycho – she could give her side of the story for all those fights her's and Connie's friends witnessed. Could I drag all that out for three hours? I could, I guessed, drag out my side of the case if I called Charlie. I didn't want to have to call him, but I would. I'd call him if I had to.

The second risk was that Vince might decide to wrap up early. All the witnesses he had lined up for tomorrow were essentially duplicative testimony from many of the other witnesses he'd called today. I knew that by looking at his list. If that happened, if Vince decided to stand up in front of court tomorrow and say he rests his case...it would be all over at that point. No way could I drag out Heather and Charlie for an entire day.

The third risk would be if Louisa wouldn't come with Anna. I'd have to issue a subpoena for her, which would take some time. I also had the feeling she'd come in to testify if I went there to ask her personally. I knew, when I saw her in the church, she was close to doing what I needed. If I could get out there, and tell her Heather was her biological child, she might come. Her coming willingly would be the only way I could get her on the stand on time.

I suddenly got an idea. "Shoot me," I said. "Shoot me in the leg."

Axel furrowed his brow. "What? Why would I do that?"

"You know how to shoot to wound, don't you? You have a suspect, you don't want to kill him, but you want to slow him down. You'd shoot him, wouldn't you? In the leg, and you probably know just where to shoot him so you don't hit major arteries or veins. Right?"

"Harper, I won't do that," he said, shaking his head.

"If you don't do it, I will. I have a gun at home. I'll do it to myself, but who knows if I'll do a decent job at it. I might go ahead and hit a major artery and I'll end up dead."

Axel shook his head. "You're crazy. You're talking like an insane person."

"Nope. Not crazy. I just see my getting majorly injured in a firearm accident as the only way to make this Heather case work. Listen, Axel, if I don't get Louisa on that stand, Heather is a dead woman. Literally. Literally. Her case is going south, and it's going there quickly. Now, I have a strong suspicion, and I mean strong suspicion, that Louisa knows where that butcher knife is. She almost told me as much when I went to see her at the church. There's no way I can get her on that stand by tomorrow afternoon. The judge won't give me a continuance. I'd be willing to bet a million dollars on that one. There's only one way to salvage this sinking ship, and that's for you to shoot me. Either that, or I drive my car into a tree."

Somehow, someway, I would end up in the hospital tonight. That was the one and only thing I could think of.

"Harper-"

At that, I took his gun out of his holster and put it in my

purse. We were in a public place, so there was no way I'd do anything with the gun right at that moment.

"Harper, give me back my gun."

"I won't." I lied to him – I didn't really have a gun at home. I wouldn't keep one with two small children around. I needed a gun, though, so I took his.

"Harper-"

"I won't give it back." I raised an eyebrow.

"You have to give it back to me."

"Arrest me," I said, suddenly thinking that was a better option anyhow. I really didn't want to shoot myself or have him shoot me. I knew that was bound to hurt. A lot. But going back to jail? A piece of cake.

"Harper-"

"I'm serious. Arrest me. Arrest me. I'll make sure to not make bail right away, so I'll be in jail until the weekend. Then I can bail out Friday evening, be on the plane to San Diego on the red-eye Friday night, which will give me two entire days to convince her to come out here." Judge Reiner would be pissed as hell, of course, but what could he do? If I was in jail, I was in jail. I couldn't try the case and Heather couldn't go forward without me.

"Arrest you? Harper, I can't."

"You will. Because I won't give you back your gun unless you do."

He sighed. "You're serious."

"As a heart attack." I stared at him, trying to convey to him, through my expression, just how serious I was. "If there was some other way, other than my getting arrested or seriously injured, I'd take it. But I can't chance it. I can't chance that I'll be forced to wrap up my case tomorrow without Louisa taking the stand. As I said, you have to help me out here. If you don't,

I'll be forced to take matters into my own hands, and it won't be pretty."

He finally sighed. "Okay. You have a right to remain silent...."

I smiled. I was going back to jail, but that was a small price to pay for the chance to win this case for Heather.

FORTY-SEVEN
THREE DAYS LATER

"Thanks for bonding me out," I said to Tammy, who had arrived at the jail with the $1,000 bond assigned to me for the crime of taking Axel's firearm. I'd been in there for almost three days, and I was going stir-crazy behind bars. I felt like a caged animal, and all I could think about was Heather's case. I just wanted to get out of there and do something.

"How was jail?" Tammy asked, an amused expression on her face.

"Eh. I'm getting used to it, to be honest. It sucks and the food is horrendous. But I picked up a couple of new clients in there, so there's that."

"You are nothing if not resourceful." Tammy seemed amused by it all, and I could see why. It was kind of funny, or it would be, if it weren't so serious.

"How angry is everybody? By everybody, I mean Judge Reiner?" I asked Tammy.

She shook her head. "When I went in there to tell him what happened, he was ready to have *my* head on a pike. He was infuriated, I'll tell you that. He threatened Heather and tried to tell her she'd have to finish the case without you. He said you were costing the taxpayers thousands of dollars with your shenanigans, except he used a stronger word than shenanigans. He also said he'll file a bar complaint against you."

"Ugh," I said. "I hate bar complaints, especially one filed by judges. What else did he say?"

"He threatened to dismiss the jury and call a mistrial. Vince convinced him not do that, though. He said it wasn't fair to him because he prepared for months for this and wants to get the case finished."

"So, what's the upshot?"

"The upshot is, you have to be back in court by Monday. If you're not, the judge will call a mistrial and fine you $10,000, which is the amount he says you're costing the taxpayers. He also issued an order, which means that, if you're not back in court on Monday, he can put you in jail for contempt."

"Sounds like he's pissed," I said. "But that's just as well. I need to get this witness on the stand, and if I get her, and her testimony is what I think it'll be, it'll all be worth it."

We arrived at Tammy's car. She would head straight to the airport and put me on the red-eye flight to San Diego. I had the address, courtesy of Anna, and I had a car lined up for me when I touched down. The plan was to find a hotel tonight and find Louisa early tomorrow morning.

"And if you can't get her to testify?"

"I'll subpoena her," I said.

"She can quash that because she's out in California. It would be unduly burdensome for her to come. Even if she has the knife and has the knowledge, all she has to do is lie to you and quash your subpoena, and you're back at square one with an irate judge, jury and prosecutor. The judge is liable to take his fury out on your client during the sentencing phase. You'll have to answer to the Bar for this, too."

"So be it. I have to try. This is a Hail Mary to end all Hail Marys, but it's either this or Heather dies in prison."

We were at the airport. "Thanks, Tammy," I said. "I owe you big for all you've done."

She sighed. "I hope this works out."

"Me too."

At that, I ran into the airport, picked up my tickets and waited for my flight.

Tammy was right. This was still a long-shot. If it didn't work out, I'd be much worse off than I was before. Heather might also be, but I prayed the judge didn't take out his fury on her. Tammy thought he might, because he was that angry.

When I finally boarded the flight, I felt myself coming down off my adrenaline high. I watched the city disappear underneath me, and I closed my eyes and did something I hadn't done in many, many years.

I prayed.

THE PLANE TOUCHED down in California several hours later, and I immediately went in to get my car. I'd stay in a local Hilton and then go on over to Louisa's the next day. I was nervous, extremely nervous, about this.

Tammy was right. Louisa could just lie to me about what she knew. Could lie to me about whether or not she had the butcher knife. If she did so, I couldn't very well subpoena her. It wouldn't do any good.

If she chose to lie, there would be little I could do. I'd go back to Kansas City empty-handed and face a judge more pissed than a nest full of hornets. He could be as dangerous as that nest of hornets, too. He could slap me with a contempt suit and hit Heather with a giant sentence, just because he's angry with me. He could drag me in front of the Bar. Plus, I now had a theft charge to go with my now-dismissed kidnapping charge. That was what I was charged with – theft of a firearm from a law enforcement officer. Axel assured me he'd work with the police department to drop the charges, but I put him into an awkward position, too.

He also probably thought I was crazy at this point. I wouldn't blame him if he did. After all, I threatened to shoot myself and begged him to shoot me. He'd visited me while I was in jail and had assured me he still cared for me, but I had my doubts. I was acting crazy, and I knew it.

I checked into the hotel, and lay down on the bed. To my surprise, I found myself closing my eyes and falling right to sleep.

THE VERY NEXT DAY, I got up bright and early. I had no idea when I could catch Louisa, but I knew I'd have a better chance of catching her in the morning than at any other time. I didn't want to give her the chance to go to the beach or to brunch or whatever she typically would do on a Saturday afternoon here in sunny San Diego. It might have been late September, almost October, but it was incredibly warm. The weather called for it to be 90 degrees. I didn't know what kind of a person she was, but most people would want to take advantage of this weather while they could.

It was 7 AM, and I had her address. It was in Escondido, a suburb of San Diego in North County. I hopped on the 15 and headed north. My heart was racing 100 MPH. This was the biggest risk I'd taken in my career. The payoff would be enormous, but there was just as big of a chance that this could turn out to be a total disaster. A total, and very expensive, disaster.

I got to her house, which was a typical ranch-style home built in the 1950s, built on acres of land. Stucco siding, shingled roof, all one level. Almond groves surrounded this place, as did beautiful bougainvilleas. The birds were singing in the trees and the place was very peaceful.

I went to the door and rang the bell.

And tried to calm my racing heart.

FORTY-EIGHT

A man opened the door. "I have a sign here that says 'no soliciting,'" he said, pointing to a small silver sign that said just that. "So whatever you're selling, I'm not buying."

The man was just over six feet tall, wearing shorts and a golf shirt. He was sixtiesh, trim and fit, with salt and pepper hair, a tanned and slightly wrinkled face, a bulbous nose and blue eyes. He was a handsome guy for his age and I could see Louisa in him. I figured this was her father.

"I'm not trying to sell anything. I'm looking for Louisa Garrison. I have some extremely important business with her and I need to see her. Please."

What if he didn't let me talk to Louisa? What then? I couldn't barge my way in there. I couldn't call the cops to make him let me talk to her. It would be over then. Over.

"She's not here," he said.

I cleared my throat, feeling my heart sink. "Can I ask when she'll be back?"

"Who may I tell her is calling?" He looked at me suspiciously.

"My name is Harper Ross," I said. I would give him my Bar Card, but thought better of it. I didn't want him to be any more suspicious of me than he already was.

"And what is this regarding?"

"It's a private business matter."

"You'll have to be more specific than that."

"She'll know what it's regarding when you tell her I'm looking for her. When she hears my name, she'll know just what I need from her."

He crossed his arms. "If you want me to even tell her you stopped by, you're going to have to-"

At that, I turned around, because I heard footsteps behind me and voices. Two female voices.

There was Louisa, dressed in a t-shirt dress with a swimsuit underneath it. She had a straw hat on her head and flip-flops on her feet. On her nose was zinc oxide, like lifeguards use while they're working. I could smell piña colada suntan lotion on her. She looked relaxed and younger than when I saw her in her office.

"I forgot something," she said to her father and then looked at me. "Hello." She looked down at the ground, and I knew she was hiding some deep shame. I could see it on her face. "Ms. Ross."

I felt my heart-rate start to decline, just a little. This was the first step, but at least I caught her. "Ms. Garrison, I need to speak with you. It's urgent. A person's life literally depends upon it."

"I know." She sighed. "I hoped I could run away and just forget about this, but you can never outrun fate." She motioned to her car, where there was a woman in the passenger's seat with a questioning look on her face. "I was heading to the beach this morning. It's tough to find a parking space if you go too late. But I need to talk to you instead. Let me call Uber, and I'll have them come and take Lynda home."

She went to her car and I saw her talking to the woman in the passenger's seat. The woman nodded, and I saw Louisa doing something on her phone. I assumed she was ordering the Uber, and I hoped that was what she was doing.

She got out of the car. "The Uber car will be here in a few minutes," she said. "Why don't we go down to Denny's? It's just down the street. We can get some breakfast and talk." She whispered. "Talk so my father doesn't hear."

The Uber car came and picked up her friend, and Louisa and I went to her car. As I sat there next to her, I could feel my blood pressure lessen more and more. Maybe this would be okay after all. Maybe I would get what I needed from her.

"I know why you're here," she said. " And I'm actually glad you are. I did the wrong thing, the absolute wrong thing, about three months ago. I've laid awake nights, every night, agonizing over it. But I've been too cowardly to do anything about it. I've prayed something would happen to give me answers. Prayed for that every night. God, give me a sign. Any sign. And here you are. My sign. I now know what I have to do."

We got to the restaurant, and I could feel my heart soaring. This was good. This was very good. She was sounding like she'd do it. Give me the butcher knife, have it dusted for fingerprints, have her tell the jury she took it and the knife was in Connie's hand when she died. Maybe even tell the jury about the reverend instructing Connie to kill Heather. That would be all I could ever hope for.

We sat down, ordered, and I looked at her. I had a pad of paper in front of me, and a pen, and I was ready to write. "Okay," I said. "You know why I came here. I need to ask you questions."

She nodded. "Yes. Yes, I have the butcher knife." She

looked out the window. "God, that feels so good to tell you that. I have it. I know I'll go to prison for doing that. Tampering with a crime scene. But the Lord has showed me the way and He brought you out here. I can't argue with that."

I felt myself completely relaxing. In place of the squeezing anxiety was a sense of peace. Of joy. I did the right thing. Heather had a chance.

"What else can you tell me?"

"About what?"

"About the Reverend Scott? Did he tell Connie she should kill Heather? I know he has been brainwashing the congregants in the church, telling them to kill their gay and trans kids. I know that. I need to know he told Connie to kill Heather while you were present in the room."

She sighed. "You're asking a lot from me. Reverend Scott is dangerous. Very dangerous. I'm in hiding here. He knows where I am, but he told me that if I ever breathed a word about what he did, I'm a dead woman. I can't give you what you want there." Her face got red. "I need to tell you, though. Since the Lord sent you, I have to unburden myself. But I can't say this on the stand. Not if I want to live."

I nodded, hoping she'd change her mind, but needing to hear it, anyhow.

"Yes," she said. "I was his assistant. His right-hand person. I was so brainwashed that I went along with it. It took a lot of praying for guidance to get my head straight on what was happening at that church. But yes. Reverend Scott is evil. I know that now. He had this vision that homosexuality needs to be wiped off the face of the earth. Transgenderism too. Transgenderism was prioritized in his eyes – it had to be wiped out first. So he told parents of gay and trans children what they had to do. Try to change them, and if they couldn't be changed, they needed to kill them. I was there when Reverend Scott told Connie that."

She had a cup of coffee and took a sip of it. She looked out the window again.

I sighed. I was right after all. My hunches were true. Now, I just had to get it out of her. Somehow, someway. "You can't testify to this on the stand?"

"No," she said. "Please don't ask me to. I'll lie if you ask me to. I know that's a crime, too, perjury, but you have to understand – if I get up there and tell the court that, Reverend Scott will kill me. Literally. I'd be risking my life even going to court to testify to anything at all. But I will. I'll testify about the butcher knife. That's necessary. But I just can't testify about what I know about the Reverend Scott and that church."

Half a loaf was better than none. "I hope you change your mind but can I get you to get on a plane? Like today? I need to get you on that witness stand Monday."

She nodded. "It's the Lord's will, obviously. If the Lord didn't want that, you would not have been sent to me."

I wanted to tell her about Heather being her daughter, although I was quite sure she'd consider Heather to be her son. I didn't want to lay it on her, however. It might be too much, too soon.

"Thank you," I said. "Thank you."

"No. Please don't thank me. I did something very, very wrong. I don't even know why I did it. I just panicked, I guess. I didn't want Connie's memory to..." She shook her head, tears in her eyes. "I loved her. I might as well tell you that. I did. I loved her. And I didn't want to think of her as violent. I knew the reverend was telling her to be violent, and I was brainwashed to believe that killing homosexuals and transgendered people was the right thing for society. It wasn't. I know that now. It was evil. I'm in a different church now, out here. It's a Lutheran

Church, and it's all about love and forgiveness. Nothing about hate or judgment or violence. It's really based on the Lord's word, not on some kind of perversion of *The Bible*. The reverend perverted *The Bible* and used it for his own agenda. I've prayed on this so many evenings, and that's what I finally discovered. The reverend is evil."

"And he must be stopped," I said. Then I narrowed my eyes. "And I think I know a way."

FORTY-NINE
MONDAY MORNING

"Okay," I said to Heather. "I think we're on our way."

I met her at her halfway house that morning. She looked ready to go. She was wearing a grey pantsuit with flared legs, high-heeled pumps, with a light-blue button-down under her jacket. Her makeup was pared-down, except for her lipstick, a light-brown that went perfectly with her skin-tone.

"You know," I said, looking at her. "Once you beat this charge, you should be a personal shopper or a makeup artist or something like that. You really have a certain sense of style. Maybe you can start with me, because I could use a stylist."

"You certainly could," she said, looking me up and down. "I mean, I'm sorry to tell you this, but your clothes are boring. Borrrinnngg."

She was right about that. I had endless navy suits that all seemed to look the same after awhile. They got the job done, in that I knew I looked professional, but I certainly didn't look like I belonged on the cover of a fashion magazine. Heather had a certain fashion sense – she had a flair, but she never looked inappropriate. And her makeup was exquisite. She had a great hand and really knew how to either make herself look understated or bold, depending on the situation.

I'd met with Heather the day before, along with Louisa. Heather initially gave Louisa the stink-eye when Louisa told her what she'd done. But Heather was also grateful Louisa was willing to come. I also went to the police station and gave them the butcher knife so they could do their forensic analysis on it. I had them put a rush on it, and Axel was instrumental in making sure the cops did just that. They did their analysis and agreed to take the stand to testify that Connie's fingerprints were on the knife and Heather's weren't.

We were ready to go.

My heart was still pounding when I drove to the courtroom, though. What if Louisa got cold feet and she ran again? She agreed to testify to everything I needed her to. I devised a plan, on the fly, really, to have Axel in the courtroom. I knew the reverend would also be in the courthouse, because I'd call him as a witness. He wouldn't be in the courtroom, because, as a witness, he couldn't be in the courtroom because he wouldn't be allowed to hear other the witnesses' testimony, but he'd be around the courthouse somewhere. And once Louisa told the court the reverend instructed parents to kill their children, including Connie, Axel would have probable cause to arrest him. Finally. He agreed to do just that – arrest the reverend and take him into custody.

"While he's out on bail, he can kill me," Louisa said, clearly worried.

"After your testimony, he'll be charged with multiple counts of murder. Just like Charles Manson – Manson never killed anybody, but he had his minions kill. Reverend Scott will be charged just like Manson. No judge will give him a bond when he has that many charges against him."

Not that I was totally sure about that, but I was reasonably sure.

"What about me? Won't I be an accessory?"

"You would be, but I can cut you a deal. Your testimony will be invaluable. I can get you a deal for immunity in exchange for your testimony against him." I put my hand on her shoulder. "It'll work out. I promise you."

She sighed. "I hope so. I'm terrified, though."

"I know," I said. "Be brave, though. You need to do this. What that reverend is doing isn't right. You can bring him down. Only you."

So, we had our plan.

FIFTY

"I won't allow you to put Louisa Garrison on the stand," Vince said to me. "You didn't make her available before trial, so you can't call her."

We were in the courtroom early, because I had to clear Louisa's testimony before the judge. I knew there would be a problem, but I hoped the judge would side with me.

"Is this true, Ms. Ross? Ms. Garrison wasn't made available prior to trial?" Judge Reiner was still irritated with me, but it seemed he'd calmed down quite a bit. After all, the train was back in the station and ready to leave. The trial was back on, and we were heading down the home stretch. That made Judge Reiner happy. "But you know you're still on thin ice, don't you, Ms. Ross? After your stunt, you're on very thin ice."

"Yes, that's true I never made Ms. Garrison available for depositions or interviews. She went into hiding. I didn't know where she was until last Tuesday, when I found out she was in California."

Judge Reiner sat back in his enormous chair and scowled at me. "Oh, so that was why you played those games? To get to her in California? I'm warning you, Ms. Ross, if you ever, and I mean ever, try something like that again, I'll have you put in the brig. I won't give you a chance to come back. You'll just be in jail."

"I understand."

"Okay, then, I'll disallow her testimony," he said. "You didn't give Mr. Malloy a chance to depose her or talk to her prior to trial, so her testimony won't be allowed."

I was prepared for this. "Okay, then, I'll call her as a rebuttal witness." I smirked at Vince. His little stunt in putting the reverend up on the stand opened the door for me to get Louisa on the stand. It didn't matter that I didn't make her available to Vince before trial, because she wouldn't be a witness in my case in chief. She'd be a witness whose testimony would contradict that of the reverend.

"A rebuttal witness?" Judge Reiner said. "Whose testimony will she rebut?"

"The Reverend Scott's."

Vince shook his head. "Judge Reiner, if her witness will just rebut the reverend, she's not relevant to this case. Nothing the reverend said on the stand was relevant to this case. None of what he said would even begin to help the jury ascertain what happened between the defendant and the deceased."

I gave Vince a look and Judge Reiner picked up on it. "Well, that's rich, Mr. Malloy. Really rich," Judge Reiner said. "*You* put him on the stand. You did. Now you're telling me his testimony should be essentially disallowed for lack of relevance? Is that your argument?"

Vince looked frustrated. "Yes and no. My argument is that I don't see where Ms. Garrison's testimony will help the jury decide anything."

"It will," I said. "Trust me, her testimony is key."

"Okay, Ms. Ross, tell me. I'm waiting here with bated breath. Tell me what her testimony will be."

"She'll testify that she was in the room when the Reverend Scott told Connie she had to kill Heather."

Vince rolled his eyes. "You're still on this, huh? You just won't quit."

"No, I won't quit. This testimony is key to my defense." I turned to the judge. "And if you don't let her testimony in, I'll have a perfect argument for the appellate court."

"I'll allow it," he said.

"I knew you would."

"But Ms. Ross, I'm going to lay down the parameters on what you can ask your witness. Her testimony can only consist of words that directly rebut what the reverend said on the stand. Nothing else. If you go fishing with this witness, I'll shut it down. I'm not above calling a mistrial, even at this point. Especially at this point. I'm still pissed about your little stunt, so I'm in no mood to give you any quarter. Do you understand me?"

"Of course." That meant Louisa couldn't testify about the butcher knife. Crap. I'd have to get the officers who were examining the knife on the stand, but what did that prove? It was a butcher knife with Connie's fingerprints on it. So what? Without Louisa's testimony about it, there would be no way I could establish the butcher knife was found at the scene.

My heart started pounding again. The issue of the butcher knife still wasn't resolved. The jury still couldn't hear about the butcher knife being found at the scene.

This whole thing wouldn't be as easy as I thought.

LOUISA DIDN'T GET to testify until the next day. As it turned out, Vince had several more witnesses to call, and then I called Heather to tell her story. By the time all this was completed, it was 4 PM, and the judge decided to call it a day.

Heather's testimony went as planned, but, as I figured, Vince would highlight the absence of the butcher knife.

"You said your mother came at you with a butcher knife, isn't that true?"

"Yes, that's true."

He walked dramatically over to the jury. "I would like to re-introduce Exhibit A, which is the police report. Could you please read it aloud?"

Heather read the report aloud, word for word.

"Do you notice the absence of anything on this report?"

Heather shook her head.

"Did you read, anywhere in that report, that there was a butcher knife found at the scene?"

"No," she said. "There wasn't a mention of that. Somebody must have taken the knife from the scene."

"Motion to strike," he said. "The last part of her testimony, as it clearly calls for speculation."

"Sustained."

He went back to the jury and handed them the police report. "Please read this," he said. "And if any of you can show me where the words 'butcher knife' is mentioned, then I will eat my tie."

The jury members giggled politely, as each one read the report carefully.

The last jury member handed the police report back to him, and he took it.

"I have nothing further for this witness."

The judge then banged his gavel. "Okay, we're all tired. I'd like to recess until tomorrow morning. Ms. Ross will continue with her evidence at 9 AM. The jury may be excused."

After the jury left, Vince came over to me. "It's not too late to take a plea," he said.

"Dream on."

"I don't know what your witness will prove, Harper. Even if she gets up there and says the Reverend Scott was an evil genius who urged Connie Morrison to kill Heather, it still proves nothing. There's still no butcher knife. There's still no way you can show there was. The jury thinks Heather is lying because no knife was found at the scene. Let's just settle this thing for 30 years, no possibility of parole, and be done. You're going to lose, Harper, and, after your stunt last week, the judge won't be kind to your client." Then he cleared his throat. "Of course, if you plead her, don't screw it up by asking her for affirmative defenses like you did last time. Just ask her if she killed her mother, she'll say yes, and leave it at that. The plea can go through that way."

I picked up my briefcase. "No dice."

As I walked away from him, my stomach was in knots. He was right. Even with Louisa on the stand, I still couldn't establish a knife at the scene. She could testify about the Reverend Scott brainwashing Connie and others to kill, but that didn't prove Connie attempted to kill Heather. All the witnesses were damning to Heather, as she apparently told most of them she wanted to kill her mother. Some didn't testify that Heather admitted to wanting to kill Connie, but these witnesses were still treated to scenes from Heather where she acted like a lunatic. None of the witnesses were completely positive for us.

I had a sinking feeling this case was still uphill, even with Louisa.

FIFTY-ONE

The next day, it was finally time for Louisa to take the stand. She was nervous, because she'd seen the reverend in the courthouse that day. "He threatened me," she said softly. "He said he knew what I would do, and if I did it, he'd kill me by the end of the day."

"Don't worry," I said. "We have Axel right here in the courtroom." I pointed to him as he nodded to me. "He's ready to go. He has an arrest warrant ready. He'll go down to the witness room and arrest the reverend as soon as you testify." The reverend was waiting in one of the empty rooms in the courthouse. I told Vince I would call the reverend after Louisa, but I wasn't, of course. I just had to say that so the reverend would be forced to stay in the courthouse.

"And if you don't call him, I will," Vince said. "To rebut your rebuttal witness."

"Go for it."

So, I was ready for Louisa. I only hoped Louisa didn't chicken out.

"Call your witness," Judge Reiner said that morning, after the jury was seated and everybody was ready to go.

"The defense calls Louisa Garrison."

At that, Louisa walked to the witness stand. Her sandy blonde hair was in a bun and she was wearing a light blue dress and tan pumps, with a colorful scarf around her neck. She looked younger every time I saw her. I wondered if it was because she was so relieved to unload her conscience. Or maybe it was because she was out of that oppressive church. Whatever the reason, she was looking younger and prettier with every passing day.

"Please raise your right hand," the bailiff said to her. "And repeat after me. I swear to tell the truth, the whole truth and nothing but the truth, so help me God."

"I swear to tell the truth, the whole truth and nothing but the truth, so help me God," Louisa said, and then turned her eyes to the ceiling, as if she was saying something to her God.

I approached. "Please state your name for the record."

"Louisa Marie Garrison." Her left hand nervously adjusted her scarf and she looked down at the table in front of her.

"Ms. Garrison, were you a member of the Church of the Living Breath?"

"I was."

"For how long?"

"Six years."

"Six years. What was your role in the church?"

"I was a member for three of those years, and a church administrator for another three."

"A church administrator. What were your duties?"

"Clerical mostly, although I assisted the Reverend Scott with counseling the congregants on certain matters."

I paced the floor. "Tell me about the philosophy of this church. Was the message that the congregants received from the Reverend Scott that of love and peace and the words of Christ?"

Louisa shook her head. "No."

"What was the message of the church?"

She sighed. "The reverend has a hatred for LGBT. An extreme hatred for them. Each week, his sermon consisted of highlighting incidents where a gay man was caught molesting a child, and then used these incidents to talk about how *The Bible* condemns homosexuality. That was the main message, although the church also talked about how women were inferior to men and how slavery was something acceptable. And that trans people were the work of The Devil."

I looked over at the jury. They were listening with interest to her story, and I nodded.

"Were these messages effective?"

"Objection," Vince said. "Calls for speculation."

"Sustained."

"Ms. Garrison," I said. "What did the reverend tell you to do with the parents whose children were gay or trans?"

"Well, many of the parents in the church had gay or trans children. If they were concerned about their children, which they often were, because of the reverend's sermons, he asked that I bring them directly to him so he could counsel them."

"What did the counseling consist of?"

"Objection, calls for speculation again," Vince said.

"Sustained. Ms. Garrison, you may only testify to the counseling you witnessed first-hand," Judge Reiner admonished her.

She nodded. "I was in the room when the reverend counseled these parents," she said. "As a woman, he thought I could relate better to the parents and they could come to me for guidance, which they usually did."

"Okay, then," I said. "You witnessed these counseling sessions, then, right?"

"Yes, I did."

"What did these counseling sessions consist of?"

"Objection, lack of relevance," Vince said, standing up.

"Your honor, I'd like to remind Mr. Malloy that the reverend testified that the message from his church was that of love and peace and that he did not preach anti-gay or anti-trans rhetoric. These counseling sessions directly contradicts the reverend's sworn testimony."

"I'll allow it," Judge Reiner said. "But if you get off-track, I'll stop you right there."

"Thank you. Ms. Garrison, what did these counseling sessions consist of?"

She cleared her throat and her hand nervously twisted her scarf. She twirled the end of scarf around her finger as she talked, her eyes focusing on the ceiling. "The reverend told the parents they were to change their gay and transgendered children. He gave them referrals to a place that does conversion therapy, which means these therapists use psychiatric methods to change these kids from gay to straight or from transgendered to...non-transgendered."

"Okay. What happened when these parents came back in after that therapy?"

"The reverend would have a follow-up counseling session with them. He wanted to ask them if the conversion therapy worked after the therapy was finished."

"And if the therapy didn't work?"

Louisa looked helplessly at the jury, and then at me, and then up at the ceiling. Her fingers drummed on the table and then her shaking hand went back to her scarf. She twisted the scarf around and around and around her finger. Tears came to her eyes as she furtively looked back at the jury.

"The reverend told the parents they must kill their children," she said softly, so softly I could barely hear her.

I looked over at the jury and saw they were straining to hear what she said.

"I'm so sorry, Ms. Garrison, could you say that a little louder and speak directly into the microphone?"

She sighed. "The reverend told the parents they must kill their children. If the parents tried conversion therapy and they came back in to speak with the reverend to tell him therapy didn't work, he counseled them to kill their kids." Once she said that, she hung her head, and a sob came from her. She started crying and she didn't stop.

I looked over at Judge Reiner and I saw he had tears in his eyes. He wiped them away, and looked over at the jury. "Let's take a fifteen minute break," he said to them. "While this witness composes herself."

I looked over at the jury, all of whom were staring at Louisa, most of them shaking their heads. It was as if they couldn't believe her testimony. I hoped and prayed I was mis-reading them.

I handed Louisa a Kleenex and she took it, blowing her nose. Her tears continued to flow and she shook her head, over and over again. "It was my fault," she said. "Those kids that died. My fault. I should've stopped it. I should've done something. I was just so scared. So brainwashed. I thought I was doing the right thing. Oh, God..." She started to cry some more.

I put my hand on her shoulder. "You're doing the right thing now," I said. "Your testimony will stop this from happening anymore." I pointed to where Axel was sitting, but wasn't sitting anymore. "Detective Springer is gone. He went to find the reverend and arrest him. Your testimony under oath here is what he needed to make an arrest. The murdering ends today. Because of you." I raised her face so she could look me in the eye. "Because of you."

At that, Vince came over to me. "What's this I hear? You're

having the reverend arrested right now? I told you I'd use him as a rebuttal witness to Ms. Garrison."

"You can still use him," I said.

"When he's under arrest and officially in custody?" Vince shook his head.

"Should I call Axel and tell him to back off?"

"No." Vince looked defeated. "I'm actually not sure what good it would do to call him, to tell you the truth. At this point, it's going to be 'he said she said' anyhow and his further testimony won't change that."

"Thanks." I turned back to Louisa. "So, see? Reverend Scott will be in custody so he can't hurt anybody ever again."

Louisa nodded. "But all those kids died because of him. And I could've stopped it." She shook her head. "I'm a monster."

"No," I said. "Not a monster. Reverend Scott is the monster. You were taken in by him just like those other parents were. You were a victim, too."

The jury came back in and I looked at Louisa. "You're okay," I said softly. "Just finish this up, and we'll get out of here."

The jury sat back down.

"Ms. Garrison, I would remind you that you're still under oath," Judge Reiner said. "You may proceed, Ms. Ross."

"Okay, Ms. Garrison, were you in the room when the Reverend Scott counseled Ms. Connie Morrison?"

She hung her head. "Yes," she said. "I was."

"Did he counsel her to kill her son, Heath Morrison?"

"Yes."

"Is that Heath Morrison, there?" I asked, pointing to Heather.

"Yes. I mean, I guess she goes by the name of Heather now, and she isn't a boy anymore. But her birth name was Heath

Morrison." She smiled at me and I nodded. I knew she'd come a long way, because she was willing to accept that Heath was now Heather.

I couldn't go further, such as asking Louisa if she'd talked to Connie and found out if Connie would carry out the murder. I knew she had because she told me in confidence that Connie told her just that and she encouraged Connie to do it. She felt horribly guilty about that, because she felt that she, ultimately, was responsible for Connie being killed. If she never encouraged Connie to try to kill Heather, none of this would've happened.

"I have nothing further."

I sat down, and Vince stood up.

"Mr. Malloy, you may cross-examine this witness."

He raised an eyebrow at me and nodded. "Ms. Garrison, did you ever ask Ms. Morrison if she would kill her son, Heath?"

"Yes."

"And what did she say?"

"She said she would kill Heath."

I furrowed my brow, wondering what Vince was doing. He was asking the question I couldn't, because it was beyond the scope of rebuttal testimony. Why would he ask that question?

"I have nothing further for this witness." He sat down and I looked at him. He smiled and shrugged his shoulders, and I suddenly understood.

Vince Malloy was helping me out.

FIFTY-TWO

"Do you have any more witnesses?" Judge Reiner asked me.

"No, your honor."

"Do you have any rebuttal witnesses, Mr. Malloy?" Judge Reiner asked Vince.

"No, your honor."

"Okay, then, you may make your closing statement."

If I had any doubt that Vince suddenly wanted to lose this case, it was erased when he stood up. "The defense waives closing statements your honor."

"Very well. Ms. Ross, please make your closing statement."

"Ladies and gentlemen of the jury," I said, looking at each one. "You heard testimony about a brutal murder. I admit my client was guilty of killing her mother. But she had to do it, ladies and gentlemen. She had to, because her mother would kill her first. The evidence showed that Ms. Morrison feared for her life because her mother would kill her with a butcher knife. The evidence also clearly showed that Connie Morrison was instructed to kill Heather Morrison, the defendant, by the Reverend John Scott. Further, the evidence clearly showed that

Connie Morrison told Louisa Garrison that she, Connie, was intending to kill Heather. Kill her because of who she is, which is a transgendered female. Certain segments of society have told Heather that she's a freak, that she doesn't belong, that she must change. Her own mother agreed, and her own mother tried to kill her for the crime of living an authentic life. Heather didn't want to hide who she was and she was almost killed for it. Think about that, ladies and gentlemen of the jury. Think about that."

I sat down and looked over at Vince. He was smiling.

"Okay," the judge said. He gave the jury instructions and sent them to deliberate. After that, they filed out of the room.

I went over to Vince after the jury left. "What's up with that? No closing statement, you got forbidden evidence in that helped me. What's going on?"

Vince shrugged his shoulders. "I just didn't feel like making a closing argument," he said.

"Okay, whatever," I said. Was Vince getting soft?

I went back to talk to Heather. "What happens now?" she asked me.

"We wait for the jury to return with a verdict. Fun, fun."

"How long does it take?"

"It could be fifteen minutes. It could be three days. We'll hang out here until five o'clock, and if the jury doesn't return with a verdict, we go home. We'll then be on call, so that when the jury returns, we have to come back and hear what it is."

I sighed. It would be awhile.

IT TURNED OUT, however, the jury didn't take as long as I thought they might. About two hours after they were dismissed to deliberate, the jury foreman came out. "We have a verdict," he said.

My heart started to race, like it always did in cases like this. No matter how things went, the moment the jury came back with a verdict was a scary, scary time. In a flash, my client's life would change. All the work, all the preparation, all the hopes and dreams and everything else came down to this one moment in time.

I looked over at Heather and I squeezed her hand.

"What does it mean?" she asked. "That they came back so quickly?"

"It could be good news. Could be bad. I never know."

"All rise," the bailiff said as the jury came back in, one by one. I glanced over at the 12 men and women who were filing into their seats. What, indeed, did it mean that they were coming back so quickly? The case was a slam-dunk for Vince, especially since the judge told me Louisa couldn't testify about finding the butcher knife. But, then again, maybe the jury found Louisa's testimony compelling, and it did explain what happened, in a way. Vince assisted me there at the end, too. I still had no idea why he did that.

"Has the jury reached a verdict?" Judge Reiner asked.

"We have your honor."

"May the defendant please rise," Judge Reiner said as Heather and I stood up. I could feel Heather's pulse beating fast on her wrist as I held her hand tightly. "On the first count of assault with a deadly weapon, how does the jury find?"

"Not guilty your honor."

I started to breathe easier, but not really. It could be that they found her not guilty of the assault and guilty of the murder. I'd seen it before.

"On the second count of murder in the first degree, how does the jury find?"

"Not guilty your honor."

I closed my eyes, trying to feel this moment. Heather was crying next to me and I nodded.

"Is this the unanimous verdict of the jury?"

"It is, your honor."

I looked over at Vince, who was smiling. I still didn't know what he was up to, or maybe I did. Maybe he, too, was swayed by Louisa's testimony. Maybe he finally became convinced of Heather's innocence. As I was all along.

"The defendant is free to go," Judge Reiner said. "I would like to thank the members of the jury for your time, patience and hard work. It's not easy to be away from your family, away from your jobs, to do your civic duty. Your work in this case, and in all cases, does not go unnoticed and is very much appreciated. You are excused."

I hugged Heather tightly, as she was crying hard. "Oh, my," she said, looking at me. "I better quit the waterworks, or my mascara's gonna run everywhere." Then she smiled. "Just kidding. I always use waterproof mascara." At that, she buried her head on my shoulder and cried some more.

The case was over. We won. Heather was free.

Now, there was just one more thing I had to do.

FIFTY-THREE

I drove Heather over to my house. Axel was coming over as soon as he got through processing in the crazy-ass reverend. Axel took Reverend Scott into custody as he sat in the jury room, reading his Bible.

"Where are we going?" Heather asked as we pulled around to my house.

"My home. I'd like you to meet my girls. And I need to talk to you about something." My heart was racing, but I knew I was doing the right thing. Heather had nobody. But maybe that would change when she met Louisa. Her birth mother.

We pulled up to my home, and I took Heather's hand. "It was a privilege to represent you," I said. "And I mean that."

She looked at me and then looked away. "Me too." She sighed. "I guess you and I aren't gonna talk much after this, huh?"

"Don't say that. You're like one of my kids now. I won't lose touch with you."

"I guess. You got your life, though. I doubt I fit into it much."

I put my arm around her. "Yes, you will. I promise you that." I gestured to her. "Come on, let's meet Rina and Abby."

We went inside, where Rina and Abby were hanging out in the television room, playing a video game. "Aunt Harper," Rina said excitedly, running over to me and looking at Heather. "Is this Heather?"

Abby got up off the floor, too, and walked over to us.

"Yes, Rina, this is Heather," I said, and Rina gave her a big hug.

"We heard a lot about you," Rina said. Abby, for her part, shyly stuck out her hand and Heather shook it.

"Very nice to meet you, Heather," Abby said.

"You too," Heather said with a smile.

"Is Axel coming over tonight?" Rina asked.

"He is. He's processing in a case, but he'll be over later."

THAT NIGHT, after all of us had dinner – me, Rina, Abby, Heather and Axel – I put the girls to bed, over their strenuous protests.

"Aunt Harper, it's only 9," Rina grumbled.

"I know, but we got things to discuss," I said. "Now go on up. You can read a book before you go to bed, but I'll be up at 10:30, and it better be light's out."

The girls went upstairs and I came into the sunroom, where Heather and Axel were waiting for me to come in. The door was open, and the soft, early-autumn breeze was coming through. The crickets were chirping outside, and dogs were barking in the distance.

I sat down. "Heather," I said. "There's something I need to tell you."

"What?"

I took a deep breath. "You were adopted. I know where your birth mother is. I need to talk to her individually, but only after I talk to you about it. I'd like to know if you want to meet her."

Heather looked shocked. Her eyes opened wide and her hand flew to her mouth. "Adopted? Connie wasn't my real mother?"

"No. I found all this out a few days ago. Before I speak to your birth mother, I need to know how you feel about meeting her."

Heather shook her head. "I got nobody, Harper. I mean, I got Charlie, I guess. He wants me to come home. But I got nobody else."

"You have me," I said. "And I mean that."

"I know. Yes, sure. I'd like to meet her."

"Good. I'll talk to her, and if she wants to meet you, then I'll arrange it."

Axel got up to get everyone some hot tea, which I was brewing. When he came back, I wanted to ask him about the reverend. "How did it go?" I asked. "Taking that crazy loon into custody?"

"It wasn't so bad," he said. "He came with me willingly, and he said he was relieved I was taking him in. Relieved. That was the word." Axel shook his head. "I guess he knew what he was doing was wrong, but he couldn't stop himself from doing it. I've seen that before."

"Are the charges going to stick?"

"They should. Now that he's in custody, I have a feeling that the church-goers, the ones who were too scared to talk, will now speak freely. And don't forget, I have those parents in custody – the ones who I suspect actually killed their children. I can convince the prosecutor to cut some deals with them in exchange for their testimony against the reverend. I have a feeling the reverend won't be terrorizing congregants for a long time."

"Good." I sipped my tea and smelled the air. "All is right in the world again."

"Well, can I meet her?" Heather said. "Call her, get her here."

"Okay." I called Louisa. "Louisa, this is Harper...can you come over right now?...see you soon."

"She's coming," I said.

LOUISA ARRIVED at my house in a half hour.

"Louisa," I said. "I would like to speak with you alone."

I took her into the television room, which also served as our den.

"What did you need to ask me?" she asked, as we sat down.

"Heather. My client. She's your birth daughter."

At that, Louisa hung her head. "Oh my God. Oh my God. Oh.my.God." She shook her head, and the tears started to flow. "How did you find out about that?"

I cleared my throat. What Anna did was illegal, so I wouldn't implicate her. "I found out through the course of my investigation."

"I never thought I'd see my son again," she said, and then she smiled. "I mean, daughter, I guess, huh?"

"Yes, daughter. She wants to meet you. Will you meet her?"

She nodded. "I have nobody right now. I have my parents, but..." She shook her head. "I'm not close with them. I was staying with them, but that was only because I needed to get out of this town. I was afraid the reverend would kill me. I didn't want to stay with them. I...my past with them isn't good."

I took Louisa's hand. "Let's go and see her," I said.

Louisa followed me into the sun room to meet Heather.

"Hi," Louisa said tentatively. "I guess I'm your-"

"Mom," Heather said, coming over to her and hugging her. "My mom."

Louisa laughed as she hugged Heather back. "My daughter."

Axel and I stood back and watched the two women.

"I guess my work here is done," I said.

OF COURSE, my work wasn't done. A criminal defense attorney's work is never done.

But I could never be prepared for who called me to defend him.

"Harper," a familiar voice was on the other end of the line. Pearl had put him through to me, telling me I apparently had a new client to speak with.

"Who is this?"

"Michael. Michael Reynolds."

My heart started to race. Michael Reynolds...my mind went back to him. The fraternity party, he and I bumping and grinding on the dance floor. Me going back to his fraternity room, where he forced himself on me. He raped me while I screamed for help, and then had his fraternity brother do the same.

"What do you want?"

"I need your help. I've been accused of murder, and I didn't do it."

My first instinct was to slam down the phone. Tell him to go to hell. Tell him he was the main reason why I had to spend thousands of dollars on therapists. The reason why I had recurring bouts of crippling depression, anxiety and panic attacks. Tell him to never, ever, call me again.

Then I thought about it.

I could use him. I could finally get my revenge. I could take his case and flush it down the toilet. He would never know the difference if I did that.

"Come on in," I said. "I have an opening today at 3."

FIND OUT WHAT HAPPENS NEXT! *Justice Denied* **is available, only $4.99**

Synopsis:

Harper defends her rapist, who is charged with murdering his father-in-law.

This is the first case she's ever wanted to lose...

Harper must deal with a dark part of her past when she defends her rapist, Michael Reynolds, who is charged with murdering a judge. Harper wants revenge, so she takes the case with the explicit desire to throw it. But as she digs deeper into the case, she understands that if she throws Michael's case, it means the real culprit will go free. Struggling with her conscience, which is fighting for her desire for vengeance, Harper must access some of the darkest recesses of her brain.

As she digs in deeper into the case, she finds a conspiracy that goes to the highest level. She's not clear, however, if Michael Reynolds is also involved.

Harper wants to see Michael convicted, even though he's her client. If he's not involved in the murder, can she try to throw his case anyhow? Doing so would go against her conscience and ethics.

But it would also set her free...

With twists, turns and lightning speed, *Justice Denied* **is one book that should not be missed by legal thriller fans!!!!** books2read.com/u/4AOl9A

. . .

FOR INFORMATION **about upcoming titles in the *Harper Ross Legal Thriller* series, sign up for my mailing list!** You'll be the first to know about new releases and you'll be the first to know about any promotions!!!! https://mailchi.mp/2e2dda532e99/rachel-sinclair-legal-thrillers

ALSO BY RACHEL SINCLAIR

For information about upcoming titles in the *Harper Ross Legal Thriller* series, sign up for my mailing list! You'll be the first to know about new releases and you'll be the first to know about any promotions!!!! https://mailchi.mp/2e2dda532e99/rachel-sinclair-legal-thrillers

Johnson County Legal Thrillers (Kansas City, Missouri)

Bad Faith https://amzn.to/3jk00tz

Justice Denied https://amzn.to/3j8s2b2

Hidden Defendant https://amzn.to/3yypUjH

Injustice for All https://amzn.to/3lmZpJY

LA Defense https://amzn.to/3A313EW

The Associate https://amzn.to/3jeXqVF

The Alibi https://amzn.to/3ykjnZL

Reasonable Doubt https://amzn.to/3C9HBYH

The Accused https://amzn.to/3jiTL94

Secrets and Lies https://amzn.to/3fowW2V

Until Proven Guilty https://amzn.to/3CbQukz

Emerson Justice Legal Thrillers (Los Angeles)

Dark Justice https://amzn.to/2Vhg72L

Blind Justice https://amzn.to/3A44DyE

Southern California Legal Thrillers (San Diego)

Presumption of Guilt https://amzn.to/3A6duQ2

Justice Delayed https://amzn.to/3lpWOiG
By Reason of Insanity https://amzn.to/3ymyz8H
Wrongful Conviction https://amzn.to/3looT6J
The Trial https://amzn.to/3jeKG1c

Made in United States
Cleveland, OH
03 February 2025

13987448R10213